FANTASY ADVENTURE

IRONHELM

by Douglas Niles

**Cover Art
FRED FIELDS**

TSR, Inc.
PRODUCTS OF YOUR IMAGINATION™

To Kavita—writing for you
is a joy and an inspiration.

IRONHELM

©Copyright 1990 TSR, Inc.
All Rights Reserved.

Distributed to the book trade in the United States by Random House, Inc. and in Canada by Random House of Canada, Ltd.

Distributed in the United Kingdom by TSR Ltd.

Distributed to the toy and hobby trade by regional distributors.

FORGOTTEN REALMS, PRODUCTS OF YOUR IMAGINATION, AD&D, and the TSR logo are trademarks owned by TSR, Inc.

First Printing, March, 1990
Printed in the United States of America.
Library of Congress Catalog Card Number: 89-51884

9 8 7 6 5 4 3 2 1

ISBN: 0-88038-903-6

TSR, Inc.
P.O. Box 756
Lake Geneva, WI 53147
U.S.A.

TSR Ltd.
120 Church End, Cherry Hinton
Cambridge CB1 3LB
United Kingdom

$25
5/03

My hand trembles such that I can barely paint this tale. I can only relate what I have seen and hope that time and perhaps sleep will allow me to plumb its depths. The time is today, the setting of the sun. . . .

Naltecona attends the sacrifices upon the great pyramid, performing two of them himself—hearts offered to Crimson Zaltec and Black Tezca. The throng crowded in the plaza, even the priests on the pyramid, seemed held in some kind of thrall. Movement slowed, perception heightened.

A great noise drew our eyes to the sky, and there appeared a beast, a huge creature the like of which Maztica has never known. Shaped like a bird, it had no feathers but was covered with leathery skin like a crocodile. A long beak, sharp and jagged, extended from its maw. The monster settled slowly to the top of the pyramid as the priests recoiled in panic. I myself fell to the stones in awe.

The beast spread and flapped its wings, sending a hurricane of wind across the pyramid, driving the priests still farther away. And then we saw the will of the gods.

Across the broad breast of the beast spread a shiny surface, like obsidian or smooth, perfect ice. I stared, awestruck, at my own dumbfounded reflection in this mirror from heaven. Others, I learned later, saw the same thing as I: a reflection of the pyramid and the assembled priesthood.

Except Naltecona.

The Revered Counselor recoiled two steps, staring into the mirror. The beast stepped toward him, and Naltecona made noises of fear. He stared for a full minute, and though none other could see the vision granted his eyes, he groaned and he wept. He pounded his chest in disbelieving fear. He spoke of two-headed monsters, of silver spears, of houses that floated upon the ocean.

Then did the beast spread its wings and soar aloft, nearly driving us from the pyramid with the wind of its ascension. Then, too, did Naltecona fall to his knees and kiss the stones before the creature's footsteps. . . .

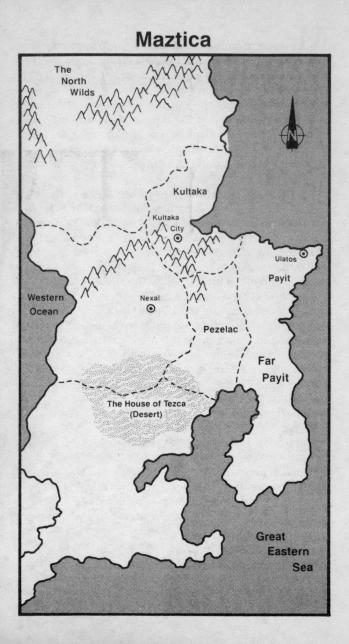

Prologue

These pages commence the *Chronicle of the Waning*, enscribed by Coton, Grandfather Patriarch of the Golden God, Qotal.

My labors, as always, are dedicated to the greater glory of Qotal, the Plumed One, Iridescent Ancestor of the Gods.

The Time of Waning comes upon us, arriving all but unnoticed by the masters of Maztica. The nobles and warriors of the great city of Nexal care for naught but conquest and battle, gaining tribute and prisoners from the subjugation of each neighboring state.

The priests of the younger gods cannot see beyond their need for more sacrifices to feed their bloodthirsty masters. Crimson Tezca, god of the sun, requires blood every day to coax his flaming self into the skies at dawn. Blue Azul, rain god, prefers to claim the lives of little children in exchange for his body's life giving moisture.

But none is so greedy for blood as Zaltec, patron deity of the Nexala. His crimson brand marks the chest of his most loyal followers, and long columns ascend the pyramids to offer him their hearts, in willing or unwilling sacrifice. Such is the glory of Zaltec!

No god of the True World is so mysterious, so secretive as bloody Zaltec. Zaltec, the great god of war! Vast ceremonies, these wars, ceremonies fought for the honor and glory of Zaltec. The armies of Nexal go forth and conquer Pezelac, that they may claim captives. They do battle with the forces of fierce Kultaka, and both sides come away with many captives for the altars of Zaltec.

In Nexal, warriors, priests, lords, sorcerers, all struggle for their own ends, complacent in the eternity of Maztica, the True World. They compete, they gain victories and suffer defeats, all for their pathetic goals! All of them are blind! All of them, fools!

Only I, Coton, see the True World as it changes. I see the commencement of its decline, the Time of Waning that has long been foretold by us, the faithful priests of Qotal. Other priests speak only of more sacrifices, grander pyramids, brighter temples. I see a time when temples vanish altogether and pyramids become heaps of unrecognizable stone!

Qotal is the vessel of my vision. His faithful are few, for most of Maztica has turned toward worship of Zaltec and his bloodthirsty offspring. Once Qotal presided as the hero of our forefathers, esteemed by the True World. It is Qotal who brought mayz to the world, so that mankind would always have food. For centuries his benign vision watched over the peoples of Maztica.

But now Qotal is supplanted by Zaltec across the True World. People follow the god of war blindly, ignorant of the peaceful wisdom offered by Qotal. Especially here, in Nexal, has Zaltec of the Bloody Hand taken the place of honor once reserved for the Plumed One.

I am sworn to silence by my station. I say nothing to the mighty of Nexal. Instead, my tale becomes the Chronicle of the Waning. As my immortal master, the Silent Counselor, so wills, I observe and record, a witness but not a participant to the unfolding of history.

The individual threads of chaos remain diverse, most of them unknown to me. My auguries show an emperor god, mightier than any ruler in the history of Maztica, yet fatally weak and flawed. But they also tell the story of a little girl, dwelling in happy innocence near the Heart of the True World; and the tale of a youth, countless day-runs distant. I know not how these strands will entwine in the course of the Waning. Only the passage of time, the swirling eddies of fate, can bring these threads together.

But when they bind, they shall form a knot of surpassing strength and cataclysmic import.

❧1❧

THREADS

He couldn't tell whether it was rain or blood running into his eyes, but his vision blurred to nothing. Night settled around him, but it was a night illuminated by hellish fires. The sharp crack of deadly magic—lightning bolts, he suspected—barked beyond the tree line, then bugles blared and he felt the pounding of heavy hooves through the ground.

Wiping his face, he found that only mud obscured his vision, and soon he could see again. Flames spouted from most of the town, and some trees had caught fire, but otherwise the night was dark. His ears told him that the battle had moved on.

He looked at the gashes in his steel breastplate and chuckled wryly. His helmet was gone, and around him lay the bodies of his men—his boys, really. They were young, cheerful; they were farmers gone to war, and they had been massacred by warriors. The bitter laugh died in his throat as he raised his eyes. Angrily he blinked at the tears that stung his eyes.

He flinched suddenly at the touch of a slender hand and turned to see an elfin face. A small woman stood before him, partially wrapped in a deep robe. Her skin was remarkably pale, almost milky white. It seemed to glow and fade in the reflected light of the flames. Suddenly a great fireball exploded not far away, and he saw her pale eyes, pupils dilated, studying him and soothing him.

"Captain, you are hurt," she said.

"The battle is lost." He sighed.

"Lost by the fools who commanded! You and your men fought well."

"And died well." He was too exhausted to feel anything except a vague bitterness. He saw the banner, the crimson figurehead outlined in silver against the bright red field, now trampled in the mud, torn by sword and dyed almost black in the blood of the young soldiers who followed it.

Horses lumbered near, their black-helmeted riders on the prowl for stragglers. The pale woman raised her hand and said something very strange, and the horsemen rode past. Mud splattered onto the pair from the great hooves, but the knights took no notice of the two survivors. Instead, the riders paused some distance away, looking toward the fires, seeking targets silhouetted in the light.

The man felt the soft protection of magic, invisibility created by the woman and now cloaking them. In another minute, the knights charged off into the night, and the man and woman heard the screams of men caught by lance or mace or hoof.

"Red is a poor color for a banner," he decided absently, looking at the bloody spots on the tattered cloth. "It will have to be something else."

The woman took the man's arm and began to lead him away, though there was no way to tell which way to go. The battlefield surrounded them, fire and smoke and the clamor of battle in all directions as far as they could see and hear.

"Disaster," he realized. "The alliance is finished. The war is lost."

"But you, Captain Cordell, you will live to fight again. And I will fight beside you."

He nodded vaguely. How did this woman know his name? The question seemed quite unimportant, the confidence of her assertion instead focusing his attention and his agreement.

More and more shadowy forms appeared, fleeing in all directions, followed by the great waves of horsemen and their riders, so eager to slay and keep on slaying.

But always the riders passed the two figures without seeing them. Once a great leering beast, twice the height of a man, sniffed suspiciously and turned toward them. The troll chomped its wicked fangs and crept closer.

The woman raised her hand and pointed, speaking a sharp, alien sound. A tiny globule of flame appeared, flickering from her fingertip and flying toward the troll. The monster blinked stupidly, and then the fireball erupted, engulfing the creature in a blossoming sphere of incredible heat and flame. It screeched piteously, falling to the ground and writhing in its death throes, as the woman once again urged the wounded captain into the night.

"Gold," he said, stopping suddenly. The battle had by now fallen behind them.

"What?" She, too, stopped, facing him. Her hood fell back, and he saw her snowy-white hair, her pale, almost bloodless skin. The tip of one ear protruded from her hair, and he saw its point, the characteristic mark of an elf. He was not surprised.

"Gold," he explained. "That will be the color of my banner. Gold."

* * * * *

Erixitl scampered up the steep trail, taking little note of the sheer drop to her left, nor of the bushy slope looming above to the right. Instead, her wide brown eyes held fast to the winding footpath. Her long hair trailed behind her, a black plume floating easily in the air, decorated with feathers of red and green.

Around her rolled a tumult of green hills, mostly covered with the same tangled brush that bordered the footpath. Occasional terraces, supporting narrow and winding fields of mayz, circled some of the lower slopes.

The brown-skinned girl darted around a sharp switchback, still climbing. Her bare feet pounded the earth in a more measured cadence now as the strain of the ascent began to tell. Still, her round face glowed with some secret happiness, and as a small, whitewashed building came into view, she broke into a sprint.

"Father! Father!" Her voice, despite the wind swirling through the yard, carried strongly. In seconds, a dark-skinned man appeared in the open door of the building.

"What is it, Erixitl? Is something wrong?" The man's dark eye's squinted along the mountainside to see if his daughter was being pursued.

"Oh, no, nothing is wrong!" The girl stumbled to the cottage and gasped for breath. The flush of exhaustion and excitement showed clearly, even through her dark, coppery skin. "*Payatli*, it's wonderful! Oh, please, Father, you must let me—you have to let me—"

A scowl came over the man's features, and the girl stopped in midsentence. He looked wearily into his daughter's eyes. Why did she not drop her gaze as was proper for a girl? This stubborn pride disconcerted her father almost as much as it annoyed the priests of Zaltec, whom Erix insisted upon studying every time her father took her down the mountain to the village of Palul.

Yet those same eyes were so undeniably beautiful, so keen and observant, that sometimes the father wondered if she did not share them with others as a gift for those blessed with her gaze. A gift from Qotal himself, shedding beauty on those he had left behind. Perhaps this was why the priests found her gaze unsettling. The worshipers of Zaltec could never enjoy such beauty.

Erixitl studied her father and noted the cloth of fine cotton in his hands. One corner of the cloth promised a look at the finished magic, for this small patch glowed with a brilliant profusion of colors—reds, greens, blues, violets, and many more hues, all bursting with a supernatural iridescence far brighter than any paint or dye could impart. As she looked at her father's work of *pluma*, or feathermagic, Erix could anticipate his next words.

"*Payatli*, eh? You don't call me 'Most Honored Patriarch' unless you wish to get out of your chores! Is that it?"

"Please, *Payatli!*" Erix almost dropped to her knees, but some inner reserve of pride held her on her feet, meeting her father's steadily darkening gaze. "Terrazyl is going to Cordotl with her brothers and her father to trade for salt! May I go with them? Look at the sky, Father! Today, for certain, I could see the temples and pyramids of Nexal! Please,

Father! You promised I could see the city this year!"

The featherworker grimaced as if in pain, and then he sighed. "Indeed I did. But your brother is attending his class at our own temple—not as grand as the Temple of Zaltec in Nexal, to be sure, but an important duty. . . ."

Erix felt growing disappointment. Her knees trembled and her lower lip quivered, but she did not show her dismay. She had forgotten that her brother would not be here today. In truth, his apprenticeship was a high honor, for should he progress to the priesthood, he would hold great status in the village. Though her father was one of the few who preferred instead the gentle worship of Qotal, the Plumed One, he did not discourage his son's ambition toward the priesthood of Zaltec.

She knew that her request was hopeless, even as her father finished the explanation.

"Someone must tend the snares, and that must be your task today. You would not leave the birds to suffer longer than necessary, would you? Or allow the feathers to suffer damage?"

Erix knew the debate was over, but her emotions pushed forth words in a reckless torrent, a torrent she regretted even as it flowed.

"But you *promised*, Father! Three times we've gone to Cordotl, and each time the haze or the rain comes so that I cannot see the city! This is my tenth summer, and I must see Nexal!" Finally she bit her tongue and stood still, awaiting the expected blow.

But no blow fell. Instead, her father replied softly, his voice regretful. "And so you will, my daughter. Now, desist in this unseemly pleading."

"Very well." Somehow she kept her voice from trembling. She turned and started for the twisting path leading past the house and sharply up the mountainside.

"Wait!" the featherworker called to his daughter, perhaps in guilt. Or, perhaps, because a frightening premonition showed him the life path awaiting this proud, strong girl. He pulled her to him in a firm hug.

"Soon, Erixitl, I will take you myself. On the sunniest, the clearest of days! We will see the great pyramid, all the temples around the grand square, and the lakes themselves—a turquoise blue that will bring tears to your eyes!"

"And the Temple of Zaltec? Will we see that?"

The man's face clouded briefly at the thought of that bloodstained altar, but he masked his feelings. "Yes, my daughter, even the Temple of Zaltec. We shall see all of Nexal from the mountainside of Cordotl."

Erix sniffled quietly, feeling a little better. She returned her father's hug, and then turned toward the narrow path. "I will see to the snares."

"Erixitl." She turned in surprise as her father called again. He took something from his pouch. "I have been waiting to give you this. Perhaps this is a good time."

She stepped forward and saw that it was a small token, made from tufts of golden and emerald downfeathers around a smooth turquoise stone. The stone rested in a small ring of jade and dangled from a leather thong. The blue and green stones gleamed, but it was the feathers that gave the pendant its true beauty. Soft and fragile, they seemed to hold the token motionless, weightless, as if it floated easily in the air. Erix scarcely dared to breathe, it was so entrancingly beautiful.

"It carries the memory of our ancestors and an earlier time of greatness," explained the featherworker. "Gold and green are the sacred colors of Qotal. The turquoise shows you his eye, watchful and benign, the color of the sky."

"Thank you, Father! It's beautiful!" Erix's heart thrilled at the delicate workmanship, the brilliant colors. She did not understand his words about the god, Qotal, for to Erix, gods were gods. But she sensed a beauty and peace within the token that differed significantly from the colorful but violent rituals of Zaltec.

"I will cherish it forever!" She embraced her father impulsively, and his own arms held her tightly for several moments.

"I hope so," said the featherworker, a trifle wistfully. He was a man of considerable talent and skill. He had created magical fans for the High Counselor of Palul, and his goods had been carried to the market in Nexal, where he had been told they commanded a fine price. Now he looked at the small medallion in his daughter's hands, and he concluded with conviction, "I hope you cherish it, for I can give you nothing greater."

Erix turned toward her chore with energy. The path she started up made the trail to her house seem like a broad avenue. Now she ascended a steep mountainside covered with verdant growth. She grasped vines and roots with her hands, climbing like a monkey, and soon gained five hundred feet. At last she reached the crest of the brush-covered ridge behind her family's home.

Here she paused, still breathing easily. She looked across the broad vista below her, green slopes falling thousands of feet to the bottom. Flat green fields of mayz lined the valley floor like a lush carpet, and indeed such it was: a carpet of food. The vale curved away to her right, and beyond it she could see another broad mountain, blue in the haze of distance.

Cordotl. The trading town that stood at the foot of that mountain, she knew, offered a clear vista of the broad valley of Nexal and its gleaming lakes. How clearly she imagined the jewel shining from the center of those lakes, the city of Nexal, the Heart of the True World. With a little sigh, she turned away, knowing that her first glimpse of that storied metropolis would have to wait.

She tried reminding herself of the importance of the feathers she now sought, of the greatness of her father's craft. Indeed, practitioners of *pluma* magic were the most important citizens of the Nexala! Of course, her father's feathermagic was of the simple, country sort. It consisted largely of feathered armor for the warriors of Palul and nearby towns, light yet sturdy vests that could shatter a flint spear tip or deflect the jagged obsidian blade of a sword; or the occasional floating litter for the speaker of the village or as a tribute to Nexal.

She had heard about, but never seen, the grand works crafted by the feathermasters of Nexal: huge litters that could bear a noble and his entire retinue; great, swirling fans that cooled the palatial homes of great nobles and warriors; or vast lifts, soaring gracefully up the side of a great pyramid with their burdens of devout priests and weeping victims.

As Erix's thoughts drifted again toward those mystical sights of the city, she avoided her previous self-pity. Instead, she continued along the path, almost eagerly seeking the feathered quarry in her family's snares, confident that one day she would not only see but also be a part of the grandeur that was Nexal.

She looked off to the right as she took up the path. There, in the wilderness to the east, lay the lands of the dreaded Kultakans, fierce enemies of the Nexala. The Kultakans, too, were a nation of warriors, worshipers of Zaltec who eagerly fed the god's gory appetite on their sacrificial altars. A small nation compared to the mighty Nexala, the Kultakans were the only nearby tribe who had never been subjugated to Nexal.

Erix followed the trail along the narrow ridgeline. To her left sloped the familiar green slopes leading back to her home, and below that to the small town of Palul. Pausing at a curve in the trail, she could even see Palul's small pyramid, where her older brother studied the ways of the priests of Zaltec. She glared at the pyramid, but then turned away, sudden guilt overcoming her jealousy. In truth, to be a priest of the god of war was an honor any male Nexala would cherish!

Continuing on her way, she came to the first snare, where one brilliant parrot hung. The bird's struggles to escape had caused its strangulation, but Erix noted with detached pleasure that few of the bird's bright feathers had been damaged. Deftly she pulled the wiry noose, made of tough strands from the gut of a jaguar, over the bird's head, smoothing the green and red feathers in the process. Then she stuffed the bird in her leather pouch and moved farther along the trail.

Several other snares along the ridgetop were empty, but she found a bright macaw in the fifth. Now the trail dropped to the far side of the ridge. She cast a wistful look bchind her and started down the eastern slope. These were the far snares, usually her brother's territory, but Erix knew their locations well.

The dirt trail twisted past a spuming waterfall, and she stopped to kick her feet through the sparkling water at its foot. Raising her face to the sky, she let the cool mist wash over her. The dust ran from her skin, and she emerged into the shady brush across the stream feeling refreshed and happier.

A screech of avian rage told her that another macaw had found a snare, and she quickly reached it and wrung the bird's neck. Ducking under low branches, she worked her way through the thick greenery, bushes that towered high over her head, as she found more birds. Her father would be very pleased.

Suddenly a harsh call drew her attention to the deep brush. She saw a moving flash of shining brilliance, disappearing, then flashing again, farther away. With a gasp of astonishment, she parted branches and looked in amazement.

At first, she thought she glimpsed the form of a brilliant snake, entwined among the dense foliage. But then a pair of large, unmistakably feathered wings fluttered. It must be a bird, but a huge and brightly plumed specimen. The colorful shape slipped quickly out of sight, and again she got the impression of a serpentine form.

She did not pause to wonder at its appearance, however. Spellbound, she crept through the brush, barely glimpsing the long tailfeathers that distinguished the creature. Her thoughts were not of capture, though she well knew that these shining plumes must number among the most valuable treasures in all Maztica. Instead, she followed the creature with a sense of reverence, herself caught in the snare of its rare and unique beauty.

She darted under a flowery vine, slipping quietly through the shallow stream, in time to see the creature take wing. It came to rest in the top of a tall tree, and Erix hesitantly edged forward, gazing upward at the proud and wondrous fowl.

She did not see the orange figure slipping soundlessly between the concealing branches, its black spots moving through the shadows like oily liquid. Erix felt, rather than heard, the large body behind her, and immediately she forgot the feathered form, forgot everything but her imminent danger.

Whirling, she saw widespread jaws, leering eyes, and horrible curving claws reaching for her shoulders. Erixitl screamed as the jaguar rose onto its rear legs, and then the scream faded into a moan of terror. The great cat bore her to the earth, and she felt its breath hot upon her face. The girl lay prostrate upon the ground, her eyes squeezed shut, her body trembling in terror, as she awaited the kiss of the deadly fangs.

"Quiet, little one!" A man's voice hissed into her ear, speaking Nexala awkwardly. She opened her eyes in shock and looked between the jaguar jaws into a snarling but unmistakably human face.

The girl's heart pounded and her voice froze in her throat. The beast that had attacked her had seemed so feline, with its animal heat and deep growl. Yet she was now held by a man wearing the skin and skull of a jaguar!

Erixitl knew of the Jaguar Knights. She had even seen members of that mystical order in Palul. Fully draped in the skin of his feline namesake, painted for battle or ceremony, armed with his intricately feathered shield and brilliantly plumed lance, a Jaguar Knight was an impressive sight. But those Erix had seen were Nexala warriors, her own people!

She knew instinctively that the man who gripped her—with fingers, she saw, not the claws she had previously imagined—was not Nexala.

She understood then that her captor must come from Kultaka. With a detached sense of disbelief, she wondered whether she was intended for slavery or for the sacrificial altar. The latter seemed more likely. Trembling in terror, her brown eyes wide and staring, she watched her captor for some sign of his intentions. Would he kill her instantly? This seemed unlikely, but that knowledge only made thoughts of the future even more terrifying.

Other figures emerged from the brush, this knight's retinue. Several of the men wore quilted cotton armor, dyed a shade of green to match the undergrowth. A half-dozen were nearly naked, clad only in loincloths made from single strips of cloth. A pair of the latter took her from the knight and expertly and quickly gagged her. Then they bound her hands before her.

The knight whispered a command in a strange language, and one of the men pulled on the rope, tugging Erix into the brush, toward the east, toward Kultaka and the enemies of the Nexala.

Behind her fell the valley of Palul, and farther away than ever before was the mystical city of Nexal, Heart of the True World.

As the girl stumbled into the brush, the green plants closed behind her, behind the knight and his men. Soon the only trace of their passage was an occasional crimson spot on the leaves—blood dripping from the claw marks that scarred Erix's upper arms.

*   *   *   *   *

"How is it that none of my wisest priests can explain a portent of this magnitude?"

Naltecona rose from his bench and stalked back and forth across the dais. His wide cape, made of shimmering green feathers embroidered into the finest of cotton mesh, floated almost weightless in the air behind him.

The great ruler stopped, and *pluma* magic slowly lifted the great cape into a fan behind his collar, like the emerald splendor of a strutting peacock. Naltecona surveyed the priests before him with a mixture of contempt and desperation.

"You, Caracatl!" He fixed the trembling cleric with an icy gaze. "What does the Grand Patriarch of Tezca have to say about this message from the gods?" Naltecona pointed at the man, whose face was smeared with pale ashes. He wore a robe of deep scarlet, and his body was thin from his many fasts.

"Most Revered Counselor," Caracatl began solemnly, just a trace of a tremor in his voice, "the fire that burns in the sky above Nexal is indeed a sign, obviously from crimson Tezca, god of the sun! Indeed, my enchantments tell me that we see the reflection of his great soul itself. It is a sign of the god's hunger, Most Excellent One. Tezca desires more blood at sunset to fuel his life-giving flame!"

Naltecona whirled from the priest, his cloak wheeling elegantly behind him. The ruler stalked past the timorous line of courtiers and attendants standing behind his throne. The brilliant plumes of his cape lashed across their faces as Naltecona passed. Though each of these was a wealthy individual, of noble rank in Nexal, to a man they wore garments of stained cotton, devoid of any ornament. Now each worthy noble trembled visibly in the presence of the counselor, and none dared raise his eyes from the floor when the great Naltecona passed.

The mighty ruler suddenly spun and faced another of the four priests standing upon the steps before him. "Atl-Ollin, perhaps you can cast some illumination on this matter. No doubt Calor wills the sacrifice of another child." A hint of irony played about the counselor's lips, but the cleric of Calor could take no note—his eyes were cast reverently downward.

This cleric, too, was a thin man. But while Caracatl's skin was lined with dirt and ash, Atl-Ollin's was scrubbed clean. Indeed, many abrasions covered his skin, where the cleric had injured himself as he vigorously applied the pumice stone that served as his ritual soap.

"I am afraid, Most Revered Counselor, that Calor has been distressingly silent in the matter of this omen." The blue-robed patriarch wrung his wrinkled hands. "None can doubt that this Star-That-Shines-By-Day, growing in brilliance as it has over the last tenday, is a portent of most cataclysmic import!"

"An honest answer, at the very least," mused the ruler as he spun once again to stride along the edge of the dais. Again the courtiers bowed nervously as the regal figure passed.

"And you, Hoxitl?" The Revered Counselor paused before a third cleric. "Pray share your tidings with us. What is the will of our First God?" Naltecona now addressed a gaunt skeleton of a man. This priest's skin stretched tightly over his emaciated frame, marred by the self-inflicted scars of penance required by Zaltec. His hands were blood-red, stained by the ritual dye used to distinguish the most loyal followers of Zaltec, those who wore the honored brand called Viperhand.

Most striking was the cleric's thick hair, for Hoxitl, like all clerics of Zaltec, used the dried blood of his victims to stiffen it into a mass of black, twisting spires.

"Zaltec seethes impatiently, Revered Counselor Naltecona. I must take the counsel of the Ancient Ones immediately. Indeed, I embark for the Highcave before dark. Only after I have spoken with them, when I have heard the wisdom of the Ancestors of Darkness, dare I speculate what means this sign."

The priest did not meet Naltecona's eyes, but neither did his voice waver. "Even so, I know that more than a year has passed without a victory feast. Perhaps our First God grows hungry."

Hoxitl, Patriarch of Zaltec, stood firmly before his ruler's gaze. Nonetheless, beads of sweat formed upon his brow. They trickled through the blood-caked peaks of his hair.

"We must have captives—many of them!—that we may claim their hearts for Zaltec!" Hoxitl dared to speak firmly, still keeping his eyes lowered. "Only thus may we drive the omen of ill from the skies!"

Naltecona did not turn in scorn from this cleric, though he shook his head in silent thought before looking to yet another priest. This one met the speaker's eyes with his own gaze of patient, silent thought.

"And you, Coton!" Naltecona spoke softly, his voice assuming a youthful wistfulness. "Would that you could speak, that I may hear you. What wisdom do you conceal behind that shield of silence?"

Coton, resplendent in a plain gown of purest cotton, nodded respectfully but, of course, said nothing. Naltecona whirled again, agitation forcing him into a restless pace. Finally he paused before his throne. In the far wall of his chamber, high above his head, was a long window. Even now he could see the winking insolence of the omen, gleaming brighter than the most brilliant of stars, though the hour was barely past noon.

"Could you be the sign of the Return? Do you warn us that Qotal comes again to the True World?" He spoke thoughtfully, then lapsed into silence.

After a moment, he turned to a courtier, his voice now firm with decision. "Prepare a dozen slaves for the ceremonies of Tezca this evening. Inform my generals to prepare an expedition against Kultaka. Their mission is the claiming of prisoners for the flowery altar of Zaltec!"

* * * * *

Many thousands of miles away, a tower slanted crazily into the sky. The narrow structure, with a conical, tiled roof, rose from a wasteland of red sand, but instead of standing proud and tall like a spire in the sky, it careened at an angle half between upright and horizontal. Defying the law of gravity, it proclaimed by its very existence the might of a greater power: magic.

Inside the tower, all seemed normal. The walls appeared to rise and fall straight up and down. A stairway curved around the inside of the tower, leading from a room at the bottom to another room at the top. The rest of the tower was a hollow cylinder. The hollow center of the place was empty, at rest, except for one careful, deliberate figure.

Kreeshah . . . barool . . . hottaisk. Over and over, the phrase rang through Halloran's head. He studied the words, the verbal component of the magic missile spell, until his brains felt like mush. But still his master made him concentrate.

Halloran climbed the stairs carefully, holding the foaming beaker before him with both hands. Two more circuits to the top of the tower, to the wizard's laboratory, to . . .

To what? The lad did not want to find out.

The wizard Arquiuius's current casting, a potent summoning spell, frightened Halloran as had none of his mentor's previous incantations. The creature within the mage's pattern had been taking shape for three days and nights now, and each hour it seemed to add another oozing pustule, bloated tentacle, or drooping moist orb. Presumably these were eyes, Hal guessed, though they numbered several dozen on the bloblike form that now occupied the entire center of the laboratory.

Kreeshah . . . barool . . . hottaisk. He repeated the words again, but his mind threatened to wander. The hour was early, before the sunrise, and he had had scant hours of sleep during the course of his master's current incantation. Still, I should be more disciplined, Halloran reminded himself, thinking of all that he owed to the wizard. Arquiuius had found him as an orphan, a seasoned street urchin who had lost his family to war, and had brought him here. For the last years of his childhood, Halloran had worked at odd tasks for the wizard. Now, as he progressed through adolescence, he was beginning to learn the secrets of arcanery from Aquiuius. Perhaps, one day, Halloran would be a wizard as mighty as his master!

Placing each footstep carefully on the smooth, worn stone of the stairway, the young magic-user made another circuit. One more to go. . . .

"What am I doing here?" He mouthed the question in genuine curiosity. Of course, he knew he possessed the aptitude that Arquiuius had recognized years ago. Now the youth could send an arrow of magic exploding from his finger, or cause an unsuspecting peasant to fall asleep at his plow. He could subtly charm an innkeeper into granting a free night's lodging, or cause a magical light to blossom in a darkened room. Never, Arquiuius recently proclaimed, had an apprentice mastered so much while still years from growing his own beard!

The steps passed too quickly, though Halloran's deliberate pace slowed even further as he approached the landing and its great oaken door.

"Why didn't I take up sword and shield like my father?" he

lamented. But he had no time to answer that question.

The great door swung silently open, as if of its own accord, and Hal tried to still his trembling hands as he stepped into the lab. The acrid smoke spilled constantly from the beaker in his hands, causing his eyes to water. Nevertheless, he was able to see that the shape in the laboratory had sprouted more limbs. In several places, large regions of moist suckers appeared in its skin, opening and closing like the mouths of primitive fish.

Arquiuius sat as he had for three days and three nights, legs crossed before him and eyes locked open. The wizard had always been thin, but now, to Halloran, he looked absolutely cadaverous. Beyond him, the window, its eerily tilted horizon showing the deserts of Thay barely illuminated by the growing light of imminent dawn. Of course, Hal knew that the tower, not the horizon, was the cause of the tilt, but Arquiuius's bizarre distortion of gravity never failed to take him by surprise.

Now, Hal, hissed a voice in his brain, and he knew the wizard spoke to him, though the old man's lips made no sound. Carefully the youth stepped around the looming shape, steadying his nerve as he extended the still-spuming beaker to Arquiuius.

Suddenly a pinkish tentacle lashed out from within the beast's magical confines. With growing horror, Halloran saw that the foul limb pressed the boundary of the shape inscribed on the floor, slowly pushing through the enchanted barrier.

Now!

The wizard's command echoed in the youth's mind. Quickly he turned back to his teacher. Hal's heart quickened in dismay at the sight of Arquiuius's face. Was that fear he saw?

The blob wriggled once more, and then a stalk of obscene flesh hurled itself toward Halloran. Reacting by instinct alone, he sprang backward, saving his life by scant inches while the lightning blow struck the beaker from his hands.

"No!" Arquiuius's voice was audible this time, and full of acute terror.

The beaker crashed to the stone floor and shattered. A cloud of red gas whooshed upward from the contents, and the young apprentice stumbled backward.

He gaped at the sight of a huge mouth emerging from the smoke, heard the wizard's shrill death cry. Row after row of long, curving teeth stretched wide, spattering drops of acid drool onto their pathetically shrieking victim.

Halloran's primal instincts claimed him. He bolted from the lab, tearing around the many circuits of the descending stairway until, breathless, he dashed out the door in the base of the tower. Here he stumbled and fell headlong. He had forgotten to adjust for the slanting gravity of the tower as he stepped into the world beyond.

Quickly springing to his feet, the young man ran into the desert. His heart pounded and his lips grimaced across his clenched teeth. *Nothing* could make him return to that nightmarish world. Even as the tower rumbled and collapsed into dust behind him, he did not slow his desperate pace.

Nor did he look back as the settling dust pile slowly brightened with the light of the dawning sun.

* * * * *

Thousands of green, red, yellow, and blue feathers joined in a vast circle of brilliant color, forming a huge canopy. The steady, silent pulse of feathermagic, of *pluma*, lifted and lowered the canopy, gently fanning the hallway. Nevertheless, the forehead of the slave stationed beneath the fan glistened with perspiration as he bowed obsequiously to the Eagle Knight approaching him.

The veteran wore a tunic of black and white feathers, entwined by *pluma* into a fiber that could stop the penetration of the sharpest obsidian blade. Crimson plumes hung freely from the knight's arms, flowing through the air as he walked, and a short cape floated easily behind him.

Wordlessly, the Eagle Knight removed his feathered helmet, handing it to the humble manservant before the great doors. He took a dirty shawl from the servant, covering his handsome features with the filthy cloth, suppressing a grimace of distaste.

The servant looked down, embarrassed by the knight's debasement—but such was the will of Naltecona.

"You may enter the presence of the Revered Counselor, Honorable Captain of Hundredmen." The servant quietly opened the door.

The knight stepped into the room, his eyes downcast, his coppery face expressionless. Immediately he knelt and kissed the floor. He rose and walked toward the dais, repeating the submissive gesture two more times before he stood below the throne of power. The warrior averted his eyes from the plumed figure before him, resting his gaze instead upon the raggedly dressed row of courtiers and clerics behind the splendid throne.

"Most Revered Counselor, I regret to inform you that our expedition against the Kultakans ended in disaster. The enemy fought well, luring us into ambush. Many of our warriors have gone to the flowered altars of Kultaka."

Naltecona reclined along the floating cushion of emerald feathers, his eyes half closed. They must not see my distress! he thought grimly. "You yourself, plus two of your comrades—and three Jaguar Knights as well—shall offer your hearts in penance to Zaltec. Pray that he is satisfied!"

"I can but hope that our First God finds my companions and me worthy substitutes." Still the knight's face bore no expression.

"We will learn tonight." The counselor rose and turned away from the man he had just condemned to death. He ignored the slowly swirling fans suspended in the air around him, then suddenly pushed in annoyance past the magical plumes to step across the dais. "We will send another expedition tomorrow! Thus will the Kultakans learn the wages of defiance!"

The Eagle Knight showed no emotion. He kissed the earth before his ruler and backed to the door, stopping twice more to repeat the ritual of submission.

"My uncle?" The voice came from one of the rumpled courtiers, a handsome young man with steely courage glinting in his eyes. Even under the dirty cotton mantle, this man carried himself like a noble. Now he alone dared speak, when all around him, the older and more experienced lords of Naltecona held their tongues.

"Speak, Poshtli," the counselor said.

"My uncle, would you not desire to teach the Kultakans a true lesson? Could you, in your wisdom, see to the rebuilding of the armies smashed in this latest venture? When they are reformed, they can join your fresh forces, and all of them march to battle Kultaka!" Poshtli bowed politely and waited calmly for Naltecona's response. He knew, as did they all, that a hasty expedition against the warlike Kultakans could only result in further disaster. As the son of the counselor's sister, Poshtli could dare offer advice to Naltecona, but he had no assurance that such advice would be either welcomed or accepted.

"Indeed," mused the ruler with a disdainful glance at his other attendants. "This I shall do. We shall strike against Kultaka only when I am ready."

The doors burst open as Poshtli suppressed a sigh of relief. An obviously agitated warrior entered, quickly kneeling and kissing the earth as he bobbed toward the throne. His cotton battle armor was visible beneath the ragged shawl he had donned at the door.

"M-Most Highly Revered Counselor," he stammered, pausing in fear of Naltecona's reaction.

"What is it? Speak to me, man!" The counselor sat erect upon the throne-bench now, glaring at the reckless intruder.

"It is the temple . . . the temple of Zaltec! Most Excellent One, please, you must come and see for yourself!"

"What do you mean by this? I *must* do nothing. Explain yourself!"

"The temple has burst into flames! I myself stood in the great square and saw the eruption. Even though no spark was touched to it, the very stone itself took to blaze! The temple is destroyed!"

Naltecona rose to his feet and sauntered down the stairs, closely followed by his horde of courtiers. He stood a full head above them all and walked with a conscious pride that made him seem taller still.

Naltecona could not entirely contain his agitation as he found himself hurrying through the door into the grand hallway beyond. Followed by his retinue and the guard, he crossed a walkway over one of the canals, which flowed directly through his palace. He then climbed a stairway and emerged onto a broad balcony.

Across the huge plaza stood the great pyramid, higher than any other structure in Nexal. Side by side atop the pyramid stood the tall temple of Zaltec and the lesser shrines of the sun god, Tezca, and the rain god, Calor, the two favorite sons of Bloody Zaltec.

Indeed, true to the guard's word, the large temple in the center smoked and crackled at the heart of a roaring blaze. The stone walls glowed red, oozing thickly downward. Before the stunned eyes of the watchers, the mighty building slowly melted away.

"There was no spark to start it, Most Revered Counselor," repeated the guard.

"Indeed." Naltecona looked for a long time at the dying blaze, his face an inscrutable mask. *What can it mean?* he wondered secretly.

"We shall have it rebuilt at once!" he barked. "Until then, the clerics will use the Pyramid of the Moon. Zaltec shall still feast tonight."

They must not see my fear!

* * * * *

The deep growls of the guardian jaguars still rumbled around Hoxitl as the cleric made his way slowly toward the mouth of the Highcave. He muffled a curse as he tripped against a rock in the darkness.

For an entire long night, he and a trio of apprentices had climbed huge, smoldering Mount Zatal. The volcano overlooked the city of Nexal and was known to house the sacred soul of Zaltec himself. Now, not far below the summit, Hoxitl and the young priests reached the entrance to the mystic cave that the patriarch knew as the home of the Ancient Ones.

"Wait here," hissed the cleric, and his black-robed assistants needed no encouragement. They nodded their heads, bobbing the spiked ends of their blood-caked hair, then sat, sober-faced, outside the mouth of the cave.

Wisps of steam and burning, sulfurous vapors swirled around Hoxitl as the high priest entered the cave. He threw back his black hood and peered into the darkness, which was faintly broken by occasional flickering pools of crimson bubbling rock.

Suppressing a cough, Hoxitl held his breath as he passed a noxiously spuming geyser. Tears came to his eyes, further blinding him.

Then he sensed the presence of one of the Ancient Ones as the shadowy figure moved from an alcove to block his path.

"Praises to Zaltec!" whispered the cleric.

"High praises to the god of night and war!" hissed the black-cloaked figure, completing the ritual greeting.

Hoxitl stared at the Ancient One as he had stared a score of times before, but he learned nothing he had not learned from previous observations. Who are you? *What* are you? he wondered.

The Ancient One stood shorter than Hoxitl, and his figure was more slight. His body was completely swathed in dark robes and cloth, down to the thin gauze that concealed his hands while still allowing him full use of his dextrous, slender fingers.

"The sign," began Hoxitl. "We must know the meaning!"

"We know of your concern, and its significance." The dark figure spoke in muffled tones, his voice coarse. "You have guessed correctly in your words to the counselor. The fire in the sky is indeed the sign of Zaltec's hunger. He must have more hearts! He starves for lack of blood!"

Hoxitl nodded, pleased with his analysis of the sign, yet deeply disturbed by this evidence of the Ancient One's wisdom. This frail figure knew what had transpired in the Revered Counselor's throne room that very afternoon!

"But there is more." The voice of the Ancient One dropped even further, to a dull rasp. "Zaltec desires the heart of a young girl, a child living in the village of Palul. Her name is Erixitl, and her life must be given to Zaltec by the close of this tenday."

"As you wish. Our temple in Palul will claim her for evening sacrifice as soon as I can send word." Hoxitl did not bother asking why this particular girl had been deemed a threat to Zaltec. The word had been given, and the life of one more peasant girl amidst the dozens of sacrifices made to Zaltec each evening would not be noticed.

"Do not fail in this!" The words of the Ancient One this time were unusually strained, Hoxitl thought. He tried to fill his own voice with confidence. After all, he was the supreme human cleric of Zaltec, wielder of the Viperhand— but even to himself, the words sounded hollow.

"She shall be dead before next we meet."

* * * * *

From the *Chronicle of the Waning*:

Dedicated to the resplendent glory of the Plumed One, Golden Qotal.

The passing of an empire and a people can be a gradual thing, measured not in days nor years but in generations and centuries. Yet the waning of the Nexala, by this scale, becomes a sudden and cataclysmic plummet to disaster.

Even so, my chronicle must pass ten years in the space of these words. More threads must gather, and those at the core of the tale must grow firm and strong.

The portents shown to Naltecona grow more dire. His armies meet continual disaster in Kultaka. Bloody Zaltec, according to his patriarch, is displeased, and more slaves and captives are offered to sate his gory appetite.

The threads of the children grow firmly to young adulthood, one as a slave girl of the Kultaka, the other as a proud soldier, mastering on the field of battle the confidence that eluded him in the wizard's tower.

And now my portents show me another, a master warrior of the same race as young Halloran. But this is a man of great power over others, capable of brilliance and cruelty, remarkable audacity and perplexing greed. He is a commander of warriors the like of which I have never seen, and under his command they seem invincible. I know that he is to be a prime instrument of the Waning.

His name is Cordell.

2

THE CONQUEROR

Two dozen galleys surged through the narrow strait, oars beating the water in powerful cadence. Two dozen banners streamed in the air, representing an equal number of pirate captains. This fleet included the most savage buccaneers of the Pirate Isles.

Wicked battering rams—copper-tipped beams mounted in the bow of each galley—turned toward shore as Akbet-Khrul, Grand Vizier of the Pirate Isles and scourge of the Sword Coast, sent his fleet racing for the beach.

In moments, each brightly painted vessel struck the sandy bank, riding well above the surf on the force of its momentum. Instantly savage crews swarmed from their vessels, massing on the beach in a broad formation glittering with scimitars, spears, and axes.

The pirates of Akbet-Khrul were the most numerous, the most barbarous of the buccaneers inhabiting the Pirate Isles. Their unequalled and ferocious cruelty had earned them prominence among those isles. Now only a small group of mercenaries, hired by the desperate merchants of Amn, stood between Akbet-Khrul and complete domination of the waters off the central coast.

"Forward to the legion's destruction!" The pirate lord himself, Akbet-Khrul, gestured toward the line of defenders arrayed upon a low hilltop. "Let not one of them escape my wrath!"

The pirates surged forward, flushed with savage confidence. There were six of them for every one of the defenders on the distant hill, and the greatest worry in their captains' minds was that the mercenary legion before them would come to its senses and flee before the pirates could reach them.

Harsh voices barked through the morning air, and even the whirling gulls ceased their cries as the army began to advance. The flocks wheeled in graceful silence over the colorful phalanxes gradually moving inland from the rocky shore.

Banners fluttered in a breeze that slowly became a wind. The pirate army, three thousand strong, spread across a mile of frontage. Its wings spread hungrily, and its greedy jaws prepared to swallow the tiny group of defenders arrayed before it.

Then suddenly the whole mass of colorful, steel-bristling pirates halted and stood restlessly, waiting.

Ten figures dressed in shining crimson silks strutted forward from the pirate mass, each followed by a pair of retainers carrying a round iron pot. The black kettles contained heaps of glowing coals, frequently emitting sparks of hissing embers.

Ten pots were suspended from tripods, ten fires quickly kindled. Slowly, at first indistinct in the sunlight but soon glowing angrily, a fire thickened and brewed in each caldron.

Suddenly, one after another, the blazes surged upward until a tall column of fire erupted from each of the iron kettles.

These columns took shape, swirling and growing, sprouting limbs, leering with flame-scribed faces, until they became not columns of fire, but *beings* of fire. These beings remained in contact with their caldrons, but strained and reached in a crackling effort to break free.

Suddenly, as if in answer to a single command, each blazing figure twisted away from its pot and swept across the plain, a cyclone of fiery anger directed against the enemy beyond. Following in the scorched path of the fire things, the pirate army roared its lust for battle and surged forward.

"Perfect."

The remark, spoken with cool self-confidence, came from the midst of the company deployed on the hilltop. A golden pennant fluttered from a long pole beside him. As the wind snapped it taut, its emblem appeared: a shrieking golden eagle, wings spread and claws outstretched. Emblazoned in the bird's breast was the staring eye of all-seeing Helm, patron god of the Golden Legion. Outlined in black, the eagle shone vividly from a background of metallic, gleaming golden fabric.

"They come toward us quickly, with little thought of tactics. Matters will reach a head in good order—it will take them some time to reach us, and when they do, we hold the high ground."

The speaker turned, with the assurance of command, from the advancing army, addressing the small group of captains at his side. He was a small man, but he spoke and moved with a confidence so ironclad that other men could not help but listen. A black beard, too sparsely grown to hide his pockmarked skin, surrounded his tight mouth. Currently that mouth curved upward in an ingratiating, genuine smile.

"Almighty Helm has granted our enemies into your hands, Captain-General Cordell." Another man, tall and bearded, his slender form cloaked in a brown robe, nodded to the leader. A shirt of chain mail showed through an opening in his robe. His hands were cloaked in metal gauntlets, and each gauntlet bore the realistic image of a wide-staring eye—the unblinking symbol of Helm the Vigilant. The man carried a tall staff and wore a mace suspended from his belt. Though he towered over the others, his movements showed the stiffness of age. His bearded face was weather-beaten and dour.

"And he has granted me the tools with which to break them, Bishou Domincus." Cordell nodded warmly at the cleric. "You have seen to the spiritual strength of the legion well, my friend. Now we shall test that strength."

"May Helm find us worthy," said the Bishou humbly, nodding his thanks at the praise.

The captain-general turned to another warrior, heartily

thumping this steel-clad companion on the back. "Now, Captain Daggrande, is the ambush prepared?"

"My crossbowmen are ready, Captain-General." Captain Daggrande was shorter still than his commander, his broad shoulders and bowed legs marking him as a dwarf. He wore a shiny steel breastplate, and his skull was protected by a shiny helm with an encircling, uptilted brim. "I'll join my men now, sir."

"Indeed." Cordell nodded, dismissing the dwarf, utterly confident of the grizzled veteran's abilities. Daggrande and his hundred crossbowmen were in many ways the central weapon of the legion, for their deadly missiles allowed Cordell to engage an enemy before that enemy contacted his armored swordsmen or cavalry.

A more penetrating concern showed in his eyes as he looked around the group. "Where's Broker?"

"He sent us, General Cordell—Captain Alvarro and myself," Sergeant-Major Halloran answered. The young horseman wore a light chain shirt and bore a slender sword and small shield. A sleek black charger stood behind him, slowly tapping the earth with one hoof. Beside him stood Alvarro, a cavalryman with hair and beard of blazing red and teeth staggered in a gap-toothed grin. Alvarro was an older warrior who currently looked with unconcealed scorn at the young speaker. "His wounds," continued Halloran, "prevent Broker from fighting today."

Cordell nodded, studying the two men. Broker, his trusted captain of horse, was lost for the battle. Indeed, from what Cordell had seen of Broker's wounds, the captain might never fight again. So his current choice was obvious.

"Sergeant-Major—no make that *Captain* Halloran—you have command of the lancers in Broker's absence. Take tactical command of the Blue and Black companies."

The commander turned to regard Alvarro, staring frankly into the man's flashing eyes. Cordell made no attempt to justify his decision to promote the younger man. He had given an order and it would be obeyed. "You have tactical command of the Green and Yellow companies. Be certain you wait for the signal to charge!"

Again the brisk nod before continuing. "I want all four companies of lancers to charge together, in echelon from the right. Blue and Black companies take the lead, behind your banner. Captain Alvarro should follow with the Yellows and Greens."

"Yes, sir."

"But wait until the trumpet sounds your charge. I want no interference with Daggrande's volleys. Let the crossbows prepare them for your lances."

Halloran smiled grimly at the prospect, and suddenly his face looked much older. "We'll ride when the trumpets sound, and not a moment before."

Cordell eyed Halloran keenly, the commander's black eyes quickly taking the measure of the young warrior. Hold on to yourself and serve me well! he thought. Cordell had observed the courage and skill of these men for many years. Alvarro was the finer horseman, the more relentless and punishing fighter. But Halloran possessed a self-assurance that seemed to attract the confidence of other men. And Hal just might have the discipline to hold the high-spirited riders in check, something the impetuous Alvarro could never do.

The roar of the pirate charge grew louder as they swept into the last mile below the legion's hill. Quickly the captain-general turned to his other captains, admonishing his sword-and-buckler men to hold firm in the center, his reserve to remain in position until called forward. The other captains turned to their own companies, and soon Cordell stood alone on the low rise except for one other.

This one was not armored like the warriors, nor tall nor broad enough to seem at home with the company. Cordell's companion was not, in fact, a manly fighter. She had white hair and pearl-colored, translucent skin. A deep, cowled hood shaded her face, protecting every surface of that skin from harsh sunlight. If the hood had been thrown back, an observer would have noticed the pointed ears characteristic of the elves. Her flowing robe, with its many pockets, marked her as a magic-user.

"When the moment is right, you, my dear Darien, should

begin the destruction." Cordell's voice was softer than it had been with his captains. He took the mage's hands in his and looked directly into her pale eyes, wondering as always at the hidden depths there. In the ten years since she had joined him on the bloodstained field of Cordell's only defeat, she had become a necessary fixture of his life and his legion. Indeed, the two of them had, together, recruited the captains who now formed the legion's core.

"Icetongue will give them pause." Darien's slender fingers gently pulled a short black stick from her robes. "But their numbers are many."

"We *will* take them today," Cordell replied. "All veteran captains, the best men I've ever commanded. The Golden Legion is the finest company along the Sword Coast, and they answer to me alone!" Darien smiled ironically at him, her lips faintly visible in the depths of her robe.

The pirate army, preceded by the smoking columns of its fiery cyclones, surged closed. The shrill cries of three thousand voices reached their ears, a dissonant backdrop to their speech.

"Be careful," Cordell warned earnestly. "But kill them!"

"I shall," whispered the hooded one, her voice ice cool. Cordell felt a slight chill. As always, he found her dispassion toward death faintly disquieting. But that dispassion was unquestionably a great military asset, and he forced the feeling away.

"By tonight, all of Amn will celebrate our victory," Cordell reminded her. "And by tomorrow, we shall have an appointment with the Council of Six itself!"

The general turned back to the pirate army. He paid no attention to the fire magic, studying instead the colorful buccaneers. The enemy moved in a shimmering wall of silken splendor, their crimson shirts, emerald tunics, and blue and golden sashes all giving the force a festive holiday appearance. And still they advanced in their broad formation.

Darien let go the general's hand, with a lingering caress. The tight smile still creased her tiny mouth.

"Come, my dear." Cordell doffed his helm, broad-brimmed

like Daggrande's, and gestured gallantly toward the field below. "We have a battle to win."

*　*　*　*　*

Hoxitl, high priest of bloody Zaltec, picked his way into the cavern of the Ancient Ones. He came in darkness, leaving his attending band of young initiates to wait on the windswept slopes near the great volcano's summit. As always, his hair was blood-caked and pointed, and ashes thoroughly covered his skin.

He wondered, as he had wondered throughout the long climb, why his counselors had summoned him. It had been ten years since last he had spoken with the Ancient Ones. Then he had reported that the girl Erixitl of Palul had disappeared into the brush, presumably the victim of a jaguar. Though Zaltec had been robbed of his sacrifice, the Ancient One had seemed satisfied with the girl's disposal.

No jaguars guarded the entrance this time, but in the dim red glow of the cavern, he saw a pair of knights, dressed in their spotted hides, casually watching him through the open jaguar jaws of their helmets. The claw necklace of one jangled as he turned his head slightly, reminding the cleric of the potent talonmagic that armored the Jaguar Knight. These warriors did not carry the typical lances or javelins for guard duty in this confined space. Instead, they wielded clublike swords studded front and back with teeth of jagged obsidian.

Quickly Hoxitl passed deeper into the cave, leaving the guards behind. Bubbling mud pots chuckled softly, like thick red slime, and every now and then a gout of steam emerged from some fissure with a sharp hiss.

A column of green smoke suddenly erupted from the floor before Hoxitl, and the startled cleric almost leaped backward. Swiftly the smoke dispersed, and he saw the black-shrouded shape standing there. Hoxitl's astonishment grew as he saw several more figures cloaked all over in cloth and gauze.

"Praises to Zaltec!"

"High praises to the god of night and war!" The Ancient One completed the greeting, and the cleric stood nervously, wondering at the unprecedented number of shrouded figures surrounding him.

"The girl has been located," said the slight form, his whispered voice nonetheless strong and vaguely menacing. "She is in Kultaka and has been a slave there these past years."

"The girl?" Hoxitl's mind tripped for a minute, then leaped backward a full decade. "Erixitl of Palul?"

"Indeed. She is owned by a man who pays Zaltec no heed, a worshiper of Qotal and former Eagle Knight. It was only through the fortuitous travels of a young Jaguar Knight that we learned of her capture."

"What—what is to be done about her?" The cleric felt disturbed by the news, only because he sensed that the Ancient Ones were somehow *afraid* of this girl.

"That is why we have summoned you. Our talonmagic will go to Kultaka tonight, aided by your spell of sending. A vessel of reception already awaits the enchantment."

Hoxitl nodded. He understood that. Though the Ancient Ones could wield far mightier talonmagic than either the clerics or the Jaguar Knights, they still needed the help of a priest for such a long-range casting.

The priest knelt on the stone floor together with the dark-swathed Ancient Ones. The latter lowered themselves with a supple grace, not at all like elderly humans. Hoxitl, as always, dismissed any speculation as to his counselors' nature, for he felt certain such questions could only lead to trouble.

* * * * *

The temple guards stood aside, each pounding his wooden drum in steady cadence. The throng, citizens of Nexala numbering a hundred thousand or more, stood in awe about the great plaza. Finally the grand procession emerged from the palace!

A collective gasp rippled through the crowd as the woman came into view. Resplendent upon her gilded litter, *supported by ten Eagle Knights, she rode in lordly luxury, casting her eyes across the multitude. . . .*

"Ouch!" Erixitl started as a drop of scalding water splashed onto her bare arm. Annoyed, she forced herself away from her daydreams to pay attention to her task, lest she burn herself more seriously.

"Young master needs his bath!" she chanted ironically. She carried the full jug of steaming water on her head, carefully following the footpath through the garden. The bathhouse of her owner's estate lay just before her.

Erix sighed as she sighed a hundred times a day, had sighed a million times over the last ten years. Truly she had been fortunate, for Huakal, her owner, was kind, gentle, and one of the wealthiest men in Kultaka. Once an Eagle Knight of great repute, he had commanded several hundredmen in the wars with Nexal. He had used his influence to purchase her immediately following her arrival in Kultaka, offering the Jaguar Knight who had captured her an unusually high sum. She had been assigned tasks in his large home before the priests of Zaltec had even had a chance to see her. Since then, he had treated her more like a slightly bothersome niece than a slave.

Never had she feared from Huakal condemnation for sacrifice—a common fate for a Maztican slave who displeased a master. Huakal had even allowed her to retain her feather token, now the only memento she carried from her childhood in Palul. She usually kept the jade object concealed under her robe, so as not to call attention to it, but nevertheless Huakal knew of it. It would have been well within his prerogatives to claim it for himself.

For ten years, she had grown up in Kultaka. Only rarely had she even seen, and never had she spoken with, anyone of her own Nexalan people. Always a pretty girl, she had become a beautiful young woman. Unlike many slaves, however, she had not been touched by her master. He had even, somehow, managed to keep his unruly son away from her.

Erix had managed to learn a little of the True World, for Huakal was a worldly man who had seen Nexal, Pezelac, and even the distant jungle lands of the Payit. Perhaps because this slave girl was clearly more intelligent than his own son, Huakal had taken the time to share some of his knowledge with her.

Still, so much of her life had been taken from her that she did not want to give up the rest of it. Kultaka was a clean, active city, but it was a shabby substitute for the great capital of her own people. She spent her days imagining storied Nexal, now farther away than ever. Even the nearest lands of her people lay across desert and mountain.

Too, there was the matter of the "young master," her owner's only son. An arrogant boor of a young warrior, Callatl never let her pass without making a rude comment, gesture, or worse. The young man wasted his days pursuing his futile objective of becoming a Jaguar Knight. Even his father had admitted long ago that he lacked the elite qualifications to aspire toward Eagle Knighthood. Though Callatl's prowess as a warrior was far short of the ideal, Erix feared him nevertheless.

Erixitl carried the water carefully, balancing the heavy jug to prevent further spillage. The vessel, a rich emerald green, bore engravings upon two sides. Each portrayed, in crude relief, the fanged image of Qotal, the Plumed One. Like her father, Huakal paid homage to this ancient and nearly forgotten god. She held the jar by the jaws of the relief, ensuring a strong grip.

The liquid within was scalding hot, and she dared not move quickly. Finally she reached the square stone building, set among roses and trickling streams of clear water, where the members of the family enjoyed their daily baths. Pushing through a curtain of hanging reeds, she entered the steamy bath chamber.

"More water, Master Callatl," she said quietly.

A strapping youth sprawled in the deep tub, taking no notice of her except to move slightly, allowing her enough space to pour the water without burning him.

She lowered the jug, ignoring the steam rising into her eyes, and carefully poured. Even so, a few drops spattered onto the bather's coppery skin.

Erix felt a sudden chill in the room, despite the steaming

bath. The reed torches around the walls seemed to flicker and fade, casting the bathhouse in darker shadows. The girl knew nothing of talonmagic, could not know that sorcery of sinister nature had just settled around her and Callatl, a spell sent by Hoxitl and the Ancient Ones, far away in the Highcave. Nevertheless she stepped cautiously backward, and her hand went unconsciously to the golden feather token, the gift from her father, that still hung from her neck.

"Stupid wench!" The young man sprang to his feet, uncaring of his nakedness. He raised his hand to cuff her, and she instinctively raised the jug to protect her face. The torches flared back to light as the talonmagic waned, but the damage had been done. Callatl's body twisted from the enormity of his wrath.

His fist crashed into the vessel, striking it from her hands. It shattered on the tile lip of the bathtub, and a jagged shard struck Callatl's knee, drawing blood.

The man stepped from the tub as Erix backed slowly away. She trembled in sudden fright, for she had never seen him so suddenly and irrationally enraged. His face might have been handsome, except for the close set of his eyes and his tight, cruel mouth. "You have teased me for too long, Temptling! Now it is your turn to pay!"

She spun and dashed for the door, but Callatl dove instantly after her. He seized her arm and twisted her to the floor.

"Stop!" she cried, crunching her fist into his already flat nose. Her struggles only served to amuse him. He seized her wrists easily and pressed her against the floor.

"Accept your slavery, *Feather Princess!*" He hissed the nickname in mockery. He had taunted her with it since noticing, years earlier, her fondness for her feathered token. "My father has been far too gentle with you!"

Real fear seized Erix, a panic that suffused her wiry frame with unnatural strength. She squirmed and jabbed, and suddenly her legs were free, the young man sprawled half across her.

"In the name of the gods, *stop!*" Her knee flew viciously upward. Callatl shrieked, mindless with agony, heedless of the sound echoing through the garden, around the court-yard and into the sprawling house.

"Beast!" she spat, punching him in the stomach as he rolled away from her. He tumbled through the shards of the pot, cutting his face and arms, but somehow he staggered to his feet. His face twisted with hatred, blood streaming from his forehead and nose, he sprang at the slave girl.

Erixitl picked up a large chunk of the broken jar. She did not notice the feathered god's image, Qotal's full visage, remaining uncracked on the piece of pottery in her hands. Callatl's fingers reached, clawlike, for her face as she slammed the shard into her attacker's throat.

The young noble gurgled helplessly as he dropped to his knees, then sprawled on his face. Dimly, Erix heard the musical tinkling of the curtain parting behind her. She turned to see the dignified face of Huakal, her owner. His patrician features grew pale as he took in the scene.

Erixitl dropped to her knees and kissed the floor as Huakal knelt beside his son. The nobleman swept his cloak of brilliant macaw feathers from his shoulders to cover Callatl. The young man coughed in agony, his breath bursting in gasps and gurgles.

Terrified, Erixitl looked into the face of the man who had treated her so kindly, who had never touched her, in anger or otherwise. His face was wrung with suffering, but his voice was steady.

"If he dies, your heart will be fed to Tezca on the following dawn."

* * * * *

Halloran made his way through a line of sword-and-buckler men. This company, commanded by Captain Garrant, stood in plain sight on the slope of the hill. The howling pirates swarmed closer, but the pace of their advance flagged slightly after nearly two miles of charging forward. The young captain suddenly realized that Cordell had selected defensive ground far from the beach for good reason.

He walked farther down the hill, toward Daggrande's company, which lay in ambush behind a low stone wall. A sense of excitement tingled through Halloran as he approached the crossbowmen and his own lancers, who waited beside Daggrande's men in a small olive grove.

This legion, these warriors, were his home. They had become the finest, most secure home he had ever known. When Cordell and Daggrande had discovered him nearly ten years ago, a gangly young tough wandering the streets of Mulsanter, Halloran could never have imagined himself feeling such a sense of belonging about anything. A hungry orphan, his magic-using days brutally ended by catastrophe in Arquiuius's tower, he had been suspicious of these silver-armored captains.

But he had served them, first as a page to the captain-general and then as a squire to Daggrande and then Broker. He had learned the ways of war, fighting and killing before his eighteenth year had begun. A natural horsemen, Halloran had found his true role as a lancer—much to Daggrande's disgust, since the dwarf had hoped to see him wield a heavy crossbow.

Now Broker was gone, terribly wounded by these pirates in the previous day's skirmish. Bishou Domincus had saved Broker's life with his healing magic, but the horseman had still lost the use of his legs. The memory of that loss gave Halloran's eagerness for battle a bitter edge. Today Broker would be avenged.

Halloran found Daggrande behind a low stone wall. The dwarf's unit of crossbowmen crouched behind the rocky barrier, patiently waiting for their captain's command. The motley collection of humans and dwarves wore an assortment of armor types, some clad in leather, others in chain. Many wore bloody bandages over wounds sustained in previous skirmishes with the pirates. All of the bowmen looked grizzled and disreputable, but Halloran well knew the lethal effectiveness of their heavy missiles.

"How much longer?" asked the young cavalryman. He tried to keep his voice steady, but anticipation of the coming battle filled him with nervous energy. His own unit of lancers waited restlessly in an olive grove behind the wall. Across the wall, still a half-mile distant but closing rapidly, came the charging wave of color, steel, and flame that was the pirate army.

The dwarf laughed, a sharp bark of sound. "Soon enough, I'll wager." Daggrande studied Halloran closely. "After all these campaigns, why are you acting like a young recruit facing his first foe?"

Hal returned his old companion's gaze with a sheepish grin. "Cordell gave me the standard of the lancers. I'll be leading all four companies."

Daggrande grinned. "You're ready for that. But what about Alvarro?" The impetuous redhead and his jealous nature were well known to the other captains.

"Second in command. He'll follow with the last two companies." I hope, he added silently.

The dwarf nodded. "Just don't lose your head. Wait till that trumpet tells you to go! Remember what Cordell and I have drilled into you, and you'll do all right."

"We hold the high ground," Hal said. "I won't give that advantage away!" Halloran's answer was deadly serious. "Cordell's right. If we time this properly, Akbet-Khrul will be broken once and for all!"

Daggrande laughed at his companion's earnestness. "And we'll be out of work!"

Halloran laughed, too, relaxing somewhat. "I expect the captain-general will find us something to fight."

"Good luck. You'd best get to your men."

"And to you. Try to shoot straight this time, will you?" Hal said, flashing a quick grin.

Daggrande huffed indignantly, but the cavalryman had already slipped into the grove. In moments, he reached his charger, Storm. The roan mare danced eagerly, anxious for battle.

"The standard, Sergeant-Major." A squire stood beside the mount, bearing the lance with the proud pennant of the Blue Lancers. The long banner, portraying a golden pegasus on a sea-blue background, snapped readily in the growing breeze.

"Captain, now." Halloran smiled as he slipped smoothly into the saddle and took the long staff. The squire grinned enthusiastically.

The olive grove screened their position from the advancing enemy, but the rows of trees provided good visibility to the right and left. He could see, within a few hundred feet to his right, the black, yellow, and green pennants of the other companies. At the far end of the line, Alvarro glowered at him from the back of a prancing stallion, his mouth split into a grimace that displayed his crooked, uneven teeth.

A full hundred sleek horses pranced anxiously as an equal number of steel-tipped lances came to rest at their riders' sides. Some of the steeds were black, others were brown or roan or gray. They were all impatient to charge. Be patient, Hal thought. Your time will come.

Halloran tried to suppress a giddy exhilaration. Helmstooth, the longsword given to him by Cordell personally, hung lightly at his side. By Helm, what a glorious commander the captain-general was! Halloran's heart nearly burst with pride at the honor that had been accorded him.

But Cordell was the glue that truly held the legion together. His skill as a commander, his eloquence as a speaker, his courage in battle, all served to unite his men and propel them toward great deeds.

Through the olive trees, Halloran could see the pirates advancing as Cordell had predicted, still preceded by their twisting cyclones of fire. The horsemen had a splendid view of the developing battle.

The scrub brush withered beneath the fiery columns, many bushes bursting into flame as the cyclones passed. Hal still counted ten of the unnatural blazes, advancing in a long skirmish line ahead of the army.

Suddenly he saw a pale white flash, like a blast of moonlight potent enough to shine in the daylight. The cone-shaped whiteness exploded from a point ahead of the army, expanding to his left. In the same instant as the flash, three of the fiery columns hissed into vapors and disappeared.

Once again came the flash of light, from the same point but this time expanding to Hal's right, and four more of the cyclones vanished.

"Icetongue!" he murmured to himself, feeling relief mixed with a little horror. All the legion knew of Darien, the elf-mage. Aloof and distant toward all but Cordell, this made her affection toward the commander seem all that much more passionate to the men of the legion. And she was mysterious, always heavily robed during daylight, for her albino skin reputedly suffered acutely from the rays of the sun.

Yet her power! Of course she had her slender wand and its deadly blast of ice. But she also could call a searing wall of fire to burst from the ground, a lightning bolt to crackle into the midst of an enemy formation, or even a swarm of meteors to smash with crushing force to the ground. On more than one occasion, those powers had secured victory for the mercenaries during a heated, hard-contested battle.

He saw the black-robed figure of the wizard, standing alone ahead of the army, and then suddenly Darien vanished. Halloran guessed she teleported herself back to the safety of the legion's position.

The pirates continued to surge closer, not visibly demoralized by the damage to their fiery skirmishers. A pair of fire columns still swirled forward to Hal's left, and one lone blaze advanced off to the right. Then he heard the thunderous bark of a man's voice, carrying even over the roar of the enemy's approach, and Hal knew that Bishou Domincus had added the might of Helm to the battle.

The pair of fire columns advancing together separated slightly to pass on either side of a small, marshy pond. As the cleric's magic took hold, however, the waters of the pond surged from their banks and swept across the field in a small flood. They swirled around the bases of the flaming columns, which hissed and writhed in agony. Slowly the fiery forms sizzled into steam. Still the army surged forward, a hundred yards away, now and closing fast.

"Now, by Helm!" Daggrande's bark suddenly carried over the battlefield. The brimmed steel helmets of his crossbowmen suddenly popped over the stone wall, followed instantly by the sharp clatter of a hundred heavy crossbows casting their missiles.

Intent upon the line of sword-and-buckler men a hundred yards farther up the hill, the pirates faltered at the sudden onslaught from the missile troops. Smoothly, Daggrande's men began to recock their cumbersome weapons, while Akbet-Khrul and his lieutenants hysterically commanded their men to renew their charge. A savage yell rippled through the air, rasping from thousands of pirate throats.

"Shoot, and again!" The second volley of bolts took a savage toll, the powerful weapons driving through the bodies of unarmored defenders and penetrating the metal shields and chain shirts of the occasional armored pirates with lethal force.

A great blossom of fire exploded in the enemy's center, fire magic working for the legion now as Darien cast two great fireballs into the midst of the pirate army. The inferno created by each spell dealt instant death to anyone caught in the effect.

Halloran felt his mare easing forward. For a moment, his hold on the reins relaxed, but then he pulled in sharply. He cast a harsh glare down the line of eager lancers, even as he wondered at Daggrande's audacity. Does he have time to shoot again?

The howling mob of pirates came on with undiminished savagery. Halloran watched the bowmen laboriously crank their weapons, certain they could not fire before the scimitars of the pirates cut them to ribbons. The leading attacker—Akbet-Khrul himself, Hal felt certain—was less than fifteen yards away when the first crossbowman raised his weapon. The pirate's face was twisted beyond human recognition, a fanatical picture of battlefield savagery.

The shrieks of the attackers pounded in Halloran's ears. I can't wait any longer! We must charge now! But then another crossbow, a dozen more, were loaded and aimed, their foes a scant ten yards away. Why don't they shoot?

In another instant, the full rank of missile weapons stood armed and ready . . . five yards. "Shoot! And charge!" A brass trumpet from the hilltop brayed its exclamation point to the order as Daggrande's bark was lost in the din.

"Forward, lancers!" Hailoran's own bellow seemed monstrously loud, though still inaudible, but the tilt of his pennant gave his men the sign. A hundred horses sprang from the grove, some leaping the wall among Daggrande's archers while others swept through a meadow off to the side, riding obliquely into the heart of the pirate horde.

Even as his horse sprang over the stone barrier, Halloran saw the effects of the last volley, delivered at deadly short range. The powerful bolts of the crossbows sometimes ripped through two pirates in succession, and all across the route of their advance he could see broken and writhing bodies.

The shock of the charging lancers completely shattered the momentum of the pirate onslaught. Hal looked for Akbet-Khrul, thought he recognized his torn body among several crossbow shafts, and then thundered forward with the exhilarating momentum of the charge.

*   *   *   *   *

Naltecona rode the feather platform to the top of the great pyramid, unconsciously cursing the slow, graceful pace of the regal lift. The high priests and magicians of Nexal, together forming his closest advisers, climbed the steep stairs below as they all sought the vantage of the high temple.

For the gods once more surrounded Nexal with signs and omens. Where once they had incinerated the temple of Zaltec atop this very pyramid, this time they displayed their displeasure not with a fiery temple, nor indeed with any sign directly striking the huge city around him. The gods vented their wrath beyond the city, where it could be seen by all of Nexal.

The great city of Nexal, Heart of the True World, lay amid the crystalline splendor of four broad lakes. Each lake was crossed by a causeway, giving access to the city from all directions. Canoes harvested wetland crops and fish from the lakes, and massive floating gardens further extended the domain of Nexal every day.

The lakes were named after the four predominant gods.

The three largest, to the north, east, and south, contained the freshest water and supported all the commerce. They were called, respectively, Zaltec, Calor, and Tezca. The smallest, to the west, was brackish and salty. This was named for the Silent Counselor, Qotal.

Now great columns of steam rose into the air, hissing from three of the lakes, billowing skyward in massive clouds that threatened to block out the sun. Sharp, unnatural waves hurled tepid water into the many canals of the city, toppling canoes and threatening to inundate low buildings. Only the brackish Lake Qotal remained calm, the only waves on its surface caused by the normal kiss of a light breeze.

Naltecona avoided looking at the lakes, but the sight of the priests and magicians offered him no comfort. In the plaza below the temple stood his many courtiers and lords, but they seemed even less useful than the advisers on the pyramid with him.

Lately the one man whose counsel helped, whose presence gave Naltecona confidence, had been his nephew Poshtli. And now that proud Eagle Knight was commanding a military expedition to punish the vassal state of Pezelac, far from Nexal. Naltecona felt very lonely, and the gloriously colored lift, slowly raising him through the air beside the temple, seemed only to emphasize that loneliness.

Almost desperately, the Revered Counselor looked up. A great emerald fan swirled with regal grace, freely floating in the air above Naltecona's head. Around him spread the blue summer sky, a great cloudless dome. Soaring into that sky jutted the three massive volcanoes surrounding Nexal. Despite the summer heat, two of the mountains wore caps of gleaming snow. The third, Zatal, was the highest, but the heat of its internal fires kept the mountaintop clear of snow.

The featherlift reached the top, setting Naltecona on the platform with the airy smoothness of *pluma*. The ruler spun through an angry circle, confronted on all sides by the portentous omens of the gods.

"More signs! Why must you plague me with mysteries and dire portents?" He shook his fist at the lakes, as if challenging the gods for whom they were named. Ignoring the anxious looks of the priests and magicians, who gasped for breath as they joined him on the platform at the pyramid's summit, he shouted, "For once give me an answer instead of more questions!"

Naltecona raged, his anger divided between the assembled advisers before him and the invisible forms of the gods beyond. What does it mean? The great ruler forced himself to regain control, but the latest evidence of the gods' displeasure made it very difficult.

The Revered Counselor paced atop the great pyramid, the grandest structure in all Nexal. A dozen priests scuttled from his path and then scurried to remain close behind him. An equal number of magicians also hovered near. The latter possessed few real powers, but practiced spells that allowed them some knowledge of future events. For this reason, the counselor sometimes demanded their services.

Nearby on the platform stood the great temple of Zaltec, rebuilt after the mysterious fire a decade before. The statue of Zaltec himself, within the temple, was now caked with the dried blood of thousands of sacrifices. The hungry mouth of the god gaped open, and this was the receptacle into which the sacrificial hearts were thrown.

"Go from me, all of you!" the counselor suddenly roared. "Wait, Coton . . . I desire you to stay."

The other high priests glared at their colleague as they started down the long column of steps. In a mythos crowded with jealous and vengeful gods, the worshipers of each deity cast careful eyes upon their rivals. That Coton, the patriarch of a long-forgotten god, one who did not even expect the sacrifice of human victims, should receive special notice from the Revered Counselor seemed to the others a dire threat.

Hoxitl, high priest of Zaltec, lingered behind as if he in particular would challenge his ruler's wishes. The cleric suddenly thought better of the idea, starting down the long stairway to the plaza below, though not before he cast a vicious sidelong glare at Coton. The patriarch of Qotal did not acknowledge his colleague's look.

Naltecona ignored the discomfort of his clerics, waiting

until all of them had descended beyond earshot. The pair stood alone, high above the city, on the flat summit of the pyramid. He fixed the white-haired Coton with an iron gaze, as if the force of his will could compel the patriarch to speak.

Then he whirled away, knowing that Coton was bound by his vow. "Why is it that the one cleric who might offer me comfort and wisdom has taken it upon himself not to speak?"

He turned back to the cleric. "All the others will instruct me for hours on end! They will all tell me that their gods are hungry, that they need more hearts, more bodies, to feed them! And we give them those hearts, and still they send these signs!" Naltecona's anguish twisted his voice as he looked skyward, earthward, anyplace away from those tormented, mocking lakes.

"What does this mean?" Naltecona's voice lost all control, ringing shrill and frantic. "You know, Coton. *You see and understand!* You must tell me!"

The cleric met the gaze of the Revered Counselor with his own eyes, compassionate and grim at the same time.

"The lake of Qotal shows no disturbance, while the others seem to boil away before our eyes!" Naltecona raged on. "How can I understand? I must know!"

Coton did not look away, but, of course, neither did he speak. In sudden frustration, the leader turned back to the unnatural vista surrounding his glorious city.

"Is this the sign of Qotal's return?" Naltecona asked the question in a subdued tone, hoping and fearing at the same time. He continued, as if ultimately relieved to have a listener who would not speak in return.

"I remember your teaching, patriarch, before you assumed your grand office and took your bothersome vow! You told us of the god-king Qotal, the Plumed One, rightful ruler of the True World . . . how he sailed to the east in his grand canoe, promising to return when the people of Maztica had proven themselves worthy of his leadership!"

For the first time, the cleric moved his gaze from Naltecona, looking to the east as if he expected the image of the

Plumed One to appear momentarily. Then Coton turned his age-wizened eyes back to Naltecona, and the counselor met his gaze with pathetic eagerness, seeking an answer in those eyes that was not to be found.

"This is the sign, I believe," said Naltecona, forcing himself to accept the evidence.

"Qotal returns to Maztica."

❧ 3 ❧

THE COUNCIL OF AMN

Cordell stroked the thin wisps of his beard, striving to contain his delight. He looked, he knew, resplendent in his green robe with its collar of emeralds and diamonds. Boots of blackest leather reached past his knees, and his ornamental steel breastplate and helm gave him a gleaming martial air.

Beside him stood Darien, her hood thrown back and her striking white hair glowing with its own iridescence. Her own gown of blood-red silk shone in stark contrast to her alabaster skin. A cluster of rubies gleamed in a lone hairpin, a shocking burst of color against the elf's snowy white hair.

"I tell you, one spell and we would have them all!" The elf spoke in an almost inaudible whisper, but the urgency of her argument was plain.

"No . . . it's too risky. The council is certain to have defenses against such an attempt!" Cordell spoke in a similar whisper.

"But do you think you can persuade them?"

"I am certain of it."

"The Council, Captain-General." A liveried guard opened the brass door with a flourish, bowing low and waving Cordell and his lady into the room.

Cordell strode casually through the door, Darien feather light on his arm. They walked on a carpet of snowy white, the elf woman's crystal slippers gliding through the woolen nap while the general's boots left faint smudges of mud.

"Captain-General Cordell, the Council of Six salutes you. You have struck a blow for Amn, and for the forces of order

❧ 52 ❧

throughout the Realms." The speaker was a member of the council, one of the ruling merchant princes of Amn. He stood in anonymous darkness across the room. His voice was deep and resonant. The general could see several figures there, above him and behind a partition that looked like the front of a great bench.

Several small candles, shaded with stained-glass screens, cast a dim light through the chamber. The council held court at the great bench, while those who entered followed the carpet to a large, circular area before the six merchant princes of Amn.

Cordell noticed with satisfaction that all six members were present. All six stood to greet him. Each face, of course, was concealed by a black silken gauze of airy weight that provided total concealment. The six were the masters of the mighty trading nation of Amn, and their identities were the most closely guarded secrets in the land.

"The end of Akbet-Khrul's pirates is a historical moment for us all."

Cordell waved off the gratitude, raising his helmet and bowing deeply. Darien curtsied with elven grace, and the six members of the council took their seats as Cordell began to speak.

"Gentlemen—forgive me, and ladies, should you be present—it is an honor to attend you. I must point out in all humility that there may be small pirate outposts still thriving in the depths of the isles. But passage through Asavir's Channel should be uninterrupted for the foreseeable future."

"Indeed!" This speaker, a man with a rather high-pitched voice, sat on the far left of the council. Cordell pictured a fat merchant rubbing his palms together in glee, though of course the mask and voluminous robe made any estimate as to the merchant's appearance purely conjectural. "You will find your payment in the chest before you, together with a bonus we trust you will find satisfactory."

"Your generosity, as always, overwhelms me." With a supreme effort of will, Cordell forced himself to avoid looking at the chest. He paused, allowing them to note and wonder at his restraint. When he sensed their growing curiosity, he resumed.

"I wish to present you an alternate proposition, however—a chance to keep your treasure, and gain more. Tenfold, fiftyfold what you have here!"

He paused for another moment to let the seed take root. All six of the merchant princes sat unmoving, waiting for him to continue.

"The trade routes to Waterdeep and all the coast are open to you now, but what of the great land trail to Kara-Tur?" The image of vast Kara-Tur, he knew, could not help but conjure images of tea, spices, rubies, and silk among the merchants.

Cordell quickly launched his arguments. "These routes are closed now by the hordes of the steppes! The spices, the arts—treasures such as this very rug beneath my feet—all the goods of the East are lost."

This reminder, painful to all profit-motivated folk, was not really necessary. Everyone knew that all land routes through the center of the continent, the trade paths for all the goods of Kara-Tur, were currently useless. A vast migratory horde of barbarian horsemen had closed all these lands to civilized pursuits.

"Lost not just to Amn, remember, but lost to the entire Realms! Hundreds of cities thirst for goods that are not to be had!

"Think, O princes, what rewards await the one who opens trade with the East . . . and the ones who support him!" They listen well . . . they will be mine.

"Surely you don't suggest that your legion open a route through the steppeland?" the squeaky merchant asked incredulously. The horde reputedly numbered more than a million savage fighters.

"Certainly not. That is a fool's task—at least, a task for fools other than myself." The members chuckled politely. They come closer, Cordell chortled inwardly.

"I ask you, Council of Amn, to fund me on an *ocean* voyage to Kara-Tur! I intend to sail to the west to reach the East!"

Two council members snorted in amusement, one shook

his head, and three others remained immobile. Cordell turned to these unmoving ones and pressed on.

"Astrologers and sages have long said such a voyage is possible. Provide me with a dozen sturdy ships, provisions, and trading goods. My ships will carry the pick of the legion. With the support of your offices, I could take to sea in six months, before the first snows."

"But where . . . how would you sail?" The deep-voiced merchant prince, the one who had greeted Cordell upon his entrance, seemed intrigued.

"West. Actually, slightly south by west. Our Bishou has consulted Helm, patron god of the legion. Also we have sought the advice of the greatest sages on the coast, have conferred with wizards from Waterdeep to Calimport!

"The auguries are splendid. One strident symbol rides above all, in every vision. With each word from our god, the Bishou sees this promise. It dominates the seeking spells of the wizards, provides the theme underlying the speculations of the sages.

"It is an image so strong that we cannot but believe it lies before us on this quest.

"That image, good council members, is gold."

I have them.

*   *   *   *   *

"It is settled, then." The old cleric looked approvingly past Huakal to the prize of the past few hours of haggling. Erixitl stood motionless before his gaze, frightened and mystified by the proceedings.

In the months since her struggle with Callatl, little had changed in Erix's life. The young man had slowly recovered, though his voice had been permanently garbled by the girl's blow to his throat. Even worse, Erix's blow to his groin had destroyed his ability to father children. But throughout his son's long and agonized recovery, Huakal had been curiously distant . . . until this morning.

Then he had summoned her to meet this man, this white-robed cleric of Qotal. Huakal and Kachin, the cleric, spoke at some length in the language of the Payit. She understood little of the conversation between the two men, but she had noticed the cleric paying close attention to her. Now they switched tongues to Kultakan.

"A chest of cocoa, ten mantles, and two quills of gold dust, then. The girl is yours." Huakal nodded with finality.

Erix's heart sank. She had been sold! Then she thought a moment about the fee that had just been detailed. A man could buy a dozen able-bodied workers for that price!

Huakal turned to Erix, his voice firm. "This is Kachin. He is your new owner. He will be taking you to Payit." She looked at him with her proud, wide eyes, disturbing him. She has never acted like a slave! Huakal thought. She doesn't know what it is to be a slave! But those eyes. . . .

The Kultakan noble walked brusquely past the girl, and she wondered if she saw tears in his eyes.

For a moment, she felt a sincere impulse to embrace him, to thank him or comfort him or say farewell. But even more quickly a sense of panic and foreboding flooded her, and she silently cursed Huakal for sending her away.

True, many nobles would have had her sacrificed without a second thought after such a fight as she had won. Callatl's scars would never heal. She had, in fact, expected, and prepared, to die.

But Huakal had spared her, selling her now instead for some absurd price to a cleric from the far fringes of Maztica. She knew little of Payit, other than that it was a land of jungles, swamps, poisonous serpents, and near-savage people.

The strange cleric's odd speech patterns and unusual dress also puzzled and frightened her. He wore a simple white cotton mantle, unadorned. He wore no feathers nor gold nor stones. His skin was very dark, his hair gray and long and tied in a single knot. His face, while creased with many wrinkles, was round and quick to smile. He moved his short, somewhat rotund form easily for an obviously old man.

Unlike the other clerics she had known, worshipers of Zaltec or his hungry offspring, this priest was obviously well fed. The only recognizable thing about him was the pendant of the Plumed One hanging about his neck, marking him as a cleric of Qotal. Perhaps the Feathered God did not require his devotees to fast as frequently as did those who worshiped Zaltec and the younger gods.

The faith of Qotal was not so widely spread as that of the warlike Zaltec, or the essential Calor and Tezca with their life-giving rain and sun. Still, Erix knew her father had revered Qotal, though this had been a private matter with him. Huakal, too, had maintained a shrine to the Plumed One. Huakal's son, like her own brother, had chosen to worship Zaltec instead of the gentle god of their fathers.

But Erix had learned to fear clerics, for they too often had but one use for a slave. And now she had been sold to a cleric who would take her to the distant shores of the True World, who for some mysterious purpose had paid an exorbitant sum for her.

She saw Huakal standing before her. Vaguely she noticed his eyes lingering on her token before he raised them to look at her face. As a woman of Maztica, she should have lowered her gaze then, but she did not, instead meeting her former master's gaze with her own penetrating dark eyes.

"You are a rare treasure, Erixitl." Huakal's voice came to her, seemingly from a great distance. The noble had indeed succumbed to emotion, and he made no effort to hide his tears as he spoke. "You are a child of grim destiny. My line has ended with Callatl, and now you are swept away. You shall go to Payit, and the land will not be the same for your being there.

"May the gods be kind to you."

*　*　*　*　*

From the *Chronicle of the Waning*:

May the wisdom of the Feathered One shine across the True World!

Now, just as swans take to the air, I see the strangers spread their wings and put to sea. But these creatures that glide ever closer to Maztica are more hawks than swans.

They come with powers beyond my understanding, devices and tools the likes of which I have never seen. I cannot imagine the uses of many of the things I am given the vision to observe. But most frightening of all my auguries is not the tools, nor the powers of these strangers.

It is the men themselves.

I sense—even across worlds of distance—that these men are somehow different. Their god is a fierce lord, perhaps more than the equal of the younger gods of Maztica. They are drawn by things, compelled by forces that I cannot comprehend. Visions of metal and stones move them with a power that leaves me mystified and awed.

I only know that they terrify me!

❦ 4 ❦

JOURNEY

Everywhere the city of Murann, the main seaport of Amn, smelled of fish. From its plastered villas and elegant gardens to its teeming slums and bustling mercantile districts, the penetrating, oily odor intruded throughout each building, penetrating walls and floors and every fiber of clothing.

But nowhere was the smell so strong as at the shore of the harbor itself, where Halloran now found himself laboring under the blaze of a hot afternoon sun. The waterfront bustled with activity—the cries of animals, the creaking of cranes and timbers, and the shouts of men. A pounding din arose behind him, where one of the greatest shipyards of the Sword Coast churned out vessel after vessel—heavy galleys for war or trade; stocky, seaworthy caravels; or large carracks, with their towering rear decks.

It was one of the latter, a short, blunt-bowed vessel with three tall masts and the characteristic raised deck at her stern, that stood at the dockside by the young cavalryman. Like the other carracks and caravels, *Osprey* carried no oars, depending upon the rigging of her sails to maneuver with or against the wind. Stores of salt pork and bacon had been stored belowdecks, and Hal now watched a group of stevedores roll huge kegs of water over the ship's aft gangplank.

Suddenly an anxious whinny pulled his attention to the bow.

"Easy now! She's not to be struck!" Halloran barked the rebuke at the swarthy stevedores who struggled to lead his mare onto a narrow gangplank.

The trio of men set back to their task with more patience, and soon had coaxed Storm onto the sheltered deck of the *Osprey*. Two other horses already stood there, under the partial shelter of a taut tarpaulin.

"And what will be the shore she next trods?" mused a gruff voice.

Halloran heard familiar clumping footsteps and turned to greet Captain Daggrande.

"The spice fields of Kara-Tur, I should think."

Daggrande snorted. "Not in the Realms I know! Sailing west to go east . . . it's preposterous!"

Halloran himself still wondered at the audacity of Cordell's mission. Nonetheless, his utter confidence in the captain-general dispelled any doubts he may have held regarding the eventual success of the voyage.

Since the mission had been announced six months earlier, a whirlwind of activity had preceded this day as the legion prepared for its most daring expedition ever. A small fleet of six carracks and nine caravels had assembled in Murann. The men of the legion had been informed of the mission and told that it was voluntary. Only a few dozen had declined the opportunity for adventure, and those had quickly been replaced.

Cordell had trained his five hundred legionnaires for shipboard transport, and the men practiced loading and unloading the horses for landings where ports and quays might not be available. Two hundred sailors were recruited, brave men or simply foolhardy. Even with the uncertain destination of the voyage, a festive sense of adventure accompanied all of the preparations.

Now the horses whinnied in agitation. Hounds barked and scrambled underfoot. They were taking several dozen of the large, shaggy greyhounds that served as camp sentries and war dogs.

Ample supplies of food and water, extra weapons and armor, and all the provisions for march and battle had been collected in warehouses along the wharf, and were now being moved by laboring dockworkers into the holds of the ships.

"Why are you coming if you think it's madness?" Halloran asked Daggrande.

The dwarf cast Hal a sly look. "Because the Cordell I know would not embark on a quest like this unless he knew there was *something* out there. My guess is it'll yield enough treasure for the lot of us to live out our lives in luxury!"

"*How* can he know? What makes you so sure?"

"It's that Bishou—him and the lady wizard." Daggrande spat. His feelings toward elves were well known, and the elven mage Darien seemed to arouse an even stronger distaste than usual in the dwarf's already cantankerous nature. He shook his head ruefully as he continued.

"I got to admit, their powers can be handy. I'll wager a year's coin that both of them have seen enough of what's out there to tell Cordell this is a gamble worth taking.

"Besides, dwarven lore is full of tales of distant lands of riches. It's said that you could once travel *under* the Trackless Sea and come up in a land to the west. One of the greatest wars between dwarves and the drow was supposedly fought miles under the sea floor."

Halloran nodded, impressed. The drow, or dark elves, were fabled as a race of great evil and vast power. Their skills included powerful magic, skilled weaponcraft, and deadly combat abilities. Nowadays they were not very common, having been driven from the territories of all civilized nations.

"They say it was the drow that ended that war," continued Daggrande, "by starting a fire so great, so enormous, that the rocks themselves melted away and the sea poured in to destroy that whole section of the underdark.

"Destroyed forever, but with lands of richness rumored to exist on the other side. And that's enough for me! After all, Cordell's luck ain't run out yet!" The dwarf's eyes twinkled. "Say, it sounds like congratulations are in order."

Hal nodded, smiling in spite of himself. "Captain of horse. The rank is permanent now! I'll have command over all four wings."

"Well, don't let it go to your head. But I'm proud of you anyways, and you should be pleased."

"One other thing, though. Beware Alvarro. He's a jealous, hotheaded type, and he was hoping to get the command himself."

"I've already noticed him scowling at me," the young man replied, nodding. "But I can handle him."

Halloran looked across the placid harbor to the rolling sea beyond. Now, before him, the enclosed port looked like a forest of denuded trees, so numerous were the masts of the vessels crowding the sheltered waters. The usual trading vessels now stood at anchor offshore, for all available quays had been given over to the loading of Cordell's expedition.

The fifteen ships lined the wharves, the largest of them no more than one hundred feet long. Each would carry a few horses and some forty men, the pick of the legion, together with a dozen or more sailors. The last of the horses had now boarded, and individual captains glared and cursed along the waterfront, tending to final details of the loading.

"Where's Cordell?" asked the young captain, realizing that the captain-general had not been paying his usual meticulous attention to every personal detail.

"He and that elf—" again a pause for a noisy spit—"spent the day bartering in the alchemists' market. Laying in a few potions for the voyage . . . or the lands beyond the voyage."

Halloran suppressed a shudder. "I think I'll trust to my own steel." He laid a hand upon the reassuring leather hilt of his longsword.

"Wise words. For me, I'll depend on the edge of my axe, the strength of my arm, and little else!" Absently the dwarf removed his small, double-bitted axe from his belt. He began stroking the edge with a whetstone while watching the activity throughout Murann harbor.

The startling blare of a brass horn brought all activity on the waterfront to an abrupt halt. "The general must be back," grumbled Daggrande, pushing the axe back into his belt. "Best hear what he's got to say."

Remaining tasks were postponed as all the members of the expedition filed between the waterfront buildings to gather in the great plaza of Murann. There indeed stood Captain-General Cordell, resplendent in a purple velvet tunic draped over his steel breastplate. He carried his brimmed helmet at his side, standing bareheaded on the podium in the sunny square.

"Who else is up there?" grumbled the dwarf, unable to see as the human members of the legion pressed around.

"His lady Darien . . . the Bishou Domincus . . . I can see some official and a young lady beside the Bishou. She's beautiful!" Halloran caught his breath at the sight of the red-haired woman standing beside the tall cleric.

"Probably Bishou Domincus's daughter." Daggrande couldn't see, but he still had plenty of opinions. "I heard she was coming along with the expedition."

"Soldiers of the Golden Legion!" Cordell's voice rang through the square, and the low hum of conversation died instantly. "We embark in a few short hours upon a mission of grave peril. The dangers we face are unknown to us, but I know that every one of you will hold true to his courage and his faith. With the aid of our almighty protector, Helm, we shall triumph over all!

"As you know, our mission is funded by the good Council of Amn," continued the leader. "We have here the council's Grand Assessor, Kardann. He will accompany us on our mission and record the treasures we gain!" A throaty roar erupted from the men.

"In the name of Helm!" The Bishou's voice now rang over the hundreds of soldiers and sailors gathered in the plaza. "May our benefactor bless our swords, making sharp our steel. May he strengthen our arms, such that our blows will fall swift and deadly as we strike in his immortal name!

"May the vigilance of his eternal gaze warn us of treachery, making swift our vengeance against those who would betray us. And may the holy light of his ironclad brilliance guide us to lands of wealth and promise, opening the fabled riches of the East to our bold exploration!" Bishou Domincus lowered his voice, mumbling a silent prayer to Helm, the legion's patron god, before he again fixed the throng with his passionate blue eyes.

"Now let us join our voices in the anthem. Martine, please lead us. . . ."

Halloran saw the woman whose beauty had so struck him step to the fore of the group on the platform. She raised her face to the heavens, and her clear, melodious voice led the men of the Golden Legion in their Anthem of War.

The song combined celebration of victory with grief for fallen companions. Its words spoke to the heart of every warrior present, and Halloran was not alone as he wept through the final chorus. He gripped his sword until his knuckles whitened, the glory of many conquests beckoning him. He stood enraptured as Martine at last ceased singing, then watched her turn with her father to stand at Cordell's side.

The Bishou and his daughter would sail with the general, he was certain, in the fleet's flagship, the *Falcon*. He wondered when he would see her again, certain that time would be too long in coming.

"Now to your ships!" Cordell cried, not loudly, but his voice rang through the square with the sheer force of command. The very sound of his voice filled Hal with energy and excitement.

"The tide falls away past midnight, and we ride to sea before the dawn, to the west, and into history!"

* * * * *

Erixitl's journey from Kultaka to Payit began strangely. Upon learning that her destination was distant Payit, she brooded about the prospects of a long, difficult march. Like everyone else, she knew little of the Payitlan people save that they were a race of rude barbarians with no culture. Of course, the cleric Kachin had seemed well-spoken and dignified enough, but anyone would expect a religious patriarch to display some education and manners. The people themselves, she suspected, were far more savage.

Thus she was astounded to find an elegant gown of softest cotton awaiting her on the morning of their departure. Sandals of snakeskin and a bright feather mantle for her shoulders completed the outfit, finer clothes than she had ever worn.

Her astonishment was compounded when she emerged from the house of Huakal to find a *pluma* litter, a luxurious bed of floating feathermagic, awaiting her. The pad was large enough to hold a reclining adult and hovered several feet above the ground. It was perhaps a handspan thick, and its surface consisted of a border of emerald quetzal feathers surrounding a mosaic pattern of wonderful, multi-colored detail.

"But a slave, riding? Carried by *pluma?*" She could not help exclaiming her astonishment in the presence of Kachin, her new owner. She saw six other slaves, strong men, standing beside large bundles. She suspected they carried goods from Kultaka such as turquoise and obsidian, perhaps traded for tropical feathers or cocoa brought by the Payit cleric to Kultaka.

The cleric regarded her strangely. The gleam in his dark brown eyes frightened her, yet there was something vaguely paternal in the smile that slowly creased his wizened face.

"A slave no longer, Erixitl. Now you are a virgin priestess of the Payit, and as such you cannot be expected to walk."

"A priestess?" Erix's astonishment made her bold. "But I know little of your god!"

"Qotal is the god of us all, whether we know it or not," Kachin replied, smiling.

She shook her head, confused. "Even so, why does a young priestess ride while you, the high priest, walks? And why did you come all this way for me? Have you no virgins in Payit?" She bit her lip, suddenly regretting her stream of questions.

But Kachin only laughed. "You are special for many reasons, dear Erixitl. And those reasons will become clear to you in time."

"But . . ." Common sense overtook her arguments, and she bit her tongue before objecting. Still, she could not help wondering what sort of man this was. What kind of religion would sanction an arduous journey and the spending of valuable treasure to *purchase* a priestess? She sat upon the litter and it gave softly beneath her, conforming to her body as she raised her legs and reclined. Her body tingled with delight at the luxury.

"Now, to the Coast Road!" Kachin barked.

The expedition also included a trio of Payit warriors, wearing only loincloths. These dusky young men carried short spears tipped with jagged obsidian blades, very different from the two-handed obsidian swords, *or macas*, carried by Nexalan and Kultakan fighters. The warriors wore their thick black hair tied in a high knot on their heads, adorned with several long green feathers. Also, these jungle dwellers dressed far more lightly than Erix's own people, scorning the padded cotton tunic that commonly served as armor.

They departed Kultaka early in the morning as the dawn mist still cloaked the mountains around them. Men and women already toiled in the vast fields of mayz surrounding the city, but by the time the haze lifted, the small pyramids of the city had fallen behind them.

The litter bore Erix sitting upright, or allowed her to recline partially or completely, at her wish. She simply moved her body into the desired position and the soft, feathery cushion adjusted its own shape to hers. The ride was luxurious, but this very luxury caused Erix to feel self-conscious, not a little embarrassed as they passed slaves and farmers toiling in their poor fields.

Erix could not dispel a strange feeling of wistfulness. Even though she had been taken to Kultaka as a slave, her life there had not been unpleasant. Indeed, her memories of Kultaka could not help but be more vivid and meaningful than her childhood recollections of far-off Palul. Now she was leaving this land, and once again her path took her away from Nexal, Heart of the True World. Silently she vowed to return someday to her own land, to set her eyes upon the wonders of that city before she died. Yet even as she made the vow, she knew that she could no more choose to go to Nexal than could a piece of driftwood select the beach upon which it would land.

The gently descending path toward the coast rolled easily under the feet of the slaves, and Erix quickly learned to enjoy the comfort of the litter. It floated along, level and smooth, moving at the pace of the rest of Kachin's party. Often she got out and walked for a time, stretching her legs while the litter followed docilely.

For several days, the little procession made steady progress. Each night they stayed in a comfortable inn, and Kachin always rented a private room for Erix. This was a land of simple country fare, yet she enjoyed the homey hospitality of the farmers and innkeepers they met along the way.

Slowly the mountains surrounding Kultaka fell away, leading to the broad coastal savannah. The dense foliage of the lower mountains gave way to dry grasslands broken by occasional villages and their surrounding fields of mayz. Each of these was distinguished by its pyramid, though none of these structures even approached in size the one in Kultaka City. And that itself, she thought, was a mere pile of stone compared to the great pyramid in Nexal!

Many times during the journey she tried to strike up a conversation with the other slaves. She gathered from their speech that they, too, were Nexalan. But they universally ignored all of her endeavors to communicate.

The three warriors spoke only Payit, so Erix conversed only with the bilingual Kachin. The cleric tutored her in his tongue, and the young woman learned Payit rapidly. Mostly Kachin told her about Ulatos, the city they journeyed toward. She wondered, as Kachin spoke of temples and arts and painting, if the cleric even understood that he was a barbarian. Erixitl decided to spare his feelings, and so she did not rebut his boasts with descriptions of the wonders she knew could be found in Nexal. He told her of his proud pyramid, covered with lush growth and brilliant flowers, and she listened politely.

Still, this god called Qotal was different and interesting, quite unlike Zaltec, the ever-hungry deity of war.

"Witness the butterflies," Kachin said one day, stopping the procession to observe the colorful creatures flitting about a vast field of wildflowers. "The Plumed Father loves them, loves the flowers that nurture them. It is this love that makes him the mightiest of the gods."

"Why, then, are the numbers of his followers so small?" Erix asked boldly. She had grown more comfortable with the cleric during their journey.

Kachin shrugged. "People—people like the Nexala and Kultakans—crave the shedding of blood. They cannot imagine a god who does not desire the same."

Erix's eyes widened at the implication of his statement. Kachin spoke as if the gods were created to suit man's need! Silently she prayed that such sacrilege would go unnoticed, for she had become fond of the old man.

"You, too, are known by Qotal and have been blessed, even if you do not know it," Kachin continued. "You carry a reminder of his beauty and tranquility."

"What do you mean?"

"That token, the feathered medallion you take such pains to hide. It speaks with a voice of its own, proclaiming the might and glory of the Plumed God. You should not cover it up. Qotal is a god of the air and the wind and the sky. His symbols should partake of those pleasures."

Sheepishly Erix removed the token from inside her gown and suspended it outside of her clothing. Perhaps it was her imagination, but the wind seemed to prance quickly around her, freshening the air with the scent of fragrant blossoms. But how had Kachin known of the token? She had concealed it carefully, fearing that he might take it from her because of its unique beauty. There seemed to be much about this cleric she did not understand.

The litter ride was languid and comfortable. Erix slept a little, other times walked beside the floating platform, often wished the cleric would discuss something meaningful. The road once again curved up mountainsides, twisting along narrow ridgetops, winding above vast, yawning canyons, and eventually descending into a region of lush valleys similar to Kultaka.

Eventually Erix saw the telltale shape of a pyramid rising from the grassy plain before them.

"Pezelac . . . this city is subject to Nexal now, but it was once an independent land," explained Kachin as they drew near the town. "The Pezelans are an artistic people, quiet and peaceful. I think you will like them.

"And when we leave here," the cleric announced enthusiastically, "we will enter the lands of Payit . . . your new home."

The Payit cleric was well received in Pezelac. The party proceeded to a large house beside a small temple, and here he was given comfortable, airy quarters for himself and his companions.

A young girl carried hot water to Erixitl's room after dinner, and the priestess enjoyed a luxurious bath. The youngster stood wide-eyed beside the tub, offering brushes and soaps and towels to her mistress.

"Why are you staring at me like that?" Erix finally said to the girl.

Quickly the girl's eyes dropped to the floor. "I—I'm sorry. You are so pretty, and I forgot myself."

Erix laughed, drawing an eager grin from the girl. "I am glad you think so. In truth, your bath has done much to make me feel pretty again."

The lass, Erixitl guessed, was perhaps nine or ten years old. She realized wistfully that she herself had been no older when she had been snatched from her home. Now that distant day seemed like a time from a different life, her home in Palul a place remembered from a dream.

"Are you the high priestess of all Payit?" the girl asked shyly.

"No, I don't think so! I don't know *what* I'm going to do there, or even why I'm going there." She thought to herself that a priest who obtained his priestesses by purchase might do anything. "Are all these Payit as crazy as Kachin?"

The girl looked frightened for a moment. "Don't say the cleric is crazed! He follows the mightiest of our gods, the one true god of all Maztica!"

"Who tells you these things?" demanded Erix, surprised by the girl's vehemence. "How can you say that one of our gods is the true god and risk the wrath of the others?"

"I *know* it's true. My grandfather is a patriarch of Qotal here in Pezelac, and he taught me about the true god before he took his vow!" The girl looked wistful for a moment, then explained.

"He learned so much that Qotal made him take a vow of silence. That means he's not allowed to talk. And since he knows more than men are allowed to know, he promised not to tell anyone else."

"I'm sorry. I didn't mean to belittle your god." Erix started to towel herself, enjoying the conversation.

"*Our* god—even the Payit!" The girl nodded her head with enthusiasm, her dark eyes serious. At the same time, she gently took the towel from Erix and completed drying her mistress.

"Only the Nexala—your people," she added shyly, "and the Kultaka glorify war, raising Zaltec to his lofty height. The Payit still await the return of Qotal. Indeed, Grandfather told me they have built two great stone faces in the cliffs of the eastern headlands, a man and a woman who look to the east in eternal watch for the Plumed God's great canoe.

"Twin Visages, it is called, and it is consecrated to the return of Qotal from the oceans of the East."

* * * * *

"Praises to Zaltec!" Hoxitl started the ritual.

"High praises to the god of night and war!" the Ancient One responded, but he seemed to the cleric to be agitated. Indeed, the dark-cloaked figure immediately continued.

"The girl has escaped again! Our counsels, from Zaltec himself—" the Ancient One paused long enough for Hoxitl to absorb the import of the remark—"have informed us that she has been bought by a cleric of Qotal. She now journeys to Payit."

"Payit?" Hoxitl was surprised. "That is far from the Heart of the True World. Perhaps she is no danger to us there."

"Idiot!" The Ancient One's voice dripped with venom. Never had Hoxitl been the target of such rage, and the feeling caused his bowels to tie themselves into a firm knot. "She is more of a threat than ever! And now time is passing us like water over a cataract!"

"Very well," Hoxitl whispered, struggling to regain his composure. "We have—that is, the temple of Zaltec has—

clerics in Payit. I will send word immediately, and she will—"

"There is no time!" The figure's voice was almost a reptilian hiss. "You will stay here for the day. We shall have need of the Viperhand." Hoxitl nodded, realizing that sunrise was but an hour away. Any powers the Ancient Ones would employ must await the coming of the next nightfall. The power of Zaltec, focused in Hoxitl's red palm, tatooed in the pattern of the Viperhand, would be necessary to propel the Sending for the distance required.

"At sunset, you will join us in the dark circle. From there, we will make a Sending. Talonmagic will carry the message to Payit in the night. We have not a day to lose. The girl must be put to death!"

❧ 5 ❧

ACROSS THE
TRACKLESS SEA

First day, aboard the Falcon

I shall keep a journal of my legion's progress as we explore to the westward. Preparations have gone smoothly, and we are well provisioned. Darien and I purchased many potions yesterday, the last additions to our stores. The rest is in the hands of Helm, aided by the sturdy backs of the legionnaires.

Predawn tide carries us smoothly from the harbor. Freshening wind off the starboard quarter speeds our departure. Land is gone by midday.

Nightfall. Headlands of Tethyr appear before us at sunset. Anticipate turn toward Asavir's Channel by dawn.

For ten years, I have gathered warriors to my banner. I believe they are the finest soldiers in the Realms. The captains are, to a man, staunch and brave. Daggrande and Garrant—my staunch veterans. Hot-blooded riders like Halloran and Alvarro. All the rest!

My heart bursts with pride for these splendid men, embarking on a mission to the unknown out of loyalty and courage. Seeing the array of our sails around me, I feel certain that we will, we must, triumph!

*   *   *   *   *

"What are you thinking, Father?" Martine joined the Bishou in the bow of the *Falcon.*

"Of the many glories of Helm," replied Domincus reverently. "Think of it, my dear! Great masses of pagans who have yet to hear of our almighty avenger! You and I shall have the glory of carrying Helm's word to them!"

"Must you be so serious, Papa?" she teased. "Think of the adventure, the sights and smells and sounds of it all! Whatever it is that we find, I'm already fascinated!"

"Do not make light." The Bishou frowned, stern creases marking his high forehead. "I fear already it was unwise to bring you on such a voyage!"

"Don't be ridiculous. You couldn't have kept me at home!"

"I know you're right," sighed the cleric. "But just the same, be careful."

* * * * *

Sixth day, aboard the Falcon

Mild headwinds caused us to take two days to pass Asavir's Channel, but all has been smooth since. Taken on water and food at Lantan Island; will be last known landfall. All provisions at maximum levels.

Crews relieved to embark again. The Lantans, worshipers of Gond the Wondermaker, are a disquieting sort, very bizarre and secretive.

Departing at dusk on course 15 degrees south of west for waters unknown.

The steadiness of the men awes me. Our journey will be long and arduous. No troops but the Golden Legion would dare even to embark!

My captains, spread among the vessels as they are, serve to embolden the men still further. I have some concerns about Alvarro and Halloran; the former still holds the latter's advancement against him. Perhaps I should have left Alvarro behind, but he is too great a fighter for such an ignoble fate. Why can he not see that his value lies in his sword, not his brain?

I will need to maintain a careful observation here.

* * * * *

"When will you finally get that axe sharpened?"

Daggrande snorted. "When this boat lands on the sandy beaches of Shou Lung, and not a moment before!" The dwarf continued with his whetstone, honing the fine steel to a hairsplitting edge.

"I thought you didn't believe we'd land in Kara-Tur!" Hal countered. He knew that Shou Lung was the greatest empire upon that distant continent.

"I don't, we won't, and I meant what I said!"

"If it's not your axe, then you're tightening the spring on your crossbow or polishing your helm!" Halloran wouldn't let up.

"What else is there to do on this blasted barge?" demanded the dwarf, huffing impatiently and turning back to his work. In truth, the sea made him edgy, and his companion knew it.

A huge, lanky dog sauntered over to Halloran and leaned against him. The creature was one of the greyhounds that accompanied the legion. This one, called 'Corporal' by Hal, had taken a liking to the young lancer and pestered him more or less constantly for food.

Amidships, Storm and two other chargers stood impatiently in the makeshift shelter the crew had rigged. A long voyage, Hal suspected, would be harder on the horses than on the men.

But suddenly Halloran paid the animals no attention, for their own *Osprey* had veered to within a hundred paces of *Falcon*, and the young horseman had eyes only for the flagship.

Or rather, for one of the passengers on that vessel. The Bishou's daughter, Martine, had just stepped from the cabin, her red hair catching the sunlight and bursting with its own fire. She walked slowly about the deck of the other ship as she did several times a day, chatting with the sailors and occasionally relaxing against the rail.

Once she had noticed Halloran watching her and had given him a friendly wave. He had shyly returned the gesture, but now he took pains to be discreet in his observations, pretending to busy himself with his horse or equipment.

Still, whenever the two ships sailed near each other, he made it a point to watch the *Falcon*, hoping for a glimpse of of Martine. When he saw her, the memory put a rosy glow over the rest of the day.

Meanwhile, Daggrande started to sharpen his dagger, keeping his own eyes anxiously over the bow.

* * * * *

Twentieth day, aboard the Falcon

Last night was the heaviest weather of the voyage; with relief, we counted fifteen vessels in the dawn. Swanmay lost a mast; morning spent in repairing damage. By noon, we're at speed again, backed by a good wind from the northeast.

The uncertainty begins to weigh upon us all. Never have men sailed so far to the west. Around us is naught but the rolling swell of the deep sea.

When will we make landfall? Some grumbling comes from the men, but it is to be expected. Strong, healthy troops are bound to grow restless over the course of a long voyage.

I grow displeased with the assessor, Kardann. The Council of Six has chosen unwisely, I fear. The man is no adventurer. He has been sick the entire voyage and already speaks of his return homeward. I fear he will undermine my ambitions unless I can keep him on a very short tether.

Unfortunately, the terms of my agreement with Amn have conferred all the power of the council into this weasel of a man, including control of the finances backing the expedition. I will have to ensure his understanding of one fact: The legion answers to me and me alone!

* * * * *

Darien moved quietly in the shuttered privacy of her small cabin. A candle flickered with the swaying of the *Falcon*, but its light was sufficient for her purposes. Indeed, she preferred its soft illumination to the harsh glare of the sun, so painful for her sensitive eyes.

Lifting a sturdy rucksack from her bench, she sought a hidden flap. Her white, dextrous fingers flipped a simple catch, and she pulled a soft volume out of its secret compartment. The leather-covered book contained dozens of sheets of fine vellum, and on each was inscribed one or more of her powerful incantations.

She took her spellbook to the small desk in the cabin, in the shadow, away from the flickering candle. The darkness caused her no difficulty, however, as she gently lifted the leather binding and began to read.

She turned the parchment pages carefully, silently mouthing the words as she read. Her full concentration focused on the tome before her as she studied and learned. Underlying her concentration was a powerful challenge burning at the core of her being.

She would be ready.

* * * * *

Thirty-second day, aboard the Falcon

Complaints and cowardice grow more apparent. This morning a near mutiny on Swallow. *I sentenced two men to hang, commuted one, and watched the other swing.*

Still nothing but the sea—not a bird nor a floating log to give us hint of land. The tumor of faithlessness must be controlled.

Evening. Now we've had wind drop away to nothing. The fleet sits with limp canvas, becalmed in the tropics. We must take action; we must do something!

* * * * *

"What are they doing?" Halloran asked, squinting into the setting sun. *Falcon* stood still in the water a few hundred yards away, her flaccid sails hanging in pathetic emphasis of their situation. The pennant of the Golden Legion hung straight down from the mainmast, its golden eagle concealed by listless contours of fabric.

The hour was late, but still the sun burned with a penetrating fire, casting nearly horizontal rays as it sank toward the western sea. No ripple disturbed the flat, lifeless surface of endless water.

"Eh? Who's doing what?" Daggrande put down his freshly oiled crossbow and joined Halloran.

"Look for yourself."

They saw the crew of the *Falcon* gathering amidships, leaving the raised afterdeck clear.

"That's the elf," spat Daggrande as a hooded figure emerged onto the *Falcon*'s deck and climbed the steps to the rear. She stood alone there, turned away from the sun, away from the facing of the little fleet.

The sound of her voice carried across the water as she raised her hands and barked harsh syllables.

"Black magic, by Helm!" chuckled the dwarf. "That pointy-eared faerie might come in handy after all!"

"What magic?" Halloran felt a chill and was unable to shake off the feeling of eeriness. He remembered the magic of a decade before, the apparition that had claimed his tutor and sent Hal himself fleeing panic-stricken into the desert. He had used none of the few spells he knew since that fearful day. The feeling of his sword beneath his hand now gave him some comfort, but he could not shake his apprehension as he watched Darien finish her casting.

Abruptly the elven mage dropped her arms and ceased speaking. Halloran jumped, as startled by the sudden halt as he had been nervous during the casting.

For a moment, the supernatural stillness closed in again, no breath of wind stirring the water or the fleet. The sun seemed to touch the water as it set, and Halloran half-expected to hear the hissing of steam from the scalding contact that looked so near.

He felt it first as a cooling touch against his right cheek. He heard a sailor shout on one of the other ships, then saw a smattering of ripples spread in patches across the sea. The pennant of the Golden Legion suddenly stirred, offering a tantalizing glimpse of its proud eagle emblem.

Then the sail of the *Falcon* billowed outward, and Halloran felt the *Osprey* lurch beneath his feet. Their own sail came taut with a snap, and the caravel's timbers creaked and groaned under the increasing strain.

Soon a pleasant breeze pushed them briskly along. Fresh from the northeast, it filled the sails with its reassuring power.

Once again the Golden Legion sailed to the west.

* * * * *

The stream twisted through dense jungle, verdant foliage more entwined, more overpowering than Erix could have imagined. She rode with Kachin in a slender canoe. The cleric deftly handled a great fan of *pluma*, and the slow whirling of the feathermagic propelled the boat with a gentle grace among the vines and fronds and water lilies. The guards and slaves followed in two more canoes, larger craft propelled by the paddles of the passengers.

Kachin had earlier explained the nature of feathermagic, and its opposite power, talonmagic.

"The power of *pluma* is the magic of feathers. It flows from the Plumed God, Qotal, and is the stuff of beauty and air and flight." The cleric had wagged a pudgy finger at Erix, assuring that her attention remained fixed upon him. "It can armor the breast of an Eagle Knight or carry a litter along the ground—even propel a canoe through the water with its gentle force.

"The darker force of *hishna* is the magic of the jaguar's claw and the snake's fang. It, too, is magic of power, flowing from Zaltec instead of Qotal. It can armor the skin of a Jaguar Knight or render him invisible in a jungle thicket. It can send a message of doom or death great distances, from a wielder of *hishna* to another. It can be used to capture and hold or to kill."

"Which is mightier?" Erix had wanted to know.

"Both . . . and neither," came the cleric's cryptic reply. "The might of the magic depends more upon the skill of the user than the type of his power."

Thoughts of menacing talonmagic were difficult, in fact, impossible, to maintain here in the forest. Blossoms of tropical brilliance exploded from every bush, while birds cackled and cawed and screeched, their feathers shimmering with a thousand colors brighter than any she had ever seen. The green water slipped easily under the hull, and Erix remained awestruck at their verdant surroundings.

A week earlier, they had passed from the palm-covered savannah of Pezelac into the Payit jungles. In the ensuing time, they had stayed nightly in small huts within the confines of crude villages, after traveling long, hot miles through the encroaching flora. Sometimes they walked along narrow trails, where Erix still rode luxuriously in the *pluma* litter. At other times, they purchased canoes and followed the winding streams through the jungle, or occasionally used the craft to cross broad, shallow lakes. Always they were surrounded by verdant foliage.

Kachin delighted in showing her the medicinal herbs that the Payit used to defend against sickness, the sweet, nectar-laden flowers given to old men who sought godly visions, and the sumptuous leaves that could be cut to produce fresh, cool water.

Together with the beauties of plants and animals, she learned of the jungle's other side, a side of discomfort and darkness, of danger, poison, and death. She had cowered from a cloud of mosquitoes thick enough to obscure vision, she had seen spiders as big as her hand, and she had even heard the forlorn howl of the jaguar as the great cat went about its nocturnal hunt.

Kachin had shown her venomous serpents, blending invisibly into the dense growth. And one night, as the members of the party shared a hot, muddy hut, her spine had chilled to a bloodcurdling scream of impossible grief.

"*Hakuna*," grunted Kachin, refusing to explain.

Even so, the three warriors nervously fingered their spears and cast nervous glances out the door of the hut.

Then one day, after a week in the jungle, the cleric turned in the canoe and spoke with animation to Erix.

"Soon Ulatos!" he said, beaming, his wrinkled face growing even more creased from the strength of his smile. "You will like our city very much, I am sure!" He spoke in his own tongue, but Erix had little difficulty following him now.

"My temple is grand, you will see! And you will have quarters there fitting a princess of the Payit!"

She wanted to ask him about that temple, about his god. She wanted to know why she had been purchased so far away and brought here. But, as always before, she could not force the questions from her lips. Instead, she looked forward in skeptical curiosity as the city came into view. She wondered what it was that caused Ulatos to rate the title of city—perhaps a small stone building among the typical cluster of thatch huts?

The stream emerged from the winding jungle, entering a broad savannah of short grass and fields of tall mayz and lush cocoa. The forest pressed in from all sides, creating a tense balance between field and wood.

But her gaze passed quickly over all this, drawn hypnotically to the structures rising above the far side of the savannah. None of her speculation had prepared her for the sight of the Payit city—and it was indeed a city.

Ulatos! Grand city of the Payit! Never had she seen temples and pyramids of such grandeur! Long, flat-roofed buildings with walls of solid stone marked the periphery of the city. Beyond these, she could see the higher walls of great houses, and then the staggered steps of several grand pyramids. One building, in the center of the city and located on a slight rise in the ground, had a dome-shaped roof.

The entire city was dominated by a pyramid that towered over all the other buildings, far above the highest trees. Perhaps it was not as grand as the great pyramid in Nexal, but Erix did not care. The pyramid's stepped sides were covered with lush gardens. A profusion of brilliant blossoms dangled from each terrace, and somehow a fountain of clear water kept a steady spray emerging from the platform at the top. There, where usually would stand the blood-caked temples used for daily sacrifice, this temple had a lush garden.

Erix stood and looked and wondered. Truly the beauties of Ulatos surprised and overwhelmed her. The Payit were obviously a people of culture and substance, far greater than most Kultakans or Nexalans would have believed.

For the moment, she even forgot that she was not free.

* * * * *

The talonmagic casting again took form, the creature of *hishna* emerging from the circled figures of Hoxitl and the Ancient Ones. Generated from the magical caldron of the Ancient Ones, powered by the cleric's symbol, the Viperhand, the form gained substance. A black shape, catlike but with a smoky indistinctness, grew in the air before them, twisting to regard each with a snarling visage.

At an unspoken command, the sleek feline form sprang from the midst of the circled figures. It flew through the great cavern, emerging from the cave and startling Hoxitl's dozing apprentices. Before they could open their eyes, the smoky shape was racing down the slopes of Mount Zatal. It circled around the city below and then shot like an arrow across the desert toward the savannah, and ultimately the jungle.

The *hishna* messenger raced faster than any living creature, faster than the fastest wind, in its nightlong flight. It left the land of Nexal, circled around Kultaka, and skirted Pezelac, finally plunging through the midnight jungle of Payit. As dawn colored the eastern horizon, the shape entered the Payit city of Ulatos, finally settling to earth. It assumed an almost substantial form, like that of a great black jaguar, and crept inside a low building. The leering skull face of Zaltec, carved in relief around the building's walls, snarled a warning at any who would follow.

The talonmagic apparition awakened the cleric of Zaltec who dwelled here, for this was indeed a temple devoted to the god of night and war. Within a minute, the cleric had dressed.

Within five minutes, he had sent messengers to the corners of the city of Ulatos, carrying urgent summons. Within a few hours, he knew, the faithful Jaguar Knights would be assembled before him.

And the will of Zaltec and the Ancient Ones would be obeyed.

*　*　*　*　*

The wonders of Ulatos seemed to grow as the canoe passed from the stream into a narrow canal. Here Kachin guided them with his paddle, for the *pluma* fan could not maneuver the craft nimbly enough to negotiate the tight confines.

No wall divided the city from its fields, but several well-defined avenues and waterways carried traffic into and out of the place. The procession finally docked beside a broad plaza, where several traders immediately approached and began bartering with Kachin. Erix understood that they wished to purchase the canoes, and soon the cleric collected a cotton mantle, a bale of feathers, and two small sacks of cocoa beans.

The young woman, meanwhile, observed that Ulatos bustled with people—bronze-skinned, black-haired people like herself. The Payit women wore plain, sacklike dresses, and the men were garbed often in mere breechclouts. Even the few richly dressed folk she saw, with feather headdresses and dyed mantles across their shoulders, wore less ornamentation in the way of feathers and gold than she was accustomed to seeing among the peoples of Kultaka and Nexal.

Kachin lifted the litter for her again, and she settled onto the soft surface, riding slowly through the city. The men she passed stared curiously, while the women all lowered their eyes. Erix looked back at the men, enjoying the unsettling effect of her frank gaze.

They passed houses of fine stone, with walls washed white with lime so that they glowed in the sunlight. Each house, it seemed, had a wide garden before it. Fountains were common, and she saw many shallow pools. In some, Erix saw brilliantly colored fish swimming lazily, while other pools held boisterous, splashing children. Lush palm trees lined the streets, swaying easily in the tropical breeze.

"My temple—the Pyramid of Qotal!" Kachin pointed proudly to the grand edifice she had seen from the city's outskirts, the garden pyramid with its spuming fountain.

"This temple is the true seat of power in Ulatos," proclaimed the cleric proudly. "The city's Revered Counselor, Caxal, fears his warriors. Too, he fears the Temple of Zaltec. So he favors the temple of Qotal, as do most people of Payit.

"Oh, Zaltec has his presence here, his temple and even a sacrifice now and then, usually some captive gained by the Jaguar Knights on their excursions. But the Payit are a peaceful people, and they do not make a great call for the god of war. Thus they do not need to pay him with hearts, as do the Nexala and Kultakans."

"The water . . . how does it rise to the top?" Erixitl asked, looking at the fountain in amazement.

Kachin chuckled. "*Pluma*. We use it to move not only air, but also water."

Erix stared in awe at the splashing streams spilling lightly down the sides of the pyramid. She could see the foliage at the top and hear the dissonant calls of many hundreds of birds. Not only was the temple a garden, but also an aviary as well!

"The birds need no cages," said the cleric, anticipating her question. "They stay out of love for Qotal. It is said that the Silent One's favorite creatures are his birds of brilliant plumage."

Next the cleric pointed to a whitewashed building with several arched doorways in its high stone wall. "Our apartments," he explained, leading her through an arch into a wide, shaded garden. Here, stone benches, surrounded by the display of blossoms Erix still found dazzling, offered many places for rest and meditation. A flowery aroma filled the air, heavy with sweet pollen.

The house itself was a low building with many spacious apartments. Reed mats lined the floors, and feather tapestries, together with gleaming disks, statues, and platters of gold and silver, brightened the walls. Servants and attendants quickly gathered in a large central hallway, all of them inspecting her curiously.

"This is Erixitl," began Kachin as the others fell instantly silent and attentive. He spoke at length, but Erix made little attempt to follow the still somewhat strange Payit tongue.

"Chicha, take the priestess to her apartments and prepare her bath." Kachin spoke to a tall young girl, a lass just approaching womanhood, who nodded excitedly and kissed the floor before an embarrassed Erix.

"Chicha is your slave, my priestess," the cleric explained. "She will see to your needs until we sup."

"I don't need a slave!" she protested, but Kachin simply smiled in his grandfatherly manner and walked away.

"Oh, I will be good!" declared Chicha, and Erix saw that the girl was on the point of tears.

"I'm certain you will, Chicha. I didn't mean . . ." She paused, wondering if one apologized to a slave. Certainly no one had ever done so to *her!* "Show me my apartments, please."

The girl excitedly led her through a reed curtain into a room with its own small veranda. A clean straw pallet lay on the floor, and a massive golden sun disk rested in a niche in the wall.

The bath proved even more spectacular, as Chicha merely pulled a plug from a hollow log in the wall to allow cool, clean water to fill the large basin. The princess stripped her travel-worn cloak and mantle away, though she kept her golden token around her neck. She felt almost giddy with excitement. A real bath again!

Erix settled easily into the water, feeling the dust and grime float away from her skin. She leaned back and closed her eyes, the bath as always giving her a feeling of exhilarating freshness and vitality.

A harsh crash made her open her eyes. She saw a male slave fall into the bathing room, his face a gory mask of jagged claw marks. Chicha screamed, and four spotted figures stalked into the room, each brandishing an obsidian-tipped club.

"Who are you?" demanded Erix, feeling more anger than fear.

Her only answer was the sharp blow of a club against her scalp. She slumped senseless into the bathwater that slowly turned pink, then red.

* * * * *

Thirty-ninth day, aboard the Falcon

Darien and Bishou Domincus have sustained us, each calling upon the deepest strains of power, bending the wind to their commands. When one collapses from exhaustion, the other takes over, carrying us steadily westward. Now, finally, a natural breeze arises, true from the east, and we sail rapidly again.

And now we have hope! Flocks of birds sighted each of last three days. Crews work with vigor, all eyes . . .

I must go, hearing a disturbance on deck.

* * * * *

"Land!"

"Land!" Halloran heard the cry and passed it along, racing to the bow of the *Osprey*. He could see the lookout atop the mast of one of the carracks, perhaps *Dragonfly*, gesturing frantically.

"What's this? Probably another cloud bank, if you ask me!" Daggrande clumped up to Hal's side, squinting forward in annoyance.

For several minutes, they could see nothing. Other men of the legion gathered around them, as all unoccupied hands stared intently to the westward.

One by one the mast-top lookouts called down their confirmations, and the breeze seemed to freshen with the expedition's aroused hopes.

Gradually Halloran saw it. Mutters of speculation, quickly growing to a rumble, spread among the men as the image before them slowly took on color, shape, substance. Finally it became a line of green, close to the horizon but extending for many miles from west to east.

Almost imperceptibly, more details became apparent: white-crested breakers upon a wide reef, a smooth shore of light sand, palm trees and other vegetation growing back from the beach. The lookouts even saw a bright stream flowing into the sea, offering the promise of fresh water.

* * * * *

From the chronicle of Coton:

May the wisdom of the Silent Counselor guide my brushes and my hand.

In the age when the gods and man were young, there came the time of the Great Dust. The rains failed ten years in a row, and heat blistered the land. This was the time of the Ancient Ones, when the cult of Zaltec began to flourish. His priests adorned themselves with blood and cried out that only through sacrifice could the favor of the gods be restored. Deep in their caves, the black-shrouded Ancient Ones watched and smiled.

Finally, in the tenth year of the drought, the speakers of the tribes heeded the call of Zaltec and the Ancient Ones. Great ceremonial battles occurred, and thousands of captives gave their hearts to fresh altars, newly consecrated to Zaltec. Gone were the flowers and butterflies and feathers offered to Qotal; instead, warm, pulsing hearts were given to the glory of Zaltec.

The rains returned to Maztica, and once again mayz ripened in vast, green fields. But the people had sworn fealty to Zaltec now, and always his hunger must be sated with blood.

Qotal, in his anger and shame, left the land of Maztica, spurning the True World. Turning to the east in his great canoe, bedecked with the golden plumes that were his symbol and his image, he rode the friendly wind beyond the ken of man. A few of his faithful priests stood at the shore, beseeching him to return.

To these few, Qotal promised to one day come again as the King of the True World. His canoe will tower like a mountain in the sea, and his footsteps will shatter the land. The peoples of Maztica will rise up in freedom and joy, when they have proven themselves worthy of his presence.

But until that time, he made these, the highest of his priests, vow their silence. Observing and watching the True World, we cannot advise nor command its inhabitants. And so we remain the Silent Patriarchs until our Immortal Master again returns.

Twin Visages

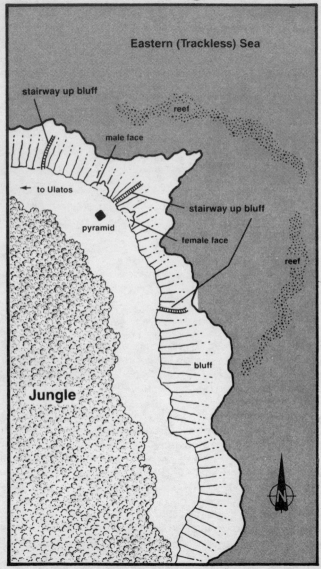

Eastern (Trackless) Sea

stairway up bluff

male face

reef

← to Ulatos

pyramid

stairway up bluff

female face

reef

bluff

Jungle

N

❧ 6 ❧

LANDFALL

Fortieth day, aboard the Falcon

*The fifteen ships stand away from shore, behind the pro-
tection of a small reef. A fair westerly wind comes from the
tropical landmass, but any hard blow from the east will
scatter the ships along the beach like matchsticks.*

*I will take that risk to plant my banner on this, the first
western shore to greet us.*

* * * * *

"In the name of Helm the Vigilant, Ever Watchful Sentinel
and Protector of the Golden Legion, I claim these lands!"
The golden pennant snapped straight in the steady breeze,
its eagle emblem flapping its wings as the fabric fluttered.
The eye emblazoned in the eagle's breast, the symbol of
Helm, now seemed to stare perpetually, even as the pennant
flapped in the wind.

The captain-general planted the staff of the pennant deep
into the sandy shore, surrounded by threescore of his men,
with the Bishou, Darien, and Kardann, the Grand Assessor,
at his side. The Bishou's daughter stood near the shore,
watching several men fill water barrels from the clear
stream. Five longboats, transportation for the shore party,
rested high on the beach.

Halloran and several other handpicked warriors stood
watch over the periphery of the gathering as Kardann began to speak, enumerating the shares of ownership: profits

from the venture to be divided among the merchant princes of Amn and the legion itself.

Hal peered curiously into the dense tropical growth pressing close to the beach. The big greyhound, Corporal, paced at his side, surprising him with his obedience.

Looking at the forest again, Halloran had the odd feeling that the jungle watched him in return. Behind him, Cordell went on to define the boundaries of his new domain, a region beginning here and extending an imprecise but extensive distance to the west.

"Hello." The voice behind Halloran fell like tinkling music on his ears; at the same time, his heart leaped into his throat and stayed there. Martine! She talked to him!

"Uh . . ." He turned to face her, feeling his face flush. "I'm Halloran! And you're Martine!"

She laughed, easing his nervousness a bit. "And this is a paradise, don't you think?" She gestured excitedly along the length of the verdant shore.

"Yes, that is, uh, yes . . . yes, it is!" He nodded foolishly, and again she laughed. Hal thought that perhaps he had never heard a lovelier sound.

"I've heard of you, you know," said the cleric's daughter, with a coy look. "The general thinks very highly of you, the way your charge broke Akbet-Khrul."

Hal stammered some kind of acknowledgment, too thrilled for articulate speech. He could scarcely believe his ears, and his luck! Here was the woman he had admired over the entire voyage, the one eligible woman on an expedition of hundreds of men—Darien, of course, didn't count—and she was talking to him!

"I'd like to walk down the beach. Will you come with me?"

Never had Hal felt so masculine, so romantic. Neither had he ever felt so shackled, nor so frustrated by the responsibilities of soldierhood.

"I'd—I'd like to," he groaned miserably. "But I have to stand guard here at the— What's that?" He squinted at the brush as he saw a large figure moving there. Martine, rebuffed, turned away and then froze as her eyes settled upon the jungle.

Corporal barked a gruff warning, and several other greyhounds joined in. All eyes turned toward the jungle as the
hesitant figures came into view.

The creatures emerging from the jungle were humans,
perhaps two dozen in number. They had thick black hair
and skin of a deep, slightly coppery brown. They were naked but for tattered loincloths, and carried nothing resem-
bling weapons. Several carried large gourds or bundles
wrapped in leaves.

Halloran stepped in front of Martine, his sword in his
hand. However, he saw no threat in the appearance of these
people. He sensed that they came in peace, but he would remain vigilant.

"What pathetic savages!" said Martine softly. Halloran had
to agree with her assessment.

Cordell had expected the spice lords of the Orient to greet
them. Thus the captain-general, too, was sorely disappointed at seeing these primitive people. The first encounter with Kara-Tur was not proving auspicious.

One native, taller than the others but still a full head
shorter than Cordell, advanced toward the party on the
beach. The general watched him, not concealing the disappointment on his face. Finally he and Darien stepped forward to meet him. The jungle dweller bowed, and Cordell
calmly acknowledged the gesture. The native suddenly jab-
bered something in an unintelligible tongue.

Then Darien stepped forward, quietly speaking a quick
enchantment. She spoke to the chieftain in the same language, and the man immediately started talking to her, gesturing around them, often pointing to the vessels anchored
offshore.

Several of the other natives, all of whom were male,
moved closer to Halloran and Martine. The pair looked curiously at their flat faces and broad noses. Each of the men
had a sharp stick driven crossways through his nose, extending several inches to the right and left of his face.

One stepped hesitantly toward Halloran, Martine, and
several other legionnaires nearby. He bowed deeply and
often before extending the gourd in his hand toward them.

Hal took it, feeling the liquid swish inside of it. Another tentatively extended a bundle of leaves, and they saw that it contained an assortment of lush fruits.

And then Hal's attention fell on the man's necklace, and his heart pounded with excitement. He felt Martine gasp beside him, thrilled to the touch of her hand as she took his arm.

"They look so poor, so miserable," Halloran whispered.

"But they're not, are they?" Martine's voice was also hushed as they both observed the band of natives. "I think the expedition is a success."

Suspended from the necklace of this native, and also several others nearby, swung a crude ornament of pure, heavy gold.

*   *   *   *   *

Erix awakened with a pounding headache, and for a long time, she could not remember where she was or how she had come to be there. She remembered that something was wrong, but what had happened?

Darkness surrounded her, and the air smelled of masonry. The stone floor had no reed mat nor straw pallet, accustomed amenities for even the lowliest of slaves. Erix couldn't tell whether it was day or night.

She remembered more, but her mind seemed to go backward. She pictured her family's cottage in Palul; she saw her father's face. With a gasp, she reached for her neck, then sighed with relief as she found her feather token still suspended there, her only remaining link to that distant era.

The picture of a Jaguar Knight snatching her from Palul came into her mind, and then she remembered Kultaka, where she had known Huakal's gentle mastership, Callatl's brutality. With a low moan, she sat up as the rest of the pieces fell into place: her purchase by Kachin, the journey to Payit.

Her head throbbed with agony as she remembered the eager grimaces of the Jaguar Knights who had intruded into her bath. Had they hurt Chicha? she wondered, desperately hoping the girl was all right. Why did they want Erix, anyway? And where was she?

Erixitl almost sobbed in despair. Her entire life had been spent following the dictates of authority. Since childhood, she had been subject to masters who had claimed her by force, or who had purchased her from her captors. Even the feather-lined comfort of her journey to Ulatos was in reality simply a softer form of bondage.

The dingy cell around her indicated that she had now been taken by harsher masters. In fact, the lack of comforts suggested strongly that she was not intended for slavery but for sacrifice. She knew that victims who might be expected to resist the Flowered Altar were often imprisoned in bleak cells until the moment of ceremony that would end the prisoner's life.

Strangely, the thought of dying on the altar did not particularly terrify her—at least, no more than had her sale to Kachin or her battle with Callatl. Instead, she began to grow angry, and as her anger grew, it turned into a fiery resentment against the fates that had swept her along for so much of her life.

"No!" She surprised herself with her vehemence.

Feeling groggy, ignoring the pain in her skull, she stumbled to her feet and leaned against the stone wall of her enclosure. She took a step and felt another wall before her, quickly ascertaining that her cell was a square about three paces on a side. She felt a low wooden door in one wall.

They will not have me! Her anger burned with steadily increasing fury, until her body began to tremble. She pushed away from the wall, growing stronger, and turned to face the door. Sooner or later, she knew, they would open that door for her.

And when they did, she would attack.

*　*　*　*　*

"I don't like it! I just don't like it, not one bit!" Mixtal, priest of Zaltec, wrung his hands and nervously bit his lip. He took handfuls of cold ashes and smeared them across his face and arms, habitually covering himself in a manner befitting a high priest of the war god.

"Be quiet!"

Gultec's voice came out a rumbling snarl. The Jaguar Knight reclined on a bench and glared contemptuously at the cleric through the jaws of his spotted armor. "Who are you to question the will of the Ancient Ones? Even I know that when your god and his counselors make a Sending, the likes of you and I had best obey!"

The two men conversed in the courtyard before their apartments, where they had been observing the night sky over Ulatos. Behind them rose a small pyramid, not far from the looming bulk that was the Pyramid of Qotal.

"But our Temple of Zaltec here in Payit is not the esteemed institution that it is in Nexal! Hoxitl must know that, but he fears to tell the Ancient Ones! I don't like it!" Mixtal raised his hands to his scalp, tearing at the blood-caked spikes of his hair.

"The sign of the Viperhand is the ultimate command," Gultec reminded the priest. "And it is granted to the patriarch of Zaltec in Nexal, not Payit. The order is Hoxitl's to give and yours to obey.

"Just be thankful we shall accomplish our task with little further difficulty," growled the warrior. In truth, the priest's anxieties made him nervous.

"And we had to take her from the *temple apartments!*" Mixtal wailed. "It's not like Nexal, where Qotal is a silent, forgotten god! Oh, no, not here! They *worship* the Plumed Father here in Payit! And they will not overlook a transgression such as this!" The priest whirled anxiously, then continued.

"Caxal will not protect us. Even he, ruler of all the Payit, fears to challenge the power of Kachin's temple!" Indeed, Caxal, Revered Counselor of the city of Ulatos, never interfered in the workings of the temples. The Jaguar Knights, headed by Gultec, formed the largest and most influential group in the city, and their might was all that kept the temples of Zaltec from banishment.

"What would you have us do?" Gultec sprang to his feet in

one fluid motion, towering over the trembling cleric. "Send her back? Ignore the ones who are your masters . . . and mine?"

"How many days?" The cleric looked at the stars once again, groaning.

"One Tenday, as I told you! We hide the girl till then—the night of the new moon. Your knife will do the rest." The Jaguar Knight took a silent step away from the cleric, his spotted cloak blending into the darkness.

"I just don't like it!" the cleric hissed behind him, but Gultec had already vanished.

* * * * *

Seventh day following landfall, aboard the Falcon

Each day brings new islands, more information, greater boundaries to these undiscovered realms. Darien speaks to these natives, and always we learn of still greater lands to the west.

I begin to suspect we have come not to Shou Lung, nor even its peripheries. Instead, we have discovered new lands, entirely unknown to East or West—lands claimed in the name of the Golden Legion!

And they are lands of richness! Our casks brim with fresh water, our holds bulge with salted game and many fruits and vegetables. Chief among these is a grain the natives call mayz, which seems to grow in great abundance.

But more than food and water, these are lands of gold. We have stopped at four islands, and each time were met by bands of native humans. Each gave us presents of food and gold, and we saw that the farther we traveled west, the greater the abundance of gold.

The villages of these island peoples are poor, but all of them tell us, through Darien, of great lands to the west, a "world that climbs into the sky." That can only mean mountains, and a mainland.

And the source of the gold.

* * * * *

Halloran stood at the base of the waterfall, letting the spray cool him. He faced away from the deep lagoon where the fleet had at last gained a sheltered anchorage, looking up at the staircase progression of cataracts emerging from inland heights. Impenetrable tropical plant life surrounded the stream before him, but a stretch of lush grasses backed the beach to either side.

"Nice scenery. Still, just an island," muttered Daggrande, joining Hal at the sandy streambank. The dwarf pulled his dagger from its sheath and clucked in alarm, flicking several grains of sand from the blade. "I won't be happy till we set foot on the mainland!"

"You won't ever be happy. Still, how do you know it's just an island? The scouting ships have only been out for one day."

"I can *feel* it in these old feet of mine."

The dwarves, in their ancient, deliberate manner, had a way of understanding things about the earth that superseded the senses of humans. Halloran believed the veteran campaigner.

They looked up the beach to the center of its arc around the cove, where Cordell, Darien, and the Bishou engaged in negotiations with a contingent of the local natives.

Here, for the first time, the delegation had included women. Now a dozen maidens stood quietly to the side as their chieftains spoke to the visitors.

"Here comes the Bishou's daughter," humphed the dwarf. "Be careful. I think she's got her eye on you."

Halloran flushed. "Don't be ridiculous!" But he wondered, hoping that Daggrande could be right. Though he had only spoken to her briefly at their various landings, she always appeared happy to see him.

Daggrande clumped away to save himself the embarrassment of speaking to the woman.

"Hello!" Martine greeted Hal cheerfully, casting an amused glance after the departing dwarf. "Perhaps we can go for that walk now."

"Of course." Halloran offered his arm, delighting in the touch of her hand. He picked his way across the shallow stream, helping her maintain her balance, though she seemed in no danger of falling.

"It's so beautiful!" She gestured at the waterfall and the lush highlands beyond. "Each shore seems more wonderful than the last!"

"I wonder at the people," mused Hal. "Such barbarians!"

"Oh, Papa thinks they're wonderful. They listen to everything he tells them about Helm. Of course, they've never heard of him before. They don't seem to know about any gods, these people, but the Bishou thinks he's converting them all!"

"Still, don't you wonder if there's more to them than what we've seen?"

She laughed again, and again he loved the sound. "Oh, I don't know. I don't really think about it. It's fun to see each new place. Don't be so serious!"

"All right." He nodded, wanting to please her.

They walked for a while down the beach, past groups of sailors and soldiers from the legion relaxing on the shore. All the men had gotten to debark at least once thus far, and more than half of them were ashore now.

Halloran looked at the forest that marked the boundary of the beach. From the sea, they had seen a steadily rising slope, leading to some moderate crests a few miles inland. Where he stood now, he could see only the trees before him, since their height concealed the rising ground beyond.

Martine exclaimed over this blossom or that brilliantly plumed bird, while the horseman wondered what lay beyond that jungle facade. What was this place really like?

"We'd better not go too far," he cautioned, realizing they had walked past the last group of men on the beach.

"Oh, stop worrying! I'd like to be someplace for once where there aren't hundreds of sweaty men around me!"

"But . . ." Halloran paused in total confusion. He would do anything to please her, and indeed her desires coincided deeply with his own. But the Bishou's dour and protective nature was well known, and Domincus could scarcely fail to observe their departure. Hal shuddered at the thought of his wrath.

A thunderous explosion of sound blasted from the jungle, striking them like a blast of air and driving Halloran to his knees. Like the roar of a great cat, amplified to an earth-shattering level, the bellow was strong enough, and star-tling enough, to knock Martine flat onto her back behind Hal. In an instant, he staggered to his feet, his sword drawn.

A creature of nightmarish appearance leaped from the jungle, pouncing to the sand ten paces before the man. Hal-loran saw a great black mane surrounding a feline face con-torted by a hateful snarl. A pair of leathery wings flapped from the creature's shoulders, sending clouds of sand swirl-ing into the air. A black-tufted tail lashed back and forth as the beast, larger than a horse, crouched, preparing to spring.

Martine's lips moved, but she lay immobile on the sand. She may have spoken, but Hal realized that he could hear nothing. The roar had deafened him.

Halloran stumbled unsteadily, lurching to Martine's side, crouching defensively to protect her from the cruel jaws and raking talons. The monster leaped, and Halloran brought his sword down in an overhand blow, striking the thing's brutish forehead.

He felt claws tear into his rib cage at the same time as his blade contacted hard bone. Hal fell backward, still in front of Martine, while the creature uttered a short, surprised screech, stopping in its tracks and shaking its head.

Instantly Hal leaped to his feet, ignoring the burning pain and free flow of blood along his side. The snarling feline face was marred by a long cut, but once again the beast growled and crept forward. Halloran knew he could not stop it a second time.

Suddenly he saw one, then several heavy bolts appear in the monster's flank. Crossbow quarrels! Some of Dag-grande's men had seen them! The creature whirled and snapped at the missiles, so Halloran thrust at its other flank, driving his steel blade deep into its flesh. A band of swords-men sprinted toward them, lumbering in the soft sand.

The monster uttered another horrible roar, directed up the beach. Halloran watched in astonishment as several of the running swordsmen stumbled and fell, apparently stunned by the roar. Before the others could close, the monster sprang back toward the shelter of the forest. Its short wings greatly speeded its flight, and in moments it had disappeared into the trees.

"Are—are you all right?" Hal asked, anxiously helping Martine to her feet. His voice sounded hollow in his skull, but it seemed that his hearing was gradually returning.

"Yes . . . but you're hurt." She looked at his chest with genuine concern. "You saved my life!"

Halloran felt a delayed reaction to the sudden deadly combat. His knees shook and his muscles felt drained. He did not resist as she lifted his arm over her shoulder and supported him, aided by several men who only now arrived on the scene.

"Get the Bishou!" she shouted, and one of the men turned to obey. Hal had visions of his last rites, his soul delivered to Helm on a silver platter.

They soon reached the main gathering, and the brown-robed Bishou Domincus came striding forward to greet them. From the glowering look on his features, Hal felt certain the cleric did indeed want to send his soul Helmward.

"Help him, Father! He saved my life! The creature . . . it was horrible! I don't know what it was!" Martine's words spilled forth in an excited jumble.

" 'Hakuna', the chief called it." Hal blinked and saw Cordell standing beside the Bishou. The captain-general's face was slightly amused, not displeased. "That was well done, Captain!" Despite Hal's pain, the commander's words sent a thrill of pride to the core of his being. He smiled weakly as Martine helped him to lie upon the beach. The Bishou, still glaring, knelt beside him.

"Helm deliver this warrior from his wounds." Domincus closed his eyes and chanted. "He fought bravely and truly in your name. Grant me the power to close his flesh, that he may strive further in your valorous cause!"

Halloran felt his pain flow from his body as if the dam re-

straining it had been breached. His arm, hanging limply before, suddenly became strong, and he struggled to rise.

"Rest here," said Martine quietly. "Don't get up yet." Her
voice was so soothing, the sand and the sun so pleasant, that
Hal had no difficulty obeying. She rested her hand upon his
forehead, and it seemed as though cool water washed over
him. In moments, he slept.

It was late afternoon before he was awakened by Daggrande. "Last boat to the *Osprey*. Unless you want to wait
here and dance with that *hakuna* again tonight, that is."

Hal sprang to his feet, feeling remarkably spry. "Are we
moving on?"

"Aye. The scout ships returned. This is an island, like I
said. But now we hear tales of real mountains and a huge
land that these folks get to by canoe. I think our next landfall will be the mainland."

"Splendid!"

"That's not all. We hear they have a real city there . . . and
a pile of gold big enough to blind you in bright sunlight!"

Halloran saw several of the native girls being lifted into
longboats, most of which had already been taken back to
the ships. Some distance away, Martine and the Bishou were
locked in a heated conversation, but he could not hear what
they said. The daughter gestured angrily, and the father
turned sourly away.

As Hal and Daggrande reached the *Osprey*'s boat, Martine
called to the cavalryman. He paused on the beach as Daggrande impatiently waited in the boat.

"I'm coming with you," said the woman. He saw a look of
unfamiliar determination on her face.

"Of course." Halloran was delighted by the news, mostly.
"But what about your father? Doesn't he want you aboard
the *Falcon*?"

"Hmph!" She flounced past him and turned to look at the
Bishou. He was aiding several native girls into another longboat. "Father seems to have been given a 'gift.'" Martine gestured at a dusky maiden. "A slave!"

Halloran looked in surprise, guessing that all twelve of the
girls had been distributed among the other captains and in-

fluential officers of the fleet, as Martine continued. "I told him that he should set her free! Helm does not sanction slavery! But he made all sorts of stuttering noises—'It would be an insult to her people,' and such!"

She cast an angry look back toward the cleric, and Halloran felt very glad that he was not the target of such scalding rage. Yet he didn't know what to say to her as she looked back at him, her eyes still flashing.

"I think he *likes* having a pretty young slave! And so I told him I would not ride on the same ship with her," she snapped. "And here I am!"

"Won't you join us, then?" said Halloran weakly.

"Send for my luggage—tonight, please," Martine continued, scarcely missing a beat.

Halloran nodded, stunned by this abrupt assault and uneasy about its possible consequences.

❦ 7 ❦

SPIRALI

A black cape rustled softly in the darkness. The sound was intentional; the Ancient One announced his arrival to his fellows. But even more than this, the silken whisper told the others that this one had made a decision, a decision for action.

"*Kizzwryll!*"

The whispered word, spoken by the Ancestor, called to life the Darkfyre. The black liquid roiled in its caldron, shedding a darkness across the gathering that washed the faces of each of those present with an inky illumination.

The Darkfyre settled within its kettle, and the Ancient Ones turned to regard Spirali, the one of their number who had just arrived.

"The cleric is incredibly weak, even for a human. We cannot trust him to fulfill the task." Spirali's voice, a low whisper, echoed hollowly in the vast cavern.

"You speak the truth." The wizened Ancestor, concealed by his robes where all the others gathered with bared heads, nodded.

"There is now a thing I must do."

Several cloaks rustled, a mute agreement with Spirali's remark and a comment about its drastic nature.

"You must not reveal yourself if it can be avoided. But if the humans fail, you *must* slay the girl." The Ancestor rasped the command gently, knowing that Spirali had implicitly understood the situation long before any of the rest of them had acknowledged the truth. Sometime our deliberateness hampers us, reflected the Ancestor. The humans move so much faster.

"I will enact the will of the council," said Spirali. With another rustle of his cape, he bowed deeply and then turned back to the darkness.

* * * * *

Erix could not see the cycles of the sun, so she had no accurate means of measuring the length of her imprisonment. She had received ten meals—each a miserable portion of cold mayz and water—and her best guess was that ten days had passed.

Other than the silent servers who brought her food, slipping it to her through a small hatch in the cell door, she had no contact with other humans. Around her yawned a seemingly vast realm of silence. A perennial chill made her suspect that she was held somewhere underground.

Not long after her tenth meal, Erix again heard sandaled footsteps outside her cell door. She sensed that only a few hours had passed since her daily sustenance, so she knew this was an unusual visit. Crouching against the wall opposite the door, she waited. The latch lifted, and a sudden wash of torchlight filled the room as the portal opened, revealing a pair of men in loincloths.

With a shriek that contained all the pent-up anger and frustration of her life, Erixitl sprang at the first man. He stumbled backward in shock as her fingers raked across his face. Instantly her victim screamed and collapsed, moaning and clutching his bleeding face.

The second man stopped in shock, and the force of her charge bowled him over. She leaped on his belly, doubling him over, and then she sprang past. She was free!

Then she slammed into something hard, something that pushed back. She fell to the floor, stunned, and felt her arms gripped by talonlike fingers. In the fading light of the torch, she recognized the horrid visage of a Jaguar Knight. His dark eyes glowered at her through the gaping jaws of his helm. The jaguar teeth, long and ivory white, seemed to reach menacingly for her face.

"That was foolish, little one!" he hissed, lifting her easily off the floor and holding her upright. "You may have blinded one of my slaves."

He shook her like a rag doll, and she felt as if her teeth would bounce from her jaw. "Now, behave!" he warned, setting her on her feet. Instantly her fist flew at his chest, scraping her knuckles on his *hishna* armor of jaguar hide. She spit in his face and he cuffed her; she kicked his knee and he knocked her down.

Finally he grabbed her unceremoniously and tossed her over his shoulder, neutralizing her struggles. "You are a spirited one, hey? Zaltec will relish the feast of your heart!"

For a moment, the confirmation of her suspicions drained her, and she slumped limply across his shoulder. She felt the knight, too, relax. And she realized that his remark had told her nothing at all, for she had never doubted that her captors intended her for the sacrificial altar.

She twisted to the side and brought her knee into the knight's throat in a crushing blow. He gasped and stumbled as she savagely struck his shoulders with her elbows. Like a wild beast, Erix twisted free as the man dropped to his knees. She saw him reach for her, and somehow she eluded his grasp, feeling his fingers slip from her arm.

Erix sprinted down the corridor, bursting through a reed curtain into a small courtyard. A wall obstructed her view of everything but the starry sky. She raced across the dark courtyard, pounding into a large gate and finding it barred.

* * * * *

Mixtal waited nervously in the courtyard while Gultec went to get the girl. He paced back and forth in agitation. The past ten days had been, for the cleric, a miserable period of suspense and anxiety. The girl had been hidden well, but her very presence had caused him constant, soul-wrenching fear.

What if Kachin gained proof of Mixtal's involvement? The thought sent shudders through Mixtal's scrawny frame. The cleric of Qotal had been persistent in his questioning, outraged in his accusations against the Jaguars.

That house of warriors had defended itself well, claiming no knowledge of the capture. The blame, it was hinted, rested upon some young warriors who had partaken of too much *octal*. Their identities were unknown, but if they were discovered, Kachin would of course be informed.

Anxiously Mixtal looked back toward the dark entrance to the cellar. What was keeping Gultec?

A group of apprentice priests awaited them outside, ready to witness the sacrifice. The ritual would be secret, performed away from the city. They all knew that the priests of Qotal, peaceable though they claimed to be, would exact a terrible vengeance should the abduction of the princess be traced to the temple of Zaltec.

And now something was wrong!

The priest saw a lithe figure emerge from the house, dashing across the courtyard toward the gate. The girl had escaped! With a low groan, Mixtal turned toward the swinging reed curtain, hoping to see Gultec in pursuit.

He heard the girl bang on the gate, and his heart sank. He had no illusions as to his own fate should she escape. The summoning from the Ancient Ones had made that clear. Mixtal ran across the courtyard and saw her moving along the base of the wall.

The cleric grasped his necklace of snake fangs, calling forth the *hishna* sorcery of Zaltec. He pulled a wriggling snakeskin from his pouch. The object writhed with a life of its own. Holding the twisting thing before him, he concentrated on the girl, seeing her turn at the sound of his voice.

"*Zaltec Tlaz-atl qoo!*"

Mixtal pointed at the girl and released the skin. The object flew through the air, darting like an airborne eel into a tight circle around Erix.

"*Tzillit!*" Mixtal finished the spell by commanding the strands to contract around his victim.

He saw the girl shrink away from the encircling magic. Her own hand seized something at her throat, a gesture that looked instinctive. Mixtal heard a sound like a burst of air, and suddenly he shouted in pain. The skin fell motionless to the ground, and the cleric blew frantically upon his blistered palms. Somehow the girl had resisted the *hishna*, and with strength enough to send shock waves of pain crackling back to the magic-wielding priest.

Groaning, Mixtal looked up again. He saw, or imagined, an aura around the feathered necklace the girl wore. His *hishna* had been defeated by something, and he suddenly felt the coolness of *pluma*, the magic of feathers, emanating from the young woman before him.

* * * * *

Erix released her feather token as if it was a scalding stone. Stunned, she watched the sorcerous attack fall away. But in the next instant, she realized that her father's gift had only offered her salvation if she could seize it instantly.

She saw a nearby tree with branches extending over the wall, and she raced toward it like a gust of wind, leaping a bench that she barely saw in her path. In moments, she would reach the safety of the tree.

Then a shadowy form crossed her path, disappearing into the predawn darkness below the tree. Erix stopped, but she could see nothing in the inky blackness.

A low growl—a deep, horrible, animal growl—emerged from the darkness, and Erixitl moaned in all-encompassing terror. She took a step backward, but her body finally sagged with exhaustion, horror, even defeat.

A jaguar burst from the shadow, its paws striking her in the chest and knocking her heavily to the ground. She gasped for air, staring upward at bright yellow eyes, the slitted pupils burning with hatred. She felt its warm drool spattering to her chin and neck.

And then the jaguar was gone, and the knight she had attacked knelt upon her.

Roughly he pulled her to her feet, jerking her sharply around and binding her hands until the cords cut into her flesh. He stuffed a filthy rag into her mouth and bound that behind her head. Then he pushed her through the gate, where she was forced into the center of a procession of several dozen young priests. She did not need to inhale the scent of caked blood to know that these were priests of Zaltec, for the scalp of each bristled with the characteristic spikes of hair.

They would perform their sacrifice outside the city, she saw, as they led her down a street and then past the fields of mayz. Soon the trail entered the jungle, but just as quickly it emerged along the coast. For perhaps an hour, they marched along the beach. Erix felt numb, barely aware of the fading light of the stars as dawn approached.

Finally the procession of priests and victim reached a steep bluff. Erix saw two massive stone faces carved into the cliff face of the bluff, a man's and a woman's image staring out across the great sea. She recognized the place as the one she had heard about from the girl in Pezelac, the place called Twin Visages. The faces, she remembered ironically, had been sculpted by worshipers of Qotal, a sign of hope and reverence in awaiting that god's return. Now they would be the site of a sacrifice to bloody Zaltec.

The priests climbed a trail up the bluff, winding between the two faces. The steep ascent took a long time, as the immensity of the escarpment only gradually became apparent. Behind, and soon below them, the rolling breakers of the sea crashed into shore, still invisible in the gloom. The approaching dawn had become a rosy glow in the east. The stars had almost all disappeared.

Now the numbness of the long march began to fade, and Erix sensed the cold proximity of her death.

Here Erixitl saw a small pyramid, a barren block of stone atop the bluff, overlooking the sea. She twisted and struggled as they approached it, but the group of apprentices simply lifted her to their shoulders and marched her up the steep steps, fifty-two in number, to the top.

The young priests formed a ring around the top platform of the pyramid while the Jaguar Knight and high priest went to the stone altar. That bloodstained block stood at one side of the platform atop the pyramid. Beside the altar squatted a bestial image of Zaltec, carved from stone. The war god's mouth gaped open, awaiting its gory feast.

Erix saw the black stains across the altar, streaking the sides and smeared across much of the platform. She twisted and scratched, but the apprentices finally held her immobile.

The rosy light became orange, then red. Erix watched, horrified and spellbound, as the sky grew ever brighter. All of the priests, too, kept their eyes upon the eastern horizon. Vaguely she felt the knight untie her bonds and remove her gag. She knew that four priests would stretch her across the altar while Mixtal wielded his obsidian knife. She saw the weapon now, tucked into his waistband, a sinister, shining black blade with a turquoise and jadestone hilt.

Then the intent concentration of the priests wavered. One whispered an exclamation, another an urgent prayer. Their attention turned toward the ocean. Erix at first took no note of the change, until even Mixtal, the high priest, looked toward the sea, an expression like fear creeping over his features.

"What is *that?*" muttered the cleric nervously.

The other priests muttered, too, and even Gultec peered through the darkness of the clearing to stare out over the sea.

"By Zaltec, they are great winged creatures!" gasped one of the young priests.

Erix stood spellbound as the dawn light spilled across the pyramid and the sea below. She saw creatures, elegant monsters, wondrous billowing white things, bigger than houses. They seemed to fly, just touching the water, and their course took them toward the shore. Their wings were huge, but they did not flap, instead seeming to stand upright, as if to slow the creatures' awesome momentum. The young priests crowded to the east side of the pyramid, all straining to get a better view.

"It is a sign from Zaltec!" groaned Mixtal.

"Nonsense!" Gultec snarled and stepped forward to push his way through the priests. Nonetheless, he said nothing for a time.

Erix stood alone with Mixtal in the center of the pyramid. The cleric wrung his hands nervously, staring to the east. The woman saw one glorious opportunity.

Her hand flashed out and pulled the dagger from Mixtal's belt. In the same instant, she drove the hilt against his scalp, just above the ear. Mixtal uttered no sound as his knees collapsed.

Before the cleric's body had fallen, Erix had leaped from the west side of the pyramid to race down the stairs and into the tenuous protection of the jungle beyond.

* * * * *

From the *Chronicle of the Waning*:

May the light of the Plumed One illuminate my miserable ignorance!

My hand trembles such that I can barely paint this tale. I can only relate what I have seen and hope that time and perhaps sleep will allow me to plumb its depths. The time is today, the setting of the sun. . . .

Naltecona attends the sacrifices upon the great pyramid, performing two of them himself—hearts offered to Crimson Zaltec and Black Tezca. The throng crowded in the plaza, even the priests on the pyramid, seemed held in some kind of thrall. Movement slowed, perception heightened.

A great noise drew our eyes to the sky, and there appeared a beast, a huge creature the like of which Maztica has never known. Shaped like a bird, it had no feathers but was covered with leathery skin like a crocodile. A long beak, sharp and jagged, extended from its maw. The monster settled slowly to the top of the pyramid as the priests recoiled in panic. I myself fell to the stones in awe.

Naltecona stood firm in its presence. His nephew Poshtli, wearing his full armor as an Eagle Knight, stepped before the counselor and raised his maca to defend his uncle. The black and white feathers of Poshtli's cloak spread from his shoulders in challenge to the monster.

The beast spread and flapped its wings, sending a hurricane of wind across the pyramid, driving the priests still farther away. Finally Poshtli, too, tumbled to the side. And then we saw the will of the gods.

Across the broad breast of the beast spread a shiny surface, like obsidian or smooth, perfect ice. I stared, awestruck, at my own dumbfounded reflection in this mirror from heaven. Others, I learned later, saw the same thing as I: a reflection of the pyramid and the assembled priesthood.

Except Naltecona.

The Revered Counselor recoiled two steps, staring into the mirror. The beast stepped toward him, and Naltecona made noises of fear. He stared for a full minute, and though none other could see the vision granted his eyes, he groaned and he wept. He pounded his chest in disbelieving fear. He spoke of two-headed monsters, of silver spears, of houses that floated upon the ocean.

Then did the beast spread its wings and soar aloft, nearly driving us from the pyramid with the wind of its ascension. Then, too, did Naltecona fall to his knees and kiss the stones before the creature's footsteps.

❧ 8 ❧

CHITIKAS

The eagle soared easily on the coastal updrafts. Far below, heavy breakers pounded a stretch of beach that vanished into the distance to the north and south.

The bird suddenly thrust its wings once and again, gaining speed and swooping into a dive. The air became moist with drifting spray, but the eagle's keen eyes penetrated the haze, studying the strange shapes on the water.

The eyes were those of an animal, but the mind that absorbed those sights was human. The Eagle Knight in avian form was Lord Poshtli, nephew of the great Naltecona himself, now flying a mission of observation for the Revered Counselor.

The eagle passed once above the cloudlike forms, carefully examining them. Still hundreds of feet in the air, the bird flew silently, unnoticed from below.

Then it dove toward the sea, a long, swooping descent that quickly propelled the powerful animal at blinding speed. The massive wings beat again, a steady cadence of power. Now the eagle climbed slowly, never wavering from a straight course, gaining only the elevation needed to cross the mountains that lay invisible beyond the horizon ahead.

It flew northwest, toward distant, iridescent Nexal.

* * * * *

Erix scrambled through the brush, ignoring the sharp thorns tearing at her limbs, mindful only of the desperate need to flee the deadly altar of Zaltec. She used the sacrificial knife to hack some of the encroaching vegetation away, but the stone blade proved an inefficient means of clearing a path. Mostly she just pushed her way between branches, occasionally diving headfirst through a tangle of vines.

After two desperate minutes of flight, she paused, stifling her own gasps in an effort to listen for pursuit. A bird cackled somewhere nearby, hidden by foliage. Fat insects buzzed around her head.

But there was no sound of even vaguely human origin. For long moments, Erix stood still, listening to the sounds of the jungle. Vaguely, in the distance, she could hear the dull roar of the surf.

The sound of the ocean reminded her of the great, winged *things* she had seen. For some reason she had already begun to doubt that they were creatures. Whatever they were, she knew their appearance had saved her life.

For a full minute, Erix stood still, wondering at the lack of pursuit. Surely they had noticed her escape! The strange objects offshore, she finally concluded, must be holding the priests and the Jaguar Knight in some kind of thrall.

Again she wondered at the spectacle, her curiosity beginning to overcome her fear. She gained her bearings, remembering that the ocean lay generally behind her. Moving slower, with more stealth than during the initial rush of her flight, she turned to the left and began to move parallel to the shore.

The pyramid of Zaltec gradually fell away behind her, and she became immersed in the heavy, wet jungle. Soaked with her own sweat, ignoring the flies and mosquitoes that buzzed around her, she laboriously worked her way to the south. Finally she emerged upon a narrow trail, and here she turned again, striking eastward for the coast.

Erixitl's arms bled from dozens of scrapes, and the thorns had torn her cotton gown into a tattered rag. But now she pushed quickly forward, forgetting all of her present difficulties in her desire to look again upon the great wings over the ocean.

At last she pushed through the dripping fronds of a thick fern and found herself near the edge of the coastal bluff. A strip of brushy ground lined the edge of the precipice, but her curiosity overcame caution. Carefully she crawled through the brush to the edge of the cliff. Worming forward, secure in the shelter of a dense tangle, she looked out toward the ocean.

The white wings of the sea-things now hung limp, smaller than when she had first seen them. Though the objects were well to her left, a mile or more away, she could see more details.

Instantly she understood: These were great vessels, like unthinkably massive canoes, and they were filled with men. Even as she watched, she saw smaller craft—more like true canoes, though still larger than the slender boats plying the waters of Maztica—drift away from the great vessels. Like great whales giving birth, each of the large craft disgorged one of the smaller boats, and these began moving slowly toward the shore.

Erixitl's sense of wonder grew. Was this a miracle in progress before her? Where did these visitors come from? Certainly they did not originate in the True World. She could see tiny manlike figures among the strangers, but she could not believe that these were actually human beings like herself. Could they be the messengers of the gods? Or even the gods themselves?

"Pretty girl!"

A voice, speaking crude Payit, jerked her attention back to reality. Erix swung around and raised the knife, but she could see nothing. Her back to the steep bluff, she scrutinized the surrounding vegetation.

"Oh, she's got a knife, too! Look out, look out!" The voice sounded amused.

"Who's there?" she hissed, crouching.

"We're all here, eh, pretty one?" A sudden burst of color startled her. She gasped, almost dropping the knife, as a brightly feathered bird exploded from the bush before her, squawking upward to rest among the fronds of a palm. "She's scared now!" Her jaw dropped as she realized that the mysterious voice belonged to a macaw.

"I'm not scared! You startled me, featherbrain!" She tossed

her head at the bird, feeling sheepish. She had heard of macaws and parrots that could mimic the sound of human voices. Then she realized with a chill that the bird had not mimicked any sound. It had remarked about things it had observed, such as her knife!

"Smart bird, that he is," lisped another voice, a low, sibilant sound emerging from a leafy bush.

Erix turned with a gasp as she saw a long, brightly colored head emerge from the greenery. It was followed by a snake's neck and a portion of a serpentine body coiling smoothly forward, slender but supple and wiry. Yet the snake eyes gleamed at her with intelligence, even perhaps a little amusement.

"A lucky girl you are today, Erixitl." The creature spoke again, its snake lips pursing softly as a black, forked tongue slipped in and out of its mouth. "Lucky girl because *I* am here.

"And I am Chitikas."

* * * * *

Tenth day following landfall, aboard the Falcon

Helm has granted us a splendid anchorage, a deep lagoon surrounded by encircling headlands. A rugged coast greets us, distinguished in particular by two monstrous images carved into the rocky bluff.

Each of these presents a human visage, apparently a male and female, many times the height of a man. At the top of the bluff stands a squat structure, pyramidal in shape.

We move quickly to put the legion ashore, leaving bare crews to tend the ships. The footmen claim the ground even now; in some hours, we will debark the horses.

* * * * *

"Who could have made them?" wondered Halloran, awe-struck. The growing light of day revealed a pair of huge faces carved into the cliff before them.

"Look at them!" murmured an unusually subdued Martine, taking Hal's arm in unconscious excitement.

He thought uncomfortably how that touch would have thrilled him a few days before. Now Martine's hand felt like a cold iron shackle, closing around his flesh. Her attentions, which once had exhilarated him, now confined and enclosed him more securely with each bubbling phrase, each coy look.

She had stayed at his side constantly during the three days she had been aboard the *Osprey*—except, of course, when they slept. Hal had willingly offered his cabin, the only private lodging on the ship, and she had accepted it as her due. He had spent the last three nights with the horses and dogs under the crude deck shelter, and he had come to appreciate those hours as his only free time.

Daggrande had avoided them as much as possible—no mean trick on the ninety-foot carrack—and Martine's incessant talking had begun to ring in his ears even in his dreams. Perhaps this landing would give him an opportunity to be a soldier again, but he doubted it.

The fleet stood offshore, resting easily at anchor. Halloran and Martine stood at *Osprey's* rail as the longboat was lowered toward the crystalline azure waters. Bright flashes of color, schools of exotic fish, darted among the coral.

But their attention remained fixed upon the gargantuan faces. They showed a male and a female, each with a broad mouth and wide nose. The faces were flat and rounded, and even the male was unbearded. The eyes, though mere carvings in granite, seemed to stare at the ships with keen scrutiny.

"Your father says these people do not know of the gods," said Halloran. "I look at these faces and I cannot help but disagree."

Martine shrugged. "Well, let's go!" she said, nodding at the longboat, which now floated beside the *Osprey*.

Halloran groaned inwardly. "We've talked about this! You'll have to wait here until we've scouted the shoreline!"

"Don't be ridiculous!" Martine turned toward the longboat.

"You can't go ashore with the first swords!" Halloran began to panic. She stepped to the short rope ladder dangling from the gunwale, and he followed helplessly. She smiled up at him as she descended with natural grace.

"Well, at least stay close to the boats!" he grunted, swinging onto the ladder as she sat in the stern of the little craft.

Halloran felt the same mixture of emotions that had belabored him for the three days since Martine had boarded the *Osprey*. Her beauty taunted him as she dazzled him with a smile, but he felt absolutely powerless in her presence, and this frightened him. The combination of emotions made him miserable.

Not to mention the matter of her father. The Bishou was a central pillar of the legion's morale, a spiritual authority to match Cordell's unerring generalship. And he served, faithfully as far as Halloran knew, a stern and unforgiving deity. True, the power of Helm had healed Hal's wounds when Domincus had prayed to the Vigilant One. But Halloran felt it a grave risk to incur the wrath of the Bishou.

Hal accepted Helm as much as he accepted the idea of any god. In truth, the god of eternal vigilance offered a useful comfort to a man-at-arms such as himself. But was he now inviting the god's disfavor by . . . what was he doing, anyway? He simply allowed Martine to have her way about things, and he knew there was nothing he could do to change that.

With a sigh, he turned to the bow and looked at those monstrous faces, now leering down at them as the boats glided into the shadow of the bluff.

* * * * *

"Wake up, you miserable dolt!" Gultec kicked the cleric none too gently.

Mixtal squinted and groaned, barely seeing the snarling jaguar face leering into his own. "What . . . what happened? . . . Where's the girl?"

"Gone. Her fighting prowess apparently overwhelmed you."

"How did—" Mixtal suddenly sat up, ignoring the stabbing pain in his skull. *"The signs from Zaltec! Where are they?"*

"Not signs from Zaltec, idiot." Gultec gestured to the east as Mixtal realized that he had been carried to the base of the pyramid. "They are men, warriors, even now gathering on our shore in great numbers."

Mixtal blinked and stared. Cold terror vied with incoherent awe in his breast. He feared the retribution of the Ancient Ones, for he had let the girl escape. At the same time, he now witnessed a miracle, or thought he did.

"What makes you so sure they're warriors?" he demanded. "They look like messengers from the gods to me!"

Gultec cast a contemptuous look at the cleric. "They sent their scouts ashore first. These investigated the forest around the beach. Now see how their numbers unfold on the sand, and they gather in organized companies."

"But they have no feathers! No clubs! And look, some of them are silver!"

Gultec growled inaudibly at the vista far below. "It troubles me, this silver. I do not see why a warrior would burden himself with such a weight. It makes me suspect they are very strong."

The Jaguar Knight turned to the priest. "Stay here and watch them, but do not let yourselves be seen. I will speed to Ulatos and warn the counselor."

Mixtal nodded dumbly as Gultec turned and trotted toward the edge of the forest on the inland side of the pyramid. In seconds, the Jaguar Knight passed from sight among the tangled branches. He placed his hands upon a horizontal trunk, vaulting easily over it to land on four soft paws. His spotted hide blended with the jungle as he sprang forward with feline grace and speed.

Soon Gultec took to the trees. He leaped from branch to branch across dizzying gaps, sinking his claws into hardwood at each sturdy bough.

Quickly the jaguar retraced the trail that had taken the human party two hours to traverse, then shifted back to his human body before emerging from the jungle. Even as he stepped onto the trail among the mayzfields, he saw that word of the strange visitors must have preceded him: No one worked in the fields, but ahead the streets of Ulatos bustled with uncharacteristic activity.

Gultec maintained a steady trot into the city. The throng naturally parted for the Jaguar Knight, and in moments he had reached Ulatos Plaza.

"Gultec, come here!" The voice called from the small pyramid in the center of the plaza, and the knight saw Caxal, the Revered Counselor of Ulatos, frantically gesturing to him. Gultec quickly climbed the twelve steps to the top of the platform, seeing that several other Jaguar and Eagle Knights, as well as the cleric Kachin, were standing there with Caxal.

"We have been invaded!" raged the counselor.

Gultec nodded. "I have seen them myself—strange men traveling in great canoes. They gather on the shore below Twin Visages. They are mysterious, but their numbers are small."

"We do not know that this is an invasion!" insisted a third voice, and Gultec turned to regard Kachin, cleric of Qotal. "We must try to speak with them, to see who they are and what they want."

Caxal looked from Kachin back to Gultec. "How many troops can we gather today?" The Revered Counselor tended to be suspicious of his warriors, but now he was frightened, and his fear took priority.

"Perhaps two hundred Jaguars, as many Eagles." The Jaguar Knight looked to Lok, Gultec's counterpart as chief of the Eagle Knights.

"Perhaps . . . certainly more than a hundred," Lok said thoughtfully. Though the two warriors were not friends, each respected the other as a man of bravery, skill, and judgment.

"We can have ten thousand spearmen gathered by evening, perhaps twice that many by tomorrow," concluded the Jaguar Knight.

"Gather them," said Caxal with finality. "Bring the troops to the top of the bluff, near the Twin Visages. But do not attack! We must learn more about them!" The group broke up, but

Kachin stepped to Gultec's side before the knight could leave the platform.

"The girl, Erixitl," hissed Kachin, his eyes blazing with a vengeful fire that Gultec found strangely disquieting. "I have learned that you took her, you or your lackeys. Her death will not go unpunished!"

The knight, a man of steely courage, a veteran battle commander, squirmed under the cleric's steady gaze.

"I don't know what you mean," Gultec mumbled, hurrying down the stairs, cursing all clerics and their gods.

* * * * *

Chitikas emerged from the concealing verdure, and Erix stood numb with astonishment. She saw first that the serpent's skin was not covered with scales, but instead with the brilliant, silky type of down found upon the breast of a parrot. The macaw that had first spoken to Erix stood motionless, watching as the snake undulated forward.

Her astonishment grew as a pair of huge wings, brilliantly plumed in red, gold, green, and blue, broke free from the leafy bower, fluttering very slowly. They emerged from the serpent's midsection, extending a man's height to each side. The snake assumed a weightless quality as more and more of its enormous length appeared, for no portion of its visible body rested upon the ground.

The serpentine shape drifted into aimless coils, slowly writhing in the air, while the wings continued their slow cadence. Its brilliant yellow eyes bored into Erix, yet she felt no menace in the gaze. Hesitantly, needing to relieve her numbed muscles, she sat on a rotten log.

"You have troubles," whispered the creature. "Perhaps I can help you."

"Sure, help!" The macaw squawked its approval of the plan, fluttering down to rest on the snake's head.

Erix finally began to relax. Somehow she felt comfortable in the presence of this strange creature. The droning of insects and the heavy warmth of the afternoon air seemed to soothe her. She sighed. The snake's eyes bored into her, seeming to whirl in opposite directions. Its body moved with liquid ease in a slow dance.

"I come from Nexala," she said dreamily. "Very far from here." And before she could continue, she was asleep.

* * * * *

Mixtal groaned again in soul-wrenching agony. The Ancient Ones would slay him, he knew, but not until an eternity of torment had been inflicted upon his miserable person. He barely noticed the twenty apprentices standing in an awkward circle around him, but gradually he sensed that they awaited his instructions, his leadership.

Several of the youths kept watch over the strange visitors, who as yet had made no effort to climb the bluff. Nevertheless, Mixtal was certain that, after making the journey from wherever they called home, these strangers were not about to limit their explorations to a stretch of wooded shoreline.

It quickly became clear to the cleric that the priests' present location at the base of the pyramid would be one of the first sites investigated by the newcomers when they moved off the beach.

"The girl!" he finally said. "Did anyone see which way she went?"

The priests looked at the ground. Their spikes of stiff hair shook slowly, like a band of porcupines performing a mournful dance.

"Inland," offered one apprentice, a strapping young man named Atax. Mixtal remembered him as one who had wielded the sacrificial knife with exceptional acumen on his initial attempts. Like any apprentice, Atax had made mistakes, requiring the sacrifice to be performed over, even once requiring three victims before the proper cut had been made. But Atax learned quickly, and his strength might now be an asset.

"We must find her!" Mixtal stood quickly. He paused at the edge of the bluff to observe the newcomers—he admitted to himself that they seemed to be men. Their great canoes had furled their wings, and it seemed to the cleric that perhaps a hundred of them had already gathered on the beach.

"Give me your knife," Mixtal demanded, claiming the obsidian blade of a younger apprentice. He tried to ignore the shame of his own blade's loss but felt a flush creeping over his features. "Into the forest! Follow me!"

For many hours of a day that grew hotter with each passing minute, the score of priests combed the jungle along the coast. They pressed eastward for a time, crossing Erix's trail at numerous points, but none of the clerics had the woodcraft to recognize it as such. Then they reversed course, moving back through the beaten zone, as the humid air settled heavily around them and morning became afternoon.

"Let's rest a moment," gasped Mixtal, collapsing against a tree. He noticed with annoyance that none of the apprentices seemed as exhausted as he was. All of their prickly hair spikes had collapsed into tangled mats, however.

"Most Holy One, perhaps we should seek help," suggested Atax tentatively.

"No!" Mixtal stood straight, vigorous once again with the alertness of cold panic. "*We* must find her! This is *our* task!"

Atax recoiled from the outburst, and Mixtal took mild satisfaction in that fact. At least there were *some* who would treat him with respect! Then Mixtal blinked, disbelieving, and watched Atax slide to the ground before him. The man was sleeping!

Raging, Mixtal spun to face his other apprentices. His rage quickly cooled into something approaching fear when he saw that *they all slept!*

"What's happening here?" he demanded plaintively. "Wake up!"

"Softly, O Holy One," soothed a voice.

"Who's that? Where are you?"

"I will speak and you will listen." The voice coaxed him gently, and Mixtal felt himself slumping to a seat on the ground. He listened.

"Searching for the girl in this fashion is foolish. Instead, you must gather warriors." Mixtal halfheartedly looked for the source of the voice, but he saw only flowers and birds, whirling colors gathering around him. He did not remember the jungle as such a colorful place, but it was really quite beautiful.

"Warriors?" he answered, from a great distance. "How?" Now the priest felt as though his eyes had been covered with a soft glaze, not painful, like looking through colorful smoke when the smoke was *inside* his eyes.

"Wait here." The voice soothed him further with its reassuring advice. Mixtal could not question the words. "The warriors will come to you. And then, if you look but a short distance, you will find her whom you seek."

And then Mixtal, too, slept, lapsing into a dream filled with singing flowers, talking snakes, and chattering, brilliant-plumed birds. He did not awaken for some time, and then only when he heard a man's guttural question.

"Priest, why do you sleep here?"

"Wha—?" Mixtal's eyes popped open and he sat up. He saw three Jaguar Knights, including the one who had just spoken, and beyond them a column of spearmen stretching to the limit of the cleric's vision in the undergrowth. Each spearman wore the breechclout typical of the Payit and carried three obsidian-tipped javelins, a caster, and a round shield of jaguar skin mounted over wood. Each had a bone or wooden ornament stuck crosswise through his nose and wore a high headdress of orange feathers.

"Warriors!" Now the priest sprang to his feet animatedly. "Wake up, you louts!" He gave Atax and another apprentice swift kicks. "The warriors are here!"

"You were *expecting* us?" demanded the knight as the apprentices roused their comrades.

"Do not question the will of Zaltec!" snapped Mixtal. "I have heard directly from the *Ancient Ones!*" At least, he thought he had. Things were happening so fast that the priest couldn't quite keep up. But he enjoyed the fear that passed across the Jaguar Knight's face at Mixtal's words.

"We have an important task to perform! A sacrifice demanded by Zaltec has escaped and is even now arousing the anger of the god. We must find her!"

"What tale is this?" asked the knight. "We have been sent

here, this hundredmen, to keep watch over the invaders. A hundred hundred even now gather to the shore. I know nothing about a sacri—"

"The invaders!" Mixtal's mind seized upon an idea. His eyes still seemed to stare through a shifting haze of smoke, but now his brain whirled with ideas, with command. "Yes, they are the ones. They have taken her from the altar of Zaltec! Don't you understand? They are an affront to our gods! We must reclaim that which is rightfully Zaltec's!"

"I have my orders, from Gultec himself," grunted the knight, nervously.

"Would Gultec want you to stand by idly while our gods are defiled because of a woman taken from us?" Mixtal felt tall, as if the warriors were child-sized people gathered around him.

The knight turned and conferred quietly with the two other Jaguars of his company. Mixtal looked down and saw them gesturing and whispering.

"We must go! I will lead you to the invaders, and you will help me reclaim our property!"

Mixtal started into the jungle, followed by the apprentices. Slowly the column of warriors fell into file behind them.

* * * * *

"There! Let's go with them," urged Martine. Halloran looked resignedly at the four swordsmen who were hacking their way up the bluff. All around them, other small groups of scouts worked their way down the beach or pioneered other paths toward the high ground beyond the shore.

"No!" Hal turned to her in exasperation. "You shouldn't even be on the beach now!" He desperately wanted to lead one of the teams, but he knew that Martine would only accompany him. He looked at Cordell, together with the Bishou and Darien, several hundred yards up the beach. Halloran sensed the Bishou's eyes upon him every time he turned around.

And Martine's bold gaze confronted him when he turned back.

"I am *not* a child, you know! I can take care of myself, and if you don't want to come along with me, you don't have to! I'm going to do a little exploring." She whirled away from him, and once again he stumbled after her.

He reached out to take her arm, but she fixed him with a glare of such intensity that his arms fell to his sides, as if paralyzed.

"What are you so worried about, anyway?" she teased.

"Another *hakuna*, perhaps. And what if the people aren't friendly everywhere we go?" Hal grew increasingly annoyed with her. He felt frustrated by the way she maneuvered him into acceptance of whatever she chose to do. But he could not show his anger. Some inner reserve kept his temper in check as she manipulated him, turning his frustration inward to seethe and simmer.

"But I have you to protect me, don't I?" She touched his arm and he started stammering. "Look at this—a stairway!" she exclaimed suddenly.

They reached the base of the bluff and saw the four swordsmen Martine had indicated earlier working their way upward through entangling vegetation. Now they could see that the path was in reality a series of broad, granite steps, climbing in steep switchbacks across the face of the bluff. Some distance to the right, the two huge faces looked out to sea.

Martine led Hal onto the granite steps, and they quickly joined the four men. Halloran wished he had brought Corporal ashore. The legion's war dogs were adept at spotting ambushes and other unpleasant surprises.

These steps, like the faces and the pyramid, evidenced a more organized and populous culture than the expedition had encountered on the islands. Even so, the level of jungle entanglement showed that they received very little use. Normally he would have enjoyed the exploration, with its splendid view of the lagoon, the strange sculpture, the steep ground. But instead, he found himself miserable, disgusted by his weakness in the face of Martine's manipulations.

It took some time to reach the top of the bluff, and Halloran watched the ships grow smaller below as they climbed. Most of the legion had debarked by now, but he felt quite isolated. He saw Daggrande lead perhaps a score of crossbowmen and swordsmen toward the stairway below and took some comfort from the sight.

"Captain?" One of the swordsmen stepped aside for Halloran as they reached the top of the stairway. Hal saw that they had reached a brushy strip of land atop the bluff, running parallel to the coast to the north and south at the lip of the steep slope. Several hundred feet back from the edge rose the verdant wall of a tropical rain forest.

"There's the pyramid!" Martine cried, pointing, and Hal saw the squat structure rising from the brush perhaps a mile to the north along the coast.

"Let's head that way," suggested Halloran, knowing they would find other members of the expedition there.

He was mildly surprised when Martine agreed.

❧ 9 ❧

FIRST BLOOD

Erix awoke suddenly. She sat up, her mind unusually clear, with none of the dullness that usually accompanied emergence from sleep. Her first thought was of Chitikas, and she saw that the serpent was gone.

It was still daylight, and very hot. Her position on the bluff offered some concealment, but she knew that the strangers would be exploring the area. Her clump of brush would not hide her from nearby eyes.

Seeking more secure shelter, she crawled through the strip of brush toward the concealment of the jungle. Quickly finding the trail she had followed earlier, she moved into the forest, glancing around frequently, alert for any sounds from behind her.

She came around a bend in the trail, and suddenly, with dismay, she knew that her attention should have been directed on the trail ahead of her. The high priest Mixtal appeared around another bend, marching toward her, his face twisted into a mask of religious fervor. He stared directly into her eyes as she lunged from the trail, tripping and falling among a tangle of branches.

Twisting behind the bole of a large tree, she listened for his cry of alarm. He could not have failed to see her, and yet now he marched right past her hiding place, his eyes still fixed in that fanatical forward glare!

Erix tried to still the pounding of her heart as she lay beneath a canopy of wet leaves. She saw the feet of Mixtal's apprentices, then the sandaled feet of a long column of warriors, march past. Slowly she realized that, somehow, she had escaped him. Mixtal had seen her and ignored her, and the others in the column, struggling to keep up with the patriarch, had not gotten a glimpse of her before she hid.

Still, the young woman remained under cover for several minutes after the column had passed. Slowly her heartbeat returned to normal, and she emerged from the foliage onto the narrow trail.

The priests and warriors were out of sight. She knew that the sensible thing would be to turn inland, opposite Mixtal's path, and strike out for freedom. The bizarre expression on the man's face remained vivid in her mind. Still, something about him had seemed so unnatural, so strange, that her curiosity was aroused.

Cursing herself for a fool, Erix silently took up the trail behind Mixtal and his column of spearmen.

*　*　*　*　*

Mixtal marched along doggedly, driven by a consuming sense of purpose. Everything had become very clear: The words whispered in his ear *must* have come from the Ancient Ones! Had not the warriors arrived just as he had been told? Now his vision, still somehow hazy and indistinct, remained fixed upon the edge of the forest before him. He stepped from the concealing cloak of the woods' and stopped in astonishment.

Mixtal rubbed his still smoke-fogged eyes in disbelief, but there could be no mistaking the sight before him. There she was, the girl who had escaped his altar at the start of this day! She was walking through the brushy clearing at the edge of the bluff, accompanied by five of the strange warriors.

"That's her!" he hissed, backing into concealment as the knights and spearmen gathered around him.

The clerics and warriors remained in the jungle, peering from the thick growth at the strangers. The five men, one of whom was wrapped in silver, walked in a small protective circle around the woman. The party move slowly along the crest of the bluff, less than a javelin's toss away.

Atax, the apprentice, looked at Mixtal in surprise, then looked at the red-haired woman before them. To him, she bore no resemblance to the girl Erix.

"Most Holy Patriarch—" he began, but Mixtal wasn't listening. Instead, the high priest squinted at the girl again, nodding eagerly. Atax still saw the flaming-haired stranger, but obviously Mixtal saw someone else. The apprentice wondered if he himself was going mad, but he suspected the madness lay across the vision of his master.

"You see?" Mixtal earnestly explained to the Jaguar Knights. "These villains seized her from our altar!"

The cleric again studied the girl. The haze over his eyes maddened him, but it seemed like the one place he saw clearly through the mist was toward this young woman, Erixitl. She was not obscured in the slightest. He saw her black hair, her rich coppery skin, even the tattered rag of her captive's gown in crystalline detail.

"We have been ordered not to attack the strangers," demurred the knight.

For a moment, Mixtal blinked in confusion. He saw the warriors looking curiously toward the girl, and then back to him. He thought again of the prospects of defeat, of facing the Ancient Ones with the tale of his failure, of losing his own life in replacement for the girl who had escaped him.

He *must* not fail! Not when he was this close, when his quarry was once again in sight. "Let the fury of Zaltec fall upon *your* heads," he snarled at the warriors. "The girl will be mine!"

Mixtal shrieked a challenge and sprang from the concealing undergrowth. He raised his obsidian dagger above his head, still screaming. Then he charged.

Propelled by instincts running deeper than military discipline, the Jaguar Knights hesitated only a split second after the cleric began his attack. Then the knights rose, a hundred spearmen rose behind them, and the warriors of the Payit followed their priest into the assault.

*   *   *   *   *

"Send Alvarro after her!" demanded the Bishou, with an angry glance up the bluff. "Halloran has no business taking her into the wilds like this!"

"Daggrande is going," replied Cordell, as soothingly as possible. He knew Halloran. Also, the captain-general understood Martine's headstrong nature, a characteristic of which her father seemed unaware, and he suspected it had not been Hal's idea to move so quickly from the sight of the legion.

"Helm's curses on that scoundrel!" snarled the cleric, looking after Halloran. "Of all the impudent—"

"Now look, my friend." The captain-general silently cursed the Bishou, but his voice remained soothing. "They will be back soon. Alvarro is busy on the right flank, seeking grazing for the horses." Cordell gestured up the coast, to the north. He knew that the bad will between Alvarro and Halloran remained far from settled, and he could think of nothing more disastrous to Hal's confidence than to send his rival to look after him.

"In a few minutes, they'll be back, and I'll have a talk with the lad. He's a good soldier."

Martine, Cordell knew, was deeply cherished by the Bishou, as a father cherishes his daughter. But her importance to the cleric went even deeper, in some way that the commander couldn't entirely understand—perhaps because she was Domincus's one remaining link with younger, more peaceful times. He had not always been a martial cleric.

The Bishou glared up the bluff. "If he allows any harm to befall her . . ." He did not finish the thought, nor did he have to.

*   *   *   *   *

The maniacal battle cry jerked Halloran's attention to the wall of jungle. He sensed the import of the sound even before he saw the knife-waving native burst into sight, followed a second later by the rank of warriors. Their orange headdresses waved in synchronization as the line paused, and the legionnaire saw them placing javelins into the notches of hand-held spear casters.

Halloran leaped in front of Martine as he saw the javelins soar into the air, raising his shield to protect her head and torso. He grunted in pain as one of the missiles grazed the fleshy part of his thigh. Another cracked against his steel breastplate, while a third stuck in his shield.

One of the swordsmen was slow to react, and a stone-tipped javelin knifed through his throat. The others raised their shields, deflecting most of the missiles, though one man took a wound in his forearm. The banded leather armor of the footmen, Hal knew, would not be as effective against these weapons as his own breastplate.

"Shields out!" he called, and the three joined him in an arc facing the native warriors, sheltering Martine behind them, their swords arrayed outward. They watched helplessly as the fourth swordsman, mortally wounded, gasped out his life from the gaping neck wound.

"Go back . . . quickly!" Hal commanded Martine, not turning to look at her. "Down the stairs! Get Daggrande!"

He glanced over his shoulder and saw the woman staring in shock at the whooping, rushing band of spear-wielding natives. Their plumed heads bobbed and their bronzed faces grimaced, twisting the sticks they wore through their noses. They whistled and shrieked, and the din they raised seemed enough to blast the leaves from the trees.

The warriors charged through the brushy clearing, stopping suddenly about halfway to their quarry. They cast back their arms to hurl another volley.

"Go, by Helm!" He turned to face Martine, grabbing her shoulder with his shield hand. She finally turned and started to run, but immediately her foot caught among the tangled brush. She sprawled headlong as Hal's heart pounded in fear. He must get her to safety! Nothing else mattered.

"Captain!" shouted one of the swordsmen.

Halloran instantly raised his shield and crouched over Martine, huddling with the other three men. The second volley of javelins, though delivered from a shorter range, found no targets among the well-shielded fighters of the Golden Legion.

The attackers renewed their rush, following the fanatical leader. Shocked by the man's blood-caked, filthy visage, Halloran stared as his attackers closed. He saw the dagger of dark obsidian, the black emblem on its hilt.

The man tried to dart around Hal, and the captain slammed his shield into the fellow's face. Immediately the black-clad figure dropped to the ground, but the mass of native warriors streamed forward in undimmed frenzy.

"Strike to kill!" he ordered, doubting their chances of survival. He cast one last look behind him and saw Martine scrambling to her feet, staring in mute shock at the swarm of shrieking, howling attackers. Desperately Halloran pulled her back into the small circle of legionnaires.

His shield crushed a stone spear tip, and his sword cut cleanly through a native's quilted armor. Another man thrust, and Halloran hacked off his wooden sword, bashing the face of yet another attacker with his shield.

He saw the flashing steel of the other swordsmen at each side. The four of them sheltered Martine in the middle, defending frantically against a whirlwind of thrusting spear tips. Halloran twisted, dodged, and stabbed repeatedly. He felt as if his life had become a focus of brown faces, waving feathered headgear, and blood.

He heard a grunt of pain as a swordsman fell, his leg slashed deeply. The three remaining men instinctively closed the circle, but then another man tumbled, claimed by a spear thrust through the bands of his armor.

Twoscore or more bleeding bodies covered the ground around them, but the numbers of the enemy were too great. Hal's arm grew leaden from the weight of his sword as he stood back to back with the remaining trooper. He did not see the priests crawling forward between them, seizing Martine, and tugging her away from the melee.

Halloran did see the first priest, the one whose fanatical charge had precipitated the battle, climb slowly to his feet, just out of sword range. For a split second, the spearmen fell back, leaving the two swordsmen to gasp for breath amid the slain forms of the attackers. Hal heard his companion cry out suddenly. The man slumped against him as a keen spear tip slipped over his belt to penetrate his vitals.

Then the priest removed a stretch of cord from his waist and held it in the air before him. It twisted, snakelike, in the man's hand. Indeed, Halloran at first thought that the object was a snake. He finally saw that it was merely the skin of a snake, though it still seemed to move as if it were alive.

The blood-caked priest barked some kind of command, and Halloran could not react before the cord darted toward him, growing and twisting into a weblike net that wrapped his arms tightly to his sides and then carried him heavily to the ground.

In another second, dozens of warriors leaped on him, completing the binding as they stripped away his sword.

* * * * *

From the chronicle of Coton:

In beseechment of the truth in the heart of the Feathered One.

The harbingers of the Waning have landed upon the shores of Maztica. Poshtli, in lofty form, observed their coming. He reports their numbers to be small, but their vessels massive.

Now is Naltecona thrown into a fit of oppression and brooding. He sees no one, speaks not at all of his anxieties. Instead, he sends more eagles to watch the newcomers, while he waits in agony for words that can offer no comfort.

The Revered Counselor now feels certain of the meaning of these many years of signs. He fears their import, but no longer doubts their meaning. Only I could dissuade him, for I know the truth. But the bonds of my vow of silence restrain me.

Meanwhile, Naltecona's army commanders, Eagles and Jaguars alike, demand to gather troops, to prepare a force to drive the strangers back to the sea. Naltecona's young nephew, the honored Lord Poshtli, is the most ardent advocate of this view. But Naltecona takes no counsel of their words.

For he is certain that these visitors are none other than the Silent Counselor and his minions, at last returned to his kingdom in the True World.

❧ 10 ❧

SACRIFICE

Butterflies of every size and color fluttered in a wicker cage of the finest reeds. Coton, Silent Patriarch of Qotal, carried the cage up the steps of the pyramid. His other hand held a colorful array of blossoms, still smelling of moist earth. Although a litter of *pluma* rested beside the base of the pyramid of Qotal, Coton preferred to climb the stairs on his own.

Besides, this structure was not nearly as lofty as the Great Pyramid, which supported the temples of Zaltec, Calor, and Tezca. Coton soon reached the top, and here he set the cage on the white quartz block that was his altar. The stone gleamed in the light of the noon sun.

The pyramid raised the lone cleric high above the houses of Nexal, and he allowed his gaze to linger in each of the four directions. Toward each side of the table-sized altar he laid an assortment of colorful blossoms. Then he raised the door on the cage.

One after another, the butterflies fluttered from the cage, bouncing erratically through the air, climbing away from the pyramid. Butterflies of every bright hue imaginable took to the air. One by one they climbed into the sky, like a dazzling thread of color reaching from the altar to the heavens.

And then they were gone. Coton, his spirit tingling after the ceremony, quickly descended from the pyramid. He was not surprised to see Lord Poshtli waiting in the courtyard below.

Naltecona's nephew wore the full regalia entitled to him

as an Eagle Warrior. His lower lip, drilled long ago, now held a plug of pure gold. His mantle and headdress blazed with a riotous array of plumage. New sandals covered his feet, bound all the way to his knees. A fan of *pluma* swirled over his head, shading him and ruffling his finery with a faint breeze.

"Coton of Qotal, I wish to speak to you. You know many things about the True World, and I know little. Perhaps all I know is that I need to learn."

The mute cleric paused for several seconds, studying the young lord. Poshtli had studied under Coton years ago, before the cleric had become a patriarch and taken his vow. The lad had been the brightest of Coton's students and a natural leader of the other, even bigger and stronger, boys. The priest of Qotal had been pleased to watch him grow to manhood.

Poshtli had shown the same sentiments for the cleric. Whereas most youths who aspired to warriorhood soon slashed their arms in penance and sought captives for the altar of Zaltec, Poshtli had turned instead to the path of the Plumed God. He sought the Eagle Knighthood, highest and most exalted military order of all Maztica.

The Jaguar Knights all followed Zaltec because the *hishna* magic of the claw required blood sacrifice, and without this power the Jaguar Knight was nothing. Warriors of the Eagle creed, however, could worship the god of their choice, and many chose Qotal. But the many years of study, the harsh tests—both mental and physical—and the rigorous discipline caused nine of ten aspiring Eagles to fall short of their lofty goal.

Even among such as these, Poshtli shone as a man of exceptional skill, valor, and intelligence. He had captured many prisoners in battle, prisoners who gave their hearts to the altars of Zaltec or were sold into slavery in the great plaza. Recently he had commanded the army of Nexal on a mission of reconquest: the subject state of Pezelac—a valuable source of obsidian, salt, and gold—had shown signs of rebellion. Poshtli's army had done a prompt job of punishing the rebellious elements while swiftly resuming the tribute paid by Pezelac to Nexal.

Now Coton sensed that the lord faced a crucial choice. Though the cleric could not speak to him, he could still listen.

"My uncle, the great Naltecona, has become the greatest of the great." Poshtli spoke softly. "He is mightier than any counselor in the long history of Nexal. Never have our people collected such tribute, held sway over such vast regions."

Cotton nodded. He knew Poshtli to be a brave warrior, but also unusually perceptive. He displayed a sense of thoughtful deliberation that Coton found exceedingly rare in the younger warriors. The cleric waited for the warrior to continue.

"Our city grows daily, claiming more and more land from the waters as the floating gardens extend their reach. More treasure, more cocoa and mayz and feathers—and more gold—all flow into mighty Nexal, Heart of the True World. More hearts are offered in sacrifice to Zaltec than ever before.

"Yet you, Coton, you come here and you release your butterflies. You place your blossoms and say nothing." Poshtli's eyes did not waver from the cleric's steady gaze.

"You say nothing because you show us much, and yet we fail to understand." Something—could it be assent?—colored Coton's eyes. "You show us, I think, what we once were and what we might be again. You show us, and we fail to see.

"Now, Coton, I have had a dream. I believe this dream is a vision from Qotal, and so I go to seek the will of the god." Poshtli paced slowly, carefully remembering the details he related to the mute cleric.

"I dreamed of a vast desert, a desert that included Nexal! I crossed the desert on foot, suffering from heat and sun, lacking water. Then suddenly I was surrounded by little men, and these men had a great wheel of silver." Poshtli noticed that Coton's eyebrows raised slightly at his description.

"In the wheel, I saw the reflection of a feathered snake, a long, sinuous thing of brilliant plumage and great wisdom.

And this snake was the voice of Qotal! I am certain of it!"

Poshtli remained silent for many minutes, patiently regarded by Coton. Finally he looked up and spoke.

"I will leave Nexal in search of this truth. Perhaps it lies with the strangers. I have seen them, flown above them, as they come to shore in Payit. Perhaps it lies somewhere in between our ways and theirs, or perhaps I may not find it at all." Poshtli stared straight into Coton's eyes. "But I must find this silver wheel!"

Coton's eyes flickered upward, to the clear blue sky. The cleric's gaze flickered once to the south, then again focused vacantly in the distance. Poshtli saw the guidance in the gesture.

"I will walk. My feet, not my wings, will carry me through the True World—perhaps to this knowledge that still eludes me, perhaps not.

"But I will find it, or die in the attempt."

* * * * *

Daggrande imagined the salt spray eating at the steel, corroding the gleaming sheen of his helmet, pocking the flawless metal of his breastplate, even gnawing at the blade of his short sword. He led a troop of two dozen legionnaires, a mixed band armed with crossbows and swords, toward the top of the stone stairway. Halloran and Martine had disappeared somewhere above some few minutes earlier.

"Damn that woman anyway!" he grumbled to himself. "Now Cordell tells me to follow Martine, to 'keep an eye on her'! What am I, a nursemaid?" Daggrande suspected, of course, that the Bishou had a hand in the order. The dwarf had seen Domincus glowering after his daughter and Halloran when the two had started up the bluff.

"I thought the kid had more brains than that," he complained. "'Course, he's only a human, but I expected more from him."

Abruptly Daggrande ceased his musings, becoming every inch the warrior. He could not define what aroused him, whether it was the scent of blood, the faint sound of combat, or something more primeval, but he instantly signaled his crossbowmen to raise their deadly weapons.

The dwarven veteran stepped carefully up the last few stairs. He saw the top of the bluff, a brushy strip along the escarpment backed by dense rain forest perhaps a hundred paces beyond.

Daggrande moved carefully onto the brushy plain, crouching, with his crossbow held ready. With the same care, he ordered his men off the stairway, deploying them in a semicircle as they reached the top.

Daggrande could see no sign of human presence save the squat pyramid a mile or so down the coast. He spent no time wondering where Martine, Hal, and the swordsmen had gone. Instead, he quickly turned the formation to the right, toward the pyramid, forming a skirmish line a hundred paces long. The legionnaires started to march, probing the brush as they advanced.

In another minute, they found the bodies.

* * * * *

Erixitl watched breathlessly, frozen in the minimal safety of a clump of bushy ferns. She saw the high priest who would have slain her leading the way, his gaunt and bony form plunging recklessly forward. He was followed by his apprentices and a company of warriors. Erix saw the prisoners, including the young woman tied just as Erix herself had been, with blindfold and gag and hands bound before her.

Most curious of all was the shining warrior who stumbled along behind the woman, neither gagged nor blindfolded. His silver shirt, she saw, was a solid piece of metal, and she knew it must be unbelievably heavy.

"Him you must rescue," came the supple voice at her ear, and she barely suppressed a scream of shock.

"Chitikas!" she gasped as the downy serpent slithered from the undergrowth to gather in a soft coil beside her. Though this was only the second time she had seen the creature, she felt a sense of joy at his arrival, as if she had just found her oldest, wisest friend. Suddenly she questioned her reaction. She gazed frankly at the winged snake. "Tell me, what's happening? Why has the priest taken that strange woman and the warrior?"

"He takes the woman, thinking she is you, to the altar of Zaltec for sacrifice."

She turned to the procession in disbelief. "How can he think she is me? We have different skins, our hair is not alike, nothing—"

"The power of *pluma* hazes his eyes." Chitikas fluttered his great wings easily, and it seemed to Erix that the gesture resembled a human chuckle. "Seeing you, the cleric moves to obey his god."

Erix remembered the greeting Chitikas had given her. "You said I must rescue him. Why? And how? What do you mean?"

The snake dipped his head, flickering his tongue back and forth before him. "This I command you, to rescue him, in return for which I save your life, for the priest thinks it is you he slays. He will seek you no more."

"No!" Erix whispered fiercely, straining to control her disbelief. "I'm not your slave, and I will not do your bidding! I escaped by myself, with no help from you! So you can change her back into herself if you want and let the priest come after me! You cannot order me to obey!"

"I cannot." Chitakas swayed his head slowly, almost mournfully. "It is the will of the gods."

"Gods? What gods? Zaltec, perhaps? Or his children, Azul or Red Tezca?" Erix's voice rose in pitch, but fortunately the procession had moved past them and disappeared into the jungle. She could not avoid a tone of scorn. "What have those gods ever done for me besides crave my heart on a stone altar?"

"There are more gods than you name. You have been the beneficiary of great attention." Chitikas now looked at her sternly, but she met his snaky stare with a proud glare of her own.

"Perhaps Qotal, the Silent Counselor himself, now deigns to speak to me, a slave girl and fugitive! Everyone knows he only talks to his highest priests, and only after they vow not to talk to anyone else!"

Chitikas lowered his head, and for the first time, Erix saw a hint of menace in the long creature's posture. His yellow eyes stared upward without blinking. "Believe as you will," he hissed softly, "but you must pay heed."

"I will leave you now!" Erix stood angrily, challenging the feathered snake to stop her.

"Very well," whispered Chitikas. With a single beat of his wings, the snake darted into the air, swirling among the dense tree trunks and almost instantly disappearing from sight.

Still glaring, Erix watched the flying serpent vanish. Then she whirled and started to move through the jungle on her own. She did not notice that she again followed the path of the priest and his prisoners.

*   *   *   *   *

Halloran stumbled down the jungle trail in a daze. Martine lurched ahead, beyond his reach or ability to comfort. He knew four brave men lay dead behind them. The prisoners now marched in the middle of the procession of warriors and priests, with two brawny spearmen flanking each of the captives.

Martine! How could this happen? He groaned inwardly, racked with despair. A small part of him wanted to rail angrily at her, for it had been her stubbornness that had gotten them captured. But mostly he remembered the look of stark terror on her face as the priests had seized and bound her. That part of him remained torn by guilt and inadequacy. He had failed!

The time before their capture, bare minutes ago, seemed as if it were another lifetime. He remembered the leering faces of the natives. The trio in the leopardskin cloaks, their faces framed by the widespread jaws of their helms, had looked the most bizarre, but the ash-streaked priest, with his twisted, fanatical grin, had been the most frightening.

The natives had been very curious about them. Immediately after their capture, Hal's steel breastplate in particular had received a great deal of attention, since many a spear or stone-bladed sword had smashed against it during the fight. The huge, scowling warrior wearing the spotted skin and skull scrutinized him with particular interest, poking the armor with his fingers, taking and keeping Hal's keen longsword. The breastplate and his steel cap with its upturned brim remained with him, however.

They had left the bodies of the swordsmen and natives on the field where they had fallen. Two of the three spotted warriors, as well as several dozen spearmen, had perished in the fight. Halloran deduced that the spotted warrior and the priest had disagreed about leaving the bodies behind, for the pair had spoken with great animation before leaving. Apparently the priest had prevailed.

Hal's mind whirled with images of disaster, and he still could not fully comprehend how quickly catastrophe had overtaken them. For what terrible purpose had they been taken captive? Of the pair, only Martine had been gagged and blindfolded. Hal thus suspected that the woman was earmarked for some special purpose, a thought that made his blood run cold.

"Martine!" he ventured to call out once, his voice a probing whisper. He saw the woman's back stiffen before him, and then his skull shuddered under the impact of a heavy cuff.

The warrior behind him growled, grabbing Hal's arm and pushing him along roughly. The spearman pressed his hand over Halloran's mouth, and the captain understood the meaning clearly.

The stifling heat of late afternoon finally began to break as a slight breeze stirred the foliage. A solid blanket of limbs and leaves blocked out any view of the sky, and Halloran had no idea as to the direction they traveled. The jungle trail twisted and turned so chaotically that he was certain they must have backtracked over their own path several times. However, something about the leopardskin-clad warrior— the man who obviously commanded the column, though he deferred slightly to the black-robed priest—made Hal certain that they were not lost.

Slowly the captain's mind started to work again as he reminded himself that inaction meant certain disaster. What can I do? His brain recoiled from the prospects of extended captivity, or worse, among these . . .

He didn't know what to make of his captors. They exhibited a higher level of military skill than the legion had encountered in any of the natives the expedition had met thus far. Indeed, Hal noted as he strained against the constricting snakeskin thong that still held his arms, these people used magic and fought in large, disciplined formations. Furthermore, the twin faces carved on the cliff and the pyramid atop the bluff bespoke of greater building skills than previously seen.

Still, the black-robed madman had attacked with a primitive savagery that chilled Halloran. His blood-caked hair, cadaverous features, and filthy aspect were unspeakably grotesque. Were all of these people so bloodthirsty, so fanatical?

This is worse than the foul beast that devoured Arquiuius, he told himself, as his thoughts leaped unbidden to that previously darkest day of his life. That disaster had motivated him to abandon his former life of arcane study and depend upon the strength of his arm and the keen steel of his sword.

Now his arms were bound behind him, and his sword was carried by another man, an enemy. For a fleeting moment, he regretted the completeness with which he had abandoned his studies. Even a swordsman could possibly use the help of a subtle magic spell now and then. Even so, he was hard-pressed to imagine how his limited assortment of spells might have aided him here.

A sharp tug on the rope brought his attention back to reality. He felt a cool breeze against his face, and the smell of the sea told him they had turned back toward the coast. The verdant canopy overhead blocked out direct sunlight, but he realized that it was nearing sunset. Somehow that fact struck him as significant.

Halloran thought again of his magic studies. He had mastered several spells, but those incantations were simply a blur of vague images now. He shook his head, wondering why he so suddenly dwelled on a time of his life that he had buried for more than ten years.

Suddenly the procession halted as they broke into a clearing in the jungle. Rough hands threw Hal to the ground. From his awkward position, Halloran saw the spearmen dispersing through the jungle. He observed several casting their javelins and then rushing quickly and silently forward.

In moments, the two prisoners were hustled into the clearing, and Hal saw the small pyramid they had first observed from the ship. Three legionnaires lay dead at the base of the structure. Obviously Cordell's first scouts had reached the pyramid only to die in this surprise attack.

The priests quickly herded Halloran and Martine toward the pyramid. The leading cleric started up the steep steps, and the warriors and apprentices prodded the captives along behind.

To the west, the sun touched the treetops. With an unconscious shudder, Hal realized that it would set in minutes.

* * * * *

"Tell Cordell there's been an attack . . . four scouts killed. Can't see Hal or the Bishou's daughter," Daggrande barked at the swordsman, who nodded quickly. "We'll try to pick up the trail."

The man started down the stairway toward the beach far below, shouting for attention, but the dwarf had already turned his men toward the jungle.

"Grabert, you worked with the rangers, right?" Daggrande asked one of the swordsmen in his detachment. When the man nodded, the dwarf continued. "Take the lead. See if you can pick up their trail."

Even as the ranger turned to follow the tracks that had battered the ground in the clearing, Daggrande shouted orders to the rest of his legionnaires.

"Here it is, Captain. They headed into the jungle," Grabert

quickly announced. Immediately the troops fell into column.

Daggrande placed two crossbowmen immediately behind Grabert, followed by himself and then staggered pairs of crossbow and sword to the final swordsman bringing up the rear. The native war party had left a wide trail, and the ranger had no difficulty following the spoor. Thus the column marched quickly through the dense jungle.

Daggrande stepped quickly but quietly, ignoring the heavy, humid heat. His breastplate rested comfortably on his shoulders, and his heavy boots tromped through the brush, impervious to thorn and thistle.

The dwarf cast a quick look to the rear and saw that his legionnaires marched at full alert. The group included a half-dozen dwarves, and Daggrande knew that humans and dwarves alike were all steady veterans, brave and skilled fighters.

But he wondered what they marched against. And a small, reluctant part of him wondered what had become of Halloran.

Daggrande worked hard to keep that part of him quiet, for he considered such overwrought concern for a companion to be dangerous to his objectivity as a commander. Nevertheless, he could not deny the fear that threatened to become panic whenever he thought of his young protege in the hands of savage tribesmen.

Idly he noticed that it was almost twilight.

* * * * *

"Come on, by Zaltec, *move!*" Gultec roared at the column of spearmen that slowly worked its way along the jungle trail. The Payit army, a hundred hundredmen strong, had started from Ulatos shortly before dusk. The serpentine columns marched slowly by Gultec's standards, but still the thousands of warriors maintained a steady trot along the network of winding jungle trails converging at Twin Visages.

Now the Jaguar Knight stood in the shadows beside the path, watching the warriors jog past. Each group of hundredmen wore its own distinctive feather headdress, each group's a different color. The natives carried javelins and spear casters that enabled the warrior to throw the weapon much farther than a bare-handed toss. Some wielded heavy wooden clubs, and many—the veteran warriors—carried heavy, obsidian-edged *macas*.

The Payit army moved smoothly, two abreast, but Gultec still felt a vague unease. Certainly they would outnumber the strangers, but the appearance of these newcomers was so unusual and their equipment seemed so mighty that Gultec could not feel utterly confident about fighting them. Then again, perhaps the encounter would not come to battle.

Suddenly a figure joined Gultec beside the trail, and he turned to see the rotund cleric Kachin studying him. The man's gray hair, still tied in a single knot, hung over his shoulder and down to his belt. The Jaguar Knight felt a momentary urge to turn into the jungle, to vanish in his feline form. Instead, he met the gaze of the cleric squarely.

"There is hesitation all around," remarked Kachin casually. "No one, not even the Revered Counselor of Ulatos, Caxal himself, knows what to make of these visitors. Do they invade us, Gultec?" The Jaguar Knight studied the cleric as the man spoke, puzzling over his simple white mantle, protruding belly, and round face. He looked so unusual, not at all like the filthy, emaciated clerics of the younger gods. Gultec found it hard to believe that this man could truly be religious.

"They are very strange in appearance, and they move as warriors." The Jaguar Knight thought carefully as he answered. "I suspect they do not come in friendship."

"Caxal is worried that these strangers are the harbingers of Qotal himself, that the Feathered One returns to Maztica at Twin Visages, even as was prophesied." Kachin spoke ironically, and Gultec regarded the cleric of Qotal curiously. It was not at all like a priest to speak in such tones about his own god.

Kachin chuckled wryly. "I surprise you. I will tell you a thing, Jaguar Knight, and you should believe it: These men are not the servants of Qotal. Their vessels do not carry the Silent Counselor back to our shores."

"How can you know this?" Gultec demanded. "Have you seen them?"

"Do you think a priest of Qotal would not know if his True Master were even now awaiting a proper welcome?" Kachin looked harshly at Gultec, his stare making the warrior feel like a worm twisting on a dangling hook.

"Listen to me, Gultec! These are men, and they are dangerous men. It will be up to Payits such as you and me to make sure that their menace does not become our catastrophe!"

The knight regarded the cleric with growing respect. This man was very different from the weakling Mixtal. For a brief moment, Gultec regretted the training that had planted him among the Jaguar Knights, the worshipers of warlike Zaltec.

The cleric seemed to read his thoughts, for he said, not unkindly, "The glory of a god does not need to be measured by the pile of bodies heaped in his honor. This is the error of the younger gods, and their bloodlust may well cause the disaster that will destroy the True World."

Kachin's tone suddenly grew harsh. "I meant what I told you in Ulatos: If you or that knife-wielding 'priest' has slain the girl, Erixitl, I will exact retribution . . . in blood."

"Then why do you offer me counsel now?" snarled the knight.

"We face a more urgent challenge than our own quarrel," replied the cleric, and Gultec could sense the deep sincerity in Kachin's voice. "I fear that the future of the world we know is at stake." Kachin's voice hushed slightly, betraying his profound concern.

Gultec growled inaudibly. He did not seek the counsel of clerics, did not like it when it was offered. Yet there was something ultimately believable in this cleric that forced Gultec to respect him. He was clearly very wise, and his bravery could not be questioned either. Never had a cleric dared to speak to Gultec as this one had—and twice in one day!

And if this cleric was frightened by the strangers, Gultec thought that they must be very dangerous indeed.

* * * * *

"Do not let her get away!" Mixtal admonished the four apprentices, each of whom held one of Martine's limbs. "She shall not escape us again!" The priest did not see the puzzled looks on the young clerics' faces, and they had given up trying to point out that the captive was other than the girl, Erix.

"Bring the man, too!" Mixtal gestured at Hal, and several warriors prodded the pair up the steep steps to the top of the pyramid. They swayed dangerously on the narrow ledges that served as stairs. Halloran wondered briefly if a fast, fatal fall might be preferable to whatever awaited them above.

Mixtal finally reached the top, where he threw his head back and laughed, delighted at last. He faced the setting sun, letting its rays fall over him as it touched the treetops. She will not escape me now! The Ancient Ones will be pleased!

He looked back at the assemblage, again cursing the haze that seemed to float eternally across his eyes. He looked to the sea. The strange winged objects seemed to be very far away, their shapes becoming shadows in the sunset.

Closer, his apprentices and the warriors gathered around the top of the pyramid. Why are they so somber? Mixtal squinted, but he could not quite see their faces . . . that accursed haze!

The apprentices pulled the blindfold from the girl's eyes and severed her bonds, jerking her toward the altar. She twitched and kicked, her eyes widening in terror, but the young men easily held her. Mixtal stared at the girl, at her coppery skin, her inky black tresses, all the details he saw and knew.

Everything became perfectly clear.

* * * * *

Halloran's blood chilled at the sight of the grisly altar. The stone block was the size of a small table, and the red-black stains smearing its sides clearly indicated its function. The squatting beast statue, with its gaping maw, crouched beside the altar. Martine screamed, the sound barely stifled by the gag, as the priests seized her.

"No!" Hal screamed, twisting desperately in the grip of the two warriors. "By Helm, no!"

The high priest, his face distorted madly, turned toward the legionnaire. The man's matted hair hung in a ragged mane around his head as he held his right hand forward and slowly clenched it into a fist.

Halloran gasped as he felt the magical thong around him tighten, threatening to crush his ribs with the pressing force of his breastplate. His head throbbed and his vision grew red. His mouth worked reflexively, gasping for air that could find no space in his lungs.

The last of his breath emerged in a ragged groan as Hal slumped to his knees, struggling to remain conscious. The pressure on his body was about to crush him, and then suddenly it eased.

Halloran collapsed facefirst, paralyzed as his lungs sucked desperately needed air. Slowly he lifted himself to his hands and knees, and then the two warriors lifted him to his feet. They easily held him as he tried to lunge toward the altar.

He could not prevent the priests from stretching Martine backward across the altar. Her eyes turned toward him, widely staring, shocked.

"No!" He roared his rage again as two more warriors restrained him. Martine lay absolutely helpless. Halloran twisted, but he was powerless to intervene, powerless to do anything.

The high priest raised his hand, raised the stone dagger. For a moment, the dark gloss of obsidian caught the last rays of the sun, a glowing reflection of the rage and murderous hate burning in Halloran's eyes.

Then the blade dropped as the priest performed the act he had performed so many times before. Martine released one shocked, final gasp, while the apprentices held her firmly, allowing no twitch of movement. Mixtal's hand moved quickly and steadily, his cut swift and deep and sure.

And then the high priest held her heart in the air. It seemed to pulse in dying cadence to the fading light of the sun.

Payit

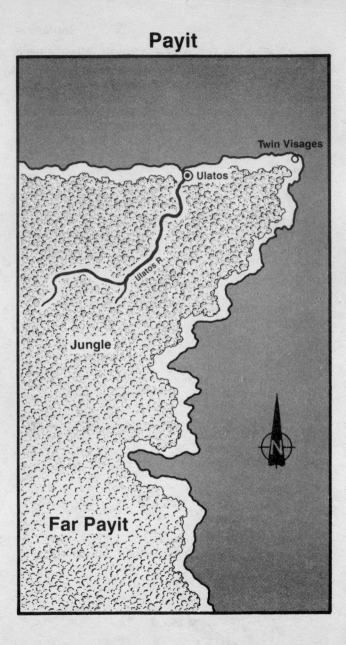

Twin Visages

◉ Ulatos

Ulatos R.

Jungle

Far Payit

❧ 11 ❧

IN THE HANDS
OF THE GODS

.

Erixitl gasped in sympathetic pain. She watched the
strange girl die, slain in her own place on the altar of Zaltec.
Suppressing a moan, she rolled back into the concealment
of her leafy shelter.

She had followed Mixtal and his prisoners toward the pyramid, to the very scene of her escape. Now sunset found her
at the edge of the clearing surrounding the pyramid, with a
clear view of the priests and the altar at the edge of the
structure's upper platform.

She sneaked another look and saw the girl's body removed from the altar, thrown unceremoniously beside it.
Mixtal placed the heart, now still and lifeless, into the mouth
of Zaltec on the statue beside the altar.

Erix heard a rustle beside her and was not surprised
when Chitikas slithered around the trunk of a low bush.
The serpent glided to her side, remaining concealed from
the pyramid.

"You caused her to die!" she accused. The downy snake
gazed at her, his yellow eyes unblinking. "Why did you do
that?"

"The man," whispered Chitikas in his soft voice. "You must
go to him, save him."

"I told you, no!" Erix shook her head angrily, wondering
again why she had followed the priests and prisoners to the
pyramid when all she wanted was escape. "How could I help
him, when he is in the hands of the Bloody One?"

"*Pluma*—feathermagic," suggested Chitikas, with the
barest flicker of his tongue. "He is held by the priest. You

can break the spell."

"No!" She turned away from the snake, and her eye involuntarily sought the spotted snakeskin thong that restrained Halloran's arms. She touched the feathered ring at her neck, remembering, when Mixtal tried to capture her in the temple courtyard, how its burst of magic had sent that same snakeskin bond tumbling to her feet.

Twilight began to settle in the clearing. Erix saw Mixtal regarding the silver-chested man. The priest started toward the stranger and then stopped, indecisive. A Jaguar Knight stepped in before the priest, and she saw the pair gesture angrily at each other.

"Why are you doing this?" Erix turned toward Chitikas again, accusing him with her voice. "Why did you save me? Why did you cost that girl her life?"

"You should understand," replied the serpent, his own tone vaguely accusing. "You have been sheltered and protected by the benign power of the Plumed One for all of your life. It is time you began repaying the debt!"

"Sheltered? Protected?" Erix's voice came out a low hiss. "I was captured as a small girl, sold into slavery! I was attacked by my owner's son, sold again, kidnapped, and very nearly sacrificed! What kind of shelter and protection are you talking about?"

"You are alive, are you not?"

"How do I owe that life to Qotal? Explain that if you can." She tempered her anger slightly, wondering what Chitikas was trying to tell her.

"I saw you once before, protected you then. Perhaps you will recall?" The snake flickered his tail slightly across her vision, a familiar gesture. Suddenly she made the connection.

"My last day in Palul . . . I was tending my father's snares! On the far side of the ridge, I saw something, and I followed it. That was you!"

Chitikas nodded smugly, then ducked as she tried to strike the snake in the face.

"You *lured* me away from the trail . . . right into the arms of that Jaguar Knight! I might still be free, might have grown up in my own home, if it hadn't been for you!" Her muscles tensed as she prepared to flee. Something in his eyes, a faint appeal perhaps, held her in place.

"Lured you I did," admitted the serpent, without a trace of remorse. "But you would not have grown up there. Indeed, you would not have been alive for many more days."

"What—what do you mean?" For some reason, Erix did not doubt the truth of Chitikas's words.

"You are a child of destiny, Erixitl, though you may be the last to know it. The priests of Zaltec and their masters, the Ancient Ones, fear you. They planned to claim you from your father's home for sacrifice, and it was only your disappearance that saved you."

Erix sagged backward, staring at the serpent in shock. Chitikas nodded. "Your ten years in Kultaka were relatively safe, until the Ancient Ones learned of your presence there. Once again they tried to kill you, but you proved stronger than they anticipated. If that attempt had succeeded, we would have been helpless to save you.

"But it failed, and the attempt—the talonmagic of the sending—warned your owner of the threat to your life. He decided that you would be safest among a people who exalted Qotal over Zaltec, and thus he arranged for you to come to Payit."

Erix shook her head slowly, not so much in disbelief as in wonder. Huakal, acting to save her by selling her to Kachin? Yet she knew in her heart that this was the truth.

"Why am I so important? Why do the Ancient Ones fear me?"

Chitikas waved his head impatiently. "I do not know."

But Erix wasn't listening. Another question had been nagging at her mind, and now she put it into words. "Why do you want to thwart the will of Zaltec? Who *are* you?"

The feathered serpent bowed his head humbly. "I am Chitikas, and I serve the Plumed God, the one true god of Maztica. I have aided you because in thwarting the will of Zaltec, he of the Bloody Hand, I further the will of Qotal."

"Qotal! Qotal!" The harsh words came from a tree above them, and Erix looked upward, into the glittering eyes of the bright macaw that had accompanied Chitikas before.

The bird's voice was loud, and Erix suddenly felt very vulnerable in her scant concealment near the pyramid.

"Qotal, the true god!" squawked the bird. "Zaltec the pretender, the buffoon!"

Erix cringed, noticing the priests and warriors atop the pyramid looking in their direction. Several warriors stepped off the platform, starting down the steep stairway on the structure's side.

"Perhaps I can deter them," whispered the serpent conspiratorially. "But remember, you must rescue the man!"

Erix didn't take the time to object, though to her, the issue remained far from settled. Chitikas disappeared suddenly, too quickly for physical movement. With a startled gasp, Erix reached out and felt the creature's downy tail slipping away, even though she could see nothing. The snake had become invisible!

She wanted to flee, but she feared that the noise of flight would only give her position away. Instead, she watched the warriors descend the temple. The priests, the Jaguar Knight, and many other warriors, together with the prisoner, remained atop the pyramid.

"False god! Zaltec is the god of gutter snakes and filth!" squawked the bird, not very helpfully.

Suddenly one of the warriors tripped on an unseen object. He tumbled down the side of the steep pyramid, cracking his skull on a step far below the top. His limp form continued to bounce and tumble to the bottom, where it lay still.

The other warriors reacted immediately, leaping and tumbling down the steep sides of the pyramid. They reached the lifeless body of their comrade and then looked around suspiciously. They showed no inclination to move away from the pyramid.

The stranger remained carefully guarded by several strong warriors, still at the top. A minute passed, and Chitikas did not return. Darkness had settled further, though the sky still glowed with the fading sunset.

Swiftly and silently, Erix turned and melted into the jungle, intending to be very far away by morning. Pushing quickly through the fronds, she turned back toward the trail.

She parted the huge leaves and stepped through. Before she could scream or react, two powerful arms reached forward and seized her.

*　*　*　*　*

Halloran stood numbly, looking from the savage warriors to the fanatical priests. He could not bear to look at Martine's lifeless, bloodless body. Nor could he stand the sight of the bestial statue, with its gaping mouth. The last memory of the sacrifice had been the priest's throwing the cool, still heart into that savage maw.

Despite his averted eyes, the image of that snarling face, vaguely human but combining elements of serpent and lion as well, remained embedded in his brain. It symbolized to him ultimate barbarism, the callous murder of innocents to feed the insatiable appetite of a monstrous god.

Martine! Why couldn't they have taken me instead?

All of his annoyance with the woman had vanished at the moment of their capture. Now he groaned under a sense of all-encompassing failure and sorrow.

His hatred burned with white-hot fury, but he could not break away from the snakeskin rope that bound him. He hated these savage warriors. He hated this hot, primitive land. And mostly he hated the ash-streaked, scarred priest who had performed this abominable rite. Halloran fixed his cold eyes on that priest, and the man flinched and finally turned away.

The priest had argued at some length with the warrior in the spotted skin, and Hal sensed that his own fate had been the topic. Apparently the warrior had prevailed, for the priest made no move toward him. In fact, the legionnaire almost hoped that he would be selected for sacrifice. In the guilt of his massive failure, he did not feel that he deserved to live after Martine had been so brutally killed. For some moments, he considered hurling himself off the edge of the steep-sided pyramid, the ultimate self-punishment for the ultimate failure.

But somewhere deep within himself, Halloran's warrior's heart burned with the need for vengeance. Without life, there could be no vengeance, and so he would have to live.

At least, he would have to live long enough to kill.

*   *   *   *   *

"Muster the legion!" cried Bishou Domincus. "Disaster threatens!"

"Quiet, man!" urged Cordell, as gently as possible. "We don't know for certain yet just what's wrong." The two men, together with Darien and Kardann, stood with a panting swordsman beside the legion's camp on the wooded shoreline. "There was no sign of Halloran or the Bishou's daughter?"

"No, sir," gasped the man. He had just descended the tall stairway from the bluff top, racing to report to the captain-general. "We found four men, all dead—along with quite a few of the natives."

"Helm's curses on his head, on his soul!" cried the Bishou, waving his fist in the direction where Halloran had last been seen.

"She may be all right! It doesn't do any good to start turning against our own, especially when we don't know what's happened!" Cordell struggled to stay cool.

"*You* don't, perhaps," groaned the cleric, nearly sobbing, "but I do! Terror has struck. My daughter suffers at the hands of evil! I know this. I can feel it!"

"Perhaps we should get back aboard the ships," urged the assessor of Amn. Kardann had grown increasingly nervous as the Bishou's distress became more obvious. Now Cordell looked at him with ill-concealed scorn.

"If there is a danger, it is certain to be a threat the legion can face. If you wish, you may reembark now. My men are staying ashore."

"Yes, perhaps that would be wise," the assessor agreed, nodding, completely missing the barbed tone of the commander's voice. "I shall oversee matters on the ships!" The pudgy accountant turned toward shore, eagerly seeking a longboat to haul him out to the *Falcon*.

"I'll send more parties up the bluff," said Cordell. By now, scouts had discovered three broad stairways climbing the escarpment. Only the central one, the one passing between the two monstrous faces, showed signs of regular use.

"May Helm grant that we are not too late!" groaned the Bishou.

* * * * *

Spirali moved when darkness once again cloaked the world, but the Ancient One traveled in ways unknown to the rest of Maztica. His journey began in the Highcave, on the peak above Nexal.

He spoke a single word, and then he was in Ulatos, chief city of the Payit. The Ancient One arrived in the courtyard of Zaltec's temple, though none could see him in the darkness. Spirali's black cloak, soft, dark boots, and cloaking hood all made him a part of the night.

A single young apprentice stood beside the temple gates. Spirali sensed at once that the place was otherwise empty. The Ancient One stalked toward the apprentice, though the youth did not see him until he spoke.

"I seek Mixtal, High Priest of Ulatos."

The youth's jaw dropped, and he stepped backward in terror. He could see a dim, dark shape before him, and he heard a voice of unquestionable strength. The apprentice stammered awkwardly, struggling to speak.

"The c-coast . . . they went this morning. They saw the strangers come. . . ."

The fellow ran out of words, and only then did he notice that the dark stranger had already disappeared.

* * * * *

"Hey, Captain, maybe this one can tell us something!" Grabert, the ranger, still leading, turned back to Daggrande with a struggling form clasped in his brawny arms.

The dwarf saw a young woman, a black-haired, copper-skinned beauty who kicked and scratched in a vain effort to escape the ranger's grasp. The man winced once as the girl landed a sharp kick, but he simply clasped her more tightly as one of the crossbowmen seized and held her feet.

Daggrande grunted, studying the girl, or woman . . . he was not sure which. Her smooth-skinned face and slender form bespoke late adolescence, but something in the girl's glaring eyes, in the firm set of her mouth, made the dwarf suspect her to be an adult.

In return, Erixitl studied these strange men who had taken her, new captors now after her one brief day of freedom. All of these strangers had hair growing out of their faces. Their skin was a sickly pale color. She especially recoiled from some of their unnatural eyes, watery blue orbs that seemed more properly the eyes of fish than men.

Some of the men were very short, she noticed, though this did not make them seem any less fearsome. If anything, the bushy facial fur and gnarled limbs of these smaller strangers made them even more ferocious-looking than their human-sized comrades. She remembered tales of the Hairy Men of the Desert, who supposedly dwelt in the arid reaches south of Kultaka and Nexal. Legends said those folk were short, broad of shoulder, and bowed of leg. Such a description matched the shorter warriors among the strangers as well.

"Well, I don't think she's the one who did the killing and capturing," speculated Daggrande. "But I don't think it would be smart to let her go until we find out a little more about what's going on."

The dwarf nodded to a couple of the crossbowmen. "Tie her up and bring her along. And be quick about it! We're moving on."

Erix couldn't understand the harsh, barking speech of the strangers, but their intentions became clear enough as the hempen rope curled around her wrists. Her struggles in the arms of these burly humans were as a child wriggling in the grasp of its mother. Soon she was bound as tightly as before, though the strangers did not gag or blindfold her.

In the meantime, the swordsman at the point of the column had pushed forward several steps and now crept slowly backward.

"Captain, look at this!" he called, with a new sense of urgency.

Erix knew he had seen the pyramid and its scene of gory sacrifice.

* * * * *

From the chronicle of Coton:

Serving as always the resplendent glory in the memory of the Golden God.

I watch the young Lord Poshtli as he leaves the city by the south causeway. He departs Nexal alone, but this in no way diminishes the grandeur of his mission.

Poshtli carries a pair of spears, an obsidian-edged maca, his bow, a quiver of arrows, and a waterskin. He will shun the lands of Kultaka and Pezelac. Instead, he will strike out over the House of Tezca, the great desert that marks the True World's southern extent.

He still wears the mantle and helm of the Eagle Knight, but he will not make this quest by wing. Instead, he laces his high sandals tight and marches toward lands as barren as any nightmarish pestilence of the gods. His goal is the truth and nothing less—a quest that might keep a man searching for a very long time.

But Poshtli has dreamed of the Sunstone. Such a dream must provide a flicker of hope, for it shows the presence, however faint, and the will of the Plumed One. And, too, this vision was given to him by the couatl, the feathered snake who is the voice of Qotal himself.

So I will choose to believe that, perhaps, Poshtli may find his truth in the great silver wheel of the Sunstone.

❧ 12 ❧

RETRIBUTION

Halloran watched the spearmen descend from the pyramid, attracted by the chattering of the bird near the base of the structure. The creature suddenly flew off into the jungle, and the leading warrior, the one who wore the spotted hide, gestured toward his comrades above. Two of them roughly urged Halloran down the stairs. The legionnaire staggered desperately but managed to retain his footing.

Soon he reached the bottom, and here all of the warriors and most of the priests gathered together. Hal sensed confusion and indecision. He looked around and, when he could not spot the high priest, he assumed that savage cleric remained atop the pyramid.

An abrupt cry of pain exploded from a warrior who suddenly collapsed on the ground. Several more cried out or gasped in sharp agony. In moments, a half-dozen spearmen writhed or lay still on the ground beside the pyramid.

To the natives, it appeared that these men had suffered some sudden, invisible, and hence supernatural disaster. Halloran, however, saw the short silvery shafts of crossbow bolts jutting from the flesh of the wounded men.

Immediately the captain ducked, breaking the hold of his captors. Dropping to the ground, he twisted desperately away and rolled to the side.

Another volley of steel death flashed from the brush, claiming more victims among the panicky spearmen. The bolts were small, but not invisible, and by now some of the natives understood the nature of the attack. These few raised their javelins, casting blindly at the brush or holding their weapons at the ready while they sought targets.

"For Helm!" The ragged cry burst from the brush, the most beautiful noise Halloran had ever heard. He identified Daggrande's voice bellowing above the rest.

"In Helm's name!" Hal cried, twisting to a sitting position and then lurching to his knees. He cursed the supernatural bond confining his arms even as he stumbled to his feet. A wiry native sprang at him with upraised club, but Halloran felled him with a powerful kick.

A ragged line of legionnaires burst from the brush, charging the base of the pyramid. Hal saw that there weren't more than twenty-five men in the detachment. He desperately hoped that would be enough.

He heard a snarl behind him and whirled to see the leopardskin-clad warrior advancing toward him. The man's face contorted into a mask of hatred as he pulled Hal's sword from his spotted leather belt. The warrior raised it in both hands and lunged, with a battle cry more bestial than human.

Halloran whirled away, but his attacker followed his evasion. The point of the sword drove toward Hal's face, until suddenly the warrior staggered backward. His snarl turned to a look of dull confusion as he stared at the silver shaft protruding from his chest. Blood, slick and black in the early evening darkness, gurgled from his lips, and the sword fell from his lifeless fingers even as his body thudded to the ground.

The legionnaires advanced in a rush, maintaining their disciplined formation. "For Helm!" they shouted again, heavy boots pounding the earth. The crossbowmen carried their bows slung across their backs now, wielding their short swords, while the swordsmen brandished their longswords and held their bucklers at the ready. The small shields protected both the left side of the man who carried it and the right side of the legionnaire to his left, so close was the troops' formation.

Halloran dropped to the ground and rolled toward his sword, forgotten by the other natives in the confusion of the attack. His heart swelled with pride at the intrepid ad-

vance of the legionnaires, outnumbered two or three to
one. Unsteadily, several of the natives stood to meet the
charge with their stone-tipped spears.

In moments, the line of swordsmen reached the base of
the pyramid. Flint and obsidian *macas* shattered against
steel shields and breastplates, while razor-edged swords
sliced easily through cotton armor and shields of *hishna*-
magic hide or *pluma*-magic fabric. Halloran saw a young
warrior swing his wooden club, its flecked-tooth blade of
obsidian flashing toward the face of a legionnaire. The
swordsman raised his buckler, and the club cracked aside as
the slim steel longsword plunged straight through the warrior's body.

The native collapsed across Hal in a shower of blood. The
young cavalryman wriggled aside, and then the line of legionnaires swept past. The other warriors, to a man, turned
and fled for the imagined safety of the surrounding forest.

*   *   *   *   *

Gultec trotted easily along the trail, once again leading the
column of warriors. His keen eyes had no difficulty following the twistings and windings of the jungle path, even in
the nearly total darkness. The Jaguar Knight knew that
columns of warriors like this one were converging toward
the coast along many such trails. By the middle of the night,
there would be ten thousand spearmen and hundreds of
Jaguar and Eagle Knights waiting atop the bluff.

Following the most direct route to the pyramid, this trail
made for good time, unlike the early-morning course that
had taken them along the circuitous coastal path. The
knight sensed the nearness of the sea in the faint smell of
the air and the moist coolness against his face. But more
than this, he *knew* their location instinctively. In mere minutes, the column would reach the pyramid.

Then the Jaguar Knight heard a faint sound, unnatural in
the jungle night. More sounds followed, and he halted, raising a taloned hand. The entire column stopped instantly and
silently behind him.

The sounds grew, a thrashing that told him that men were forcing their way through the underbrush. He heard muffled curses, in Payit, and soon sensed the nearness of many sweating, frightened men.

A figure pounded toward them along the path, breathing heavily. The man did not know of Gultec's presence until the knight stepped from the shadows and seized him by the throat. He recognized the orange headdress of a nearby village. This warrior must have been one of the first on the scene.

"What is the meaning of this?" demanded Gultec, his voice a rumbling growl. "Why do you flee like a young girl?"

The man's eyes widened in even greater terror. He croaked something indistinguishable, and Gultec slightly relaxed his hold upon the man's windpipe.

"The strangers!" gurgled the fleeing warrior. "Sorcery! They attacked us! They killed many! It was death to remain!"

Gultec's body tensed with the news, but he was only mildly surprised. So these strangers were here for war! Well, the warriors of the Payit would see they got what they sought!

"Where are they now?"

"The pyramid—by the Twin Visages!" The man virtually squealed the answer.

Casting the terrified villager aside, Gultec started forward at a renewed trot. In a minute, he would deploy his men through the jungle surrounding the pyramid. But first he would see what these strangers were about.

* * * * *

"Halt!" barked Daggrande. The line of swordsmen stopped instantly as the last of the natives disappeared into the jungle. With a quick look, he saw that none of his men had suffered any serious wounds. At least a dozen natives had fallen to their crossbow bolts, perhaps an equal number to their swords, but Daggrande wasted no time on self-congratulations.

"Over here!" gasped Hal, squirming out from beneath the slain warrior's body. Several legionnaires helped him to his feet. "I never thought I'd be so glad to see your whiskers!" He grinned as the dwarf clumped over to him. Hal's hands and arms were still pinned to his side, or he would have embraced the old campaigner.

"Humph! I never thought you'd be fool enough to get caught in a simple ambush!" Daggrande's anger, Hal discerned, masked his relief at finding Halloran alive. Nevertheless, the rebuke struck home, especially as the dwarf continued. "I found the bodies of four good men back there!"

"They killed Martine, too." Hal looked up, all his rage and revulsion flooding back. He wondered if the high priest, the murderous fanatic, remained atop the pyramid. Unconsciously he strained at his bonds, eager for vengeance.

"We've got big trouble," grunted the dwarf. "Let's get back to the beach." The dwarf pulled out his dagger and started to saw at Halloran's binding. "What is this stuff, by Helm? My blade can't mark it!"

"It's magic," groaned Hal. "But I thought you'd be able to cut it. These people have priests or sorcerers . . . I'm not sure which. One of them, the same one who killed Martine, used this to wrap me up."

Halloran fixed his gaze on his companion's face, the horror of the scene on the pyramid choking his voice. "Daggrande, he—he tore her heart out! They murdered her in cold blood!"

The dwarf nodded seriously, his brow knitted with concern. Unknown to Hal, Daggrande fretted more about Hal's fate at the hands of the Bishou than over Martine's untimely death.

Halloran looked around, though it was fully dark now, as if he hoped to spy the priest who had bound him. Instead, he saw two crossbowmen moving toward them with a squirming, brown-skinned prisoner between them.

"What's this?" he asked.

"We found her in the jungle," explained Daggrande as the trio reached the rest of the legionnaires. "I couldn't let her go. I thought she'd warn the others about us. No sense in keeping her now, I guess."

The girl held her head high, her black hair tossing like a stormy sea around her slender, lovely face. Her eyes gleamed with anger—a burning fire that Hal found disturbing—but her rage seemed only to enhance her beauty.

Erix looked at the strangers with a mixture of fear and fascination. They were unquestionably savage and powerful warriors, for all around them were bodies of fallen Payit warriors and priests. She looked quickly but could not find Mixtal's corpse among them. The high priest, she assumed, had escaped with the rest of the warriors. The two soldiers who had held her while their comrades attacked now half-carried her to the company at the base of the pyramid.

Erix saw the tall one, Mixtal's prisoner with the sandy beard, and she was glad that he had not perished under the high priest's knife. She remembered the attention Chitikas had directed toward this stranger. She felt a strange sense of relief to see him among his fellows, as if she desired his rescue but had not wanted to perform it. He was, however, still bound with the *hishna* snakeskin.

Suddenly the two men who held her arms released her. The short one with the furry face gestured at her, indicating the jungle, and in that instant, she realized that they were releasing her.

She quickly stepped back from the two strangers while her mind whirled with possibilities and fears. She didn't trust these mysterious people. She had seen grim evidence of their fighting prowess. Yet she dared not flee here only to fall into the hands of Mixtal, who must still be near.

* * * * *

Gultec's rage almost compelled him to burst from the undergrowth and slay the invaders single-handed. Only the utmost exertion of self-discipline allowed the warnings of his brain to prevail, compelling caution.

His keen night vision showed him the bodies of a score or

more Payits, presumably slain at the hands of the two dozen strangers now gathered at the pyramid. The invaders were clearly warriors of great prowess. Therefore, he would not attack until he gathered his warriors around them.

The men filed quickly and silently through the jungle. Ten ranks of hundredmen slipped along the periphery of the forest, led by stealthy Jaguar Knights on each flank. Gultec remained in the middle of the force, waiting only long enough to allow the spearmen and knights to gather behind him.

Soon a thousand warriors stood ready to attack.

* * * * *

"It's dulling the blade!" complained Daggrande after another attempt to saw through Hal's bonds. One of the legionnaires handed Hal his sword, but the snakeskin binding his arms to his sides prevented him from raising the weapon above his waist. The dwarf cast a glance at the jungle, and then to the trail leading down the bluff, to the beach and the rest of the legion.

"Let's get out of here. Maybe that elf-wizard—" he paused to spit, then continued—"can do something about this rope."

Halloran reluctantly had to agree, though he felt terribly vulnerable standing there with his hands and arms held tightly at his sides. He felt the eyes of the girl on him again. He tried not to stare, but he found himself looking back. Her wide brown eyes did not move away, as had those of the other native women he had encountered. He detected a hint of fear within them, but also a prideful challenge that seemed to mock him.

And then the night air exploded with a shrill chorus of screeches, whistles, and shouts. The sound crushed in from all sides, and the legionnaires saw movement in the darkness.

"Form square!" bellowed Daggrande. The captain was appalled at the volume of noise, but his movements were crisp and precise. He tucked his dagger in his belt, slung his battle-axe from his wrist, and raised his powerful crossbow.

The legionnaires stood shoulder to shoulder, longswords and crossbows alternating. Following Daggrande's command, they created a four-sided wall of steel, facing outward on all sides. Now they could see the attacking shapes closing in from the darkness.

"Fire!" At the instant of Daggrande's command, the ten bowmen released their missiles and seized their swords. There would be no second shot this night.

"Helm curse this thing!" Halloran roared his frustration, shaking his head like an angry lion. Despite his bonds, he tried to shoulder his way into the line.

He saw the girl move suddenly, stepping toward him, and he looked at her in astonishment. She stopped to look up at him with those wide eyes, which even in the darkness seemed to penetrate to the depths of his soul. Then she reached for him, and he saw that she held something in her hand, something that looked like a small cluster of feathers. Something gleamed like a shining stone in the midst of the plumage.

The shocking clash of steel against stone rocked the clearing. Hundreds of Payit warriors met Daggrande's two dozen and the legionnaires stood firm. The screams of the wounded joined the din, with some of the legionnaires falling as well as many natives.

The girl touched the feathered object to Halloran's side. His heart leaped as he felt the bonds give way, falling in a loose coil about his feet. He instinctively reached down and grabbed the ensorcelled thing that had restrained him. Hal was amazed to see that now it was a mere snakeskin, colorful and scaly but no more than six or eight feet long. He would have sworn that it was much longer when it held him. Nevertheless, he stuffed it into his belt.

In an instant, it seemed, the first attack fell away. Halloran stood at a corner of the square, watching the warriors waiting restlessly several paces before him. They were packed tightly to the limits of his vision, an uncountable number. He was vaguely aware of the girl standing behind him. For a moment, he thought of encouraging her to leave the square, to return to her own people.

Another volley of shrieks arose, this time to the side and above them. The bulk of the pyramid had vanished in the darkness, but he remembered the height and size of the object. He imagined the natives making use of that height.

Halloran instantly pictured the javelins arcing through the sky, and he stepped backward to seize the girl and hold her underneath the protection of his armored arm and shoulder. The missiles scattered around them, and then the spearmen surged once more to the attack.

Hal raised Helmstooth and stepped into a vacant space in the square. The captain faced a kaleidoscope of attacking spearmen and club-wielders. His sword quickly grew slick with blood, his arm weary of battle, and yet he knew that the attack had just begun.

*   *   *   *   *

Kachin joined the rush toward the strangers, more out of curiosity than aggression. Indeed, he carried no weapon, but the priest of Qotal wanted to see these invaders up close. Like the warriors, he had been disturbed by the reports that the soldiers attacked a group of Payit at the pyramid. One panicked warrior had gasped a tale of a sacrifice interrupted by surprise attack.

This intrigued Kachin. A sunset sacrifice in this remote location was mysterious. He hoped against a cold, forbidding fear that the ceremony did not explain the disappearance of Erixitl. Yet he felt almost certain that it did.

Kachin saw the strangers standing in their tight line as the mass of warriors struck them from all sides. He saw flashing silver and waving feather banners. The air resounded with shrieks and crashes and whistles and shouts, and then a momentary still settled in as the Payit fell back, just far enough to avoid the deadly steel. The priest saw many bodies scattered around the invaders, but a few gaps had opened in their previously tight formation.

Through one of these gaps, Kachin saw a flash of black hair, and then he gasped. Erixitl! She was being held by the strangers!

More and more of Gultec's column emerged from the jungle, massing around the little square. Many spearmen climbed along the sides of the pyramid, not as far as the top but gaining positions high above the legionnaires.

"Hieeeiiii!" A volley of screeches burst from the warriors on the pyramid, and a hundred spears took to the air. The missiles, launched from the height of the pyramid, dropped among the tightly packed soldiers below. Several found their marks in the shoulders or backs of the legionnaires.

The warriors on the ground surged forward, striking the square with savage force. This time the little formation began to give way. Several legionnaires fell, and each fallen trooper left a hole in the line.

Kachin got a glimpse of Erix again. She had been grabbed by one of the strangers, a very tall man, before the javelin volley fell. It had almost looked to the priest as if the man had shielded her body with his own, but Kachin could not be sure. Now he saw her struggling in the man's overbearing grasp.

The priest pushed his way to the forefront of the battle, ducking low among the swinging, surging warriors. He saw a gap in the legionnaires' line—indeed, it was now more gap than line—and dove through.

Kachin rolled across the earth, springing to his feet before the startled Erix. Her eyes flashed with recognition as he pulled her from the grip of the tall stranger.

* * * * *

Daggrande sensed the square collapsing and knew he was going to die, that his entire detachment would perish here in the shadow of this Helm-cursed monument. The dwarf's battle-axe chopped the arm from a spearman. He spun on his foot, swinging the weapon at arm's length to disembowel another even as his shield deflected the spear thrust of a third.

He saw another legionnaire fall, blood spurting from his torn throat. Several of his men were borne to the earth under the sheer weight of the attacking numbers.

"Look out!" he shouted, seeing a native lunging toward Halloran. The attacker didn't look like a warrior; he wore a white robe and carried no visible weapon. Yet the dwarf saw him hurl himself at Halloran with abandon.

Daggrande sprang to the side of his old friend as Hal cut down one of the fearsome spotted warriors who were visible among the attackers.

And then things changed, quite suddenly.

* * * * *

Chitikas hovered in an easy circle above the battlefield, invisible to all the participants. The serpent greatly enjoyed the savagery of the fight, but his attention concerned primarily the man and woman in the center of the legionnaires' square.

He saw the woman step to the man's side, and a reptilian smirk twisted the feathered snake's still invisible features. Then Chitikas arched his scaly eyebrows as he saw a man—a priest, it seemed—rush toward the girl. At the same time, a dwarf joined the man.

But the press of attacking Payit grew overwhelming. It was obvious that soon the man would be dead. Shaking his head, annoyed at the need for unseemly haste, Chitikas acted.

* * * * *

Hal saw the pudgy white-robed man emerge from the mass and spring toward him. He turned to meet him before realizing that the man was coming after the girl, not him. He saw Daggrande's stocky form at his side. The dwarf's axe cut a deep gouge in the leg of an attacking warrior, and the native went down like a felled tree.

A bright light suddenly washed over the clearing, and the combatants all froze in momentary indecision. Hal blinked against the brightness and saw a whirling circle, the source of the light, descending from the sky toward the battle—toward *him!* He knew instantly that powerful magic threatened them. Grimly he raised his blade, facing the potent and supernatural attack.

He dimly noticed the natives backing away, bowing their heads in fear or reverence, bending toward the earth in supplication. He saw the girl beside him looking upward also, her face washed in the cool light.

The whirling circle dropped quickly as the legionnaires stood transfixed. Vaguely Halloran saw that the ring was made from the body of a huge flying snake. Its vast, brilliantly colored wings blurred from the speed of their motion, but were nonetheless visible. The glow emanated from the snake's body itself. Though not equal in brightness to daylight, it flared brighter than any source of nighttime illumination known to Maztica.

The broad ring, several paces across, settled around Halloran and Erix. The snake shifted and swirled its coils, embracing the pair. It could not avoid entangling Daggrande and Kachin at the same time.

Then the light disappeared, and with it, the four vanished within its grasp.

* * * * *

Mixtal gaped at the surreal scene below. He peered over the edge of the pyramid's top, from where he had watched the events below as night had fallen. The priest's mind seemed to settle into a damp puddle somewhere in the pit of his stomach, overwhelmed by the events of this still-early evening.

First the Jaquar Knight's objections thwarted the sacrifice of the enemy soldier. Then the girl had returned from the dead, still held by the strangers. He knew he had sacrificed her once, for the cold body still lay beside the altar. Battles of increasing size and ferocity had whirled around him. Then the couatl had appeared! The mystical creature of ancient history and legend, here, now!

And finally the sudden disappearance of the serpent and the four caught in its coils stunned Mixtal's brain into complete surrender. Collapsing on the stone surface, he wept.

Mixtal did not see the dark figure on the pyramid with him. He did not see the slender form, swathed completely in a black robe, bend over the body beside the altar, the body of the young woman, Martine.

But the priest heard the soft rustle of silk. He lifted his head to behold the Ancient One striding toward him, feet moving silently over the paving stones. Dimly Mixtal saw a pair of wide, pale eyes gleaming at him from the depths of a black cowl.

"So, cleric, you have made your sacrifice?" The voice came softly to Mixtal's ears.

"I did," he said, nodding. "You saw."

Spirali looked back at the pale corpse before turning scornfully back to the priest. "You have failed!" he spat. "Failed Zaltec!"

Spirali reached a black hand forward, seizing the cleric by the throat, squeezing. But the attack ran deeper than a mere physical clasp.

Mixtal's eyes widened in a gape of unparalleled horror. His tongue protruded; his cheeks sucked futilely for air. And as he suffocated, he felt his soul drawn from him by the unspeakable might of the Ancient One. Mixtal knew as he died that his death would bring annihilation, a complete consumption by a vengeful force of unspeakable evil.

Spirali threw the husk of the man, a dried, stiff remnant, to the stones. The Ancient One looked at the now-mummified face, sneered at its terror-stricken features.

"Failed Zaltec, perhaps," he whispered. "But more importantly—far more importantly—you have failed the Ancient Ones."

* * * * *

From the chronicle of Coton:

May these tales be preserved to shine in the light of the Plumed Serpent's glory.

Naltecona, greatest and most omnipotent ruler of the True World, mighty Naltecona, Revered Counselor of the

Nexala and holder of the Seat of Flowers, who governs the lives and deaths of men with a wave of his hand, supreme Naltecona, blessed with the wisdom of his ancestors . . .

Naltecona has decided.

After months of fasting, after long consultations with his wisest clerics and magicians, he has decided. After the dozens of sacrifices consecrated to the younger gods, captive warriors slain, that the Revered Counselor may gain the insight he needs, Naltecona has decided.

He has heard the counsel of his war chiefs, who have urged him to muster his army and meet these invaders on the shore with a full display of the might of Nexal.

He has listened to gibbering sorcerers and soothsayers, who tell him the strangers are the incarnate forms of the Feathered Father, Qotal, returned to Maztica at last.

He has heard the fears, conveyed through Eagle flight, of the Payit warriors, who even now stand and face these strangers, perhaps in battle, perhaps in counsel.

All this has Naltecona heard, that his decision can be made with the wisest counsel, the greatest knowledge possible. All this he has heard, and he has decided.

He has decided to do nothing. The mighty Nexala, masters of Maztica, will sit and wait.

❧ 13 ❧

THE SHRINE OF QOTAL

Cordell looked up quickly, disturbed by the undisciplined shouts suddenly drifting in from the beach pickets. He knew his guards, posted along the fringe of jungle at the base of the bluff, would not yield themselves to such an outburst without cause.

"Domincus, Darien!" He called his chief lieutenants to his side, and the trio trotted rapidly through the grassy sand. Darkness hid the nearby bluff and its gigantic stone faces, but Cordell knew the voices came from the base of the precipice, near the main trail toward the pyramid at the top.

The Bishou rushed ahead of Cordell, his face drawn and haggard. "Almighty Helm, I depend upon your mercy!" chanted the cleric. The captain-general, too, feared the news from the scouts, though for more pragmatic reasons than the Bishou. Had he lost the use of Halloran as a captain? It was a possibility that needed to be faced.

A single word caught his ear as he approached: "attacked."

Cordell reached the picket to find two swordsmen supporting a third. The latter gasped for breath. His skin was torn in many places, and blood covered his body. Cordell recognized him as Grabert, a reliable veteran.

"Martine!" roared the Bishou before Cordell could speak. "What happened to my daughter—tell me, man!"

"Where's Daggrande!" demanded Cordell, ignoring the Bishou's glower. The bleeding man stiffened at his commander's voice, doing his best to stand like a legionnaire as he reported.

"Daggrande and Halloran are gone, sir. It was sorcery! A

bright circle, a ring that floated in the air, settled down around them. Then they disappeared, together with a couple of the savages."

The man dropped his eyes, avoiding the Bishou's gaze. "I'm afraid, sir . . . that is, I heard Halloran say that the savages killed Martine. On top of that pyramid, I think."

The Bishou bellowed his grief until his voice faded to a strangled gasp. He slumped to his knees, turning his face to the heavens. Shaking his fists at the sky, he roared his rage so savagely that the men around him stepped back several paces. "The curses of Helm fall upon your heads! May your ignorance be obliterated by the strike of his almighty hand!" For a moment, the cleric paused, and then he rose to his feet, his wild gaze meeting Cordell's.

"You *must* send the legion against them! We will wipe them from the face of the earth!"

The captain-general's eyes flashed darkly, but the Bishou was too blind to see the warning there. "The legion performs at *my* command," Cordell said softly. "But you should know that we *always* destroy our enemies. I will not let this attack go unavenged."

By this time, perhaps ten legionnaires had stumbled down the stairway from the top of the bluff. Many of the troops on the beach had also gathered as Grabert finished his report. The Bishou moaned as Grabert told of Hal and Martine's capture, and Daggrande's pursuit.

"Then hundreds of 'em attacked, sir, coming out of the jungle with spears and clubs. We were completely surrounded. Daggrande got us into square, but too many men had fallen."

"And how did you escape—you and these other men?" The question came from a black-robed figure beside Cordell. Darien had remained unnoticed until now.

Grabert stiffened at the question, but he did not meet the wizard's eyes. "When that ring appeared, the one that snatched Daggrande and Halloran, the savages fell on their faces, like they were frightened or maybe awestruck. And we ran for the bluff, those of us lucky enough to still be alive."

Cordell looked at the elf woman at his side, and she nodded in understanding.

"I will return soon," Darien said softly. No one saw her gesture or heard the words to any spell. But all of those gathered saw her disappear from sight, instantly invisible. They knew she went to observe the legion's newest enemies.

* * * * *

Halloran felt the ground drop away, and then a ring of swirling color surrounded him. His hands flailed madly, seeking a handhold as he fell. He felt the squirming body of the young woman beside him. A tugging at his waist told him that Daggrande, too, held on.

Dimly he realized that he wasn't really falling. He felt weightless, but there was no rush of wind, no sense of motion. He tried to look around, but all he saw was the ring of color, expanding into an all-encompassing kaleidoscope.

And then solid ground once again materialized under his feet. The colors faded to a milky glow, and he saw that he had somehow arrived inside a stone building. The native girl had clung to his arm during the mystifying journey, but now she pushed away from him and stared, panic-stricken, around the chamber.

They occupied a circular room, perhaps ten paces across, with walls made of carved stone blocks. An opening on one side displayed a series of stone stairs leading upward into darkness. Above and beyond the opening, the faint twinkling of starlight illuminated the night sky.

"Helm's curses on this sorcery!" Daggrande had fallen upon landing and now sputtered angrily as he climbed to his feet. His hands clenched his bloody axe menacingly.

Hal saw the fourth person, the older man in the white robe who had tried to seize the girl. He alone seemed calm. Indeed, Hal watched in amazement as he knelt and bowed toward an image at one side of the room, opposite the doorway. The man's long gray hair, tied in a single knot, fell to the floor as he bowed.

"Qotal!" gasped the girl, stepping away from the image.

Erixitl, too, recognized the image of the god, with its fanged jaws and encircling mane of feathers. She saw with sudden and startling clarity the truth of what Chitikas had spoken of earlier: that the faith of Qotal had lurked in the background of her entire life. Both her father and the Kultaka noble Huakal had worshiped the Feathered One, albeit quietly and privately. Kachin, cleric of Qotal, had purchased her for an exorbitant price in the name of that temple. She was the object of great attention from Chitikas, a feathered snake made almost in the image of the Plumed Serpent form of the god.

She looked with new eyes at the benign cleric, saw him regarding her with an expression of cherubic innocence. His face, lined with wrinkles as it was, beamed with a quiet smile for Erixitl alone.

Many questions suddenly rose within her. Why did the gods place such value on her life . . . or her death? What had compelled the followers of Qotal to manipulate her across the breadth of the True World? To make her a slave? Or a priestess?

And now Chitikas had brought her to this shrine, the sacred place dedicated to Qotal, at the close of this tumultuous day.

She looked at the fanged, grinning stone image of the Plumed God, and then at the serpentine form of Chitikas, covered as he was in downy feathers, and she wondered.

Halloran faced the garish stone image carved into the wall of the round chamber. He saw the face of a serpent, with gaping jaws and a wide mane surrounding the head. The mane, Hal saw after a moment, depicted a wide collar of feathers.

Suddenly he looked upward, wondering at the pale glow. He saw the long snake's body whirling through the air, beating its brilliant wings easily. The snake's body itself was the source of the illumination! His sword hand started upward with a will of its own until he forced himself to lower the blade. He felt certain that nothing good could come of attacking this glowing serpent, at least not yet.

"Who are you?" he demanded. "What do you want?" As

soon as he challenged the thing, it slowly settled to the floor, resting on its long tail while most of the body floated gracefully before him.

"Better to ask you, stranger. What do you want?"

The voice hissed in his mind, though the creature had made no sound. Awestruck, Halloran stepped backward, realizing that the beast's powers dwarfed his own mortal abilities.

The girl spoke, her voice smooth and quick. He could not understand her words, but suddenly the meaning entered his mind.

"Chitikas! Why have you brought us here? Who are these men?"

The serpent, Hal realized, not only communicated its own thoughts to him, but it also translated and passed along the words of the native girl.

"I don't like this," growled Daggrande, his voice a coarse whisper. "Let's get out of here!"

"We must stay here and listen." The white-robed man rose to his feet and turned toward Daggrande and Halloran. He, too, spoke his own language for telepathic translation. "The couatl is the sign of ultimate good, disciple of Qotal himself. I, Kachin, priest of Qotal, beseech you to listen."

The cleric nodded at the carved visage, and Hal understood that the serpentine face, with its mane of feathers, depicted this god, Qotal.

"Priest?" spat the legionnaire. "A priest such as the one who tore the heart from a defenseless woman? What kind of priest is that? What kind of *god* is that?" Halloran trembled with rage as the memory of that event came back to him in all its horror.

Kachin sighed. "No, not such a priest, though you have seen this face of the gods of Maztica."

"What possessed that monster? Why was she killed?" Halloran demanded.

"The tale is unpleasant, and complicated. That cleric is a patriarch of Zaltec, god of war—and night, and death, and other incidental things, but mainly war." Kachin spoke quickly, his words becoming thoughts in Hal's mind with equal speed.

"Across the land of Maztica are many who worship Zaltec, and all of them seek hearts to feed to their god. The priests take these hearts, usually at sunrise or sunset, in great numbers."

"That's barbaric!" snarled Halloran, appalled. "What kind of a god would demand such a thing? And what kind of people would obey?"

"Do not make judgments too sweeping," urged Kachin. "Though the creed of Zaltec spreads far across the land, here in Payit are many who hearken to the call of Qotal."

Erix spoke suddenly, surprising both Kachin and Hal. "Qotal is the source of *pluma*, the feathermagic that broke your bonds," she told Hal. "A god who thrives on life and beauty, not blood."

The girl turned and explained many things to the cleric. The serpent did not translate her words, but Hal understood the basic message: She had fled from the priest who killed Martine and had been captured by Daggrande's men.

"All right," Hal growled, interrupting her. "We'll stay here and listen, as you suggest. But I want some explanations!"

"I don't like this," grumbled Daggrande softly, but he remained beside his comrade.

"*Remember, stranger,*" hissed the serpent, "*I could have left you to die at the pyramid. There was no escape for you there.*" Halloran winced at the power, and the underlying sense of menace, in the message thrumming into his brain. For a moment, he wondered if the snake intended to attack him.

At the same time, Halloran realized that the creature spoke the truth. The battle at the pyramid had been lost. He thought of the legionnaires of Daggrande's detachment, all of them probably dead now. How many times this day must he stand helpless as companions died?

"I have told you that I am Kachin," said the rotund priest, suddenly nodding. His words were translated even as the snake held its unblinking gaze upon Halloran. "And this is Erixitl."

Hal nodded curtly, still staring at the snake. Abruptly a wave of power knocked him backward. Something had struck his mind, a blow that was not physical but nonetheless stunning.

"*Speak!*" commanded the serpent. "*Do you strangers have no manners? Speak your names!*"

Hal bit back a sharp reply and nodded stiffly. "I am Captain Halloran. My companion is Captain Daggrande."

"*And I am Chitikas Couatl, devoted servant of Qotal, and the one who has just saved your lives.*" The serpent undulated through the room. Slowly the golden glow emanating from its body faded until the chamber disappeared into darkness.

"*You humans complain about the most ridiculous things! You don't understand things that should be obvious to an infant!*" The voice was a menacing growl in their minds.

"*The True World stands at the brink of disaster. Evil threatens life upon all sides, from all directions. And you bicker proudly about your might and your fierceness!*

"*It is in your power to do things, to act against this blanketing scourge. You, Captain Halloran, face a quandary. You are not an evil man, yet great evils shall be asked of you.*

"*Only you, Erixitl, once of Palul, have touched the spirit of Our Esteemed Father.*" The creature directed its gaze to Erixitl, and all four humans could feel the focus of its attention change, even in the inky darkness of the chamber. "*And even you have been reluctant, not showing gratitude proper for one who owes so much.*

"*So I will leave all of you to think upon my words. Only when the true blossom of understanding shrouds you can the will of the Feathered One become life.*

"*But still, for the spirit you have shown me, however briefly*"—the serpent again hissed softly to Erix—"*I will give you a gift . . . a gift of learning.*"

They all felt a brief pulse of power, something that seemed to twist the air in the cavern and then vanish. "Sorcery!" grunted Daggrande.

"It is sorcery in truth, short man," said Erix. The three males gaped at her in awe, for the words were carefully pronounced in stilted Commonspeech, the language of Waterdeep and the Realms.

"How is it you speak the words of the strangers?" gasped Kachin.

"This is the gift of Chitikas Couatl," replied Erix in amazement. She spoke in Payit, then turned and repeated the words in Common.

"Where'd Twisty go, anyhow?" grunted Daggrande, the first to notice that the snake seemed to be gone.

"You should show Chitikas more respect," Erix chided Daggrande gently, then turned to look at Halloran with that frank curiosity that he found so unsettling.

Halloran returned her stare, half in challenge and half in confusion. Even in the darkness, her luminous eyes were visible, studying him with bold intelligence and a hint of reproach. He wanted to rage at this savage woman and her companion, wanted to curse them for their obscene god. But even so, he remembered her act of kindness, when she had used her feathered necklace to free him from his bonds.

"Why did you free me?" Hal asked slowly. He pulled the snakeskin from his belt and held it toward her. "This held fast against our sharpest steel."

"I do not know what 'steel' is, but the—" Erix paused and searched for a word in her new language—"the *hishna*, the magic of scale and claw and fang, stands in opposition to *pluma*, the magic of feathers and air. I freed you because my necklace of *pluma* gives me power over *hishna*."

Erix pondered for a moment, puzzled. "I do not truly know why I chose to use this power to come to your aid. You are certainly the most frightening men I have ever seen. And in truth, you smell as though you have not bathed in many days.

"Chitikas told me to help you, but I did not want to. It was only when the Payit attacked that I desired you to have a chance to at least fight for your life."

"Thank you," said Halloran, as puzzled as Erix by her decision.

Daggrande had walked over to the doorway and looked at the sky. Now he turned back with a more practical concern.

"Does anyone know where we are?"

* * * * *

Spirali sat cross-legged upon the altar. The heart that had been torn from Martine lay beside him, cold and still. The Ancient One slowly worked his magic, seeking through the night the power that would tell him where his enemy had gone.

The appearance of the couatl had surprised and angered Spirali. Not one of the creatures had been detected in over two centuries, and Spirali's dark-dwelling leaders had pronounced them extinct. They would be displeased by Spirali's report.

But they would be very pleased with Spirali if he could announce that the beast was dead, presumably extinct again. So now he sought the deep emanations of power that would tell him where the couatl had gone. And even if the serpent escaped him, the Ancient One might learn where the girl had gone as well.

Spirali stiffened almost imperceptibly. There! In another instant, he disappeared.

His journey through the spaceless and timeless void that had been the couatl's pathway was instantaneous. Spirali arrived among a grove of flowers in a jungle clearing. He sensed that dawn was near, and this increased his urgency.

A dark stone doorway marked a vine-shrouded temple before him. Spirali closed his eyes, but the concentrated emanations of the couatl were no longer present.

Nevertheless, he heard voices coming from the temple. One of them he recognized as Erixitl's.

* * * * *

"The bluff teems with warriors—at least a thousand, with more emerging from the jungle every minute." Darien explained her observations to Cordell and the Bishou. They didn't question how she gained the information, both knowing that the elf woman could become invisibile, levitate or fly, assume the shape of an animal or monster, and employ other magical abilities as she needed. Her methods could not be questioned, and her results were invaluable.

"We must attack these pagan savages, now!" Bishou Domincus railed at the sky, shaking his fist at the enemy unseen in the darkness above.

"I'm ready to lead an attack," growled Alvarro eagerly. "We'll spit the devils on our swords!" The gap-toothed redhead had willingly echoed the cleric's cry for battle, and now they pressed an all-out attack.

"Be silent!" Cordell's tight voice instantly quelled their ranting. The commander continued, his voice low and tense.

"Think of our tactical position! We stand at the foot of a bluff. By Helm, they could use *rocks* as weapons!" Fury and frustration strained Cordell's voice. They hold the high ground!"

"This bluff seems to mark only this headland," interjected Darien. "To the west, the land drops off quickly." Cordell raised his eyebrows. "You have been busy tonight, my dear."

The elf shrugged, her pale eyes veiled. "I sought some sign of Daggrande or Halloran. Unfortunately, I saw nothing to indicate where they might have been taken by this glowing ring."

"Very well. They were good legionnaires, but we have to assume they are gone."

"Hiding!" snorted the Bishou. "The young man avoids facing me, shirking the responsibility for his criminal carelessness!"

Cordell sighed softly but did not reply to the Bishou's threat. There will be time enough for that should we ever see Hal again, he thought. "We shall sail along the coast, find a shore, and land, as the vigilant eye of Helm is my witness!"

Cordell looked into the Bishou's moist eyes. The captain-general's determination was a black fire burning in his heart as he vowed, "And there, in the open, the legion will await the savages. I assure you, my friend, that your daughter will be avenged!"

* * * * *

"This is the Forgotten Shrine," explained Kachin for Erixitl's translation. "We are east of the mayzfields, within sight of the Flowered Temple of Ulatos."

Erix explained for the benefit of the strangers. "Ulatos is the great city of the Payit, not far from your landing point. Your ships lie a march of perhaps two hours to the east." The translations of distance and time came easily to her. She realized that in both areas, the language of the strangers was far more precise than her own. Obviously they were a people who liked to measure things.

"Why did that priest kill Martine? Why did he choose *her* for his sacrifice?" The memory of the gory ritual burned in Halloran's mind like a nightmare that would not go away.

"The priest was mad," explained Erix. "He thought the woman was me." Maddened by Chitikas, she added to herself.

"You mean this war was started by a bewitched cleric?" howled Daggrande. "I might have known!"

But Halloran was thinking about her answer. "Why does he want to kill you?"

"I . . . don't know." The sight of her eyes left him absolutely convinced that she told the truth.

"Come, Erix," urged Kachin, in Payit. "Let us hasten to Ulatos. We should leave the presence of these strangers."

"But what about the danger in Ulatos?" Erix vividly remembered her abduction from the temple.

"I will see to your safety personally. The sanctity of the Silent Counselor's grounds shall not again be violated."

Erix turned back to the two legionnaires. "You will find yourself on the shore as we emerge from this shrine. Your friends lie to the east. Kachin and I return to our city, to the west." She started toward the door, then stopped and looked back at Halloran.

"May your journey pass in peace."

Halloran looked at the woman again. She seemed so much older than Martine, or himself, for that matter. He suspected that she had not yet seen twenty years, yet she carried herself with a maturity and grace that fascinated him almost to the point of awe.

Yet Martine's terror-stricken face appeared in his memory again. He had failed his responsibility to her! She had been killed because a mad priest took her to be this woman in front of him. Perhaps that should make him angry at Erix, but instead it only made him more curious.

"I hope that we meet again," he said, bowing.

Halloran preceded the others up the stairway leading out of the shrine. The twilight of approaching dawn filtered dim light through the foliage around them, and he saw a wide beach through the trees.

Erix followed him out of the shrine, then paused to look at him one last time. Kachin followed her, stopping in the door-way.

Suddenly the cleric's eyes widened. He sprang forward, pushing Erix roughly to the side. The black arrow intended for her heart lodged instead in the cleric's rib cage. Kachin gasped in deep pain and dropped to the ground.

Daggrande raised his crossbow, quickly sighting on the dark blur he thought he saw among the foliage. The black shape rolled to the side, evading his missile but revealing its presence by the movement.

Halloran charged the manlike figure, his silver longsword seeking flesh before him. Even though dawn's light had come as a rosy hue in the east, he could see nothing of his opponent but whirling shadow. Then he caught the dull glint of cold steel.

Helmstooth clashed against another metal sword. The enemy's blade was black, but rang like true steel. Again and again the weapons met, silver and black. Sometimes sparks flared from the violence of the contact. The fighters dodged and ducked among the trees, hacking into trunks and through branches in their desperate attacks and parries.

Hal guessed his opponent to be of human size, perhaps a little smaller but possessed of a supple, wiry strength. He noticed that the swordsman was cloaked entirely in black, including his gloves, boots, and a silken mask. More importantly, the dark one's skill with the blade matched the best swordsmen he had ever seen.

With savage, silent violence, the dark figure rushed Hal, slicing his face and narrowly missing his bowels. Then the legionnaire kicked the wiry form away and stabbed once, twice, again, each time missing by a mere inch.

Halloran attacked and parried with all the skill in his arm and his brain. The dark figure seemed to flow away from his shining blade, deftly swirling beyond the point, and then the razor-edged return thrust whistled past Halloran as he used all of his speed to avoid sudden death.

Daggrande cocked his crossbow and aimed, but he could not get a clear shot into the melee. Even as red dawn blossomed to pink, as flowers and insects became visible among the fronds, the mysterious attacker remained shrouded in shadowy darkness. His garments, if such they were, seemed to float around him like a cloud of smoke, obscuring his limbs but in no way impairing his movement.

The fighter pressed Halloran back again, the blows coming more swiftly than ever. The legionnaire parried and retreated. Slowly he felt himself losing the fight. His arm felt like a leaden weight, and his brain began to struggle against fatigue. Still the dark stranger attacked, with no sign of strain or exhaustion. Dawn's pale illumination began to brighten the clearing around them, and Halloran fought for his life.

Then suddenly the black form darted away from him, rolling into the foliage. Like smoke, his shape seemed to dissipate. Hal lunged forward recklessly, his longsword lancing out toward his opponent's suspected location.

But his strike met only succulent greenery. He hacked at the fronds, but there was nothing there. As the first rays of the sun flickered across the treetops above them, Halloran and his companions realized that the attacker was gone.

On the ground, Kachin coughed, the pink froth of his life-blood trickling through his lips.

*　*　*　*　*

Dawn showed the great wings spreading across the water. Gultec, atop the pyramid with Caxal, the Revered Counselor of Ulatos, and Lok, chief of the Eagle Warriors, watched the white shapes unfold like the blossoms of a day-flower opening to the sun.

The Jaguar Knight felt a terrible unease as he watched. Oddly, he missed the presence of Kachin. That cleric, among all the men he knew, seemed capable of offering wisdom and sound guidance in this hour of dire danger.

And Gultec did not underestimate the danger posed by these strangers. Nearly two hundred of his warriors had been slain in short minutes of combat, a horrifying death toll even to the veteran campaigner. At the same time, only ten of the strangers had been killed.

Gultec felt certain that the other strangers at the pyramid would have perished, except for the appearance of the couatl. But at what cost to his own troops?

A sense of menace grew in his mind, and suddenly he spoke to Caxal and Lok. "We must send the warriors back to the city . . . quickly!"

"The city?" Caxal looked at him suspiciously. "But the strangers are here now!"

"I think they will fly soon. See how they spread their wings? The army of Ulatos is here, and the city lies undefended."

"No!" Caxal barked. Lok, the Eagle chief, started to speak but closed his mouth in the face of the counselor's glare. Caxal squinted, studying the great water creatures—he could not think of them as boats—and trying to control the fear raging in his breast.

Gultec turned away from the counselor, his temper flaring. Normally, in such a state, he would have stalked away. But this day, these occurrences, seemed so momentous to the Jaguar Knight that such ordinary concerns of pride faded to insignificance.

The white wings did indeed fly. "See how their beats stir the wave tops," Lok said, pointing. They all watched the white wakes foaming behind each hull as the strangers rode their water creatures around the reef. They followed the coast toward the west, in the direction of Ulatos.

Caxal watched the flight of the strangers in a stupor. This

was the first he had seen of their might, and awe filled his body with numbness. Suddenly he shook his head.

"We must race to Ulatos," he declared, oblivious of his two war chieftains, who looked at him in scorn, "to defend the city against the invaders!"

* * * * *

From the chronicle of Coton:

Now our destiny has only to be born.

The Eagles continue to report to Naltecona. He hears the news of their departure with joy. He smiles and relaxes and beckons to his priests and nobles.

"See? The strangers leave us. They are no threat, surely not the cause of ten years of portents." He cheers himself, but no one else, with the heartiness of his words.

Then more Eagles fly to the palace of Nexal, and the Revered Counselor hears of the strangers' approach to Ulatos. For a time, Naltecona is despondent, and then again the smile of understanding crosses his features.

But now he understands things that no one else can see. "It is their folly to go to Ulatos, for that is the heart of the Payit lands," he assures his attendants. "Surely the Jaguars and Eagles of the Payit will rally to destroy them," he explains to the nobles.

And indeed the warriors of the Payit gather, many thousandmen of the city and the surrounding towns. More warriors arrive daily from Payit lands deeper in the jungle, mysterious regions unknown even to Nexal.

But only Naltecona believes they may solve his dilemma.

❧ 14 ❧

ULATOS LAGOON

The cleric of Qotal gasped and wheezed, each breath coming shorter than the last as his lungs slowly filled with blood. Erixitl wept softly beside him, holding Kachin's hand in hers. The cleric forcefully stopped her when she tried to tend his wounds, shaking his head to indicate certain knowledge of his fate. This man suddenly meant a great deal to Erix, and the thought of his loss left her frightened and lonely.

Halloran stood awkwardly off to the side, while Daggrande looked fruitlessly for some indication of the dark attacker's nature or trail.

The shrine, Hal saw now, was a round, dome-shaped building in the rain forest. It was covered with vegetation and stood very near to the shore. He wondered how far they were from the fleet's anchorage. He did not allow himself to consider the possibility that the legion had moved on. Nothing Halloran could imagine seemed as frightening to him as the thought of being stranded here, never to see men of his own world again.

Erix moaned and leaned across Kachin's suddenly still body. Halloran looked away, realizing with surprise that this man's death saddened and angered him.

The attack had been cowardly, and the cleric had given his life to save a maiden, a clear statement of the relative merits of attacker and victim. But also this cleric had acted as a decent and reasonable man.

Indeed, Kachin had almost seemed civilized, Hal admitted. Too, he was discomfited by this unusual girl who had magically learned his language and who regarded him with those luminous eyes.

"Well, there's no sign of that thing, or person, or whatever it was," reported Daggrande. "Now let's get going back to the fleet."

"Wait!" Halloran suddenly felt reluctant to leave. He turned to the girl. "I'm sorry about your friend."

Again she disturbed him, this time with the extent of the pain he could see in her face. She studied him with a wounded innocence that finally forced him to turn away. "Will you help me bury him, please?" she asked softly.

"We have to go!" Daggrande objected. "Cordell might already have decided to move on!"

Halloran sighed and looked at his old friend. "You go ahead. I'll help her and catch up as soon as I can."

The dwarf looked at him incredulously for a moment but made no move to leave. "I never did think you had much in the way of a brain. But I'd best stay here and help you get the job done. Then"—and his voice dropped to an ominous growl—"we're going!"

Erixitl selected a spot beside the shrine of Qotal, the god Kachin had served all his adult life. The fringe of forest along the coast was lined with many rocks, for the beach here was more gravelly than it had been below Twin Visages. All three of them helped carry rocks to the burial site, then slowly built a mound over Kachin's body.

Erix worked steadily, ignoring the questions that began to grow in her mind. Where should I go? What should I do? Fiercely she forced those questions aside until the grave was completed. Finally the work was done, and all her uncertainties settled to the fore of her mind.

A small part of her wanted to return home, to Palul, to finally see Nexal, the great city she had never seen. She knew no one in Ulatos—indeed, in all Payit—and she had come here as a purchased slave. Erix understood that, though Kachin had called her a priestess, she did not have the training or background for such an exalted calling.

But if she was not a priestess, neither was she any longer a slave. She feared the forces of Zaltec, for they had attacked her more than once, yet it seemed that greater things had been set in motion by the arrival of these strangers. And those forces would threaten her everywhere in the True World, perhaps with even greater savagery near their highest temple in Nexal.

Too, there was the matter of Chitikas's gift to her. She was probably the only Maztican who could communicate with the strangers. They were indeed a frightening, even horrifying, lot. The prospects for peace between Halloran's people and her own looked very grim, especially after the melee at the pyramid. In her heart, she wondered whether war was inevitable.

Could her destiny, the destiny Chitikas had spoken of, involve the prevention of this conflict? She doubted whether this was possible, but at the same time she felt compelled to try to do *something*.

She would return to Ulatos. If the strangers sailed up the coast, this would be the first city they encountered. She would get there first and offer her abilities as a translator. Then she would do everything she could to prevent a war.

"Now I—we—must go." The man called Captain Halloran looked at her with a certain sadness in his face. Once again she bravely met his gaze. Indeed, he had begun to look less horrid than she had first thought. His pale blue fish eyes still unsettled her, and he, like all of these strangers, seemed surrounded by that unpleasant odor. Obviously bathing would be difficult on the strangers' great flying houses. No doubt they would resume normal human hygiene now that they had landed.

She looked up at his genuine smile, his tall, powerful form. He was the most magnificent warrior she had ever seen. True, Erix had never been one to be swayed by the prowess of a fighting man, but never before had a warrior saved her life. And every one of his acts seemed tempered with honor and decency.

"I will show you the way back to Twin Visages," she offered. They stepped from the verdure onto the gravelly coastline, and she turned to the right. "There, perhaps one or two hours from here."

"Where will you go?" asked Hal, looking at the long stretch of stone and jungle.

"I journey there." She pointed to the left. "To the city of Ulatos, heart of the Payit lands." She did not add her fears of war, nor her thoughts of prevention.

"I wish you a safe journey," he said, bowing. "Perhaps we will meet again."

She looked at him with humor. "I think perhaps we will!"

He did not understand, and she pointed past him. Daggrande groaned as they looked out to sea, and Halloran's heart sank. All of his fears came back. He was stranded on a distant shore!

Fifteen sets of sails jutted above the horizon. The legion sailed along the coast, headed in their direction. But the ships were too far from shore for the pair to have any chance of hailing them as they passed.

* * * * *

The wind cooperated splendidly, carrying the fleet seaward, beyond any shoals that might have lurked around the headland of Twin Visages. After they had safely passed from the lagoon into the deep sea, the breeze shifted, gently ushering the caravels and carracks along the luxuriant vista of this new shore.

Cordell watched the tangled jungle press forward to the sea, and he guessed that they passed a river delta. Indeed, dozens of canoes darted back and forth through the lush greenery, and he knew that the natives of this land observed them as they sailed westward.

"These are puzzling people," remarked the captain-general to Darien. The pair stood alone atop the raised afterdeck of the *Falcon*. The elf woman's hood was pulled completely over her head in order to protect her skin from the blazing afternoon sun. "In many ways savage, yet they show organization and considerable energy."

"I suspect our Bishou's notion of their godlessness is mistaken," said Darien.

"Whether they're led by gods or sorcerers, or both,"

vowed Cordell, "they will come to regret the impetuous attack on my men!"

After the delta, a line of hills rose from the river valley. In the shelter of these hills, almost as if the land extended an encircling and protective arm, the Golden Legion found its anchorage. The shore along the bay was smooth and grassy, with numerous villages and small temples scattered among the fields.

The canoes of the natives maintained a constant vigil as the caravels dropped anchor. Here longboats probed the shore, and soon the reports reached *Falcon*: The anchorage was deep, the shore firm and suitable for the debarkation of horses and men.

The Bishou climbed to the deck as Cordell gave the order to move the ships closer to shore. The cleric had grieved loudly over the death of his daughter, but now he approached the general with a quiet, grim look.

"Helm in his mercy has given me a sign," explained the Bishou abruptly.

"Indeed," answered Cordell cautiously.

"You need a commander for the lancers, since Halloran has disappeared." The Bishou glowered.

"Yes . . . I have had some thoughts on the matter."

Domincus shook his head. "Helm has shown me directly that he desires Captain Alvarro to take command."

Cordell tried to suppress a grimace. The Bishou often used 'visions from Helm' to urge the general to follow some course of action he knew was not entirely agreeable to Cordell. Naturally the commander needed to consider the opinions and suggestions of his spiritual adviser, and Domincus often took advantage of the fact.

"I was thinking of someone a bit older, more seasoned. Alvarro can be somewhat . . . impetuous," began the captain-general, but the Bishou interrupted.

"It must be Alvarro! I have seen this!"

Cordell did not want to antagonize his old comrade at this stage of his mourning, nor could he risk the demoralizing effect a public argument might have upon his legionnaires. He knew Alvarro to be a brave and dashing horseman, albeit a trifle rash. He had a reputation as the best swordsman in the legion. The general finally overcame his objections.

"Very well. Captain Alvarro shall have command of the lancers."

* * * * *

"They gather their flying houses in the lagoon," explained Gultec. He breathed heavily, for he had just returned to Ulatos from a hurried reconnaisance.

"Excellent!" Caxal declared, beaming. The Revered Counselor had come more and more to relish the coming clash with the invaders, almost to the point of what Gultec considered rashness.

"Now you must take the warriors down the plain and await them above the shore. Allow them to land before you attack." Caxal gave his instructions quickly.

"Perhaps, my counselor, we should conceal a portion of our force in the trees along the delta," suggested Gultec. "I remember all too clearly the fighting prowess of these warriors. We would do well to hold some of our troops in reserve for a surprise attack."

Caxal fixed Gultec with a darkly suspicious look, the implications of which caused the Jaguar Knight's blood to boil. "Do you fear these warriors, Gultec?" The counselor's voice was smooth, unusually considerate, but the question was a mortal insult to a captain of Gultec's stature.

Once again all his emotions urged him to turn on his heel and leave the presence of the Revered Counselor. Yet thoughts of destiny, of the historical importance of this moment, held his rage in check.

"I will personally lead the warriors across the field," Gultec agreed stiffly. "We will meet the invaders at the shore."

* * * * *

The Bishou smoldered in his cabin as the fleet swung easily at anchor. In his rage, he had abandoned his slave on the shore below Twin Visages. He only spared her life after Cordell intervened on her behalf, reminding him that Helm's vengeance should be directed at those responsible for evil, not its innocent victims.

Now Cordell and Alvarro stood on the raised deck of the *Falcon* and observed with anticipation the flat plain beside the river delta. The jungle shore was gone here, replaced by golden fields of the tall, plump grain these natives tended. "Mayz," the islanders had called it.

"Yes, Captain-General, I understand. I will command the horses well!" Alvarro beamed, his widely spaced teeth standing like scattered tombstones in a cemetery. The sun caused his red hair to blaze like firelight.

"And may I say, sir, that you will not regret your choice. That young fellow, Halloran, was simply too green to—"

"Enough!" snapped Cordell. "Go back to your ship. Be prepared to debark the horses after nightfall."

"Yes, sir!" Alvarro couldn't conceal his delight as he turned away. His eyes drifted idly over the verdant shore less than a mile away. Was Halloran still alive there? Alvarro belched, not really caring.

Darien joined Cordell as Alvarro stepped into the longboat beside the *Falcon*.

"See how that ridge of land encircles us here?" said the commander. "I think we've found ourselves a splendid anchorage!" All soundings indicated a good depth below them, even though their ships were anchored within a few hundred feet of shore.

"Look there." The general pointed to his elf woman. "Those are man-made structures rising above the trees."

Indeed, the pyramids of Ulatos were in plain view from their anchorage. The tangled swamps blocked the delta below the town, but less than a mile to the west beckoned a broad savannah of grass and mayz.

"The Bishou will be pleased," said Darien, with a sly, private smile.

"To be sure." Cordell paid her little attention. "Excellent. We will land the entire legion here. The savages will quickly learn the folly of attacking the Golden Legion."

"Let the war begin," whispered Darien, so softly that even her man did not hear.

* * * * *

Spirali rested inside the dark shrine of Qotal. He felt no sense of irony at taking shelter within a building devoted to the rival of Zaltec. In truth, Spirali felt little of anything.

The fight with the swordsman had exhausted him, but only daylight had forced him to teleport away from the battle. Even so, he was not certain he could have bested the human.

Indeed, these invaders were of a breed quite different from the natives of Maztica. Of course, he, like the other Ancient Ones, had long known of the lands across the sea, the lands referred to by their inhabitants as "the Forgotten Realms" or "The Sword Coast," or by other exotic names.

For many years, it had been the task of the Ancient Ones to prepare the land for the coming of these strangers, prepare it so that Zaltec would feed well and the Ancient Ones would grow strong.

Spirali regarded his problems coldly, dispassionately. Yet he nearly cursed when he thought of the girl escaping his arrow. That the missile had claimed the corpulent cleric was little satisfaction.

Now the hot sun blistered the world outside this stone building. Even the pale light spilling down the stairs burned his eyes and forced him to avert his gaze.

He could only wait until nightfall.

* * * * *

The white sails had remained visible against the horizon for several hours as Halloran and Daggrande, led by Erixitl, pressed westward along the shore. Eventually the fleet overtook them and continued on farther to the west, never coming closer to land.

The shoreline was mostly smooth beach backed by jungle, and they made good time. Along the way, they encountered several small groups of fishermen on the shore. These natives took one look at Halloran in his steel breastplate and blond hair or the grizzled visage of Daggrande scowling from beneath his heavy brows and quickly fled into the jungle or took to sea in their long canoes.

"I'd like to get my hands on one of those canoes," said Halloran as another trio of fishermen desperately paddled their slim craft through the surf, away from shore.

"Perhaps we can find one when we reach the delta," replied Erix. "I can take you that far before I turn toward Ulatos."

Late in the day, they saw the billowing canvas veer landward, and Hal's heart thrilled to the hope that the fleet would drop anchor and allow them to rejoin their companions. He tried, unsuccessfully, to bury the bleak sense of failure that would accompany his return. He felt, again, his guilt over Martine's loss. Somehow his shame seemed even more tarnished when he realized that he had been enjoying Erix's company for some time without a single thought of the Bishou's daughter. What kind of a man am I? he wondered.

"That is the delta, where the ships go now," explained the woman. She remembered descriptions of Ulatos she had heard from Kachin, complete with details and maps sketched on the ground. "I know there are many canoes—traders and fishermen and flower gatherers—working among the mangaroo groves."

The shorelands here were more open, and Daggrande clumped along ahead of the man and woman. Halloran saw large fields of the plump, rich vegetable they had sampled at every landing in Maztica. "I see you, too, make use of this 'mayz' plant," he observed to Erix as they passed a particularly lush field, separated from the beach by a row of palm trees and a narrow, straight canal.

"What place in the world could live without mayz?" asked Erix in bewilderment. "It is the food sent to man by the gods, brought by Qotal himself before he fought with his son Zaltec and was driven from Maztica."

Hal smiled. "We have grown to adulthood never knowing of mayz until the last few weeks. It is a wondrous plant, but unique to . . . 'Maztica'?" he pronounced tentatively, to her shy laughter.

"Maztica. Maztica meaning 'the True World.' But perhaps the world is a larger place than we have known." She turned and looked at him.

"Tell me, where is it you come from? Are there many humans there?" Erix had decided for herself, beyond any sense of doubt, that these visitors were men and not gods. Complex and interesting men to be sure, but as mortal as herself and her people.

"It is a place called the Forgotten Realms, from lands along the Sword Coast. My general is a great man, a man named Cordell, and he has led his legion here in search. . . ." He suddenly let his words trail off. Their mission, the plundering of these people's gold and the conquest of their lands, suddenly seemed less righteous than before, now that he was here, face to face with Erix.

It had been a simple matter when the inhabitants of these lands had been faceless savages, rude barbarians. The legion's mission became even more just when the natives attacked him by surprise and then performed the shocking ritual of Martine's sacrifice.

But now he had seen the courage and kindness of these people as well. No legionnaire had ever died a braver death than had Kachin, stopping the arrow intended for Erix. And that young woman had shown herself to be wise and patient, even in the face of events that could easily have overwhelmed her.

Such thoughts, he reminded himself sharply, were disloyal, perhaps even treasonous. Roughly he forced them from his mind, replacing them with the vivid memory of Martine's brutal sacrifice, the chilling cruelty of the priest. Whether he had been mad or not, many others followed his orders with apparent willingness, so even in madness he had not been alone.

Nevertheless, Hal felt certain that there was more to these people than Bishou Domincus, or even Cordell, suspected. This was a complex issue, and Halloran disliked complex issues on principle. Unconsciously he scowled, then smiled at Erix's sudden expression of worry when she saw his face.

"My mind is wandering," he explained.

He saw that they approached a region of densely tangled vegetation extending far into the sea. Stretches of glassy water were visible, winding among the trees, which Erix called "mangaroo."

"See how the limbs entwine?" she said. "The mangaroo creates its own islands as it expands. There is the Ulatos delta. They say it is always growing, that islands creep farther into the ocean every day."

"We've got to find a canoe!" declared Hal, suddenly anxious to return to the fleet. She looked at him sharply, surprised by his sudden, rudely abrupt declaration, but then shrugged and led him onward.

A small dock marked the border of the mangaroo delta—it looked like a swamp to Halloran—and here they found several canoes left by the hurriedly fleeing natives. They selected a large dugout, made from a single log that had been hollowed by fire and patient chiseling.

"I will leave you here," said Erix quietly, disturbed and slightly frightened by the sudden tension in this tall man. "May you have a good journey to your great canoe, your 'ship.' "

Daggrande lowered himself into one of the wobbling boats as Hal turned to say farewell. He found his tongue frozen in his mouth. This native girl disturbed and intrigued him in a way that Martine never had. Halloran's conscience troubled him deeply as he realized that the legion's mission would almost certainly make them enemies.

"Thank you for all your kindnesses," he finally blurted. "I hope that we meet again, and that fate is kind to you until that day." Bowing awkwardly, he climbed into the stern of the canoe. He and Daggrande each took a paddle, and soon the nimble craft disappeared among the winding mangaroo groves, heading for the open sea.

Erix watched them sail away, fighting a powerful sadness growing in her heart. She would remember the pale, tall soldier, with his mighty prowess and his strange, burning sense of drive. Truly if the other strangers were his equals, the invaders were a powerful and deadly force, perhaps equal to the might of Nexal itself.

Suddenly she shuddered. Her thoughts had briefly touched on both the city of Nexal and these strangers. For a stark second, her brain had flashed with a vision of distant Nexal in ruins, black smoke shrouding the sky above her lakes.

In her imagination, these strangers were everywhere.

*   *   *   *   *

"Do not debark the horses until dark," ordered the captain-general. "We have seen no sign of mounted travel here. Perhaps they will provide an unpleasant surprise for the foe come tomorrow."

His captains were gathered before him on the deck of the *Falcon*, receiving their final instructions. Cordell had commanded that the legion debark before nightfall. The troops would bivouac on the shore, in full view of the native army.

The captain-general once again turned his eyes to the plain beside the delta, where thousands of warriors, under many dozens of colorful banners, pennants, and fans, gathered to await them. They remained perhaps a mile back from the beach, within easy striking distance.

Beyond the plain rose the high white buildings of the city. Particularly intriguing was the tallest pyramid, with its green gardens draping in elegant terraces down its broad sides. High atop the pyramid, a crystalline fountain shimmered and gleamed in the late afternoon sun.

"General, why should we not remain aboard the ship tonight and land the entire legion in the morning? We leave ourselves terribly exposed to night attack!" The speaker was Garrant, the captain commanding a company of sword-and-buckler men. He raised objections running through the minds of many of the men.

"We land tonight precisely to show them we are not afraid!" Cordell answered forcefully, but he clearly welcomed the question. His voice softened. "I know, Captain Garrant, that your men will bear the brunt of such an attack should it develop. I am gambling that it will not. I can afford the gamble because I know your company will protect the legion if I am wrong."

Pleased with the compliment, the captain nodded his understanding, if not his approval, of the plan.

"My lord general?" asked a plaintive voice. Cordell turned, gritting his teeth, to regard the weasel-faced accountant, Kardann.

"Yes?"

"The treasure, my lord! I beg you to consider the treasures we have already gained. We carry a small fortune in gold nuggets and crude ornaments from the islanders!" Kardann bobbed his head as he spoke, with frequent glances toward the shore.

"Should we not see that treasure safely out to sea?" he blurted. "Not held here, close to shore, where the savages could swarm out in their canoes and take it?"

Cordell looked at the assessor in astonishment. "It's preposterous to think they could claim even one of our ships by force! I'll have no more such talk!" The assessor's words may already have caused a distraction, he feared—at a time when he needed the entire concentration of his men directed toward the upcoming conflict.

Cordell half-turned toward the afterdeck, then changed his mind. Normally he would ask the Bishou to bestow Helm's blessing upon this undertaking, but Domincus still muttered and paced, staring intently landward. Cordell feared his address could do more harm than good. *Get hold of yourself, man!* he silently willed. *I need you. The legion needs you!*

"It's the deserters themselves!" howled Domincus, suddenly pointing to a small craft approaching the anchored flagship. Cordell and the captains stepped to the gunwale and saw a native canoe emerging from the nearby stands of delta trees. Halloran and Daggrande were plainly visible, alone in the boat.

"Bishou Domincus, we must talk," said Cordell quietly.

Even hushed, his voice had the strength of a steel rod. The captains stirred behind him, and the general knew that he needed to tread carefully between the vengeful cleric and the pragmatic needs of his men.

The Bishou glared at Cordell suspiciously, but he knew enough not to bluster loudly before the legionnaires. "Surely you don't mean to welcome them back!" he hissed in disbelief. "The young man was guilty of criminal cowardice in allowing my daughter to be slain. And both of them deserted our men in the face of enemy attack!" The cleric's voice grew shrill with his anger.

I cannot antagonize him now. I need him tomorrow. Cordell sighed, a heavy and obvious gesture. "Your daughter's death is a great tragedy, my friend. And to be sure, she had been entrusted to young Halloran's care at the time. This, then, must mark against him.

"But he is a skilled lancer, a natural horseman, and a brave soldier. And Daggrande is my best captain! You cannot claim both of these warriors on the eve of battle!"

"But the guards told us! They disappeared during—"

"They were snatched by sorcery! Even through your anger, you should recognize that!" The Bishou turned away sullenly as Cordell continued. "I will give you Halloran, in chains. After the battle, you can punish him as you deem fit. But Daggrande goes free, with no sanction from you. And you will not refer to either of these men as cowards, in my presence or in the presence of any member of the legion. Do I make myself clear?"

Obey me! The captain-general focused his will and his command upon the cleric. *We need you, Bishou. But we need Daggrande, too.*

"Very well," Domincus grunted. "I want Halloran clapped in irons and locked below. I will say nothing to the men. I have no need to punish the dwarf."

"Good." Cordell nodded, still annoyed that his lieutenant's vengeance would cost him a good officer. "Now let us see to the landing."

The Bishou joined the captains, and Cordell summoned his cabin boy. The lad listened carefully while his commander outlined the preparations to be made in fashioning a cell belowdecks for Halloran.

* * * * *

The golden eagle banner fluttered proudly atop the *Falcon*'s mainmast. Halloran felt a surge of emotion as he approached that flag and the ship below it. Tears clouded his eyes, and he saluted the pennant as the canoe drew alongside the *Falcon*. Shame, too, threatened to overwhelm him. The tragedy of Martine's loss weighed heavily on his mind. He did not know what to expect when he boarded the flagship.

The carrack rode quietly on the placid lagoon, and Daggrande and he had no difficulty ascending the rope ladders dropped to them from the deck above.

Halloran stopped in shock as he stepped aboard the *Falcon*'s deck. Without a word, four brawny sergeants seized him and clapped metal cuffs about his wrists and ankles.

Hal bit his tongue. He saw the glowering figure of Bishou Domincus beyond his guards and suspected the explanation. Perhaps he deserved no better treatment, he told himself.

"Here, now!" growled Daggrande, turning to defend his friend. But Captain-General Cordell stepped up to him and raised a placating hand. The dwarf glowered suspiciously at his commander. Cordell's words struck Halloran with greater force than any physical blow could possibly deliver.

"Captain Halloran, you are charged with desertion in the face of the enemy. You will have a chance to speak in your own defense after the matters of tomorrow are resolved. Until then you are confined to a brig belowdecks of the *Falcon*."

Cordell looked Halloran squarely in the eyes as he spoke. The young man sought some hidden message there, some gleam of communication that would tell him that Cordell knew he was not a coward, would not have fled a battle. This man's high regard meant more to Halloran than anything in the world.

But instead he saw inky-black depths that showed him only the strength of the commander's murky soul.

"Your sword, sir!" Cordell's voice strained as he barked at Halloran.

Numbly the young captain ungirded Helmstooth. Slowly,

looking at the weapon in disbelief, he handed it to his commander. Cordell turned away from him, setting the weapon aside before turning back to the assembled legionnaires.

"Command of the Pennant Lancers is conferred to Captain Alvarro, effective immediately."

Halloran heard his unit transferred to the oily hands of the unscrupulous horseman, a final outrage as he stepped through the hatchway toward his dark and musty cell.

❧ 15 ❧

IMPRISONED

The desert stretched in all directions, bleak, dry, and hot. Where once Poshtli had seen a myriad of wondrous colors, hues of gold and red and brown in a million varieties of shadow and light, now he saw only emptiness, wasteland, and death.

His waterskin had been empty for days. No stranger to the desert, the Eagle Knight had survived by hacking the plump cactus known as the Sand Mother wherever he could find it. The sweet moisture within the plant had sustained him until the desert became so dry that even the Sand Mother could not live.

Poshtli's eagle-feather mantle spread around him as he slumped to the ground. He squeezed a handful of powdery rock, crushing it into sand as if he would force water from the stones. He began to wonder, for the first time, if the desert had defeated him.

The eagle feathers, black and white . . . now covered with dust, they could spread into wings and carry him from this place of death and despair. He shook his head weakly.

No! he thought determinedly. I have set out on foot, and on foot I will complete this journey. The god, the Plumed Father himself, had spoken to Poshtli in a dream, commending him to this quest. Somehow he would find the silver wheel, the artifact that might explain the meaning of the strangers' coming. If they did not herald the return of Qotal, their arrival still was a thing of great significance to the True World.

It was Poshtli's mission to find that truth, to learn the nature of that significance. How he would learn it, and if he would even survive his quest, were just now points of some doubt.

Then the rocks began to talk.

*   *   *   *   *

The longboat slipped through the darkness to nestle against the seaward side of the *Falcon*. A dark figure grabbed a line and quickly pulled himself onto the deck. He nodded curtly at the legionnaires guarding the ship and went to the door of the forward cabin.

Bishou Domincus opened the door in a wash of candle-light. He admitted the visitor and then quickly closed the portal, darkening the deck.

"So good of you to come, Captain," greeted the Bishou, pouring two glasses of brandy.

"I got your message. What do you want?" grunted Alvarro.

The Bishou frowned, his long face creasing unpleasantly. He narrowed his eyes as he handed Alvarro a glass. "I fear that justice may not be served in a certain case of treason within the legion."

Alvarro's gapped teeth split into a sly grin of understanding. "Go on," he urged.

"You are in a position to benefit from swift justice in the case in question, and I desire such justice to be done. Believe me when I tell you that you owe command of the lancers to my intervention and strong recommendation."

Now Alvarro's red beard twisted into a frown. He did not like this turn in the conversation, and the Bishou immediately changed his tactics.

"If Halloran were to meet his end aboard ship, before his trial—while I am safely ashore, with Cordell—I can ensure that the investigation into the . . . execution would be minimal."

Alvarro turned and paced two steps in the small cabin, then turned back. "I want more than revenge. I want gold," he hissed.

"I'm certain that we can agree upon a price," replied the Bishou.

* * * * *

The featherbanners streamed in the air, lifted by *pluma* into a weightless colorful cloud over the army of Payit. The whole plain of Ulatos became a sea of shades and hues. Great fans swirled over the most important leaders, the chiefs of a thousand men. From all the lands of the Payit, from the depths of the jungles and the breadth of the wide coastal savannah, the warriors gathered on the field beside Ulatos Lagoon.

Gultec stood at the heart of the gathering with several other Jaguar Knights, on the flat roof of the large house they had claimed as their meeting place. The whistles and shell trumpets of different bands shrilled and honked in the growing twilight, and new arrivals often marched in under torchlight, advancing like slow, flaming serpents from the surrounding jungles.

It made the knight uneasy, this gathering of the entire army in the open, a mile from the camp of the strangers. Dense jungle and the mangaroo swamp of the delta surrounded them, and Gultec knew they could conceal ten thousand men or more close to the enemy route of advance. But Caxal, the Revered Counselor, flushed with his insulted pride, had ordered otherwise.

The enemy forces had quickly come ashore in their longboats, deploying into companies and advancing a hundred yards from shore. For some moments, it had seemed that they intended to attack at nightfall, a tactic unthinkable to Gultec and the other warriors of Maztica. But now it seemed as if the strangers, like normal men, would wait until sunrise to fight.

Fires marked the scope of his army's camp, and Gultec indeed felt a surge of pride as he saw the vast mass of warriors across the plain. Twenty-five thousandmen, each composed of ten companies of a hundred, had answered the alarm of invasion. They were all independent formations, each commanded by a highly ranked Jaguar or Eagle. Each hundredmen included an auxiliary force of perhaps a half-dozen Eagles or Jaguars, knights who had proven exceptional valor in many campaigns.

Some bands were armed with bows and arrows, others with slings. These they would position carefully to bombard the enemy. Then the many thousands with javelins or *macas* would close to complete the capture.

At least, that was the plan.

* * * * *

Erix walked quickly among the fields, passing the houses of farmers. She did not want to go to Ulatos, but neither did she want to sleep on the shore of some canal.

A plump woman patted mayzcakes before one of the residences she passed. It was a small house, adjacent to a narrow canal. But it was freshly whitewashed, and the green fronds of the roof shone with bright freshness. The woman waved cheerily, and Erix waved back and smiled. She hesitated, and the gray-haired matron called her over.

"I am Tzilla," she explained, nodding politely as Erix introduced herself. "Why is a pretty girl like you walking alone at such an hour?" Tzilla asked. Her tone was teasing, but Erix sensed real concern in her voice.

"I am alone here, and I seek a place to sleep."

"My house is your house, my daughter," said Tzilla formally. "Will you share my table?"

"I would be honored, mother," Erix replied gladly. In moments, Tzilla put her to work stirring the beans bubbling in a clay pot among the coals of a fire. The woman sliced peppers and tomatoes, and soon the pair sat comfortably on reed mats and ate a delicious meal.

Erix was surprised that they were joined by neither Tzilla's husband nor anyone else. "Forgive my impertinence, but you have a very large house. Are you here alone?"

Tzilla looked surprised. "My husband and sons gather with their hundredmen on the plain before Ulatos. Have you not heard?"

"Of the strangers? To be sure. I have seen them."

"But you do not know," said Tzilla with a sly look, "that the warriors of Payit have gathered on the plain, very near the strangers. Our army will destroy them tomorrow!"

Erix's face betrayed her shock even before she stammered a reply. "So . . . soon? There will be battle tomorrow?" The thought of the battle at Twin Visages, multiplied a hundredfold, chilled her.

Tzilla nodded sagely, her voice dropping to a conspiratorial whisper. "These strangers are great savages! They attacked a group of priests on the shore. They kidnap our women! They fight like demons, but they are men and can be killed."

Erix sat stunned at the swift outburst of rumor. "All of the men of Ulatos, and those within a day's march in all directions, have gathered here! Never has the Payit nation put together such a force!" Tzilla talked on, detailing the pageantry and colors.

But Erixitl had trouble listening. She remembered the metal armor that shattered spears, the silver weapons that cleaved shield and bone like grass. She saw the savage faces of the legionnaires, their tight discipline. She remembered a bare two dozen slaying hundreds of Payit.

Suddenly Tzilla's description faltered as she described the *pluma* banner depicting a green parrot, the symbol of a nearby village.

"I'm sorry," Erix said, noticing the woman looking absently at the dough before her. Tzilla shook her head, and Erix saw tears in the woman's eyes.

"I babble like an old woman, and I'm far from an old woman yet!" Tzilla forced herself to laugh, but the sound was hollow and she quickly gave up. "I am so terribly frightened!"

"I am, too," Erix said. "I was hoping there could be peace. I wanted to make peace!"

"It is too late," sighed Tzilla. She looked at Erixitl with surprise as the younger woman climbed to her feet. "Where are you going?"

"I must go to the army!" Erix cried, suddenly infused with an idea. Perhaps it was not too late! Perhaps tomorrow does not have to be a day of war!

"Don't be a madwoman!" Tzilla seemed truly alarmed. "Caxal is determined to avenge the insult to his priests! And Gultec, who commands the men of Ulatos, is said to be eager for a fight. The armies will be in a frenzy of dancing tonight. The gods themselves couldn't stop that battle."

"I know of Gultec," admitted Erixitl, suddenly feeling foolish. "He is certainly the most fearsome warrior I have ever seen. . . ."

She trailed off, guilty with the lie, remembering Halloran and his legion. Yet there was no need to terrify this woman with tales of the deadly enemy who faced her husband and sons. At the same time, she sensed the futility of her mission. Gultec would merely turn her over to the priests of Zaltec, and the battle would proceed.

"No matter, for tonight," soothed Tzilla. "We can only pray to our gods, and what the gods will, shall be."

*　*　*　*　*

The heavy door slammed. Halloran collapsed glumly against the wooden bulkhead in the bilge of the *Falcon*, his shoulders slumped to keep his head from knocking against the low ceiling beams. The chains around his wrists and ankles chafed, holding him upright, his arms shackled to the wall.

But he took no notice of his physical pain. Far more grievous was the spiritual hurt, the sense of betrayal that had numbed all other sensations and left his soul teetering beside a yawning black chasm of despair. The legion was his home, his family . . . even his life! And now it had turned upon him, condemned him for a falsehood that Cordell could not help but recognize.

My general! How could you do this to me? Then his emotions surged through his body, tearing tears from his eyes and sobs from his throat. Hanging limply from his chains, he wept until he could find no more tears.

The soft swaying of the carrack at anchor slowly soothed him. The stink of bilgewater thickened the air around him, and finally he began to take note of his surroundings.

It must be dark now, he guessed. Thin beams of light filtered into his cell through cracks in the floorboards above him, but it seemed more like lamplight than daylight. His tiny compartment offered no amenities, not even a wooden bench. The manacles had been screwed directly into the timber behind him.

The feeling of hopelessness left him exhausted. What good were his struggles when the capriciousness of fate could place him in circumstances like these?

"A curse upon Helm!" he hissed. The gods, he saw, were nothing more than man's excuses, his reasons for doing things terrible and inhuman. Vain, unpredictable and everchanging, the gods were no source of comfort to him.

A man needed something more real, Halloran saw. Something tangible, like the strength of his arm or the keen edge of his steel. Even the arcane power of magic was something *real*, something that could be counted on, even when things were blackest. A god might as soon turn his back upon a follower as listen to his troubles.

Hal thought again of his magic studies under Arquiuius, which seemed like a lifetime ago. What were those strange words he had drilled on so hard to learn, the words of the magic missile spell? He shook his head ruefully. Spells and weapons were as useless as the gods to him now. He was left with his wits, and his wits didn't seem to be functioning at the highest level.

Hesitantly he jerked his arm, wincing against the pain in his raw wrist. But the chain moved! Again and again he tugged, ignoring the blood that now spattered across his skin from the chafing. The bolt had been sunk into the wood between two beams, a very insecure arrangement! Now he finally pulled it free.

He looked at the metal cuff and saw that it closed with a simple latch, impossible to open with the cuffed hand but no obstacle to a man with one hand free. In seconds he unlocked both of his wrist irons, and his ankles followed shortly thereafter.

Dimly he heard the creaking of longboats, the gentle thump of wood against the *Falcon*'s hull. He heard the soft nickering of horses, and he knew that the legion was debarking its lancers. The ache returned to his heart when he realized they would ride to battle without him on the morrow. He remembered Alvarro's gloating grin as the chains had been locked around Hal's limbs. What would be the fate of his beloved lancers under such brutal command?

The light filtering through the overhead beams suddenly disappeared. He heard a cabin door close above, and he noticed that the ship had become perceptibly quieter. Most of the legion must already be ashore.

But what could he do now? He was slightly more comfortable, to be sure, and the exertion of escaping from his irons had distracted him from his despair. Halloran slumped against the bulkhead and thought.

Could he betray the orders of his general? Wasn't it enough that he had been sentenced to this cell? If he escaped, then he truly would be a deserter, worthy of every epithet in the Bishou's vocabulary.

His reverie jerked to a halt as he heard a soft noise. There it was again—a subtle click of metal, coming from the door to his cell. Someone's turning a key in the lock . . . and he's doing it secretly.

For a moment, his heart lifted with the thought of escape. Then caution took over, and he quickly leaned against the wall, feigning his shackled position. The door swung open, and he caught the unmistakable odor of a horseman. The man stepped into the cell and then closed and locked the door behind him.

Alvarro unshuttered a lamp very slightly, but it was enough to fill the cabin with light. The man's red hair looked black in the shadows, but the dagger in his hand gleamed like true steel.

"You'll die unmourned, traitor!" he hissed, thrusting the dagger toward Hal's chest, knowing his victim was shackled to the wall.

Hal dodged the thrust and punched Alvarro, hard, on the nose. His left fist knocked a precious tooth from the man's already shrunken gums, and the attacker slumped, unconscious, to the deck.

Alvarro's gloved hand fell open, and Hal glimpsed a small key. He grabbed for it, but his aim was errant in the dim light, and the object fell to the floor, slipping between two planks into the bilge before he could catch it.

With a hushed groan, Halloran slumped against the bulkhead. The sudden tingle of victory in mortal combat quickly faded in light of the lost key. And even if he had the key, he wondered, could he bring himself to flee the legion? Where could he go?

But if he stayed, he became Domincus's prisoner, a sop thrown to the cleric by Cordell in compensation for the loss of his daughter. Now he knew the nature of that compensation, and though he had foiled one murderous attempt, how long would his luck last?

The answer was obvious. Perhaps if he could escape, he might even find some way of proving his worth to Cordell. To stay here meant certain death. He picked up Alvarro's knife and stuffed it into his belt. He found a pouch full of gold coins at the man's waist, taking it as just punishment.

Next he examined the door to his cell, finding it locked securely. He had no skill, and no tools to even attempt to pry open the lock.

He bumped his head and suddenly remembered the cracks in the overhead bulkhead. Perhaps the low ceiling might prove to be an asset. Stepping over Alvarro's unconscious body, he felt along the boards. There! What was that? With a careful examination with his fingertips, he recognized the shape of a latch, and soon he had traced the outline of a trapdoor beside it.

It took but a minute to release the catch. Halloran then pushed upward with all of his strength, but he could not make the wooden platform move. Collapsing against the bulkhead, he stared upward in mute frustration. He sensed freedom, if he could but push his way up and out of here.

Awkwardly he braced his feet against the hull and his back against the inside wall. Lifting himself off the floor, he pressed against the trapdoor again, but again it would not move. Angrily he punched the wood, bruising his knuckles. But that time he felt something move.

Pushing again, he felt the trapdoor move heavily upward. It had been stuck, the wood moist and moldy with age, and his blow had broken it free. Grunting from the energy of his exertion, he pulled himself upward and squirmed from beneath the trapdoor.

He felt something smothering his face, but he quickly realized that he had emerged underneath a rug. Crawling forward a few feet, he at last felt cool air on his face. In an instant, he pulled free of the rug and stood up, looking about the small cabin.

He found the porthole and threw open the hatch. Harsh white moonlight instantly spilled through the opening, lighting the inside of the cabin. Halloran knew immediately that this was the cabin of the elf-wizard, Darien.

A crowded desk was covered with sheaves of parchment and scrolls. Many candles stood in holders around the room. A small chest on the floor stood open, and within it, he saw the tops of a dozen or more glass vials.

The most interesting feature of the room was the porthole. He estimated that he could squirm through the opening with little difficulty, dropping into the warm water eight or ten feet below. His plan developed quickly: He would swim to shore and find the legion, concealing himself until the battle. Then he would await the proper opportunity to enter the fight and redeem himself.

Of course, that opportunity might not be instantly forthcoming. He suddenly realized that he might be stranded ashore for some time before he would have a chance to confront Cordell under the right circumstances. He would have to prepare for that event.

A bundle of leather caught his eye, and he hefted it, finding a sturdy backpack with a heavy reinforced panel in the bottom. Suppressing a guilty twinge, he took several bottles from the chest of vials, hoping that he could decipher the labels in daylight. He knew enough of magic potions to know that those bottles, if his suspicions were correct, might save his life.

He searched for food but found nothing he could take as rations. He did not want to emerge from the cabin to search the rest of the ship, so he decided to make do with what food he could find ashore. He did find a length of rope and a blanket, both of which he stuffed into the backpack.

Finally he found a large leather bladder, designed to hold water or wine. But it would hold air just as well, and he hung it outside the porthole and inflated it.

Holding the backpack and bladder outside the porthole, he pushed himself forward, twisting slightly to get his broad shoulders through the opening. His legs followed easily, and he slid awkwardly down the hull, striking the water with a loud splash.

For several minutes, he bobbed in the shadow of the high stern, certain the noise of his fall would attract attention. But no sound disturbed the darkness above. In the distance, he could hear the sounds of the legion settling into camp—the barking of hounds, the shouts of officers, the curses of sergeants, and the crude laughter of the men.

Halloran turned away from that sound as he swam across the placid lagoon. Ahead of him beckoned the line of mangaroo trees that marked the edge of Ulatos Delta.

* * * * *

Erix slept lightly on the pallet Tzilla provided, not through any lack of comfort but because of a nagging restlessness that allowed her no peace. She arose before dawn, washing quietly in the clear canal beside the house. She wrapped her mantle around her shoulders and was starting past the house when she heard movement.

"Here, my daughter," Tzilla whispered, stepping out of the doorway to press a heavy bundle in Erixitl's hands. She felt the pliable softness of mayzcakes and smelled spicy beans.

"Thank you, my mother," she replied, drawing a warm pleasure from the ritual exchange between a young woman and a matron.

"Travel well and swiftly, girl. These are troubled days in the land of the Payit. May your god watch over you!"

Erix bowed deeply. "Your kindness is blessing enough. I hope your husband and sons return from the battle unwounded and with many prisoners."

She started down the trail in the first light of dawn. The mist still filtered among the palms lining the trail and the clumps of mangaroo trees to her right. She skirted the swamp of the delta, then turned westward before she reached Ulatos. She wanted to witness the plain, with its great and irresistible array of military splendor, before she returned again to the great city of the Payit.

Passing between the city and the mangaroos, she noticed that the mist had dispersed. Then she saw a haze of color before her, and she knew she had found the armies on the Ulatos Plain.

She could see little of the troops themselves, for the slowly undulating ground concealed them. But to her left, the air was aflutter with brilliant feather streamers, the whirling fans of *pluma*, and the great banners of the war chiefs. To her right, she saw the pennants and flags of the strangers, smaller in number and less colorful to be sure, but just as martial.

Then the sounds of trumpets and conch-shell horns, whistles and shouts, the clashing of spears against shields as the Payits thundered the challenge, all echoed across the clearing. Erix settled down to wait, noticing that the field was fringed with many other people, old folks, some women, and a few youths not quite old enough to serve as apprentice warriors. All had come in curiosity or fascination to see the strangers and watch the Payit army destroy them.

And then the pennants and flags began to move.

* * * * *

From the chronicles of Coton:

In the hope of the Plumed Father's return, may he know the depths of our need!

Now does Naltecona fast again. He makes many sacrifices at dusk and plans many more for the dawn. All of his sages hold their tongues, and none dares offer counsel.

The Revered Counselor awaits the decision before Ulatos,

with a sense of calm that has previously eluded him. But he has convinced himself of his own truth with single-minded determination, and he will allow the battle to determine his mind.

His decision is based on two points. Each is simple, and each is so deeply ingrained in Naltecona's mind that none can offer the slightest voice of dissent, save upon penalty of his life.

If the strangers are destroyed, they cannot be gods.

If the strangers destroy the Payit, Naltecona will know their godhood. Then will he prepare to welcome Qotal back to his ancestral throne.

Ulatos and Helmsport

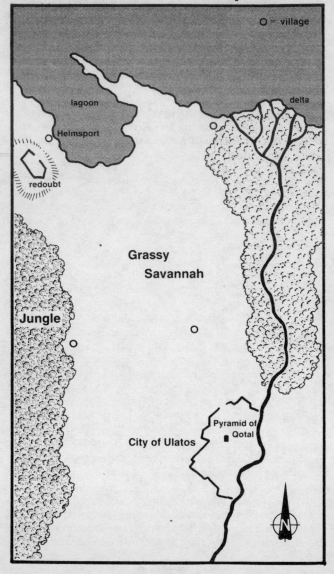

O = village

lagoon

Helmsport

delta

redoubt

Grassy
Savannah

Jungle

Pyramid of
Qotal

City of Ulatos

N

☙ 16 ☙

FEATHERS AND STEEL

Emotion tightened Gultec's throat as he absorbed the spectacle. Never in memorable history had so many warriors of the Payit gathered in one place, for one campaign. The whistles and shouts, the crashing of weapons against shields, the pounding of feet against the ground, all created an aura so overpowering that the Jaguar Knight could do nothing but allow the sensations to wash over him.

The colors dazzled his eyes. The pennants and plumes and symbols and banners all floated magically. Many of the warriors danced as they passed him, and their tall feathered headdresses swayed like graceful birds. Jaguar Knights prowled among the companies, their spotted armor appearing clearly for a moment and then vanishing again in the whirl of color. Eagle Knights preened and strutted, proudly aloof from the activity around them.

The grandeur of the army overcame all of the chieftains standing on the housetop, and for several minutes, none of them spoke. There was little they could do, for the moment, in any event.

Gultec finally began to see the army, more than twenty thousand strong, in a more practical eye. He alone among the dozen or so chiefs here had fought the invaders already. Gultec felt that he alone possessed a satisfactory respect for their prowess.

But even he had trouble imagining the strangers, numbering perhaps half a thousand, standing against the array of force around him. Forty Payit would attack for every one of the strangers. Surely they would overwhelm and destroy the foe!

True, the attack would be made across the open plain by Caxal's order. Still, Gultec had managed to interject one measure of caution into the plan, if the men of Ulatos had the discipline to obey.

In the leading division of the army, marked clearly by banners of golden feathers, advanced three long columns, each a thousand men of the city's own guard, men Gultec and Lok had trained for years. Now those men had been given a strange and difficult task.

Their Jaguar and Eagle chiefs had ordered these troops to advance toward the strangers, to make great noise and show, and then to swiftly withdraw when the strangers attacked. The command was exceptionally difficult because the warriors considered such a withdrawal insulting and unwarlike.

Gultec had done his best to insist upon the tactic, for he had placed thousands of slingers and bowmen behind this first rank. He had assuaged the insulted warriors' pride with the promise that, when the missiles had done their work, the men of Ulatos would be the first to meet the enemy in melee.

Now he could only wonder if they would have the discipline to obey.

* * * * *

"They come on quickly in the center, my general," announced the lookout. Cordell saw the advance plainly but did not admonish the man. Better to receive too much information during a battle than too little.

The captain-general had just joined the lookout atop the observation tower his men had constructed during the night. The sturdy square structure, thirty feet high, had been raised so that the general and his officers would have a good view of the flat battlefield.

Darien and the Bishou remained below, together with Cordell's signal officers and their clusters of flags. Now, as the haze lifted, he saw the surge of color opposite his center, like a wave of silk ribbons flickering across the ground.

Arrayed to meet them stood the sword-and-buckler men of Captain Garrant, protecting both flanks. Behind and between the swordsmen, Daggrande's crossbows stood in compact ranks. Other companies of swordsmen and longbows stood farther to each flank. But the five hundred men looked considerably overmatched by the mass of natives across the plain.

Hidden to the rear of the legion, near the base of the square tower, were Cordell's strongest weapons, or so he hoped. Gathered in four wings of ten or twelve riders each, the lancers remained hidden from the enemy in several ravines back from the shore. Each wing could charge into the fray within moments of receiving its order.

But the horses would stay hidden for now. Instead, Cordell would let the native warriors taste the cold death of the legion infantry.

The advance in the center became a charge, great blocks of spearmen and swordsmen each clearly marked by the colorful swath of its headdresses. The native army swept across the plain, thousands of men rushing Garrant's and Daggrande's companies amid a tremendous cacophony of sound.

"Signal the charge . . . for Garrant and Daggrande only. Now!" Cordell barked. In the next instant, two flagmen raised the pennants of these companies, selecting for each the banner with the bright yellow fringe.

"We'll see what these savages are made of," Cordell said, to no one in particular.

*　*　*　*　*

"It's the yellow flag, Captain!"

"Company, advance! On the double!" Daggrande bellowed the command without bothering to check the corporal's observation behind them. He had served with Cordell long enough to have expected the order.

He saw the swordsmen advancing to the right and left. He ordered a dozen men of his company to fall back to each side, providing missile protection for the outside flanks of Captain Garrant's company.

"Tighten up there!" he called as his ranks started to waver. Sergeants growled their way along the line, keeping the crossbowmen advancing in tightly packed straight lines, even at a steady jog. The dwarves, especially, huffed and panted to maintain the pace, but Daggrande knew they would not falter.

The swordsmen on their flanks also remained tightly packed as the natives howled closer and closer. Garrant's men suddenly broke into a run, hoarsely invoking the name of Helm as they charged.

And then, before the two groups could clash, the natives paused. We're breaking them already! Daggrande glimpsed a brief prospect of victory, but immediately discarded it in alarm.

The colorful horde slowed its rush, then stopped altogether, still a hundred paces or more away from the charging swordsmen. They continued to taunt and whistle and clash their weapons against their shields, even as they started to fall back. Then they quickly sprinted away from the armored swordsmen, but Daggrande sensed that these were not troops in terrified retreat.

Indeed, so did Captain Garrant.

"Halt!" Garrant bellowed to his companies as the spearmen drifted away. Most of the swordsmen finally ceased their charge, though a few still lumbered on.

"Stop, you idiots!" The captain finally collected his companies, forming again into tight ranks and falling slowly back around the crossbows.

Suddenly the plain around them swarmed with new troops, warriors who had been lying concealed in the tall grass while the legionnaires charged. These attackers quickly sent a shower of stone-tipped arrows soaring toward the companies. Other natives raced forward, swirling slings and sending heavy stones flying toward the invaders.

"Fire! Reload! Fire at will!" Daggrande bellowed his command and cracked off a bolt into the mass of archers before his troops. He bent to crank another shaft into the weapon as the enemy missiles began to fall.

"I'm hit!"

"Helm's curses, I'm down!"

Men cried out all around Daggrande. Arrows slashed into the legionnaires, but their armor stopped most of the stone heads from penetrating deeply. The stones from the slings were more painful, occasionally crushing a cheekbone or smashing an eye with a blow to the face.

Daggrande's men reloaded their weapons, ignoring the steady barrage of missiles showering around them, and fired another volley into the natives. While the arrows of the Payit inflicted painful wounds, the crossbows of the legionnaires cut a broad swath of death through the ranks of archers. The heavy steel bolts lanced through the quilted cotton armor as if it were not there. Sometimes a bolt passed clear through a victim to inflict further damage beyond.

Still the natives stood firm, firing again and again. The wounds became more severe, and Daggrande saw several of his men fall and lie still, or writhe in excruciating agony. Their own volleys of steel death slashed into the native archers, and hundreds of bodies soon bled their lives onto the field. But always more archers raced forward, more slingers advanced, to step across their fallen comrades and shoot.

"Company, advance! Charge!" Daggrande heard Garrant's command and immediately echoed it with his own. Only by driving these archers back could his own formation retire safely.

The swordsmen rushed forward. The crossbowmen raised their weapons and fired, laboriously reloading as they, too, broke into a run. The name of Helm resounded from every throat.

The archers stood bravely, launching missiles at point-blank range before they died from the swift strikes of Garrant's swordsmen. In scarce moments, the legionnaires had hacked their way through the bowmen and slingers. With still greater shouts to the glory of their god, the two companies of legionnaires rushed toward the bulk of the native army.

* * * * *

Gultec stood amazed at the carnage inflicted upon the archers, at first by the metal darts of the invaders and then by their long silver knives. But now these men had rushed far ahead of their companions. The men of Ulatos stood ready to meet them, javelins and *macas* poised for combat. The warriors who had performed Gultec's opening feint now closed to crash into the strangers' ranks.

The enemy warriors expanded their line to meet the natives. The men with the metal darts dropped their casters and took up metal daggers, long weapons but not as great as those carried by the men with the metal shields.

But all of those keen weapons cut easily through the armor and skin covering the men of Ulatos. Even Jaguar Knights, protected by *hishna*, talonmagic armored hides of the great cats, fell easily before the deadly silver blades.

Still, Gultec knew they had to exploit this opportunity, even as the men of Ulatos died to provide it. "Now!" he urged Lok beside him.

The Eagle Knight hesitated for just a moment before nodding. "Now!" he cried, raising his fist. Behind him, his standard-bearer twirled his great feathered symbol. "Send in the Eagles!"

More than two hundred warriors, resplendent in their black-and-white-feathered costumes, capped with the colorful beaked helmets, waited behind the house where the chiefs stood. Now these warriors suddenly wavered and crouched. Their costumes blossomed into true wings, and the forceful beat of their power sent miniature whirlwinds through the grass.

The eagles rose into the air, shrieking, their voices harsh and powerful enough to penetrate the din of the battlefield below. Black and white feathers shone gloriously on each of the magnificent birds. Their claws extended, they slowly climbed into the sky. Soaring forward, they passed over the melee raging on the ground. Legionnaire and Payit alike fell back, gasping for breath and watching the graceful formation.

Then the eagles tucked their wings and plummeted earthward, diving toward the bare ground behind Daggrande's and Garrant's companies.

*   *   *   *   *

"Time for you to go, my dear," Cordell said quietly. He and Darien stood at the front of the observation tower, watching the approach of the eagles for a moment, seeing them settle toward the earth behind the two companies. The rest of the legion's infantry advanced steadily on each flank, but Daggrande's and Garrant's companies were still far ahead.

The elf woman was completely swathed in her hood and robe to protect her albino skin from the hot sun. Nevertheless, she heard Cordell and nodded.

In the next second, she disappeared from sight, vanishing with a sorcerous suddenness that unnerved the signal officers with Cordell on his battle tower.

Her teleportation spell took her instantly to the ground below the descending eagles. She swiftly looked skyward, squinting against the bright haze that nearly blinded her. Holding up a finger, she pointed at the lowest eagle and barked a harsh command.

A sizzling missile of light bolted from her finger to explode in the breast of the bird. It screeched and tried to arrest its descent, but another blast, and another, sizzled into its bare flesh. With a pathetic flutter, the bird's wings collapsed and it crashed to earth, a shapeless pile of feathers.

Darien turned her attention immediately to another bird, shearing off its wing with several more magic missiles. At the same time, she sensed more of the birds circling behind her.

Wheeling like a swordsman, Darien snatched Icetongue from its sling at her belt. Raising the wand, she uttered the command word, once, twice, and again, moving the wand slightly each time.

At each command, the wand winked its soft, silent attack. A wash of bright, cool light surged outward in a cone from the end of the wand. The frosty blast enshrouded the eagles and killed them with cold, shocking the knights with its supernatural, deadly power.

A half dozen birds fell from the first blast, frozen stiff in the air, with their wings spread and beaks gaping, and then smashed to pieces when they crashed to earth. More died with the second blast. The rest of the eagles shrilled in rage and closed in. More and more of them fell to Icetongue, but now they soared into an enclosing circle, talons extended. They would destroy this alien sorcerer with their god-given bodies, then become humans to strike the enemy soldiers from behind.

Darien abruptly dropped Icetongue, letting the wand swing freely from its thong. She stood straight and still as the ring of eagles soared inward, shrieking.

Then she raised her hands to the sky, and as her hands came up, an orange ring of fire erupted from the ground around her, sheltering Darien inside a circle of deadly heat.

Many of the eagles were too close to avoid the fiery wall. Eager fingers of fire tore feathers from their wings, ripped down from their proud feathered breasts. The eagles fell by the score, scarred and singed and blistered. Many of these were not killed by their wounds, but Darien ignored them, knowing they would be no further threat.

The surviving eagles, less than half the original force, settled somberly to the ground, well away from Darien. She watched them as they blurred and expanded into their human forms, quickly moving to surround her.

Darien took the opportunity to cast a fireball spell, incinerating several more of the warriors. Then, knowing that she had done her job, she teleported back to Cordell's side, leaving the Eagle Knights to close their empty ring.

*　*　*　*　*

"Every man must attack! We can hold nothing back!" Gultec was the first to recover his voice after the chiefs had seen the devastation of their proud eagles. Now he leaped from the rooftop to the yard below, brandishing his *maca* above his head and howling the deep and resonant challenge of the Jaguar Knight.

The other chieftains instantly followed. Standards hastily passed from the rooftops to eager hands. All across the field, the great army of Payit surged forward, following their feathered banners to war.

Gultec raced forward toward the enemy. A red haze fell across his eyes as he pictured the slaughtering done, the slaughtering still to do. His war cries came as inarticulate howls, but they touched a deep and warlike nerve among the warriors. Fresh thousands surged toward the forward companies of the invaders. Many more Payits advanced to engage the white warriors on each flank.

Gultec surged into battle with a sense of euphoric joy. The moment of decision had come, and it was his decision. All around him, the noise and color of his countrymen gave him strength and delight.

The Payits surged around the forward companies now, surrounding them. Gultec felt a warm rush of admiration for the fighting of these soldiers, their tight formations, their weapons of unbelievable might. He would go to them now as a warrior.

His destiny propelled him, told him that this fight would be the climax of his life.

* * * * *

Halloran reached the shelter of the mangaroo swamp just as dawn's light filtered through the overhanging verdure. Still resting on the inflated bladder, he drifted easily along the winding stretches of water, searching.

Soon he found that which he sought: a lone canoe. The vessel floated motionless and empty, tied to a rickety wooden landing, with no one in sight. Hal slipped over the gunwale of the craft and unlashed the twine rope before paddling quickly away.

He saw enough of the sunlight to gauge his directions, working his way to the western fringe of the delta. There his ears confirmed his sense of direction.

The chaos of battle noise in the distance was an unnatural

din, beautiful and frightening at the same time. Familiar sounds like the blare of trumpets mingled with the shrill noises of the natives.

The mangaroo passage grew too narrow for the canoe and Halloran climbed out, worming his way toward the battle. Soon the entwining trees parted to reveal the grassy plain. Halloran stayed well back among the trees, for he saw several natives before him, apparently gathered to watch the battle.

He found an unusually stout mangaroo. It was not tall, but he was able to climb to perhaps twice his height.

It was enough to give him a clear view of the carnage.

* * * * *

Daggrande stabbed and slashed, carefully coordinating his movements with the legionnaires on either side. The company fought bravely, but was forced to slowly give ground, forced backward by the tremendous press of bodies. Even should each man slay ten of the enemy, it seemed twenty more would step into the gap.

Now the veteran captain sensed the threat to the flanks of his company as the tremendous numbers of the attackers swept around him to the right and left. He tried to hasten the withdrawal, but dared not move too quickly. He knew, as did all the officers, that it was only their disciplined formation that gave them hope of survival against the mass of enemy warriors.

The prospects of that survival grew more bleak with each passing minute. Brave legionnaires fell to the ground, their bodies dragged down among the ranks of the natives. The withdrawal came to an abrupt halt as the natives swept around the rear to surround Daggrande's and Garrant's companies.

Daggrande thought of his commander in his distant tower. He knew Cordell could see the situation.

Now, my general! thought the dwarf. Now, or it will be too late!

* * * * *

"Now, by Helm!"

Cordell's shout anticipated the dipping banners, the pennants of his lancers, by a split second. The signal flashed as the flags swirled down and up. Trumpets blasted from each of his four wings of horsemen.

The hooves of the chargers pounded the turf as they quickly darted from the ravines. Each wing spread in a line abreast of each other. The general saw Captain Alvarro leading the first wing. Black streamers tied to his helmet clearly marked his position for the rest of the riders. Several lanky greyhounds ran at the heels of the horses, barking excitedly.

Cordell unconsciously held his breath. The extent of the native attack, the organized tactics and huge formations, stunned and awed him. He had grievously underestimated them.

Now he had one attack left. If the lancers failed, the Golden Legion faced imminent destruction.

* * * * *

Gultec found Lok standing quietly in the midst of the melee. The Eagle Knight's feathered armor was singed and bedraggled looking. He did not seem to be wounded, but he swayed quietly, ignoring the chaos that swirled all around him.

"Are you hurt, my brother?" Gultec asked quietly. The euphoria of his battle joy still wrapped him warmly. He felt it as a tiny bubble of peace around Lok and Gultec. The comradeship warmed Gultec's heart, causing him to confer the respectful title upon Lok.

"I ache for Maztica, brother," whispered the Eagle Warrior softly. "Even as we live, she dies."

"How can you say this?" chided Gultec. "The battle is undecided. Can you not feel the surge of our strength around us?"

The bubble of peace threatened to burst, but Gultec

willed it to remain. He tried to focus on the Eagle Warrior and saw that Lok regarded him with something akin to pity.

"Can you not feel the end approaching, my brother?" asked Lok. "Can you not see it coming?" Lok's eyes wandered slowly away. The Eagle Warrior slowly slumped to the ground.

And then Gultec saw the substance of Lok's vision.

The monsters came rushing through the dust of the battlefield. They were huge beasts, big and brown, with snorting nostrils. Their feet crushed the ground to dust below them, and the sound of their approach was like thunder.

The monsters advanced in a line, as if the creatures had the minds of soldiers. Indeed, as they closed, Gultec saw that the beasts had the upper torsos of men, complete with arms and heads and weapons. But their lower bodies were grotesque, bearing a resemblance to deer, only much more massive, a thousand times more terrifying. Deer were passive and timid creatures, but these beasts bellowed and snorted and chomped. Flecks of foam covered their mouths, and lather spattered from their flanks.

Behind these giant things came smaller monsters, with wide, drooling jaws and long pointed teeth. Their tongues dangled, spattering foam. Heavy collars, bristling with spikes, protected their necks. They looked like huge coyotes, impossibly savage and fierce.

The monsters crashed into the Payit, into those warriors who had not turned and fled at their first appearance. Gultec saw the head sail from a spearmen. He saw one of the monsters drive a long spear through the body of another Payit. Still a third went down screaming and kicking beneath the plunging feet of one of the creatures.

Gultec stood and watched, his euphoria a distant memory. The sight of the beasts was so horrid, so shocking, that he could not raise a weapon to defend himself, nor turn away to run. He could only watch as his destiny, the triumph of his life, fell to shambles around him.

Somehow the monsters did not destroy him, passing instead around him and killing most of the warriors in their path. The Jaguar Knight watched the monsters wheel, even at considerable speed maneuvering like disciplined warriors. He saw one who seemed to be their leader, lumbering forward with black streamers trailing from his helmet. The face of this monster, a humanlike face, was contorted into a grimace of truly hellish cruelty.

The beasts rode forward and cut down a fresh band of warriors, plowing into a full thousand with crushing force. The warriors swarmed around, some of them attacking bravely, but the monsters kicked and leaped and whirled, soon breaking free to continue their rampage.

Gultec saw other bands of the monsters. The beasts roamed the battlefield at will, the thunder of their feet beating the death knell of the Payit. Back and forth they charged, and none could stand before them. The entire army began to melt away, warriors fleeing toward their homes or kneeling to tend wounded comrades, their weapons forgotten.

But the monstrous attackers did not forget. Gultec saw them riding to the far fringes of the field, still slaying, even though there was no semblance of resistance anymore. The members of the Payit army simply wanted to escape.

Gultec did not think that any of them would succeed.

* * * * *

Erix stood with the old people near the fringe of the delta. All morning the battle had been a scene of immense confusion, noise, and color in various patterns of chaos. The bystanders had been unable to tell how matters progressed.

Erix sensed the approach of disaster before most of the others. She felt a vague premonition, like a primeval warning, and moved back several hundred feet until she was close to the mangaroo tangle of the delta.

Then the monsters had come.

Erix moaned with horror and fell to the ground, paralyzed by fear, as were many of the other observers. This paralysis meant death in most cases, as the beasts with their humanlike cunning and cruelty, their supernatural speed and power, raced among the Payit and butchered the warriors and the helpless watchers alike.

The sight of the massacre sickened and numbed her. She saw a small child torn from its mother's arms, killed on lance point before the woman was trampled under the flashing hooves of the monster. She watched an old man standing valiantly before his gray-headed wife, and saw the creatures thunder past, clubbing the husband to earth and laughing as the old woman knelt to hold her dying mate.

She watched spellbound from her knees as the monsters swept closer. Their leader, a great, red-bearded manlike form with wild, flaming eyes and black streamers trailing from his helmet, saw her crouching. The light flared in his eyes, and his lance tip lowered. The monster lumbered toward her, and she saw her death approaching. At its heels raced a smaller, shaggier creature, slavering and yowling.

Erixitl faced the charging rider, wishing she could slay him with her eyes. She could not, so instead she calmly climbed to her feet before his charge. Around her lay the battered and bleeding wreckage of Maztica. She sensed her world ending, saw it writhing in torment everywhere.

It seemed a good day to die.

*   *   *   *   *

From the chronicle of Coton:

TALES OF THE PLUMED ONE IN MAZTICA

There came a time of war, and the brothers Zaltec and Qotal each made ready with sacrifice. The masses of men gathered eagerly, relinquishing their hearts and bodies and minds to the will of their gods.

And Zaltec claimed ten thousand warriors as his sacrifice. Eagerly, in song and verse, they ascended the pyramids in the time when pyramids reached the sky. Laughing and singing on the top, they offered their hearts to Zaltec, and the god was pleased.

But Qotal made his sacrifice of thirteen butterflies, each a different color, each brighter and bolder than the last. And his sacrifice was not the death of the butterflies, but their freedom. Each, in turn, he raised to the heavens and re-leased.

Then came the war. Zaltec strived to gain dominance over the gods, but Qotal would not yield. In the end, Zaltec tumbled from the pyramid and crawled away. He left behind him the supreme form of the elder god, Qotal, reigning at the height of his glory.

But ever after, in the dark of the night and the privacy of his treacherous thoughts, did Zaltec know Qotal as the Butterfly God.

☙ 17 ☙

ENEMIES AND FRIENDS

Alvarro soared with the momentum of the charge, the invincible feeling of power that surged through him as he led the lancers through the tattered ranks of the enemy. He had killed many of these natives already, more than he could count.

The horses rumbled on, unstoppable, the sleek, fierce greyhounds running beside them. Alvarro delighted in the effect of the war dogs, for the natives seemed to fear the hounds nearly as much as the lancers.

But still targets abounded for his lance, victims awaited the cut of his sword. The killing became a ritual for him, a process he could continue indefinitely.

He took no note of the fact that they had ridden beyond the enemy warriors. Still he hacked and slayed. The twelve horses of his wing thundered among the old people, the women and children who had come to watch the battle. Now the horsemen rode them down, far faster than they could flee.

Alvarro sensed, dimly, that he should turn, but the momentum of his attack had taken on a life of its own. Instead, he flew forward in his orgy with death, and still he killed.

Something caught the captain's eye, and he wheeled his mare sharply as his wing thundered on. He saw an extraordinary young woman standing on the field, staring at him. She was slender and very beautiful, but her arresting feature was her eyes. They found Alvarro and accused him, baring his soul to himself in all its ugliness.

The sight enraged him, and he lowered his lance, spurring his steed on toward the lone woman as bloodlust contorted his soul.

* * * * *

Halloran watched the battle with keen interest, balanced in his tree, concealed by its leafy branches. He feared for Daggrande's company as those ranks charged forward. He cheered the valiant stand of Garrant's men, and finally breathed again when they were relieved by the charging cavalry.

He watched the lancers with a twinge of envy, knowing that he should be riding at their head. He felt a grudging admiration for Alvarro's audacity as the riders circled among the mass of Payit warriors. The colorful banners trailing from the lances, the smooth precision of the horses and riders, all characterized the riders of the legion he had helped to train.

But his admiration turned to puzzlement as he saw the lancers ride beyond the native army and keep riding. And his puzzlement turned to shock, and then to horror, as he saw the butchery perpetrated by his—no, not his; he knew for certain they followed Alvarro now—horsemen.

The savage riders cut along the fringe of delta, and several thundered past a hundred feet from Halloran's lookout. He slid quickly to the ground as they passed. Hal forgot all thought of heroic intervention on the part of his comrades, for he felt no kinship to these brutal assassins.

The lancers killed without regard to the nature of their victims, whether warrior or bystander. The horses trampled those Payit who did not get out of the way, and the dogs growled and snarled and snapped, causing more consternation by their savage appearance than from any actual damage they inflicted.

Halloran saw the black charger wheel away from the others, recognizing Storm. He saw the black streamers trailing from the rider's helmet, knowing this was Alvarro's banner. His enemy had even claimed Hal's mount! A greyhound followed Alvarro and Storm as the lancer looked to his next victim. Halloran watched Alvarro's lance drop. I should have killed him when I had the chance, he thought ruefully. Murderous hatred burned in Hal's heart.

Then, for the first time, he saw Erix on the battlefield and recognized her as the horseman's intended victim.

Not Erixitl! "You bastard!" he croaked, scrambling forward. "By Helm, no!" The thought of her death on this field seemed like a final nightmare to his life—a nightmare he could not allow.

Alvarro rumbled forward, taking no note of Hal as the young legionnaire stepped out from the trees. Halloran desperately felt the inadequacy of his only weapon, the slender dagger. Even had the blade been weighted for throwing, it stood no chance of stopping or even distracting the racing lancer.

Magic! Now was the time when arcane powers could aid the swordsman's arm. But Halloran knew no magic, had known none for ten years.

Kreeshah . . . What was that phrase? Damn! The words tickled his brain with a long-buried memory. Alvarro's foaming charger galloped past as Hal desperately tried to think.

Kreeshah . . . barool . . . hottaisk! That was it!

"*Kreeshah . . . barool . .* ." Halloran pronounced, very loudly. He pointed his finger at Alvarro and his black charger as the lancer rushed toward Erix. "*Hottaisk!*"

A tiny flash of light sparkled from his finger, hissing like an arrow through the air and trailing sparks behind it as it flew. The magic missile surprised Halloran with its vigor. It struck Alvarro squarely in the back as the horseman loomed over the strangely motionless girl.

Alvarro shouted in pain and surprise as his horse bucked sharply. His cavalry lance fell to the ground as he forcibly brought the charger under control, cursing the burning wound in his back.

"Run! Head for the trees!" Halloran rushed toward Erix, puzzled by the girl's apathy.

She regarded him with a passive expression, vaguely sad. Her eyes instantly wrapped him in their luminous web.

"A deserter *and* a traitor!" Alvarro's hoarse voice came as a cruel taunt. Hal reached Erix as the rider turned and drew his razor-edged longsword.

"But not a butcher!" Halloran's voice carried to Alvarro's ears. The man's red beard split into a grin as he kicked the horse forward. The greyhound, too, raced forward, but now Halloran recognized Corporal. Surely, he hoped, that dog would remember him.

Hal seized the heavy lance, ponderously lifting the tip to face the rushing rider. The weapon was lethal when backed by the momentum of a charging horse and well-seated rider; it was little more than a heavy pole in the hands of a footman.

The horse thundered closer, and Hal suddenly knelt, resting the hilt of the lance on the ground behind him. Steadying the weapon carefully, he sighted upon Alvarro's armored chest.

The captain hacked with his longsword as he closed, attempting to knock the lance out of the way. But Halloran held firm against the stroke, and in the same second, the wooden tip crashed into Alvarro's chest, splintering the lance even as it drove the rider from his saddle.

The greyhound snarled toward him, and Hal stared into the dog's eyes. "Corporal, no!" he shouted. The dog halted in astonishment, looking at the two men in confusion.

The red-haired lancer lay on his back, moaning. Halloran sprang forward and snatched the man's longsword off the ground. For a moment, he considered thrusting it into Alvarro's body, fair payment for the man's orgy of slaughter. But he could not bring himself to do it, especially with Alvarro's taunt of "traitor" still ringing in his ears. Instead, he tore Alvarro's belt and scabbard away, girding the man's longsword on his own belt.

Then Hal looked around. The black charger, Storm, stood placidly some hundred paces away. The other horsemen of the captain's wing had separated, each pursuing his own victims. They ranged about the field around them, and it would only be seconds before one of them noticed their leader had fallen.

* * * * *

Erixitl slowly realized that she was not about to die, though the nature of her deliverance escaped her. Something had angered the monster just before it killed her, and the beast had leaped and snorted and bellowed its rage from both its mouths.

Then she had recognized the stranger, Halloran, and it slowly occurred to her that he was saving her. But why? Wasn't he the servant of these monsters, like all of his companions? She looked at him wistfully, numbed by the brutality of his kind.

She had felt a thrill of admiration for him as he lifted the spear, desperately fighting the monster. It seemed sad that he would die here, now, with her. Surely no man could stand before the rush of the hellish two-headed monster.

But he broke the monster's body!

Erix gasped in astonishment as Hal's blow tore the top half of the creature away, smashing it to earth. The beast's torso twitched on the ground, but her blood chilled at the sight of its great body lumbering on. The beast looked even more like a deer now that its human part had been ripped away.

Too, it seemed to lose some of its terrible nature. She saw it pause to nibble on the trampled grass among the bloody bodies it had, moments earlier, slain.

Her astonishment was compounded when Halloran barked a command at the small monster and the creature obeyed! It, too, did not look nearly so fierce when it responded to the man's command.

Halloran still dashed around in agitation, followed by the small monster. Now she saw him seize the long knife and start toward the lower half of the greater monster. She understood now: Each half must be killed separately.

But the man did not strike the beast. Instead, he seemed to speak to it. Nor did the monster attack or flee the man, instead standing docilely while Halloran stroked it.

Then Halloran joined the beast! She watched him replace the torso he had torn away. The recreated monster wheeled toward Erix and lumbered in her direction again. But the sensations came too quickly now, and her lively mind was overwhelmed.

By the time Halloran reached her she had collapsed, unconscious, to the ground.

* * * * *

I see a coyote, speaking to me very slowly. I cannot understand him, but he stands over the body of a man. A buzzard, dark with dried blood, lands before me and greets me very politely. He calls me "Most Excellent and Enlightened Lord Poshtli," and I am pleased.

The body between coyote and vulture stirs, struggling to speak. The man is dead, has been long dead, yet he sits up and talks to me. I see that it is my uncle, the Revered Counselor Naltecona.

The coyote, hungry, plucks at an arm of the corpse. It is always hungry. The buzzard pecks at a cheek. My uncle helps them; he pulls pieces of his body away and feeds the scavengers, an arm to the coyote, an ear and an eye to the buzzard.

Then the body of my uncle changes.

Poshtli blinked at the short, bald figure that squatted before him. Slowly the Eagle Knight looked around from the stone bed where he lay, seeing that he was in a cave of some kind. Yellow sandstone walls reflected in golden hues the light of a small fire.

"You speak with the gods, Feathered Man," said the fellow sitting beside him. "Will you speak with me now?"

Poshtli studied the strange speaker, for he had never seen anyone like him. Short and powerful, with bowed legs and broad shoulders, he was a misshapen man. His head was bald, but his face was covered with a whiskered profusion of hair that descended across his belly. The fellow's skin was sun-bronzed, dried like old leather but not as dark as Poshtli's. The stranger stood, and the Eagle Knight saw that he was perhaps four feet tall.

"Who are you?" asked Poshtli, discovering that his tongue felt like an old sandal.

"Eh? I'm Luskag, chief of Sunhome. Funny you should ask that. I've been wondering the same thing about you."

Poshtli's mind cleared. He remembered tales, dismissed as fantastic legend, of the Hairy Men of the Desert, dwarflike people who lived far from any human settlement, past a supposedly uncrossable waste of desert.

"I am Poshtli, of Nexal," he explained, sitting up with difficulty. "I owe you my life."

Luskag nodded. "You came farther than any man I've seen, but no one can live for long in the House of Tezca. Though that's not why I saved you." The dwarf handed Poshtli a flask of water, and the warrior sipped a few drops as Luskag continued.

"Sometimes humans come into the desert and die there. Other times, we desert dwarves save those humans and bring them here, to Sunhome. When we save someone, we must have a reason.

"I saved you because of my dream. I dreamed of a great buzzard, and he circled you, alone in the House of Tezca. And I came to you, gave you water and life, and the buzzard was pleased.

"I don't know why I should want to please a buzzard, but this was somehow important to me." The dwarf looked at Poshtli as if he hoped the lord would have an explanation.

"I dreamed of a buzzard, too . . . just now, before I woke up," explained the Eagle Knight. "But I don't know what it means."

"Why did you come into the desert?" asked Luskag.

"I seek a vision of the future, some way to bring meaning to the events of the True World. Strangers, powerful men, have flown to our shores. Naltecona, the Revered Counselor of Nexal, has been beset by omens and visions. One night, I had a dream. The Plumed One, Qotal himself, spoke to me, telling me that I might find the truth my uncle seeks. But I could never find it in Nexal.

"The vision showed me an image of heat, sand, and sun, that I took to be the House of Tezca. And within that desert, I must find a great silver wheel. This is why I came here, seeking this knowledge."

Luskag sighed, shaking his head in resignation. "It is as I feared."

"What did you fear? Please explain!"

"There is a place near here. One may go there for knowledge or truth, but often at terrible cost—perhaps even a man's life, or his sanity. But this is why men venture into the House of Tezca, and why, sometimes, we bring them here."

Luskag fixed Poshtli with a cold stare. "And that is where your answer lies. I must take you to the Sunstone."

* * * * *

Erix recovered her senses slowly, first realizing that her nostrils ached from a gagging, putrid odor. Next she felt an ache in her abdomen, and finally she sensed motion—but not the gentle rocking motion of the canoe. Abruptly she understood, and the knowledge filled her with profound fear.

She lay across the back of the monster!

The pain came from a protruding shell on the beast's back, for she lay straddled across it, behind the monstrous head but in front of the human torso. She did not look, but felt certain the man was Halloran.

Looking down, she saw that they moved quickly over sand. The nearby sound of waves told her they raced along the beach.

Abruptly she twisted around and sprang away from the creature. She heard Halloran shout as she landed on the sand and sprawled full length. The pounding of the creature's heavy feet ceased instantly, and before she could scramble to her feet, the huge stranger had broken free of the beast and stood on his own feet before her.

"Why did you do that?" he asked. "I won't hurt you!"

"What—what *are* you?" she cried. "What kind of beings are you that kill with such abandon, such joy? And what are these monsters that . . ." She gestured angrily at the beast that now stood placidly on the shore. As if sensing her interest, the monster raised its head and made a soft nickering sound.

Suddenly the nature of the horses became clear to her. They were animals, great creatures to be sure, but mere animals that carried these men about and were subject to their will.

She saw with her penetrating eyes that her words caused Halloran pain, and she remembered that he had fought against those of his people who would have killed her. The memory brought her anger back afresh.

"Why did you not let me die?" she demanded.

Now anger flashed in Hal's eyes. "Why? Because it was *wrong*, what they were doing. It was wrong for you to die there!"

"You are strange, even for a stranger, Halloran. You come here on a great journey with these people, and then when they fight, you turn against them."

Once again she caused him pain, she saw, and this time she regretted the hurt. "My people have turned against me," he explained. "They would have killed me, and so I fled." *And they blamed me for the death of Martine*, he added silently. He suddenly wanted to accuse her with this fact, but he held his tongue.

"When I saw you on the battlefield, there was but one thing I could do. I did it. We rode away from the field, and ever since we have been following the coast to the west."

"Am I your captive?" she asked boldly.

"What? No! Of course not! I wanted to right a wrong done before my eyes, to help you. That's all! And I thought you would be safer here with me than on the field with the legion."

"Then I am free to go?"

Suddenly Halloran felt a terrible fear, an unreasoning sense of loneliness that threatened to dwarf his earlier feelings of despair. He did not want this girl to leave him. She offered his only hope of communication, his only knowledge of this land. But he could not, would not hold her against her will.

"Yes, you can leave. You can go anywhere you want. But I hope you'll stay with me and help me. I'm alone here. I can't go back to my people."

The sight and sound and smell of him filled Erixitl with amazement. But she was already growing accustomed to his bizarre appearance. He had proven himself a man of bravery and honor. She knew his companionship would be interesting. As for the smell . . .

"Very well. But first," she said to him pointedly, "you must take a bath."

He looked at her in puzzlement and saw that she was serious. "Then," she added, "we'll have to find shelter. It will be night soon."

* * * * *

"The treasure must be counted and assembled quickly!" Kardann urged Cordell. The captain-general noted wryly that the assessor had disappeared before the battle, presumably by returning to the fleet. Now that victory had been secured, however, he showed up with quill and parchment in hand. Nevertheless, he proposed a course of action exactly in line with Cordell's own wishes.

"We will march into this city—I understand it is called 'Ulatos'—tonight," Cordell said. "Darien has informed the chiefs, and they will be prepared to meet us." Once again, the elf's language spell had speeded understanding. Afterward, she had returned to the ship to study the spell, so that she would have it ready for the evening, in case more than one tongue was needed in subjugating Ulatos.

"And the gold?" Kardann asked anxiously.

"We will be rich men by dawn, I assure you," Cordell said as Kardann turned toward the battlefield.

"What about the bodies?" asked the assessor of Amn. "Have they been checked for ornaments, bracelets, that sort of thing?"

"Of course!" snapped Cordell. The necessity of the task did not make it any more palatable to him. "There was considerable gold. It's been gathered at the tower." He pointed to the observation tower on the battlefield, and Kardann hurried away. Cordell felt a vague sense of relief, amplified when he saw Darien coming toward him.

"Greetings, my dear!" Cordell was surprised. He had assumed she would be gone for hours, studying her spell.

Now, in the orange light of the bonfires, her pale white skin reflected the red haze of her anger. "What's the matter?" asked the captain-general.

"Your plan for Halloran backfired," she said, too softly for anyone else to hear. She took great pains to speak when the Bishou's attention, in particular, was directed elsewhere.

"You mean he didn't escape?" Cordell pursed his lips. "I'm disappointed in him. I thought I made it easy enough."

"Oh, you did that," Darien agreed, her tone biting. "He escaped . . . and more." Cordell raised his eyebrows, and she continued. "He stole my spellbook—perhaps not intentionally, but it was concealed in my backpack, and he took it along with him!"

Cordell winced and looked away from the elf's pale and angry eyes. They both knew the seriousness of the theft, for a wizard needed to consult her book after each spell in order to relearn the enchantment. Without her book, Darien could use each of her spells but once, then would be unable to relearn them until either the book was recovered or an alternate form of the spell was found and copied.

"There is a rumor among some of the men," Darien continued unmercifully, "that he attacked and unhorsed Alvarro, stealing his charger and fleeing the field."

"Helm curse him!" Cordell hissed his anger. "I give him a chance to redeem himself and he betrays me! I cannot allow this!"

"Obviously," agreed the wizard dryly. "But what do you propose to do about it?"

"Did he get all of your spells?"

"He got a copy of each, but I have some sheaves of notes and scrolls about that will help me relearn most of them. It will take time to copy the scrolls into a new book, though. He also stole some potions from the crate."

Cordell blinked his black eyes, his expression cold. "Very well. We can spare no effort. Halloran must be found and killed. Quickly."

"That might be accomplished more easily than you think,"

noted the wizard with a slow, cruel smile.

"How is that?"

"One of the potions he stole is the decoy . . . the poison. If he touches it to his lips, he'll be dead before he can lower the bottle."

* * * * *

Spirali walked among the bloody bodies on the field in amazement. As an old member of a very old race, his training had prepared him for many things. But the evidence on this battlefield left him cold and frightened, for the first time wondering if there were forces that even the Ancient Ones could not control.

Nightfall made the battlefield a hellish place. The grass had disappeared, everywhere trampled to mud. Great fans of feathers, once-brilliant banners, and countless plumed headdresses lay in the mud, a fit epitaph to the fortunes of the Payit army.

Silently women and children moved through the dark, seeking a familiar face among the multitude of dead and wounded. Slaves carried bodies to a great trench and laid them carefully, but anonymously, within. Several thousand Payit had been slain and the normally important ritual of individual burial was of necessity forsaken.

Priests of Qotal and Azul passed among the wounded, tending those they could, but their limited healing magic was overwhelmed by the extent of the disaster. For the most part, the warriors bore their wounds stoically, though an occasional cry—usually from a man in delirium—echoed across the field.

But these trivial human concerns meant less than nothing to Spirali.

The Ancient One looked toward the city, where great fires commemorated the victory of the foreigners. By all rights, by a plan laid through centuries, the foriegners should have met complete disaster on this day. But now they danced about the plaza, with its mound of gold, in a way that added to Spirali's sense of foreboding. Indeed, it seemed that these humans were as dedicated to the pursuit of their goals as the Ancient Ones were to theirs. And they were so much more passionate!

His alarm left him but one alternative. Thus Spirali disappeared from the field at Ulatos, flashing himself with the power of teleportation to the Highcave.

He arrived beside the bubbling caldron of Darkfyre as it was being nourished by the Harvesters. The latter, black-robed like Spirali but smaller of form, bowed respectfully.

The Harvesters stood around the caldron of the Darkfyre as they did every night, tending the immortal blaze, feeding it with the fruit of their harvests, garnered from across the lands of Maztica. And thriving on its food, the Darkfyre twisted and flared.

Indeed, Zaltec was happy, for once again he ate well.

The Harvesters labored diligently, and soon the feeding was done. Silently each slipped away into the darkness. The task of the Harvesters was finished until the following night.

Spirali rustled his cape, the sound harsh and jarring through the vast, echoing chambers of the cave. In moments, the Ancient Ones gathered around the Darkfyre. Spirali remained silent, as did all of them, until the frail, shrouded form of the Ancestor emerged to claim his seat above the caldron.

"The strangers have vanquished the Payit in battle. In one day, they have conquered Ulatos and destroyed the army."

Capes rustled in mute statements of surprise, even astonishment.

"Impossible!" hissed one voice, the harshness of her tone offending the sensibilities of the other Ancient Ones. Her cape swished softly, a careful apology for the outburst.

"It is indeed disappointing that the Payit performed so poorly. Nevertheless, the roots of our power have always lain in Nexal. We can be sure that the strangers will not fare so well when they face the warriors of Naltecona!" The Ancestor looked about the chamber before continuing.

"The connection of these strangers with the lands of the Old Realms makes it imperative that we do our work quickly and secretly. Were these strangers to learn of our nature, our plans for Maztica might suffer disastrously.

"They will doubtless learn of Nexal," he mused, his voice like dry reeds rustling in a breeze. "What of the girl?"

Spirali's head fell. "The cleric failed. He is dead. I attempted to slay her, but also failed." It would, of course, be inappropriate to explain the circumstances, such as the arrival of dawn, that contributed to his defeat. He awaited the verdict of the Ancestor, fully expecting death for his own failure. No slightest whisper of silk disturbed the chamber for countless minutes.

"You must return and seek the girl. Her death is more important now than ever. If she is allowed to fulfill the terms of the prophecy, the effect could be catastrophic. But it is essential that your identity remain a secret. Do you understand?"

"Very well." Spirali bowed, the clasp of his black-skinned hands before his body conveying his gratitude for the second chance. "I respectfully report that I shall need help on this task."

"What sort of help do you require?" asked the Ancestor.

Spirali answered, and a soft rustle of astonishment circled the chamber. Such a step had not been taken for centuries! But the Ancestor considered the request very seriously, and finally the venerable leader nodded.

"Very well. You may call out the hell hounds."

Spirali nodded, pleased with the aid and relieved that no punishment had been declared. He knew that he would not get another chance. After warming his hands and his body beside the Darkfyre, Spirali worked his way deep into the vast cavern.

He followed a winding, narrow tunnel until he reached an opening, where this passage joined the wide vertical shaft in the heart of the volcano. Heat pressed against his face from deep, liquid fires flickering far below.

The Ancient One bent over the plummeting shaft and raised his voice in a long, ululating wail. Twice more he repeated the sound, and then he waited.

Far below, a bubble of hot gas burst from the burbling

lava. Fiery red, seething with contained energy, it rolled and rumbled up the shaft, straining against its contained pressure. Higher and higher it climbed, growing in speed and force. It twisted and bubbled with contained energy, finally slowing as it approached the level where Spirali waited.

When the gas bubble reached the Ancient One's level, it paused for a second. Inside, Spirali saw a seething mass of long, pointed teeth, of blazing red eyes and smooth, shadowy shapes. A dark creature sprang from the bubble into the corridor beside Spirali. More and more of the great wolflike animals joined him, until the entire pack had collected around him.

Each of the animals was dark in color, ranging from a dirty brown to rust, like dried blood. Great black tongues flopped from their mouths, and their fangs were long, sharply pointed, and as black as midnight. Only their eyes gave the creatures color, for these wicked orbs gleamed and flickered with a light indistinguishable from the bubbling fire below.

As soon as the great dogs had all sprung free, the bubble resumed its ascent. Quickly it burst from the mouth of the volcano, spreading into a great fireball in the sky. Far below, the citizens of Nexal watched in awe as the orange globe blossomed against the star-speckled void and then disappeared.

"Welcome!" hissed Spirali, stroking and scratching the slavering beasts. "Are you ready to hunt, my hell hounds?"

* * * * *

Darien sought a shady clearing in the garden before Caxal's palace. Here she could work without exposing her pale skin and sensitive eyes to the murderous sunlight. Sitting upon the grass, she laid her components around her with extra care, for without her spellbook, she had but one chance to perform this spell.

She placed a small bowl upright on the ground, crushing several dry leaves into it. Next to this, she placed a silver longsword—Helmstooth, Halloran's sword, taken from him when he was arrested—and a small box of glowing embers. She found a dry twig and placed its tip in the tinderbox, blowing on it until it flickered with flame. Then she touched the twig to the crushed leaves.

The powdery stuff immediately puffed into flame, filling the bower with a sweet aroma. Darien now pulled a small piece of horn from a pouch on her robe. Stroking it with her long, slender fingers, she concentrated on her casting, whispering words of deep and arcane power, searching across surrounding planes for the one she sought.

Her mind drifted across the plane of fire, where heat of all types blazed eternally. Rocks flowed in liquid eruption, and the air itself crackled and hissed. Only the arcane power of her enchantment preserved her, and even the unemotional elf felt a sense of relief as she left the fiery realms behind.

Next came water, not so threatening but also not her objective. She quickly moved into the plane of air, and here she would find the aid she needed. Resting now in an intangible space of cloud and wind, she let the magic do her work. The spell of summoning thrummed louder than ever, and soon she felt it meet resistance.

Come to me. I demand you to obey! Slowly at first, but inevitably, the creature answered her call. Instantly Darien returned her full attention to her body, which had never left the garden.

For a long minute, she sat alone among the encircling leaves. Then she felt another presence. With a final sense of release, she exhaled, for the spell had been successful. Darien suppressed an almost giddy sense of relief as leaves parted and the grass beside her flattened from an unseen weight.

The invisible stalker had arrived.

"You are to find a man named Halloran," Darien said softly, her eyes once again shut. The invisible form made no reply, for it could not speak.

"Here is a sword he once carried. It will give you his spoor. We do not know which way he has gone.

"When you find him, you are to kill him instantly. Do not delay his death, for he is a resourceful man." The invisible stalker remained beside her. She could sense the creature's resentment of her commands, but it would do her bidding, for it was bound by the power of her spell.

"Now go!" she said, opening her eyes and watching the leaves rustle as the creature departed.

*　*　*　*　*

From the chronicle of Coton:

Painted in the certain knowledge that the Waning of Maztica is upon us.

A lone eagle arrives in Nexala. He brings a tale of tragedy and disaster too extraordinary to be believed. The strangers, he tells us, are the servants of great monsters. These beasts ride upon clouds of smoke and make thunder with the crashing of their feet.

They are powerful and swift, stronger than many men. But they are also cunning, for they have the minds of men. They fight with weapons, and also with their invincible flesh.

The Eagle Knight tells us all he has seen as tears flow from his eyes. His heart breaks from the weight of his tale, and he dies upon the floor before Naltecona as he completes the story.

Naltecona's eyes widen. His skin grows pale until he resembles the description of the foreigners' white, bloodless complexion. His mouth hangs open, working at words that will not come forth.

"More sacrifices!" he finally cries. "We must consult the gods!"

And the priests and their captives form a procession. Naltecona wields the knife himself. He seeks the wisdom to decide, asking the gods to provide him with the knowledge and will he himself lacks.

Of course, they do not answer.

♣ 18 ♣

CONQUEST

At sunset, the surviving people of Ulatos gathered in somber ranks along the avenues of their lush city to witness the entrance of the conquerors. Though the battle had never reached the city itself, every resident of Ulatos knew the tale of this day's fighting. Nearly every family had lost a father or brother, or even a younger sister or grandparent caught up in the massacre.

First came the measured columns, six abreast, of Garrant's swordsmen and Daggrande's crossbows. Banners flew above the men, and trumpets and drums paced their step. They advanced in a steady, even cadence, faster than a normal walk. The legionnaires marched precisely, stealing glances to the right and left at the many splendors around them. They saw gardens and flowers such as they had never imagined, and clean white houses. Water flowed in many places, always clean and clear.

Next came twenty-one horsemen, three abreast. The blue and yellow pennants flew from their upraised lances, and the riders took great pleasure in wheeling and bucking and prancing with their mounts, to the great awe of the onlookers. Alvarro rode at their head, on a black gelding he had commandeered from one of his men. Often he pulled savagely against the bit, causing the horse to rear and kick while the red-headed captain brandished his sword.

Cordell rode into Ulatos in the center of the Golden Legion, mounted and followed by horses bearing Darien and the Bishou. The other twenty horses, and then the last companies of foot soldiers, completed the grand procession.

The legion moved along the wide avenues quickly, soon reaching the large plaza at the heart of the city. Trees and flowers grew in profusion around the square. Several narrow canals reached the fringes of the plaza, crossed by the avenues on wide wooden bridges.

Dominating the plaza was the great green bulk of a verdant pyramid, higher than the one near Twin Visages and also distinguished by the profusion of vines and flowers growing from each of its terraces. Atop the temple splashed a high fountain of clear water, and the liquid leaped down the stepped sides of the edifice in a merry trickle, as if to mock the solemnity of the humans gathered below.

The soldiers broadened their ranks to cover the square as Cordell and Darien dismounted. The two walked slowly toward the figures awaiting them at the base of the green pyramid.

One man, distinguished by his resplendent mantle and his collar of green feathers, stepped forward and bowed low. He began to speak, but Cordell cut him off.

"Are you the chief of this city?" the captain-general demanded as Darien quickly translated. The man, shocked and frightened by Cordell's rudeness, stammered and then responded.

"He is Caxal, the 'Revered Counselor' of Ulatos," Darien interpreted.

"Tell him to bring me all of the gold in the city—now. We shall also require food and quarters. But first the gold. They are to bring it here." Cordell gestured to a raised square in the center of the plaza, a foot above ground level.

Darien translated, then Caxal turned and spoke urgently to the lords and chiefs behind him. "Tell him that if they attempt to conceal any of their gold, their city will be destroyed!"

Caxal's expression was desperate as he spoke to Darien. "We will bring you all of our gold. Please know that we are not rich. This is not Nexal! We are but the Payit, and our gold is yours."

Showing interest, Cordell nodded to Darien. "We will learn more about this place 'Nexal.' But for now, let us count the gold before us!" He turned back to the counselor of Ulatos.

"Caxal, you are to lead your lords to every house in your city. You will claim all of the gold in my name and bring it to me here. When you have finished, my men will search. If we find that you have deceived us, your city will be destroyed!" The counselor hastily turned and collected his nobles, sending them scurrying off in all directions.

"My general, the pennant," Bishou Domincus urged, joining the pair at the base of the pyramid. Several men-at-arms and the sergeant bearing the legion's standard also came up.

"To the top!" exclaimed Cordell, with a flourish. The little party climbed the pyramid. At the top was a lush garden, complete with clear bathing pools, grassy walkways, and beds of brilliant blossoms. At the center of the square area stood a raised dais, with a statue upon it.

"A demon!" cried Domincus, spitting upon the image of the Feathered Serpent, Qotal. "Tear it down!"

Instantly the men-at-arms toppled the squat carving, knocking the leering dragonlike head off its encircling mane of feathers in the process. In moments, they had rolled both pieces of the statue over the edge, where they tumbled down the side and smashed to rubble in the plaza below.

Already, Cordell could see, natives hurried to pile objects in the center of the plaza. He could see the metallic gleam of gold on many statuettes, chains, and bracelets. Other objects, swathed in cloth for the moment, he imagined were ingots and large chunks of the precious yellow metal.

"The pennant! For the glory of Helm!" Bishou Domincus tossed back his head and shouted. He snatched the standard from the sergeant and leaped onto the now-vacant dais. His gauntlets, each emblazoned with the blazing eye of his god, gripped the flagpole as he raised it high. With a powerful blow, he planted it in a crack between two rocks. The pennant unfurled, its golden eagle emblem snapping taut, the great staring eye of Helm in the eagle's breast glaring imperiously about the city.

Behind the pennant, the crystal plume of the fountain slowly sank back into its pool. Then it died altogether.

* * * * *

The smokeless fire cast a warm glow against the shiny walls of the grotto. Halloran emerged from the clear pool, his skin raw from scrubbing. Corporal still swam joyfully in the shallow stream, while Storm grazed on a profusion of tall grass.

Hal discarded the root Erix had provided him, an herb that had frothed with the water to form something she called 'soap.' It had proven so effective that Hal now felt uncomfortably clean.

He slipped into his leather jerkin and woolen leggings with some relief, ignoring Erix's wrinkled nose. They both relaxed now, comfortable and reasonably safe for the moment, in any event. Hal had located this steep-sided rocky niche, only a few hundred paces from shore but masked by verdant growth on all sides.

"We will find you a mantle," she said. "Clean and cool. You will like it."

Hal grunted noncommittally. In fact, he immediately noticed the itching of his present rough fabric against his skin. Pools of sticky sweat formed quickly where the heavy leather padding clung tightly to his body. But the bath had been grueling enough. Helm's curses if he would allow anything else.

"Here. I have food." Erix handed him a flat object, which he recognized as a mayzcake. The islanders had introduced the legion to this nourishing staple, the mainstay of the Maztican diet.

"Thanks." Hal bit into the cake, and suddenly tears sprang from his eyes and his mouth blazed with fire. Desperately he swallowed the food and gulped many mouthfuls of water. "What's—what's in this?" he gasped.

"This? Just beans. Oh, and a little pepper. Do you like it?" She smiled curiously.

"It's . . . splendid," he whispered, quickly cooling his gullet with more water. Even the water only seemed to spread the fire around, like oil thrown upon a blaze.

Still, rations were rations, and these were the only rations available. He tried smaller bites and slowly came to appreciate the sharp, distinctive flavor. His eyes watered freely and sweat burst from the pores on his skin, but he noted with surprise that, in this tropical heat, the spicy food actually made his body feel cooler—on the outside, at any rate.

"Tell me about your land," he prodded as they finished eating. "That city, Ulatos . . . is that your home?"

"No. I come from far away, near the Heart of the True World."

"The True World?"

"Maztica. The whole known world. Maztica's greatest nation is Nexal, for the Nexalans have conquered many of the other tribes. Kultaka is another strong land, enemy of Nexal. Here we are in Payit, the land farthest removed from Nexal. Payit is the only land that is not an enemy of Nexal, but it is not a conquest either. The Payit are too far away for the Nexalans to worry much about them."

"But what of the bloody priests, such as the one that killed Martine?"

Erix sighed. "The followers of Zaltec, such as that priest, are far more numerous among the Nexala and Kultaka than among the Payit. But always we can find worshipers of Qotal, such as good Kachin. He was the patriarch, the highest of high priests, of the temple in Ulatos." She turned to him, suddenly curious. "You said that your own people attacked you. Why?"

Hal told the tale of his arrest and escape, and as he spoke, the events seemed like distant history, a story that had happened to someone else. The whole fabric of his life had been shattered, and yet he felt like the same person now as when he had served Cordell's legion.

Yet as he sensed the impact of what had happened, he began to realize that Cordell, Alvarro, Bishou Domincus—none of them would be content to let him escape. They would come after him with all the powers at their disposal, and Hal knew these to be considerable. In that same instant, he made another decision.

"When I spoke to you of staying with me, I forgot . . . that is, you can't," he began, awkwardly. He forced the words out. "You *can't* come with me. I can't be around you!"

"Why?" Erix demanded.

"It's not safe. The legion is sure to chase me, and they'll probably find me. You would . . . well, you'd get in the way if I had to fight," he lied.

Erix leaped to her feet. "And just what will you do? Do you think, with your hairy monsters and your metal shirt, you can go where you please in Maztica? Do what you will?

"No, Captain Halloran. You will be killed, and your heart will be fed to Zaltec or Tezca. Only with me do you have a chance to stay alive. And don't worry . . . if something attacks you, I won't get in the way."

Halloran blinked in surprise at her outburst. He hadn't intended to offend her. Couldn't she see that he only wanted her safety? That no place in Maztica was likely to be as unsafe as by his side?

"You don't understand!" he blurted. He wanted to explain to her his terrible guilt over Martine's death. She had to see that he could not be responsible for another such violent fate! But even as the reasons, the explanations, whirled through his mind, he began to feel that perhaps he didn't understand things fully either.

"I'm not a slave!" Erix declared forcefully. "And I will not be dismissed like some bothersome child!"

She took several steps away from him and then looked back, her eyes softening. Some of the tension left her body. "You are a brave man, Captain—especially so, that you would send me to safety even though it would leave you helpless in my country.

"But you need me," she finished, sitting again beside their small fire. "You have saved my life when I would have given it up. That is a debt I will not easily ignore."

He looked at her in gratitude, realizing how very fearful he had been about her departure. "You're right. I need your help to survive. And I'm grateful that you're offering it." He shook his head, angry at himself. "I'm sorry about what I said. I don't believe for a minute that you'd get in the way. But you must listen to me: There could be great danger, terrifying attacks that you cannot imagine. If something strange happens, I want you to get away from me quickly. Do you understand?"

She nodded at him, still glaring. He was certain that she understood, but quite uncertain that she would obey.

With a sigh of resignation, Hal adjusted his backpack, currently employed as a pillow. "What's this?" he wondered aloud.

He examined the leather satchel, particularly the bottom, where he thought it had been reinforced. He realized instead that something flat and solid had been inserted into a secret compartment there.

After a moment, he found a concealed flap and pulled it upward, revealing a leather-bound tome wrapped in a black ribbon. Pulling the heavy book out, he gasped in astonishment.

"What is that? Is it good?" asked Erix, puzzled by the look of mingled wonder and fear on Hal's face.

"No . . . not good. I don't know how bad." He looked directly into Erix's eyes. "It appears that I have inadvertently stolen the spellbook of the wizard, Darien." He explained the significance of the find, knowing that this tome held a copy of each magical spell in Darien's arsenal.

"Of course, they aren't useful to anyone except a trained magic-user. You can go mad trying to read a spell that is beyond your abilities. More than likely, it just won't make any sense."

Yet as he spoke, the smooth leather cover seemed to beckon invitingly from his lap. His eyes wandered downward, intrigued and tantalized. He held the book, shut, for a long time, eventually noticing that Erix had dropped off to sleep.

How much do I remember? he mused, over and over. Finally he flipped the book open to its first page.

A searing flash burned his eyes, and he slammed the cover shut, blinking. Yet within the brief instant of that flash, he had recognized symbols, words of arcane power.

Carefully he opened the book again. This time the flash was not so bright. He forced his eyes to remain fixed on the page and was elated as he identified the enchantment.

A sleep spell! This was one he had once known.

Could he learn it again? Carefully he scrutinized the symbols. Some of them became clear to him, but others seemed to waver on the page, just beyond the reach of his understanding. His head began to throb, but still he studied.

Finally it was sheer fatigue, and not magic, that caused his head to drop back and his eyes to close.

Halloran dreamed of Arquiuius. The old wizard counseled him on his magic missile spell, cuffing his ears when he mispronounced a syllable or let his attention wander. In the dream, he studied the spell and attempted it dozens of times, always failing in one crucial aspect or another.

Then suddenly he got it right, firing the enchantment off in a sparkling trail. He leaped up, thrilled with the success, but his tutor passed it off with a gruff "That is acceptable." Immediately Arquiuius gave him another task, the learning of the light spell. He labored over the new incantation, trying to cast it again and again, but he could not capture the rhythms of the enchantment.

Arquiuius left him and went to sleep. Still the youthful Halloran practiced, and still he failed. Tears of frustration rolled down his cheeks, but no one offered sympathy. Again he studied, his eyes straining under weak candlelight to read figures that seemed to slip elusively across the page.

Over and over and over he tried the spell, and each time his task grew more difficult. But always he went back to it, and now, finally, he felt that he was getting close. He was almost there!

He shouted a word, something from his distant past, and suddenly sat upright in fright. Instantly the inside of the grotto blossomed with cool, white light, harshly gleaming against the dark night above.

Did I do that? was Hal's first thought. Then he heard the howling.

* * * * *

"If the white men want the gold of this house, let them come and take it themselves! Now leave me!" Gultec growled at the plump nobleman, a nephew of Caxal's. The little fellow squealed in terror and fled down the street as the Jaguar Knight angrily slammed the gate.

For some time, Gultec brooded in the garden before the House of Jaguars. Several of the younger warriors crouched listlessly in their chambers, while others wandered aimlessly among the flowers and ponds. Most of the rooms were empty now, their former occupants lying on the field beyond the city.

Why was I spared? Why, when so many young knights, so many fathers and brothers, so many with so much to live for, perished? Why was I, who have nothing, spared?

Gultec pulled his flint dagger from his belt and cut long slashes in his forearms. He watched the blood drip to the ground, but his act of penance brought no healing to his spirit.

He stood and stretched, catlike, looking at the House of Jaguars wistfully. This elegant mansion, home for members of his order who had no wives, no families, had sheltered him for more years than he cared to remember. Always it had been a symbol of the invincible might, the unassailable pride of his order.

Now that might had been broken on the field of battle. The pride lay in shambles across the treasure-littered plaza of Ulatos, where the nobles of the city hastened to do the bidding of their new masters.

Once again came the banging at the gate, and this time Gultec recognized the voice of the Revered Counselor.

"Open up, Gultec!" groaned Caxal. "I've got to talk to you!"

Angrily the warrior threw open the portal. He looked with scorn at his chieftain as Caxal stumbled inside. The man's expression was tearful, his position cowed.

"Gultec, you must give up the gold in the house! The foreigners demand it! You have much gold; you will make them very happy. They feed on the yellow metal and need it to live!"

"Let them come and take it, then. Let me die a warrior's death facing them!"

Caxal looked at the Jaguar Knight with compassion. "This I would tell them, but they will not come after you only. They will raze the city if we do not yield our gold!"

Gultec wanted to shout at him, even to attack him. Some part of the Jaguar's pride desperately needed to blame the counselor. If only Gultec could have deployed the army in the forest, as he had desired.

But in his heart, Gultec knew that his own tactic, while it might have saved more warriors, would not have held the strangers out of Ulatos. Ulatos had been doomed, and it was Caxal's destiny to preside over the first city of Maztica to fall to the invaders. For the first time, he felt a measure of pity for this pathetic chief.

"They will come tomorrow to search the houses," urged Caxal. "Think of the children, Gultec!"

The Jaguar Knight tried to think of the children. He tried to think about anything, but all he saw was a black void. His life was behind him. He had failed at his destiny. Now there was nothing.

"My house is your house," he said softly. He walked away from Caxal, seeking the darkest corner of the garden. Here he squatted and faced the wall as the gold from the House of Jaguars was taken to the plaza.

Gultec watched the young Jaguars meander dejectedly from the house. One by one, they carried golden ornaments up the street to the House of the Captain-General, as Caxal's palace was now called. They went to answer their new lord's command.

None of them spoke. Never had Gultec imagined a scene of such tragedy, such utter humiliation. Every Jaguar stood ready to accept death upon the battlefield or honorable capture and sacrifice upon an enemy's altar.

But the warriors now entered the palace and did not emerge. They remained there, prisoners of the invader, Cordell. The captain-general had loudly proclaimed that sacrifice was now forbidden, and none knew why he gathered the warriors to himself.

Gultec could not make himself rise. He sat in the garden until night fell, and then waited throughout the long hours of darkness for the soldiers to come and take him. When he resisted, they would kill him.

Inside the warrior, a great, caged feline paced angrily back and forth, growling and snarling at the confining bars. But outwardly Gultec showed no expression, moved no muscle for the many hours of night. The pacing became a restless obsession, though still with no outward display.

And with the passing of hours, he knew that even his enemies had forgotten him. His destiny had been destroyed on the battlefield, crushed by the might of his enemy. Now that enemy would not even grant him the dignity of a warrior's death.

His life finished, Gultec rose and left the garden under the rosy glow of dawn. He did not turn toward the palace. Instead, he went south, out of the city and through the cleared fringe of fields. At full daylight, he reached the jungle's edge.

Now a great spotted cat sprang into the middle branches of the trees, above the choking growth along the ground. Supple muscles rippled under the smooth pelt, and bright yellow eyes probed the greenery for the sight of game. The great cat was hungry.

And Gultec was free.

* * * * *

Footprints marched steadily down the beach, appearing one after another to mark the track of the invisible stalker. Helmstooth, Halloran's silver longsword, swung about three feet above the ground, just as if a human warrior held the weapon at the ready. Like the needle of a compass, it swung tentatively for a bit, then quickly steadied in the direction of its quarry.

The stalker possessed inhuman patience and tenacity. It could only be drawn to a physical world such as this one by the command of a powerful wizard. The stalker was compelled by the summoning spell to perform the task assigned, and so it searched for the man named Halloran. Not until it found him and completed the command would it be free of the wizard's will.

It had searched the battlefield of Ulatos for hours before finally locating the spoor. The man had mounted a horse, and the steed had thwarted the stalker's previous efforts at detection.

But now it followed that horse along the beach, and the footprints and sword made steady progress. Suddenly they stopped as the stalker sought a spoor invisible and undetectable to mortal senses.

Then the footprints turned from the beach and entered the jungle. Leaves rustled, as if to mark the passage of a short burst of wind, and soon the sword danced toward the entrance of a rocky grotto. Within, it sensed the dying coals of a fire.

And its quarry.

* * * * *

Cordell pried the gold nugget from the belly of the delicately carved turquoise statue. He freed the metal and let the statue drop and smash on the hard stone of the plaza. Placing the heavy nugget between two of his molars, he grinned as the pliable metal conformed slightly to the pressure of his bite.

Though the time was past midnight, great bonfires lit the plaza and the men of the legion showed no weariness as they watched more and more gold brought before them. Like Cordell, they tore the golden elements from artwork, compressed wiry statues into compact lumps of metal, and pulled the feathers and shells from delicate pictures embroidered with gold.

Long into the night, the captain-general toiled at his enjoyable task, until finally fatigue claimed him. He would meet with the assessor in the morning, and for once he looked forward to the meeting.

* * * * *

Halloran sat up in alarm, his magical dream forgotten even though the soft light still washed through the grotto. Corporal stood nearby, growling softly. The legionnaire listened to the distant howling, carried by the night breeze, and the sound sent an uncontrolled shiver down his spine.

"Erix?" he called softly. "Wake up."

She sat up quickly, and he sensed that she had already been awake for a little while. "Do you recognize that sound?" he asked.

"No . . ." She looked at him, and he had never seen her so frightened. "Is that more of your monsters?"

He shook his head and cast a glance at Corporal. "Greyhounds don't bay when they follow a trail. When they do bark, it doesn't sound anything like that." The musical, mournful cry again ululated through the night, still distant but intensely menacing.

"But you made this light, did you not?"

"Yes . . . that's one of the magic spells I told you about. I don't know if I could do it again. I was having a dream, and when I woke I cast it."

Erix looked around, her expression a mixture of fear and wonder. The cool white light filled the narrow niche, reflecting softly off the rocky walls. They had slept comfortably in the sheltered grotto, Hal wrapped in the blanket and Erix in her plain cotton mantle. But now neither of them wanted to rest.

The howling came again, noticeably nearer. Hal recalled the various powers and enchantments available to the Bishou or Darien, wondering if this might be the work of one of the spellcasters. "I think we'd better move on," he suggested. Erix was already up, rolling her mantle into a tight bundle.

Halloran lashed his backpack, blanket, and other supplies to Storm while Erix quickly splashed some water on herself. She joined him beside the horse as he was examining something from his pack.

"What is that? Water?" Erix asked, seeing a large vial in Hal's hand. He held two smaller bottles in his other hand.

"No. They're magic potions of some kind. I took them when I escaped from the ship. I don't know why I did. Magic gives me the willies."

Erix's brows knitted. "What do they do?"

The howling echoed again, still distant. Corporal paced nervously while Hal thought about his answer.

"I don't know for sure. You drink them, and something magic happens. The labels explain it all, I'm sure, but I've never seen writing like this."

"Perhaps you should throw them away," urged the woman quietly. "We don't need them, and what if they're dangerous?"

"Oh, I don't know," Halloran said airily. "They might come in handy." He set the two small bottles back in the pack and unstoppered the large one. Squinting into the bottle first, he raised it and took a short sip.

"Halloran!"

When Erix screamed, Hal quickly dropped the bottle and spat. He fumbled to push the cork back in, wondering why he couldn't see the bottle. Come to think of it, he couldn't see his hands, either. He was invisible!

"Halloran? Where are you?" Erix whirled around, panicking.

"It's—it's all right. I'm right here." Already his form began to grow visible, and in moments, he looked normal again. "This is a potion of invisibility! I didn't take enough to do more than fade for a second, but if we need to, we can drink a dose and disappear!"

"Forever?" Erix was clearly dubious.

"No . . . for an hour or two, I suppose. I know they're only temporary, but I haven't had much experience with potions." He reached for one of the small bottles.

"Wait!" urged Erix. "It does seem that they may be useful, but let's leave the others for a later time. We should be moving on now."

The howling abruptly faded, changing in pitch and volume. They could still hear it, but it did not seem so imminent.

Corporal suddenly growled and sprang to his feet. A gust of wind swirled through the grotto, rippling the stream water and rustling the grass along the bank. Hal looked up but saw nothing, even though light still washed their camp. Once more the howling echoed in the distance. Then Corporal barked loudly.

The sound saved Halloran's life. He whirled to look behind him just in time to see a silver sword driving toward his throat. Twisting away, he leaped to his feet. A sudden wind blazed the dull coals of the fire back to light, and Hal gaped in astonishment at his attacker.

Or rather, his lack of an attacker. The silver sword danced in the air, apparently animated by itself. His astonishment grew as he saw the weapon clearly.

"That's Helmstooth—my own sword!" he cried. The blade, given to him by Cordell himself, had been taken away when he was arrested. Now, as if under its own power, it was attacking him!

As the weapon darted forward again, he saw splashes in the shallow water below it, marking the passage of invisible feet. He snatched the sword he had claimed from Alvarro from the nearby saddle and parried the attacker's next blow.

But the enchanted sword flickered back and forth too quickly for Hal's eye, and the legionnaire stumbled backward to avoid another deadly thrust. His shock turned to fear as he realized that this inanimate attacker could kill him. He tumbled backward through shallow water, and something splashed after him.

Corporal leaped at the attacker, snarling and biting at the air. The greyhound twisted in the water as a sudden gust of wind whipped up froth. A column of swirling air suddenly lifted the dog and hurled him to the shore.

Halloran darted at the invisible shape, hacking back and forth, trying to knock Helmstooth to the ground. The whirlwind turned back, and spray flew in a howling column, blinding Hal. The force of the air buffeted him backward, and he sprawled on the shore.

The once placid grotto became a cage to him now, the limestone walls barring him from maneuver . . . or flight. The rocky barriers formed a deadly arena, where life would be the winner's prize.

Halloran scrambled desperately to his feet as Helmstooth came at him again. Diving away, he once again tumbled headlong in his desperate attempt to evade death. The sword chopped at the ground behind him, and he rolled away, bumping his shoulder on a sharp object.

The sword lifted above him, ready for the kill, when something thumped into the invisible figure and knocked it aside. Hal saw Erix holding a sizable log, originally intended for their fire. But the whirlwind shape came swirling back, and Halloran knew they could not best it with physical attacks.

The sharp object jabbed at him again as he struggled to his feet, and he realized that he had fallen onto his backpack. The top of one of the small potion bottles was barely visible, jutting from the side pocket. It had been that bottleneck that had poked him.

Erix swung again, knocking the invisible sword-thing backward, but then the wind swirled around her, smashing her to the ground. Hal's throat tightened with a cold terror that dwarfed his earlier fear. Then the sword turned back toward him. It was not interested in killing Erixitl of Maztica.

Desperately Hal pulled the little bottle from the pack. *I hope this does more than make me invisible.* Popping the cork, he threw back the bottle and gulped its entire contents in one swallow. In the next instant, he raised his sword and parried another slashing blow.

Once again the swirling wind raced through the camp. Spray blinded Hal, and he braced himself for the crushing force that had twice knocked him over. Closing his eyes against the stinging needles of water and dirt, he leaned into the wind and struggled to keep his balance.

But the wind did not swirl so forcefully this time, at least, not against his whole body. He felt it pounding his belly and his legs, then just his legs. He opened his eyes as the spray fell into mist and the wind jerked, annoyingly but not dangerously, at his calves.

He looked down at the fire, down at Erix, saw the starlit

horizon stretching for miles around the grotto . . . around the grotto! Even the twenty-foot high walls that had concealed their camp now looked like a trench around him. I'm a giant! he suddenly realized. For a moment, he reeled with vertigo, so dizzying was the sensation.

But his feet had grown proportionately, and his balance remained steady. He crouched lightly, dropping into the trenchlike grotto, every bit as nimble as he had ever been.

Halloran saw the silver sword slash in for another attack, and he kicked the irritating thing away. Slowly he grasped the significance of the potion: It had increased him to a height of perhaps thirty feet. His weapons and clothing had grown right along with him!

Erix sat, awestruck, gaping up at him. The invisible stalker whirled in again, and Hal raised one huge foot, stepping down hard on the struggling form. His massive weight pressed the thing into the water.

A froth of bubbles exploded around his giant foot, but he could feel the substance of the monster still wriggling beneath the pressing weight. For several minutes, he stood still, and slowly the struggles faded. Finally bubbles burst from the water all around his foot, as if a great air sack had burst.

Feeling nothing resisting him now, he reached down and plucked Helmstooth from the bottom of the stream. Holding the sword like a toothpick, he looked around for any sign of the attacker, but once again the night was silent.

Erix stammered something unintelligible, and once again he looked at her horrorstruck face.

"Don't worry," he soothed, his voice like the rumbling of thunder. "It won't last long."

At least, that's what he hoped.

* * * * *

"Up here, inside the mountain," explained Luskag, barely breaking a sweat. "That's where we'll find the Sunstone."

Poshtli gasped an inarticulate reply. The combination of the steep climb and the high altitude made it virtually impossible for him to move, much less speak. Nevertheless, he followed the desert dwarf in their slow, steady ascent.

Clad only in sandals and loincloths, they made the grueling climb under the blazing light of the morning sun. The climb was not treacherous, just a steady, long uphill grind in an atmosphere that offered precious little air to breathe.

The mountain spread across a vast area of desert, rising from a tumult of lesser peaks to dominate the skyline in all directions. Dirty white snowfields, streaked with mud from melting, adorned the heights of the cone-shaped peak, and finally the climbers neared this region.

"The mountain was born at the time of the Rockfire," explained Luskag when they both paused to catch their breath.

"You've talked about that before," noted Poshtli, between gasps. "What's the Rockfire?"

Luskag looked at him in surprise. "I thought surely the tale was known to all. The Rockfire marks the birth of the desert dwarves, but the death of all of our kindred dwarves."

Poshtli looked at him in puzzlement, and Luskag continued. "The time was many generations ago, by dwarven reckoning—that means even more, measured in human generations—though no one knows exactly. The dwarves were locked in conflict with their archenemies, the drow elves . . . the dark elves.

"It was a conflict that wracked the far corners of the world, for the underearth at that time was linked by tunnels and caverns, such that a dwarf could cross under the great ocean, past the vast snow realms of the north and south, anywhere he wanted, without poking his head above the earth.

"And this region was the domain of many peoples—dwarves and dark elves, of course, but also the deep gnomes, the mind flayers, and many others. But none were as evil, as calculating, as the drow.

"The drow maintained a magical focus, deep under the earth, that they called the Darkfyre. Into this, they fed the bodies of their slain enemies, and the Darkfyre grew in power. Finally it overwhelmed those who fed it and grew of its own will into a great force, of cataclysmic destruction—the Rockfire.

"It consumed the world of the underground, destroying most of it. Mountains such as this were born in the fire, while whole cities and nations of the underdark were demolished." Luskag paused, and Poshtli sensed the pain of the tale, a pain that appeared as fresh as if the disaster had occurred only yesterday.

"The dwarven race was annihilated, except for a few small tribes, such as my ancestors. And even they found that life underground was no longer possible, for the hallowed caverns of antiquity, those that survived the fire, became caldrons of poison gas or pools of hot, molten rock. So the dwarves came to the surface, and now we live our lives in shallow caves, very near the baking heat of the sun. Now we dwarves, here in the House of Tezca, are the last survivors of a proud and noble race.

"But one good thing, too, came from the Rockfire. That was the complete destruction of the drow. At least now we live in peace, unthreatened by their evil machinations."

Poshtli lowered his eyes in respect for his companion's pain. He wondered at the power that could destroy a whole people, a whole nation. The dry wind swirled around him, and he felt a sudden chill.

Luskag's pride was evident as he raised his bald head and looked across the House of Tezca. The barren, hot desert became muted with distance, when viewed from this lofty vantage. The reds and browns and yellows flowed together in soft shades. The harsh and jagged skyline became a thing of beauty —distant, aloof, and unassailable.

"And the Sunstone . . . that, too, was born of the Rockfire?" asked Poshtli, with a glance toward the summit.

Luskag nodded and climbed to his feet. "And we'd best get moving if you would consult the stone today. The sun will be high in the sky shortly, and we must reach the top before then."

Poshtli grunted acquiescence and stood stiffly. They had climbed most of the way up the mountain, but the last bit was the steepest, strewn with loose rock and dirty patches of snow. His mind became a haze of fatigue. Sweat dripped into his eyes, blurring his vision. They had brought no water. Luskag had informed him that the body and soul must be bared by the climb. One who sought the insight of the Sunstone must be pure and show his devotion by such abstinence.

Finally they crested the summit, and Poshtli saw that they stood upon the rim of a vast volcanic caldera. Through his fatigue, he looked down into the yawning crater and gasped with amazement at the sight of the Sunstone. His body tingled; his mind came sharply alert. This is a place of the gods! he realized in awe.

A great disk of silver lay flat in the crater, like a lake of molten metal. The inside of the caldera was dry and lifeless, a baked surface of black rock. But the disk, nearly the size of the great plaza of Nexal, seemed to gleam with a life of its own.

Poshtli could not have torn his eyes away even if he had wanted to. He squatted on his haunches, spellbound. He sensed Luskag sitting beside him, also facing the inside of the mountain.

Slowly, majestically, the sun crested the opposite side of the crater. Higher it climbed, warming them with its heat, but never did their eyes waver from the silver disk. Poshtli saw the metal begin to move, starting to swirl slowly in a great circle.

Faster and faster the metal whirled, and more magnificent, more enthralling grew the spell. The Eagle Warrior and the desert dwarf did not move, did not twitch a muscle or blink.

Finally the sun reached high across the mountain. Its light struck the disk in a scorching reflection, pouring brilliance in its concentrated beams.

Poshtli felt the force wash over him, almost knocking him backward. Grimly he fixed his gaze against the glare, feeling his body grow warm, then hot. His vision had suddenly become a white nothingness, but then a hole opened in the vast blank.

In the very center of his vision, the hole grew, until he could see through it, into a region of clear blue sky. He looked through the hole in his vision and saw buzzards circling, wheeling downward, away from him.

Poshtli forgot his pain, forgot the heat. He dove with the buzzards, which had now become eagles. Soaring, he remembered sensations of flight, but never had they created such joy.

With sudden, sickening abruptness, he flew with the eagles over a vast black wasteland. Through the ashes, he could see the outlines of canals, a tumbled mound that might have been a pyramid, the swamps that outlined what once had been lakes.

Nexal! He cried for the city, his voice a harsh wail. This was truly Nexal that stood below him, but a Nexal of death and disaster. There were no people here, but strange, frightening *things* wandered among the muck and ruin: creatures of grotesque appearance, malformed shapes, and bestial, hateful eyes.

Poshtli still looked through the hole in his vision, though now he tried to look away—but he could not. He thought the sight would drive him mad. Despair threatened to burst his heart.

Then he saw, before him, a woman of indescribable beauty. She stood among the blackened ruins, and the darkness fell back from her. Where it recoiled, the city did not reappear, but at least the land emerged, green and whole again.

Poshtli's avian form reeled under the brutal assault of the vision. He twisted and squirmed in the air as if he would escape the horror below it, but it seemed that everywhere he turned he faced new scenes of devastation.

Then he saw jungle below him, broken by patches of savannah. The sun appeared in his vision, rising directly above an overgrown pyramid. Poshtli's vision fell toward the pyramid, and here he saw a strange sight: a beautiful woman, fighting desperately for her life. He saw a pack of coyotes snapping at her legs.

Beside her stood one he recognized as a white man from

across the sea. He, too, fought the coyotes. Poshtli saw that the attackers were small, shaggy creatures of several colors—pale yellow, brown, and black.

The next thing he knew was Luskag's hand on his shoulder, shaking him. He sat up and blinked, unable to remove the glaring yellow spot from his vision—the spot where the hole had been. Dimly he realized that it was night.

"Come," said Luskag. Poshtli saw that the dwarf, too, blinked often. "Were the gods kind to you?"

"They were," Poshtli said softly. "I know now what to do."

* * * * *

Kardann, the assessor, reported to Cordell at noon. The captain-general kept the bookkeeper waiting outside the grand house while he dressed. Kardann fidgeted nervously on a stone bench in the courtyard, taking little note of his surroundings in the spacious palace that had once been Caxal's.

The house was huge, with an enclosed garden and bathing pool. Beyond this open area, whitewashed walls enclosed the high, airy rooms of the huge flat-roofed building. While most of the buildings in Ulatos seemed to be of wood or thatch, this one was made of stone.

Cordell soon emerged from his apartments to meet the Council of Six's representative.

"Of course, I worked under execrable conditions," began Kardann. "It's not like weighing nice minted coins. My estimate includes an error factor of plus or minus ten percent."

His apology out of the way, Kardann beamed. "My preliminary assessment, however, yields the pleasant sum of one million, one hundred thousand pieces of gold, once forging and minting have been accomplished. The gold seems to be of genuinely high purity, though my assumptions have been cautious there as well."

Cordell whistled softly. "That is splendid news, sir. Simply splendid!"

Kardann lowered his head modestly and then cleared his throat, looking hesitantly back at the captain-general. "May

I ask, Your Excellency, whether you now plan to embark for home?"

Cordell looked at the man in astonishment. "Of course not. We have barely scratched the surface of this land!"

"Begging the general's pardon," wheezed Kardann, "but some of the men have been talking about the distances, and our small numbers. Surely it would be wise to return to Amn for additional provisions and reinforcements?"

And perhaps another assessor, you filthy coward? Cordell looked at the man with barely concealed scorn. "You had best set aside any thoughts of returning to Amn, my good bookkeeper." His voice took on its customary edge of firmness, the tone of a captain's captain. "Double-check your figures. And strive for a little more accuracy this time, if you please."

With a dark look backward, Kardann slipped away, stiffening and nodding as Cordell called after him. "Send in Captain Daggrande."

The dwarf clumped in and raised his hand in salute. "Town's quiet, General."

"And that chief, Caxal?" asked the commander.

"He's waiting outside."

"Very well. When my lady Darien emerges, we shall summon him. Remain until then, Captain."

In moments, the elfmaiden came from the private apartments across the wide courtyard to join them in the large, open room that served well as a central meeting hall. As always during daylight, the albino's body was swathed completely in her robe.

Two guards ushered Caxal through the door, and Cordell immediately began to speak, with Darien translating.

"You have done well with the gathering of gold. I am sure we will now have peace between our peoples. But there is one more thing you must do."

Caxal scowled but then quickly wiped his face clear of expression. Cordell continued. "All of those warriors who are chiefs, the 'Jaguars' and the 'Eagles,' must be brought to me. We have many here, detained when they brought the gold. But you must find the rest and send them to us. When they are all safely locked up, then your city will return to life as usual."

For a moment, Caxal stood taller. "My city will never return to life as usual," he growled. But then his shoulders sagged. "I do not know why you would lock up a man, unless he fears to escape the altar. Are you making sacrifices of them?"

"Of course not, by Helm!" Cordell's face flushed. "That barbaric practice is forevermore outlawed! Here, in Ulatos, and wherever else I take my legion!

"The warriors will be placed in a room and kept there until we ascertain that Ulatos will give us no further trouble. They must report to me by sunset today."

"But they will surely die!" protested Caxal. "They are not the kind of men who can live caged in a room. You will surely kill them!"

"That's a risk I'm willing to take," barked Cordell. "This interview is concluded."

Caxal bowed, shaking with emotion. He held his eyes downcast as he backed toward the door.

"Wait!" Cordell stopped him. "There is another thing. I wish to learn more of this place you talked of, this 'Nexal.' Bring me some of your people who have visited there or lived there. I'm sure you know of such people."

"As you wish." Caxal nodded again and hurriedly slipped out the door.

"Do the men have comfortable quarters?" Cordell asked, turning to Daggrande.

"Indeed, General. Splendid. Food is plentiful. The Payit have no ales nor spirits," admitted the dwarf wistfully. "This 'octal' they drink has a most pungent aroma and curious taste. But the men have made the most of it."

"We will remain here for two days. We'll let the men enjoy themselves a bit, find some women, that sort of thing. Go easy on them if they get a little out of control. One other thing, though, Captain. Any legionnaire caught hoarding gold is to be thrown in irons and displayed in the plaza as a lesson to his fellows. See that the word is passed.

"Then, Captain, I have a task that will require your special abilities." Daggrande looked at his general quizzically, and Cordell smiled slightly as he explained. "I wish to build a fort beside the anchorage where the fleet stands. You will be in charge of the construction, rotating half of the legion on work detail while the others stand to arms."

Daggrande nodded in quick comprehension. "Good choice, sir. That rocky hill just back from the shore?"

"Exactly. But we'll need a jetty, too. Later, perhaps, a breakwater, but for now, we'll start with a breastwork and a place to dock a carrack. Now, enjoy some time before I put you to work."

The dwarf nodded and clumped away. Captain Alvarro stepped in as his comrade departed.

"Ah, Captain," began the commander. "I will tell you why I have summoned you. We have been accepted rather prettily here, but I believe one more gesture is necessary to ensure the lasting obedience of the Payit."

"Yes, General? What do you suggest?"

"I want you to observe these warriors we have in captivity. Find four or five that show some spirit, that seem like leaders. Bring them to me, in the plaza before this house, this evening hence." The captain-general smiled grimly at his lieutenant, his eyes glittering like black sapphires.

"We will make sure that the warriors of Ulatos remember that they have been conquered by the Golden Legion."

* * * * *

From the chronicle of Coton:

As darkness gathers around the shores of Nexal.

Zaltec holds all of Maztica in thrall. Qotal tantalizes us with the promise of his return, with the sign of the couatl, with the visions to the Eagle Knight, but he gives no sign of arrival. And now an Ancient One is abroad in the land.

He follows his pack of hounds—black, fiery beasts from the netherworld, the world of Zaltec and the Darkfyre— and he seeks to kill the future before it can begin. For thus can Zaltec's triumph be assured.

But now the Ancient One moves with fear as well, for the

pieces of the future are falling into place. He must slay her, and he must keep his nature a secret. Even the Ancient Ones, it seems, fear the might of the strangers.

The girl is still a child of pluma, and, too, she is the beneficiary of unpredicted aid. The white man accompanies her not as conqueror but as companion. Together they challenge the darkness, but that darkness is vast, and they are very small indeed.

❧ 19 ❧

HELMSPORT

"What happened to you?" gasped Erix, leaning back to stare at the towering figure of Halloran.

"The potion . . . one of the small bottles! It must have been a potion of growth!" Erix clapped her hands over her ears, and Hal looked around self-consciously, imagining the echoes of his deep voice rumbling through the narrow, stone-walled gorge. He squatted in the grotto, noting that the light spell had vanished sometime during the fight.

"And that . . . *thing* that attacked you . . . I couldn't see it! What *was* that?" Erix stepped closer to Halloran, hesitantly reaching upward and touching his knee as if to ascertain that he really stood before her. Even squatting, he still loomed over her, but at least their faces were closer. He made an effort to speak quietly.

"I don't know. I've heard about such things . . . invisible stalkers and servants that wizards can summon. I think it was one of those . . . that it somehow tracked us here."

Erix frowned in concentration. "Listen . . . the howling. It's gone!"

They both remained still for a few moments, listening. Hal noticed that the sky was growing light from the approaching dawn. "I don't think this invisible fellow had anything to do with the howling," he ventured. "It's quiet now, sure, but that doesn't mean whatever it is has given up the trail."

"Do you think others know where we are? If the stalker can find us, maybe its master can, too!"

"Or mistress . . ." said Hal, thinking of the wizard Darien. He knew she would never forgive him for the theft of her spellbook, and he suspected she would be relentless in her pursuit of vengeance. By the same token, that loss might limit her powers enough to make pursuit difficult.

"You've got a good point," he said. "I think we'd better get out of here right away." Rosy light now colored half the sky, but the jungle remained still. The low rumble of surf, on the beach beyond the grotto, was the only sound.

Suddenly Halloran doubled over, his giant form toppling like a felled tree. He dropped to his hands and knees, retching uncontrollably. For a second, he suffered a terrifying sensation of falling as the world spun madly around him. His body twisted, racked by convulsions, and he sensed the grass slipping from his hands as he moved involuntarily.

Finally a sense of normalcy returned. He remained kneeling, supported by his hands, and slowly caught his breath. He no longer felt nauseous. Most importantly, his size was once again that of a human, not a giant.

Erix helped him to his feet. "Are you hurt?" she asked. "You looked like you were in terrible pain."

He nodded, suppressing a groan. "I was, for a minute there. I'm glad that's over."

Erix shook her head slowly. "I don't like it, this magic that changes you so. I think we should pour the other potions out!"

"That one surely proved useful! Who knows how helpful the invisibility potion might be, or that other one? I should find out what it is."

He reached into the saddlebag and pulled out the other small bottle. Like the invisibility and growth potions, it was marked by an indistinguishable label. He popped the cork out and raised it.

"Wait," said Erix, her voice quiet but urgent. "It's so soon since the effects of the other. At least wait awhile before trying it."

He was about to ignore her caution, but something in the strain of her voice told him she was really concerned. "All right," he said and put the bottle away.

* * * * *

"These are the warriors who have been causing the difficulties?" demanded Cordell.

Four men had been dragged to him in chains. Now they waited on their knees before the captain-general in the plaza of Ulatos. They were filthy, wearing only torn breechclouts. It was hard to believe that they had once been Eagle and Jaguar Knights.

"These are the ones," grunted Alvarro, cuffing one man who dared to raise his head at Cordell's voice.

The horseman knew what his commander had in mind, and the whole charade was a game he found quite entertaining. The men were not troublemakers. Their only offense had been to glare at him instead of casting their eyes down like the other prisoners. The Payit warriors generally became morose and apathetic under captivity. It was as much spirit as any of the captives had shown, but that was all the excuse Alvarro needed.

"Valez, are you ready?" Cordell asked.

"Yes, my general!" Valez, the legion's master smith, nodded. He knelt before a hot pile of coals and quickly pulled forth a long iron. Its tip was the image of the staring eye of Helm, and now it glowed cherry red.

The group stood on the raised platform in the plaza, with Darien and a strong contingent of guards. Many natives had gathered in the great square around them to witness the sorcery of the white men. Darien stood with Cordell, ready to translate when the time was right.

The first prisoner did not know what was happening. Two legionnaires threw him roughly to the ground and knelt on him, pressing his head sideways against the stones. Valez moved quickly, pressing the red-hot iron to the man's cheek.

The knight's flesh sizzled sickeningly, and a cloud of smoke hissed into the air. He screamed, but the legionnaires held firm. In a second, Valez pulled the iron away, and the knight rolled across the hard clay surface of the plaza. He sobbed uncontrollably, and though the legionnaires did not know it, his tears were tears of shame, not pain.

In short order, the other three knights were similarly

overpowered and branded, though each struggled frantically against the debasement. But in the end, each of the four wore the glaring eye, branded forever onto their faces.

"The hand of Helm is everywhere," pronounced Bishou Domincus solemnly. Domincus glared at the branded men as if their very presence was an affront to his god.

"Indeed." Cordell nodded. He was worried about the cleric. Since the death of his daughter, the Bishou had become obsessed with the notion of Helm's vengeance against transgressors. And his mind, clouded by hatred, saw all Mazticans as transgressors.

However, such vehemence had in fact proved useful in the subjugation of Ulatos. So vigorously had the Bishou preached his tale of Helm's might, so vivid was the proof of his superiority in the form of the recent battle, that the Payit seemed to have no difficulty accepting Helm as a superior god. Domincus told them that Helm had personally vanquished the pagan gods. Now the Mazticans turned out daily to hear the Bishou harangue them in a language they could not understand. They recognized the glaring eye in Helm's banner, however, and began to treat it with the respect due a mighty god by prostrating themselves when the flag was raised or lowered.

"Let this be a final reminder of our mastery and the punishments meted to our enemies!" proclaimed Cordell for Darien to translate. The elf woman, robed and masked as always when she ventured into the light of the sun, looked with satisfaction at the prisoners.

She was impressed once again with the general's wisdom. The legion could not afford to keep a large garrison in Ulatos. Yet the city must know, and always remember, that it had been conquered. Even when no legionnaires were in sight, the citizens of the city would look at these four warriors and they would remember.

"Now, to the palace," spoke the captain-general, turning and marching quickly back to his residence. Darien and the Bishou accompanied him through the courtyard, where he found Daggrande and Kardann awaiting him.

"The headman, Caxal, is here, General," explained the dwarf.

"Did he bring anyone with him?"

"Yes, sir. He's brought several of his fellows to tell you about that city, Nexal." The dwarf gestured toward the inner courtyard of the building that had once been Caxal's house.

Cordell quickly strode through the vine-fringed archway. He found Caxal seated on a stone bench, with six men resting on the ground beside him. The captain-general paused long enough to allow Darien to catch up and take position beside him. Meanwhile, the Payits all flung themselves on the earth and pressed their foreheads to the ground.

The rest of Cordell's captains, Garrant and the commanders of the longbows and spearmen, joined them here. Kardann, too, hurried to catch up, wheezing for breath but quickly readying his quill and scroll as Cordell spoke.

"I want you to tell me anything you know about the land of Nexal, both the people and the city itself. I will not harm you. I will reward those who share their knowledge with me. Now, speak."

Cordell paced back and forth beside a flower-studded lily pond, dictating his words for Darien to translate. The men remained kneeling on the grass before the captain-general.

"You." He addressed a tall man who wore a humble white mantle. "Have you been there?"

"Indeed, Most Commanding Lord. The city of Nexal is the greatest city in all the True World. Beside it, Ulatos is nothing more than a squalid collection of hovels."

"And gold?" prodded Cordell. "Do the Nexalans have gold?"

"Oh, yes, Most Magnificent Conqueror! The most humble of lords wears plates upon his chest, ear and lip plugs of solid gold. They collect gold in tribute from all the tribes they have conquered.

"The marketplace of Nexal is like no other place in the world, Supreme One! The markets alone cover a plaza the size of this entire city. There will Your Magnificence find more gold, feathers and turquoise, pearls and jade, all manners of treasures, sorcerous things, objects of feathermagic and talonmagic.

"There, too, are the great treasuries! Naltecona's alone, concealed somewhere in his palace, holds more valuables than our entire humble city. And each of his counselors has built a palace, and each has such a storeroom, never opened in the long history of Nexal!"

"How do you know of all this, man?" The captain-general grew suspicious at the extent of the man's enthusiasm, but the native hastily and abjectly explained.

"I have traded with the Nexalan merchants, the *potec*, who travel all Maztica. They sometimes come to Payit, especially for cocoa and plumage that cannot be found in less verdant lands. They talk freely of their city, and they tell how they must pay taxes to Naltecona for his treasure room, just as their fathers were taxed by Naltecona's father.

"Once I journeyed to Nexal with a band of *potec*, and lived a year in that grand city. I spent long days in the marketplace, bartering and learning their ways."

"What of their army?"

"The warriors of Nexala are more numerous than the grains of sand on the shore," answered the trader. "They have prevailed over all their foes, conquering all of their neighboring nations save one. That one, Kultaka, has fighters who are as fierce, if not as numerous, as the Nexalans."

"This city, Nexal . . . is it walled?"

"It is protected by lakes on all sides, O Hallowed Warrior. You must cross long causeways to reach the city, and each of these has many wooden sections that can be removed. It is a city of canals and plazas and avenues. There are no walls surrounding it."

Gradually the others confirmed or embellished upon the trader's story. Most of the details referred to colorful murals, grand temples, and bloody gods. None could accurately estimate the size of the Nexalan army, but by all accounts, it made the Payit force look like an understrength regiment by comparison.

Cordell also gained an approximate understanding of the city's location, thanks to a map of many colors, with surprisingly detailed terrain features, drawn by the trader. After the natives had been rewarded with glass beads and ushered out, the captain-general turned to his followers.

"Daggrande, how does the loading progress?"

"The gold was finally loaded this morning, General. A share to each ship."

"Splendid. We will remain here for one more day to allow the men some more opportunity to enjoy our fruits of victory!"

"May I ask," Kardann began hesitantly, "has the captain-general considered the suggestion that we return to Amn for reinforcements? With the treasure we have already gained, the council would be sure to fund a much larger fleet!" Several captains nodded and muttered assent to the suggestion.

"The legion moves west!" barked Cordell. "We have barely scratched the surface of the opportunities here. Don't you know that once we return home, every small-time wizard and copper-plate pirate on the Sword Coast will head for Maztica?"

"Surely the base you speak of will serve as ample protection of our claims! You can leave a force to hold the fortress until the fleet returns with more men!"

"I fear your understanding of tactics is not as great as your counting of numbers, my good assessor." The commander spoke gently, hoping to humiliate the accountant rather than browbeat him. Captain Daggrande grinned at the jibe, but Cordell was mildly alarmed to note that several other captains seemed to be taking Kardann all too seriously. "Were we to abandon this shore now," he pressed, "we would stand to lose all that we have gained so far. These people will only understand our mastery if we hold it before them, not just for a day or a week but for months, perhaps years!"

Kardann started to sputter, but Cordell silenced him with a look. "By the time that happens, I intend to have the entire land under the banner of the Golden Legion!" He paused to make sure they understood the depth of his commitment.

"Make the most of your day here," he suggested breezily. "We toil again very soon, this time upon the building of Helmsport!"

* * * * *

Gultec's stomach growled again, and the lanky jaguar rose and stretched in feline bliss. He rested upon a massive bough, high above the jungle floor. Sitting up, he cleaned himself thoroughly. His hunger was present, but not yet urgent.

Eventually the spotted cat sauntered down the branch, springing easily to a lower limb, and down again into the crotch of a neighboring tree. His nostrils twitched, alert for the spoor of game.

Gultec made his way along the middle level of jungle branches, avoiding the tangle upon the ground but remaining well camouflaged among thick foliage. For perhaps an hour, he hunted, catching the scent of nothing edible.

Lengthening shadows stretched through the small open patches in the deep jungles of Far Payit. The jaguar's spotted form moved among the shadows, his orange and black pelt blending perfectly with the gathering darkness. His stomach started to growl uncomfortably.

By now the great cat skulked through forests far removed from Ulatos. He had worked his way southward, hunting and prowling and sleeping as occasion demanded. Now he was farther south than he had ever been before, in a region of Payit little known to the city dwellers of Ulatos.

Gultec began to move with unaccustomed urgency, for the hunting had been lean for several days now. Hunger prodded him along, sometimes through the trees and occasionally along the twisting trails below. He pounced on a small rodent and devoured it in one gulp, but the tiny meal did little to sate his appetite.

Perhaps it was the urgency of his hunger that made him careless. It had been many days since he had encountered any sign of humans, and thus his vigilance was relaxed. The great cat need worry about no other enemies, for even the powerful *hakuna* generally took no note of another feline predator.

In any event, Gultec slipped silently along a trail as night fall settled around him. His padded paws fell silently on the soft grass of the ground. Every few steps, the great cat paused to sniff the air and look around.

Impatient, he picked up his pace to a trot. Once an irritated growl even rumbled from his throat before he recalled the need for stealth. As he paced along the trail, he heard something rustling ahead. A current of breeze carried to him the delightful scent of a plump turkey—food enough to fill the great cat's belly.

Gultec crouched and crept forward, slinking soundlessly on his belly. There! He saw the turkey, standing oddly still at the base of a great tree. The bird fluttered and twisted, but it did not move from its location. Even Gultec's keen eyes did not see the narrow tether holding the bird in place.

With one lightning bound, Gultec sprang toward the bird. His attack was planned perfectly: He would land once, ten feet from the bird, and instantly spring again for the kill.

His paws settled to earth, already preparing to push him forward, but the earth proved yielding, crashing away beneath his weight. With a screech of feline rage and panic, Gultec fell through the network of branches concealing the deep pit and plummeted to the bottom with a heavy thud.

Instantly the jaguar sprang at the sides of the pit, his powerful muscles carrying him upward a prodigious distance before the steep, smooth walls sent him tumbling back down. Again and again the cat hurled himself toward the top of the pit, and again and again he fell back.

Finally, exhausted and ravenous, he settled into a crouch. His unblinking eyes stared upward at the night sky, beginning to sprout stars above his pit. For all his rage and all his strength, Gultec could not deny that he was trapped.

* * * * *

Several dozen men remained in Ulatos, while the rest of the legion moved to the sheltered anchorage barely three miles away. There construction of Fort Helmsport began as two hundred legionnaires, armed with pick and shovel, assaulted the rocky crest a short distance from the sandy shore.

Darien used a powerful earth-moving spell to begin a jetty out into the lagoon, and now men labored with wheelbarrows and shovels, extending the pier into deeper water. The wizard and the captain-general, meanwhile, moved from the palace to their quarters aboard the *Falcon*.

Late at night in this luxurious cabin, two figures lay in the great bed. Cordell snored deeply, while Darien lay wide awake, her pale eyes staring across the cabin, her elven senses seeing everything despite the pitch darkness.

A sense of danger gripped the elf woman, and she sat up in the bed. Something unseen warned her of attack, and she placed her feet on the floor. Her robe, with its many packets of spell components, hung beside her.

Suddenly a gust of wind rushed through the crack under the cabin door. Darien's keen vision, unnaturally sensitive to such conjured creatures as the invisible stalker, recognized the thing instantly. In the next moment, she perceived its intent.

The stalker reached out for her, a sudden gust of wind whirling in the cabin, extending invisible but powerful tendrils of air toward Darien. She sensed immediately that it wanted to kill her.

But Darien's spell was ready. She spat, her saliva flying toward the invisible attacker. "*Dyss-ssymmi!*" she cried, raising both hands before her face.

With a horrible sucking sound, the wind twisted into a vortex and whirled in an ever smaller cyclone in the center of the room. It writhed as it shrank and then puffed into nothingness. Her spell of dismissal, she knew, had sent it back to the plane of air.

Cordell had awakened at the sound of her spell, and now he stretched an arm around the elf woman, amazed and impressed by her calm demeanor.

"What was that?" he asked. He sat up in the bed, blinking. He had seen nothing of the attacker, though he had heard the wind.

"My stalker. It has failed to kill Halloran, thus it sought me out instead. It is a risk of the spell." Darien shrugged, the attack already forgotten except for its implications.

"And this means Halloran still lives. If he had perished from the poison, the stalker would not have come after me. It would simply have gone away."

Cordell flopped backward with a sigh. "Helm's damnation! That lad makes things very difficult."

Darien squinted in anger, an expression Cordell could not see. "Difficult, perhaps. But he will not escape!"

"What makes you so certain?"

"Where can he go? We have control of Ulatos, and through the city, we can keep tabs on the entire nation. Sooner or later, someone is bound to report him. He'll probably leave a whole wealth of stories behind everywhere he goes." Darien leaned over Cordell, gently pressing him back on the bed.

He grinned. "Come closer. I'd like to hear you scheme some more." And he pulled her down to him.

* * * * *

"There is no way that I can repay the kindness you have shown me. It has meant my life, and much more, to me." Poshtli bowed deeply to Luskag, blinking and finally looking to the side. The golden dot still burned before his eyes.

But the vision had been worth the price. If he could but complete the tasks before him, a city, a whole people, might be saved.

"You have been a worthy companion, Poshtli of Nexal," said Luskag sincerely. The dwarf mopped the sweat from the top of his bald head, then reached into a quiver slung at his belt.

"I would like you to take these on your journey," he said, offering Poshtli six slender arrows. The Eagle Knight took the gifts reverently, bowing deeply.

The arrows bore no marks to distinguish them, but each was perfectly straight, made from an exceptional reed. The heads were of shiny obsidian, deftly chipped from flawless rock. Tiny fluffs of feather marked the tail of each arrow, and though the feathers were small, it was here that Poshtli sensed the true strength of the gift.

The desert dwarf chieftain and a score of his dusty, suntanned warriors had gathered in the center of Sunhome to bid farewell to the stranger, one of only a handful of humans ever to have found Sunhome, according the Luskag. Many of them had come seeking the Sunstone, but only a few had departed alive.

The village itself was simply a circle of ground-level cave homes around the inside of a box canyon. A clearing in the center of the canyon floor had long ago been smoothed, and here Poshtli nodded to the others, then turned back to Luskag.

The Eagle Knight wore his full regalia, black-and-white-feathered cape and beaked helmet, with his bow and arrows, his spear, and his *maca* all suspended from his belt or harness.

Suddenly Poshtli whirled around in a circle. The desert dwarves scurried backward as he raised his arms, causing the feathered cape to swing in a wide circle. Then he squatted and beat his wings, falling several feet and then swooping above the ground.

The Eagle Knight enjoyed the stunned expressions on the faces of the dwarves. His wings beat steadily as his sleek form circled, climbing into the canyon above Sunhome. He cried a challenge and a farewell that echoed through the canyon long after he soared from sight. A cold mountain updraft lifted him and carried him eastward.

Poshtli flew steadily toward the sunrise, as his vision had shown him.

Vast reaches of land passed below him, and desert slowly turned to savannah, then mountains, and finally jungle. The eagle subsisted upon the power of *pluma*, for Poshtli did not stop to eat nor to sleep, though the sun rose and set during his flight.

He flew on through the damp, heavy air above the jungles of Payit, and now his muscles thrummed with renewed energy. He sensed the goal of his flight in the distance. Somewhere ahead he would find the green pyramid.

*　*　*　*　*

Halloran and Erix pressed through the forest for a full day, gasping through hot, moist air and ignoring a surrounding swarm of biting insects. Occasionally they found a narrow trail and mounted Storm, while Corporal trotted ahead or behind. The dog panted constantly in the heat, and Hal began to wonder if the greyhound could keep up for long.

They tried to work their way inland as much as possible, avoiding human settlements. Hal felt that any pursuit by the legion would come along the shore, the only terrain suitable for horsemen over any stretch of distance. Indeed, sometimes he considered abandoning the loyal mare, but he always discarded the idea, hacking extra-hard at the ubiquitous vines to open a passage large enough for Storm.

Finally the long day came to an end, and they collapsed in exhaustion. They camped in a place indistinguishable from all the surrounding jungle, a space between two tree trunks, with the overhanging vines and drooping ferns hacked away. It was all Halloran could do to pull the saddle off Storm before collapsing on the ground. Corporal already snoozed, albeit with an occasional whimper or twitch.

They had not found fresh water all day, but Erix found several thick-stemmed plants. When cut, these yielded a precious trickle of water. After a minimal meal of beans and mayzcakes, Erix fell asleep.

Halloran once again pulled open Darien's spellbook and tried to force himself to concentrate on the pages. The words still seemed distant and indistinct. Though he had cast the magic missile spell against Alvarro, he found himself struggling and failing in his attempt to relearn it. The light spell was a little, but not much, more familiar. Finally he drifted off to sleep, with the spellbook resting across his body.

Near midnight, Corporal's whine awakened them both. The source of the dog's agitation was quickly audible: a sharp, ululating howling rose into the night and resounded through the forest like the voice of doom.

"It's closer," whispered Erix, awestruck.

In the back of his mind, Halloran had sheltered the notion that perhaps this nocturnal pack was not connected to him. After all, he knew of no spells usable by the Bishou or Darien that could conjure up anything like this. But their appearance on this second night in a row confirmed his worst suspicions.

"They're a *lot* closer," he said grimly, looking straight into Erix's eyes. He wanted to dive into the warm pool he saw there, seeking comfort and shelter. But he knew this was not to be.

"What *are* they?" Erix questioned him earnestly.

She tried to conceal her fright, but was not completely successful.

"I'm not sure. Sorcerous, some kind of black magic things, I'm sure . . . very powerful, very deadly. They sound, in a way, like a pack of hounds on the hunt, but the noise is too unearthly for that." He took a deep breath and continued.

"Remember when I told you that we'd have to split up if it ever got too dangerous? The time has come. You can't stick with me any longer. I can't outrun those creatures, and when they catch me, it won't be pleasant. I might be able to hold 'em off, but you'll be far safer elsewhere."

She laughed at him then, and Halloran just stared back, not amused. "I mean it! We'll have to split up. It's the only chance you have!"

"Did you ever stop to think that this pack might be chasing *me?*" she asked, standing up and then helping him to his feet. "Maybe we should just stick together and try to help each other out," Erix suggested.

Halloran looked at her in surprise, ashamed that he had not considered that possibility. He had known since the death of Kachin that Erix had powerful and murderous enemies. Indeed, that attacker had broken off the fight at dawn, exactly when these hounds had ceased their howling the previous night.

Wearily, aching in every joint, they prepared to move out once more. The howling was more distinct than the previous night, yet still somehow indefinably distant.

They plodded along through the rest of the night, and gradually the sound drifted away behind them. But humans and animals both were near the point of total exhaustion when sunrise finally ended the cries of the beastly pursuers.

Finally, just as dawn turned to daylight, the jungle opened slightly into a flat savannah of grass, reeds, and, wondrous miracle, a clear pond! They both splashed into the water as the sun came up, drinking and washing and cooling off.

Only as the first rays lit the ground around them did Halloran look up to see three buzzards wheeling through a lazy circle above them.

* * * * *

"Higher! It needs five more feet!" Daggrande barked at a group of legionnaires who leaned on their spades in exhaustion. With dark looks at the dwarf, they chopped into the earth and shoveled more dirt onto the rampart that now ringed three quarters of Fort Helmsport.

Despite his shouts and curses, the dwarf could not restrain his pride in the work of the legionnaires. In a few short days, they had moved a prodigious amount of earth. Soon they would have a commanding and easily defensible base overlooking a fine natural harbor and a long stretch of the coast of this nation called Payit.

Below them, the little fishing village would never be the same. The wide, once-grassy field surrounding it had been churned to mud. A small smithy had been established near the stream, which now flowed brown and silt-laden into the bay, while black smoke from the forge filtered across the plain. A road, already reduced to a strip of mud, led from the fort to Ulatos. Steady supplies of food—cocoa, mayz, turkeys, venison, all the choicest delicacies of the Payit— arrived daily, and the legion ate well.

As the fort's construction progressed, rocks and earth had also been dumped into the bay, and now a solid jetty extended perhaps a hundred feet from shore. An additional pier, crossing the **T** of the jetty, took form, and carracks and caravels pulled up to the solid barrier. No longer did all loading and unloading depend upon the ships' small boats.

Daggrande continued his inspection of the rampart. The hilltop would soon be circled by a ten-foot-high dirt wall, with a five-foot deep ditch on the outside. A small opening had been left, free of ditch and wall, but Darien claimed to know a spell that would fill this gap in a moment. Daggrande did not doubt her.

The dwarf moved around to the far side of the redoubt, facing inland. This entire length had been the first completed, and no one was working here now. Daggrande climbed to the top of the wall and looked south. The belt of coastal plain surrounding Ulatos quickly met a deep jungle. The legionnaires had heard tales of a land called Far Payit, in the distant reaches to the south, but little was known of that heavily forested reach.

The natives of Ulatos had proven most cooperative, arriving at Helmsport laden with food, *octal*, and featherwork, but no more gold. These days Cordell studied his map, consulting again and again with the men who had seen Nexal. Images of that city—gold-lined images, Daggrande felt certain—had begun to dominate the commander's thoughts.

The dwarf himself didn't like the prospect of a long campaign on this foreign shore, so far from a supply and reinforcement base. At least here, beside Ulatos, they were close to their ships. The fleet represented ultimate safety against a people whose largest craft was the canoe.

Nexal was an inland city, many days' march from the sea. Surely even Cordell would not be so rash as to lead his small group, a bare five hundred men, into the heart of a nation whose army must number many tens of thousands! But beneath all his reflections, Daggrande was a legionnaire, sworn to obey his captain-general. And such he would always do, or die.

Daggrande's musings were interrupted by the sound of hushed voices. Scowling, he looked along the length of the wall, then into the redoubt behind him, but he saw nobody near him. Leaning slightly forward, he looked down the outer slope of the wall and saw several captains, including the usually dependable Garrant. Leaning farther, but crouching so as to remain hidden, the dwarf recognized the hat of the Assessor of Amn, Kardann.

It was the latter who spoke.

"He means to see us die here for his own aggrandizement!" Kardann's urgency carried even through the whisper of his voice. "Any sensible man would send for reinforcements and build up an army here before marching inland to seize more land!"

"Aye," grunted Captain Leone, a brave but unimaginative captain of longbowmen. "I've heard the army we fought here is nothin' next to the men they can muster inland."

"We must send to Amn for more forces!" persisted the assessor. "It would not mean abandonment of this base. We'd only need to send a few ships, enough to get the treasure safely back."

"It's the sensible thing to do," grunted another captain. Daggrande didn't recognize him beneath the brim of his helm.

"Perhaps we should all talk to the general . . ." suggested Garrant.

"No!" hissed Kardann. "He fears too much for his own power. We would only scare him into doing something rash. Instead, I have another plan. . . ."

A sudden wind whirled off the bay, and Daggrande ducked backward, startled. The whispers of the warm breeze drowned out the whispers of treachery from below, but Daggrande had heard enough.

It was time to find the captain-general.

* * * * *

By day they stumbled until fatigue claimed them, collapsing into whatever minimal shelter the land might offer. They would steal a few hours of sleep in the afternoon, but then night fell, and soon the howling commenced again. Each night it drew closer, until it resounded through the forest, as if the pack were about to burst through the nearest line of trees. Still, after four nights of desperate flight, keeping always to unpopulated lands, barren wildernesses of jungle and swamp, they had yet to catch sight of their pursuers.

Halloran thought many times about stopping and fighting the faceless pack, challenging them with Helmstooth. But something in the sinister noises from bestial throats convinced him that such a challenge would be folly.

And, too, the thought of this woman facing a death as bloody and violent as Martine's was too terrifying for contemplation. The bitter image of the sacrifice still tortured Hal's memory. He felt certain that Erixitl's death would drive him mad.

They progressed slowly through the rough terrain, still encountering no sign of human habitation—at least, current human habitation. Many brush-covered mounds dotted the land, especially among the clearings. A close examination of several proved them to be overgrown pyramids, from a time long past. The land grew more open, still covered with jungle in patches but also offering areas of open meadow or grassland.

Corporal proved his fine greyhound's instincts over and over as he darted into the brush or across a short stretch of prairie, often returning with a turkey, rabbit, and once even a monkey. With this limited supply of meat, and the many fruits offered by the jungle, they did not suffer from hunger.

But still the driving, terrifying howling greeted them at night, driving them onward, always growing closer. They spoke little, sharing a pervasive sense of fear. Only in the mornings, after the howling had ceased for the day, would they sometimes pause for rest and quiet conversation.

"Who was she?" asked Erix one morning.

Halloran knew whom she meant, but he wasn't sure how to explain how he felt about Martine. He and Erix had just collapsed in a relatively open jungle clearing several hours after dawn. Since the pursuit grew closer every night in any event, they had decided that it didn't make sense to exhaust themselves during the day.

"She was a headstrong girl. I was charged with her safety."

"Was she your . . . wife? Your woman?" asked Erix tensely.

Halloran looked at her in surprise. "No." Suddenly the memory of his infatuation with Martine seemed foolish and embarrassing. Her death would remain a shocking barbarity in his memory, but it was the death of an innocent victim, not the loss of a true love. He shook his head emphatically. "No. She was the daughter of our priest. He brought her along with the expedition."

He remembered all the other ways he had once hoped to describe Martine, as his lady, his lover, even his wife. But all of those images now seemed ridiculous and absurd. The woman he desired was nothing like Martine. His woman was coolly intelligent, courageous, forgiving. . . .

She was Erixitl. Halloran looked at her, and this time he allowed himself to fall into those deep, dark eyes. He felt their warmth around him, and then he was holding her and nothing else seemed to matter.

"You frighten me, Captain Halloran," she whispered to him as they lay together on the soft grasses. "But I am not afraid."

* * * * *

Daggrande did not find Cordell until evening, when he saw the captain-general on the shore beside the jetty, admiring the project with Domincus and Darien. Torches lined the pier, reflecting in the clear water of the lagoon and illuminating the work that would proceed far into the night. The dwarf scowled in concentration as he remembered the treachery he had overheard upon the wall.

"Splendid work on the harbor, Captain, simply splendid!" Cordell gestured at the T-shaped pier. "The earthworks are proceeding well, too. We were up there earlier."

"Thank you, General." Daggrande, stoic figure that he was, nevertheless invariably thrilled to praise from his commander. He nodded politely. "Excuse me, sir. There's a matter I need to discuss with you."

"Go on," urged Cordell.

"It's . . . well, it's a matter of some confidentiality, General." Daggrande wasn't about to assume that any of the captain-general's lieutenants were definitely loyal.

"These two have my utter confidence," said Cordell. "Speak!"

"Aye, General." Daggrande cleared his throat. "I was on the wall today, inspecting the work. I overhead some scuttlebutt from the far side."

"Indeed? Our good assessor, perhaps?"

The dwarf nodded in surprise. "He talks treason, General! He seeks to recruit officers and men to steal away some of the ships and take them back to Amn—with the treasure!"

Cordell showed no reaction, except that his coal-black eyes narrowed with tension. For a long moment, he remained immobile.

"Well done, Captain. I didn't trust the little weasel, but neither did I suspect him to be this bold." The captain-general's voice was tight, clipped. "But with this warning, hc can be stopped in his tracks. Indeed, that is the only solution."

Slowly his face creased into an oily smile.

* * * * *

The attack came at dusk, silently and swiftly from the darkening jungle. No howling preceded it. Only Corporal saw the hell hounds, as Hal and Erix still slept peacefully in the grass. The greyhound barked, the sound shrill and frantic with tension.

Halloran sprang to his feet in time to see Corporal lunge toward the trees around their clearing. A great shape loomed there, half again as big as the greyhound. Hal saw red, glowing eyes and a tooth-studded maw spread wide.

Corporal lunged toward the attacker, unmindful of the other hell hounds coming into sight behind it. Halloran saw the greyhound spring, while the wolflike predator before him simply crouched. The beast spread its jaws, revealing huge black teeth.

As Corporal leaped for its throat, the monster belched a great cloud of flame. The greyhound twisted and yelped once, before fire wrapped the dog in a torturous, fatal shroud. Hot, billowing flames crackled from the hell hound's widespread maw, tearing the life from the loyal dog with its infernal heat.

The greyhound toppled to the ground while Halloran sprang forward, shocked and enraged by the attack. Helmstooth cut through the air in a silver flash, and the hell hound's head flopped onto the ground.

But then he looked up and saw more dark shapes charging through the darkness. They seemed to be all around him.

*   *   *   *   *

From the chronicle of Coton:

Silently obedient to the last, I yearn for a sign of hope or promise.

Naltecona has decided to send the strangers presents, as a token of his welcome—and his fear. The decision he left to the gods has been made by men, and now he greets those men as gods.

He has learned from his scouts and spies that the white men desire gold, so the Revered Counselor will send them gold to sate their appetites. He will also tell them of the great and grueling road to Nexal and inform them that they should not undertake such an arduous journey.

His lords and priests have counseled against this course, universal in claiming that gifts of gold will not cure the strangers of their appetite for the yellow metal.

But Naltecona is obstinate, and so the presents depart the city, a colorful caravan of slaves, litters of treasure, and ambassadors and spies of the Revered Counselor's court. They will bear the gifts to the strangers.

Once these men have seen our gold, I fear we shall never keep them away.

☙ 20 ☙

MEETING AND DEPARTURE

Gultec finally gave up trying to leap over the high walls of the pit. After some hours, he heard men approaching. Several minutes later, they reached the mouth of the pit. Soon he glared upward, growling, into the faces of perhaps two dozen brown-skinned, loinclothed tribesmen. Before he could move, a tangle of heavy nets fell into the pit, blanketing him.

He snarled and slashed and bit as several men dropped into the pit to complete the binding. The nets wrapped him tightly, and he was quickly hauled to the surface. He had the minor satisfaction of drawing blood from several of his captors, but now they dragged him unceremoniously along the ground, out of reach of any more victims.

For perhaps an hour, he slid across the ground, bruised and battered from the rough surface. He couldn't see much through the many layers of net, but suddenly he realized that he was no longer surrounded by looming jungle.

He growled and stumbled to his feet as several layers of nets were torn away. Blinking his yellow eyes, he looked at the most massive pyramid he had ever seen. Deep in the jungle, here in the heart of Far Payit, where only crude savages were supposed to live, someone had built this huge edifice!

All around the great pyramid spread flat green fields of grass or clear blue ponds. He saw other buildings, also great, though not as huge as the pyramid, spread among patches of thick jungle growth. A wide field, surrounded by three high walls, lay next to the structure. In the field,

Gultec saw several men dashing back and forth in pursuit of a round ball.

His captors dragged the jaguar toward the pyramid. Instead of ascending it, as Gultec had expected, they threw the net into a black opening set into the base of the structure like an open doorway. Instantly Gultec twisted and thrashed, but it took him several minutes to tear free from the nets. By that time, a door had been closed behind him.

Deep, rumbling growls reverberated through the jaguar's heavy chest. Gultec saw a passage leading toward the center of the pyramid, and he began to slink along this black corridor. He silenced his growls and crept forward noiselessly.

The corridor continued ahead for some distance, though not to the center of the pyramid, Gultec guessed. Then it opened into a large room. He smelled jaguar spoor, and the fur on his back bristled.

A second later, he saw the great cats sprawled about the room, some grooming themselves, some sleeping, some watching him with interest.

And then he noticed the other inhabitant of the room. An old man sat on a stone step directly across the chamber from him. He wore only a loincloth, and his hair was long and white. Lines creased his face, making it look like the wrinkled map of some mountainous land. The fellow stared at Gultec, ignoring the other jaguars. Those felines apparently were equally indifferent to his presence.

Gultec tensed. He crouched lower, his belly touching the floor. Slowly he began to slink forward.

The old man raised his hand and passed it once before his face. At that instant, Gultec's body contorted. He pitched onto the floor, in seconds changing violently from feline to human form. Stunned, he lay on the floor, slowly realizing that this man had affected the change. Shocked and awed, Gultec sat up and regarded the man, who rose and slowly moved toward him.

"Come, Gultec," he said softly. "You have so very much to learn."

* * * * *

Poshtli tucked his wings and dove toward the pyramid, certain at once that this was the place shown to him by the vision. The sun disappeared behind the tree-lined horizon as he landed upon the summit of the brush-covered structure. Soon it would be time.

For the first time in days, the Eagle Warrior stretched into his human body, reclining atop the mossy shell of the pyramid while he carefully massaged his muscles back to flexibility. He enjoyed the sight of a round moon, nearly full, climbing into the sky.

When he felt more comfortable, he arose and looked at the pyramid, going to the east side of the platform at the summit. The sides were steep and fully overgrown with brush and mosses, so that a human could scramble his way up or down, but with some difficulty.

The Eagle Knight cleared a small shelf just below the top, on the east face of the pyramid. There he carefully laid out the six arrows given to him by Luskag. The crude materials gleamed silvery bright in the moonlight. Then he laid his own quiver, with its two dozen arrows, beside the others.

He found a comfortable sitting position and waited. His *maca* rested across his lap, and his bow was in his hands.

* * * * *

A huge, rust-red hell hound—the color of dried blood, thought Halloran—lunged past the charred body of the greyhound, Corporal. The monster's jaws opened wide as the legionnaire dove to the side, and he barely avoided the gout of flame that singed the brush behind him.

He sprang to his feet and drove the hell hound back with a stab to its chest, his blow more painful than injurious to the beast.

A horrifying sense of impotent rage possessed him as he saw three of the creatures charge toward Erix. The woman stood with her back to a tree, a stout stick in her hands. But the crude weapon could not even reach the hounds as they crouched before her, jaws gaping for their deadly blast.

"No!" cried Hal, savagely chopping into another hound and springing over the dying beast in an effort to reach Erixitl. He knew he would never get there in time.

The trio of hell hounds spat their scorching breath directly into the young woman's face. Hal screamed as he saw the yellow flames blossom, surrounding her with an incinerating wave of evil magic.

The flames faded away, and he saw Erix again, standing in shock. The jade and feather token she wore at her neck now glowed and sparkled with a magical force of its own.

Then Halloran reached the fray, dropping one hound with a stab to its heart. The other two turned on him, but Erix clubbed one with her stick, knocking it to the side. The other blasted Hal with a gout of flame just as his sword pierced the creature's chest and heart.

Gasping, Halloran fell backward, his left arm blistered and charred. The hell hound fell dead, but more appeared from the darkness. He heard a panicked cry from Storm, and then the mare pulled free of her stake and galloped off into the night.

"This way!" he panted, pulling Erixitl away from the tree. Another hell hound, and another, charged in close. This is the end, Hal thought grimly.

Erix put her hand on his arm as the hell hounds breathed, and the fire crackled around them like a living thing, seeking their skins and their lives. But the power of *pluma* protected them, the aura of Erixitl's feathermagic token cloaking them like a soft shield.

The dead branches of a fallen forest giant crackled into flame behind them, and Hal counted close to a dozen hell hounds closing in around them. The flames leaped higher, and Halloran saw a black figure behind the pack, a hooded but lightly dressed form with a bow and a longsword.

"The Ancient One!" gasped Erix, as Halloran drove back the nearest hounds with a barrage of thrusts and slashes.

"Come on!" he gasped, leading her away from the pack of dogs. One of the creatures, already wounded in the leg, sprang directly into his path. The hound tumbled to the ground as it landed, and Hal killed it with a straight thrust to the heart.

Erix jumped after him, and they sprinted through a narrow belt of forest, dense brush and trees that separated the large clearings that dotted the area. The dogs crashed behind them through the jungle as they both fought for breath. Hal's arm burned, sending great sheets of pain shooting through his body, especially as the thorns and bark of the forest tore at him.

In the moonlight, Halloran saw Storm across the next clearing. The horse galloped along the perimeter of jungle, seeking a path of flight. He also saw a small cone-shaped hill in the center of the open area.

A hell hound burst from the edge of the jungle behind him, and Halloran split its skull open, even as Erix's hand on his shoulder protected them both from the monster's flaming breath.

Get the high ground, hold the high ground! The basic maxim of legion tactics came back to Halloran as hopelessness threatened to drag him down. Already he and Erix stumbled toward the center of the clearing, toward the low hill that loomed higher and higher as they ran. The nearly full moon, still low in the eastern sky, shed its impartial light across the scene.

More dogs broke from the forest, streaking across the open ground toward the humans.

Get the high ground!

Halloran recognized the hill as an overgrown pyramid, like other ruins they had seen on their flight. At the same time, he realized they would never reach the structure before the hell hounds dragged them down.

He turned to face the dogs, Erixitl beside him. The first of the slavering beasts leaped toward them, then suddenly crashed to the ground with a yelp of pain. It kicked once and lay still.

Something flashed past them, a blur in the moonlight, and then another hell hound collapsed. This time, Halloran saw the arrow, sparkling like a crystal shaft, protruding from the beast's neck. Still a third dog dropped, and renewed hope arose in Hal's heart. He wasted no time wondering about the nature of their miraculous deliverance.

"Run!" he shouted, propelling Erix toward the pyramid and stumbling after her. They threw themselves against the first tier of the structure and clawed madly upward through the brush. Ignoring the pain in his blistered arm, Halloran pulled himself upward by his feet and his right hand.

Finally they stopped, grasping the undergrowth to keep from slipping down the steep side. Halloran looked over his shoulder and counted six hell hounds dead in the clearing. A few more probed tentatively around the base of the pyramid, but he doubted whether the creatures could reach them now.

"Come on," urged Halloran. "Let's get up to the top."

"Look!" whispered Erix in horror. He turned and followed her gaze, instantly spotting the black-clothed figure stepping into the moonlit area of the clearing below. The figure crossed toward the pyramid below. As it did, they saw several arrows dart from above them toward the advancing form, but each sizzled to ashes before it could strike the Ancient One.

Here, finally, they sensed the ultimate challenge of their flight. This dark figure had tried to kill Erix before, with implacable drive and consummate skill. Only the timely arrival of sunrise had driven it away. Now it came on again, employing the aid of this hideous pack. And this time the night was young.

The masked face looked upward, and Halloran imagined triumph and mockery on the unseen expression. Yet that sense of mockery only increased Hal's own determination.

"I'd rather face him than the dogs," he grunted, leading Erix steadily upward.

*   *   *   *   *

Cordell set Daggrande to his task immediately. The plan to counteract Kardann's treason would be swift and irrevocable. The dwarf took a picked unit of fifty loyal men, embarking in the longboats to the fifteen vessels bobbing in the deep natural harbor. They labored for some time, making many trips back and forth from shore.

Finally the captain-general sent for the assessor, asking Kardann to meet him in the nearly completed redoubt. Just past sunset, the moon rose in the east, shedding its bright, full light across the lagoon and the legion's camp, all visible from the mouth of the fort.

The commander waited, alone, as Kardann struggled up the steep hill. Work progressed on the other side of the compound, now nearing completion of the fourth and final wall. When the assessor reached him, Cordell politely waited for the man to catch his breath.

"A grand spectacle, is it not?" he asked rhetorically while Kardann panted and gasped. The carracks and caravels swung placidly in the moonlit lagoon. Campfires speckled the shore, and torches lined the jetty. Kardann did not notice the extra activity along the waterfront. Cordell would have been surprised if he had.

"Come, my friend, we must talk," he urged when Kardann was more comfortable. He led the assessor into the redoubt, where now they were surrounded by high earthen walls.

"There are some," Cordell began gently, "who would have me believe that you seek to turn my men against me. They claim you wish to mount an expedition homeward while our work here is still far from finished."

"My feelings are well known to the captain-general," replied Kardann stiffly.

"Surely as you witness the treasures brought from Ulatos, as you see how easily that city falls under our sway, you have reconsidered?"

The assessor's jaw trembled as he struggled to keep his voice under control. "I tell you, it's madness to think you can survive here! With your small group, brave and skilled as they are, you can only meet with disaster! Let me take word to Amn of the riches here. I can return with five, ten times this number! Then we can proceed safely about our business!"

Cordell sighed in apparently genuine sadness. "Haven't you seen that a few can do much when they work together?" I wonder how Daggrande fares? Idly he noted that the moon had climbed higher, exceptionally bright. The clear skies promised perfect illumination for the night's activity.

"My dear captain-general," Kardann wheezed, struggling to appear reasonable and firm at the same time, "I have been entrusted with safeguarding the interests of the good Council of Amn. It is my responsibility to see that the profits are handled in a reasonable fashion. Sir, I must demand that you provide me with ships, and the bulk of the treasure, for return to the coffers of its rightful owners!"

"You demand?" Cordell seemed depressed. "Dare I resist such a pronouncement of authority?"

"You mustn't lose heart," soothed Kardann, elated by Cordell's attitude. "You and some of your men can stay if you wish. Indeed, you can stay and garrison this fort!" Kardann was delighted. He had just had a tactical idea.

Daggrande should be done by now, Cordell decided.

"Your ships, then," Cordell said, beckoning Kardann out of the enclosing walls of the fort and back to the mouth of the redoubt, with its view over the placid lagoon.

"Choose your ships, Kardann," announced the general as they again came into view. "Choose the vessels to take you back to Amn!"

His voice was as hard as ice.

Kardann stared at the lagoon, gasping again. He struggled to speak, tried to force words from his throat. But an overwhelming sense of panic, of utter helplessness, threatened to break him entirely.

The ships still floated in the lagoon, easier to spot than ever, for each was marked by a crackling orange blaze. The moonlight illuminated a climbing plume of black smoke over each vessel. Daggrande had done his work well. Decks, masts, hulls, cabins, everything combustible caught fire and burned. The carracks and caravels swiftly gave way to the oil-spread conflagration that ravaged each one of the vessels. The flames spread quickly to every timber of seasoned wood, burning each until the hulls fractured and water sizzled over the flames, extinguishing them as the ships slipped, one by one, to the bottom of the lagoon.

"Come, Kardann," urged Cordell as the assessor turned to regard him with horror-filled eyes.

"Choose your ships."

*　　*　　*　　*　　*

Halloran saw the proud warrior as soon as he crested the top of the pyramid. The man regarded him curiously for several moments. Halloran returned his attention, looking at the broad cape of eagle feathers, the high, beaked helmet—and the long wooden bow that had saved their lives.

He helped Erix onto the summit, then pointed at the figure of the Ancient One that had started to climb below them. The man nodded and spoke.

Erix replied, then turned to Halloran. "He says he is Poshtli, an Eagle Knight from Nexal. He is here because of a vision, and we are part of his vision!"

Halloran looked again at the warrior, his curiosity turning to amazement. "Let's thank him after the fight's over," he said curtly, still watching the climbing figure.

"The strangers can be very rude," apologized Erix, speaking to Poshtli. "But he is a great warrior. We thank you for saving us, but do you know whom we fight against?"

The Eagle Warrior shrugged. "I know that I fight *for* the preservation of Nexal, and that is all I need to know. Still, those beasts are horrible, like monstrous coyotes with the power of Tezca in their bellies."

"They serve Zaltec," corrected Erix. "This black thing, below us here, this is an Ancient One walking the True World."

"Soon he will walk the world of death," grunted Poshtli. Impassive, he raised his *maca* and went to stand beside Halloran. The two awaited the Ancient One at the very edge of the top, not wanting to grant him any advantage.

The masked figure paused below them, well out of sword range. They heard a sound, a muffled word, and suddenly the Ancient One floated straight up into the air! Poshtli growled something and Halloran suppressed a shudder.

The figure floated free of the pyramid, slowly drifting upward. When it reached a height equal to Hal's, it stopped and hung motionless in the air. The body looked human, though it was wrapped in black silken garments and leather boots. The moonlight reflected brightly, but this shape before them seemed a void of darkness in the night.

Suddenly they heard another command, a soft magical word, and then they were shrouded in complete darkness. "Helm's curses!" Hal stumbled backward, away from the edge of the pyramid, knowing that the Ancient One had cast a spell.

He heard Poshtli shout a challenge, followed by a splintering crack. Halloran imagined the wooden *maca* meeting that black steel longsword, with only one possible result. He heard a thud and a grunt. The legionnaire finally broke from the area of darkness, a bloblike bubble of magical fog that prevented all light from entering or leaving.

A dark form exploded from the darkness, and Halloran barely had time to raise Helmstooth. The deflection saved his life as the black steel of the Ancient One's sword slashed through the sleeve of his shirt but missed his skin by a hairbreadth.

Hal backed away, keeping himself between the attacker and Erix. The bubble of darkness slowly dissipated, but he still could not see Poshtli. The warrior had been swept off the pyramid by the Ancient One's attack.

They clanged blades several times, and the dark figure moved with shocking quickness. Again Hal was forced to retreat just to maintain his guard, Erix moving nimbly ahead of him, making sure they didn't get cornered.

Hal's blistered arm stung with each abrupt move that he made. Sweat ran into his eyes, and he frantically blinked it away, cursing the momentary blur in his vision. Still his foe assaulted him with that blinding, whirlwind speed.

Lunging desperately, Halloran began an attack that slowed the dark-swathed swordsman, even forced him to stumble back for several steps. But instantly the black figure recovered, and again Hal struggled to protect himself against a series of lightning blows.

The Ancient One made a dart to Hal's left, and the legionnaire lunged to block, cursing as his foot caught among the tangled brush on the pyramid.

Instantly as Hal fell, the attacker cut back to the right. The black steel did not come seeking the man, but instead darted after Erix. Hal twisted to his feet, fear energizing his reactions as the murderous figure closed in on the woman.

Once again his mind groped for a spell, any magic he could use to prevent disaster from striking Erixitl. He tried to think of the magic missile again, but the words would not come. Instead, he remembered the dream, falling asleep and then waking up to light. The command words to the light spell drifted through his mind impudently, useless and mocking. But it was all he had.

In desperation, he shouted the spell, not certain if his pronunciation was proper or if his hands were correctly positioned for the casting to work. If only he could delay the dark one for two seconds. . . .

The cool wash of light surprised all of them. It emanated from Erixitl's feathertoken, a medium glow that clearly illuminated the top of the pyramid. Hal again leaped forward, but started in surprise as the Ancient One reeled away, clutching his hands to his mask and screaming an inhuman, high-pitched shriek as the light seemed to sear his eyes with pain.

The figure turned away from Erix, hissing its rage, just as Helmstooth darted toward its chest. The blow was strong and true, but Hal's blade jarred against a shirt of black chain mail, almost unnoticeable under the black silk shirt.

The Ancient One quickly recovered his balance and forced Hal backward again with savage, lightning strokes. The figure held its arm raised, blocking the bright light. He felt himself approaching the edge of the pyramid, struggling to turn away, but now the masked attacker sensed cold, cruel victory, and the attacks came with unrelenting force.

Halloran parried to the left and took a gash in his right arm. He slashed back to the right and cried out as the black steel bit into his blistered left flank. Then his foot felt only air behind him, and he knew he could retreat no farther.

Helmstooth wavered before him as he maintained a careful guard, but the Ancient One took his time about this attack. He raised his sword arm high, its tip pointed low, toward Halloran, as Hal desperately struggled for room to maneuver. The attacker's black-gauntleted hand moved slowly back and forth.

Then the swordsman's arm moved suddenly, but not to attack. Hal saw a great shadow momentarily block out the moonlight, and then powerful talons seized his sword arm and twisted. The harsh cry of an eagle rang in the Ancient One's ears.

Poshtli's beak slashed downward in a savage bite as his powerful wings pummeled the black head. The flying eagle tore at the Ancient One, his talons scratching at the scalp as the swordsman desperately tried to deflect the blows. Halloran darted to the side, getting his feet on solid ground, and attacked.

The bird suddenly pulled upward, flapping toward the night sky as the black steel blade swept toward it. A few feathers floated down, while one of the eagle's powerful talons remained clenched at the figure's hooded mask. With another beat of those powerful wings, the bird lifted away, and with him went the silken mask.

Halloran almost held his stroke, so shocked was he by the visage of the Ancient One. His face was twisted by hatred, but Hal saw the tall shock of white hair and the pale, almost luminous eyes, both contrasted by the ink-black skin. The slender physique and pointed ears left no doubt in his mind as to the nature of the creature.

His hand almost hesitated in his amazement and fear at this element of old-world evil, here flourishing in a new land. He almost delayed, but he did not.

Helmstooth darted like a hungry fang underneath the Ancient One's arm as the dark attacker struck upward at the eagle. The tip of the blade penetrated deep, avoiding the impervious steel of the chain mail and striking straight to the creature's heart.

The black-skinned face contorted into a leer of disbelieving horror. The wide, pale eyes bulged outward from the slender face, and the Ancient One's mouth worked soundlessly. Halloran swiftly withdrew his blade, holding it poised for another thrust.

But the enemy began to sag. A sound, like the dolorous sighing of a thousand condemned souls, groaned forth from his mouth, followed by a spray of dark blood. The luminous eyes fixed Halloran with a gaze of implacable hated that, as the body slumped, faded to the vacant stare of the dead. Poised on the edge of the pyramid, the body slipped over the lip and tumbled through the brush, toward the green earth below.

"The drow is dead," said Halloran curtly, watching the dark elf fall.

*　*　*　*　*

Captain-General Cordell gathered his Golden Legion in precise ranks. All the footmen were present, and most of the horse. A few patrolled the lands around Ulatos, claiming tribute from the surrounding villages.

The companies gathered beside the redoubt they now called Fort Helmsport. Ten thousand natives, mostly warriors but also many dignitaries and even some women and children, had gathered to witness this ceremony of their new rulers.

"Men of the legion!" Cordell's voice rang across the field and the lagoon. The blackened hulks of several ships were visible jutting from the water. The rest had sunk in deeper areas, and while they were all visible from the hilltop, most of them did not protrude above the surface.

"Our course is now determined! There will be no turning back, for one or for many. The legion will fight, it will succeed or fail, as a whole!

"And I tell you this, my brave men, my magnificent soldiers: *The legion will succeed!* Helm has provided us with righteousness! Our arms and steel provide us the strength! And our hearts give us the courage to prevail!

"We know many things about this great land of Maztica. We have an important, wealthy colony here, with a fine capital city. When our work is done, each and every one of you will receive rewards in lands and treasures.

"But first, our grandest task lies before us. We have seen some of the peoples of this land. But we have heard of another land, another people, a place whose richness pales the treasures we have already gained.

"That land is the true center of Maztica, the source of riches and gold beyond imagining. It is the land and the city: Nexal.

"There, we know, are coffers of gold claimed from all the nations of Maztica. There are treasures worthy of our mightiest efforts, riches to make all the Sword Coast thirst for our good fortune.

"And I tell you this, my brave and loyal soldiers: Our task shall not be finished until the flag of the Golden Legion flies over Nexal, until that treasure, that city, is ours!"

Thunderous roars of approval rose from the men, frightening the natives, who did not understand what had happened. Then, by columns and by companies, the Golden Legion prepared to march.

* * * * *

The eagle settled to the top of the pyramid, moonlight shimmering across the bird's smooth feathers. The creature's form changed quickly, and Poshtli joined Halloran and Erix at the edge of the overgrown platform. Far below, at the base of the structure, the body of the Ancient One, the drow elf, lay twisted and broken.

Following the death of their master, the remaining hell hounds slinked toward the shelter of the jungle. Nevertheless, the three humans remained atop the pyramid for a little while, resting but alert.

"Your wounds must be tended," noted Erix. Halloran's arm was a mass of pain, and Poshtli had suffered a deep gash in his leg—his eagle's leg—when the drow struck upward at him. The cut had closed when the knight returned to his human form, but the leg remained very weak. "Let's get to the bottom, and I'll find something to wash and wrap them with."

Halloran wondered about Storm, whether or not the hounds had reached the loyal mare. He desperately hoped not, but he could see no sign of the horse across the moonlit clearing.

Working his way carefully down the steep side of the pyramid, Hal climbed alone. His arm was usable, so Erix helped Poshtli, whose leg wound made walking difficult. They descended slowly, without mishap. At the bottom, Hal whistled once and Storm galloped across the clearing. The mare had sought refuge in the shadowed edge of the clearing. Erix found some of the barrel-trunked plants that had provided them with water and used this liquid to cleanse their wounds.

Halloran forgot about the pain as his mind whirled with implications and implausibilities. "The drow . . . the Ancient Ones . . . Zaltec!"

He explained to Erix, and she translated for Poshtli, what he knew about the drow. They were subterranean elves of utmost evil, crafty in ways both arcane and mundane. Potent and numerous, they were known throughout the Forgotten Realms, but in most places they had been driven deep underground.

"And now they are working with a priesthood, one of unparalleled savagery, with an unquenchable thirst for blood. *Why do they want all those hearts?*"

Poshtli then told of the visions he had been shown. "The Sunstone showed me a woman of Maztica and a man from another world. If I could find them, find *you*, and bring you to Nexal, then perhaps might the doom of the city be averted.

"This knowledge of yours, the proof of this drow, may be the reason for my quest. Will you come with me to the city at the Heart of the True World?"

Halloran felt a sudden sense of weightlessness, realizing a kind of freedom he had never imagined. The Golden Legion was behind him forever, a part of his former life. The legion had turned on him, so he felt no trailing bonds of guilt. He lived in a new world, a world with untold wonders and unimagined secrets. And he, better than anyone else in that world, was in a position to see those wonders, learn those secrets.

Erixitl took his hands in hers and looked closely into his face. The moonlight filled her liquid eyes and overflowed in a warm cascade, wrapping Halloran in a feeling of rare joy.

"I'm going with you," she said. "Wherever you decide to go. But I've always wanted to see Nexal."

Halloran's mind was already made up, but her confirmation made the decision complete. He felt proud and invincible, flushed with their victory and escape. He had a good sword, a steady horse, and a spellbook. He had two bottles of magic potions. And he also had two loyal companions, a woman who had proven herself a true friend—or more— and a man of courage and skill who had risked and almost lost his life to help them.

Together they would go to the city of gold.

*   *   *   *   *

From the chronicle of Coton:

Alone in Nexal, I await the coming of the fates.

The gods arise in Maztica, taking note of the change that begins to wrack the land. Zaltec seethes, while young Tezca and Azul observe and tremble.

The god of the strangers, called Helm the Vigilant, is a new force in the True World, a powerful and forbidding presence that intimidates the younger gods and threatens the very foundations of life.

Zaltec does not fear Helm, but his anger grows at the impudence of Helm's followers. They seek to ban the offering of hearts to the god of war, and this he cannot allow. So the Ancient Ones gather in their Highcave, and the high priests of Zaltec work their magics. The power of the Viperhand, borne by Hoxitl, will be called upon to unite the cities and nations of Maztica to war against the strangers.

The return of the couatl causes hope to fire in my breast, for always the feathered snake has been the harbinger of the Plumed One. But the temples of Qotal remain empty, and his silent priests consult auguries and visions, with no promise of imminent hope or joy.

Still the true god does not return.

DragonLance Saga

PRELUDES II

RIVERWIND, THE PLAINSMAN
Paul B. Thompson & Tonya R. Carter

To prove himself worthy of Goldmoon, Riverwind is sent on an impossible quest: Find evidence of the true gods. With an eccentric soothsayer Riverwind falls down a magical shaft--and alights in a world of slavery and rebellion. Available in March 1990.

FLINT, THE KING
Mary Kirchoff & Douglas Niles

Flint returns to his boyhood village and finds it a boomtown. He learns that the prosperity comes from a false alliance and is pushed to his death. Saved by gully dwarves and made their reluctant monarch, Flint unites them as his only chance to stop the agents of the Dark Queen. Available in July 1990.

TANIS, THE SHADOW YEARS
Barbara Siegel & Scott Siegel

Tanis Half-Elven once disappeared in the mountains near Solace. He returned changed, ennobled--and with a secret. Tanis becomes a traveler in a dying mage's memory, journeying into the past to fight a battle against time itself. Available in November 1990.

DragonLance Saga

HEROES II TRILOGY

KAZ, THE MINOTAUR
Richard A. Knaak

Sequel to *The Legend of Huma*. Stalked by enemies after Huma's death, Kaz hears rumors of evil incidents. When he warns the Knights of Solamnia, he is plunged into a nightmare of magic, danger, and *deja vu*. Available June 1990.

THE GATES OF THORBARDIN
Dan Parkinson

Beneath Skullcap is a path to the gates of Thorbardin, and the magical helm of Grallen. The finder of Grallen's helm will be rewarded by a united Thorbardin, but he will also open the realm to new horror. Available September 1990.

GALEN BEKNIGHTED
Michael Williams

Sequel to *Weasel's Luck*. Galen Pathwarden is still out to save his own skin. But when his brother vanishes, Galen foresakes his better judgment and embarks on a quest that leads into a conspiracy of darkness, and to the end of his courage. Available December 1990.

FORGOTTEN REALMS
FANTASY ADVENTURE

EMPIRES TRILOGY

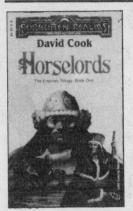

HORSELORDS
David Cook

Between the western Realms and Kara-Tur lies a vast, unexplored domain. The "civilized" people of the Realms have given little notice to these nomadic barbarians. Now, a mighty leader has united these wild horsemen into an army powerful enough to challenge the world. First, they turn to Kara-Tur. Available in May.

DRAGONWALL
Troy Denning

The barbarian horsemen have breached the Dragonwall and now threaten the oriental lands of Kara-Tur. Shou Lung's only hope lies with a general descended from the barbarians, and whose wife must fight the imperial court if her husband is to retain his command. Available in August.

CRUSADE
James Lowder

The barbarian army has turned its sights on the western Realms. Only King Azoun has the strength to forge an army to challenge the horsemen. But Azoun had not reckoned that the price of saving the west might be the life of his beloved daughter. Available in January 1991.

NEW  BOOKS

DARK HORSE
Mary Herbert

After her clan is massacred, a young woman assumes her brother's identity and becomes a warrior--all to exact revenge upon the chieftain who ordered her family slain. With an intelligent, magical horse, the young warrior goes against law and tradition to learn sorcery to thwart Medb's plans of conquest. Available February 1990.

WARSPRITE
Jefferson Swycaffer

On a quiet night, two robots from the future crash to Earth. One is a vicious killer, the other is unarmed, with an ability her warrior brother does not have: She can think. But she is programmed to face the murderous robot in a final confrontation in a radioactive chamber. Available April 1990.

NIGHT WATCH
Robin Wayne Bailey

All the Seers of Greyhawk have been killed, each by his own instrument of divination. And the only unusual sign is the ominous number of black birds in the skies. The mystery is dumped on the commander of the City Watch's night shift, who discovers that a web of evil has been tightly drawn around the great city. Available June 1990.